The U.S.A. Book of Lists

The Ultimate Compendium of All Things American

★

by Stephen J. Spignesi

New Page Books
A division of The Career Press, Inc.
Franklin Lakes, NJ

THE U.S.A. BOOK OF LISTS
Cover design by Foster & Foster
Printed in the U.S.A. by Book-mart Press

To order this title, please call toll-free 1-800-CAREER-1 (NJ and Canada: 201-848-0310) to order using VISA or MasterCard, or for further information on books from Career Press.

The Career Press, Inc., 3 Tice Road, PO Box 687
Franklin Lakes, NJ 07417
www.newpagebooks.com
www.careerpress.com

Library of Congress Cataloging-in-Publication Data

Spignesi, Stephen J.
    The U.S.A. book of lists : the ultimate compendium of all things American / by
Stephen J. Spignesi.
        p. cm.
    Includes bibliographical references (p.).
    ISBN 1-56414-484-4 (pbk.)
    1. United States—Miscellanea. I. Title.

E156 .S67 2000
973—dc21   00-034856

DEDICATION

Dedicated with gratitude to the men and women, past and present, of America's Army, Navy, Air Force, Marine Corps, Coast Guard, and NASA Space Program.

Contents

Introduction

The U.S.A. Book of Lists

"Education is too important to be left solely to the educators."
—Francis Keppel

Many Americans do not seem to know much about America. However, it seems as though every other TV commercial uses the name of our nation to shill something. America loves a certain steakhouse. Car salesmen will try to convince you, by singing about America and showing their car, that buying their vehicle is your patriotic duty. Listen for it. You'll hear it.

My hope is that you will find *The U.S.A. Book of Lists* to be an entertaining read, a fun reference, and an intriguing way of looking at, and learning more about, this great land of ours and the people in it.

There are features in this book about America's beginnings: her presidents, states, culture, and much more. There are also the various facts and figures that make America such an interesting place to study. There is information about UFO sighting locales in America, places where some people say miraculous phenomena occurred, Thomas Edison's most interesting patents, and the most frequent injuries for which an American will visit an emergency room. In addition, I have a guest contributor from America's earliest years who wrote eloquently about a certain legendary "Midnight Ride" of his that is now a famous moment in American history.

For those of you who would like to know even more about the United States and her history, there is also an astonishing array of documents and resources and a few Web sites you will undoubtedly find useful in your quest. For example, each state's Web site is provided in a separate chapter in this book.

Remember: There is nothing trivial about American trivia.

Chapter 1

The 10 Articles of the Bill of Rights

The first 10 amendments to the U.S. Constitution are known as the Bill of Rights. It is testimony to the genius of the Founding Fathers that today, more than two centuries after they were written, almost all of these 10 articles are still relevant and critical to the ongoing legacy of the United States. The Bill of Rights is impeccably phrased and are a magnificent codification of the tenets of a truly democratic society's system of government. In a mere 458 words, the Founding Fathers defined the best of all the systems of government. As I said…genius.

ARTICLE I

Congress shall make no law respecting an establishment of religion, or prohibiting the free exercise thereof; or abridging the freedom of speech, or of the press; or of the right of the people peaceably to assemble, and to petition the government for a redress of grievances.

This is the big one that is the essence of a free society: free speech, freedom of religion, freedom to gather at will, and the freedom of a citizen to complain to the government, without the fear of jackbooted thugs breaking into their home to take them away in the middle of the night. No wonder people from all over the world want to become Americans.

ARTICLE II

A well-regulated militia, being necessary to the security of a free State, the right of the people to keep and bear arms, shall not be infringed.

This is the Bill of Rights' problem child. Even now, its meaning is hotly debated. Gun owners look to it as a constitutional guarantee of their privilege to buy, sell, and own guns. Anti-gun and gun control advocates dismiss that interpretation, calling its right to bear arms an antiquated throwback to a time when ordinary citizens needed to be armed in case they were suddenly called into military service. The debate continues.

ARTICLE III

No soldier shall, in time of peace be quartered in any house, without the consent of the owner, nor in time of war, but in a manner prescribed by law.

There really isn't much relevance to this article these days: The idea of the military quartering personnel in people's homes—or even asking permission to—is ludicrous and it is difficult to imagine a scenario in which this would be necessary.

ARTICLE IV

The right of the people to be secure in their persons, houses, papers, and effects, against unreasonable search and seizures, shall not be violated, and no warrants shall issue, but upon probable cause, supported by oath or affirmation, and particularly describing the place to be searched, and the persons or things to be seized.

This is still a relevant article, as it requires that law enforcement (that is, the government) has to have probable cause to want to search someone's person or premises. Second, law enforcement must obtain a warrant from a judge before they can proceed. The tenets of Article IV are abided by every day all across America.

ARTICLE V

No person shall be held to answer for a capital, or otherwise infamous crime, unless on a presentment or indictment of a Grand Jury, except in cases arising in the land or naval forces, or in the militia, when in actual service in time of war or public danger; nor shall any person be subject for the same offense to be twice put in jeopardy of life or limb; nor shall be compelled in any criminal case to be a witness against himself, nor be deprived of life, liberty, or property, without due process of law; nor shall private property be taken for public use, without just compensation.

This important and still relevant article protects citizens from being tried twice for the same crime, from testifying against him- or herself, and from being indicted for a capital or felony crime without the review of a grand jury.

ARTICLE VI

In all criminal prosecutions, the accused shall enjoy the right to a speedy and public trial, by an impartial jury of the State and district wherein the crime shall have been committed, which district shall have been previously ascertained by law, and to be informed of the nature and cause of the accusation; to be confronted with the witnesses against him; to have compulsory process for obtaining witnesses in his favor, and to have the assistance of counsel for his defense.

America's legal system abides by the dictates of this article on a daily basis and the Miranda ruling ("You have the right to remain silent…") was based on its requirements (as well as those of the preceding article).

ARTICLE VII

In suits at common law, where the value in controversy shall exceed twenty dollars, the right of trial by jury shall be preserved, and no fact tried by a jury, shall be otherwise reexamined in any Court of the United States, than according to rules of common law.

Another guarantee of a jury trial if desired.

ARTICLE VIII

Excessive bail shall not be required, nor excessive fines imposed, nor cruel and unusual punishments inflicted.

The concerns of this article are still timely. Opponents of the death penalty have cited its "no cruel and unusual punishments" clause as an argument against capital punishment.

ARTICLE IX

The enumeration in the Constitution, of certain rights, shall not be construed to deny or disparage others retained by the people.

This article says that just because the Constitution does not spell out a specific right, that does not mean that that right is denied to American citizens. Basically, this means that the Founding Fathers preferred—insisted, actually—that the government err on the side of too many freedoms rather than enumerating rights on an individual basis and risking leaving one out.

ARTICLE X

The powers not delegated to the United States by the Constitution, nor prohibited by it to the States, are reserved to the States respectively, or to the people.

This article is critically important for a free democratic society. It states that all rights not specifically granted to the federal government belong to the states and the people. This is truly a clear and simple premise, yet it is one of the most visionary of all decrees incorporated into the Bill of Rights.

Chapter 2

The Order the **50** States Joined the Union

THE ORIGINAL 13 COLONIES

1. Delaware	December 7, 1787		8. South Carolina	May 23, 1788
2. Pennyslvania	December 12, 1787		9. New Hampshire	June 21, 1788
3. New Jersey	December 18, 1787		10. Virginia	June 25, 1788
4. Georgia	January 2, 1788		11. New York	July 26, 1788
5. Connecticut	January 9, 1788		12. North Carolina	November 21, 1789
6. Massachusetts	February 6, 1788		13. Rhode Island	May 29, 1790
7. Maryland	April 28, 1788			

STATES THAT JOINED

AFTER THE DECLARATION OF INDEPENDENCE

14. Vermont	March 4, 1791		26. Michigan	January 26, 1837
15. Kentucky	June 1, 1792		27. Florida	March 3, 1845
16. Tennessee	June 1, 1796		28. Texas	December 29, 1845
17. Ohio	March 1, 1803		29. Iowa	December 28, 1846
18. Louisiana	April 30, 1812		30. Wisconsin	May 29, 1848
19. Indiana	December 11, 1816		31. California	September 9, 1850
20. Mississippi	December 10, 1817		32. Minnesota	May 11, 1858
21. Illinois	December 3, 1818		33. Oregon	February 14, 1859
22. Alabama	December 14, 1819		34. Kansas	January 29, 1861
23. Maine	March 15, 1820		35. West Virginia	June 20, 1863
24. Missouri	August 10, 1821		36. Nevada	October 31, 1864
25. Arkansas	June 15, 1836		37. Nebraska	March 1, 1867

38.	Colorado	August 1, 1876	45.	Utah	January 4, 1896
39.	North Dakota	November 2, 1889	46.	Oklahoma	November 16, 1907
40.	South Dakota	November 2, 1889	47.	New Mexico	January 6, 1912
41.	Montana	November 8, 1889	48.	Arizona	February 14, 1912
42.	Washington	November 11, 1889	49.	Alaska	January 3, 1959
43.	Idaho	July 3, 1890	50.	Hawaii	August 21, 1959
44.	Wyoming	July 10, 1890			

The Declaration of Independence—the document that started it all.

Chapter 3

The **10** Greatest American Speeches

"Choice words, and measured phrase,
above the reach of ordinary men; a stately speech..."
—William Wordsworth,
Resolution and Independence

As the end of the 20th century neared, Texas A&M University and the University of Wisconsin-Madison conducted a survey of 137 rhetoric experts and asked them to name the most important and influential speeches of the 20th century. Artistry was to be factored in as part of their selections and the following list is what the experts came up with. Interestingly, only two of these speeches are presidential inaugural addresses. However, an amazing seven of these speeches are by U.S. presidents. As a group, these speeches—which are ranked in order of greatness—paint an evocative portrait of America in the 20th century.

1. MARTIN LUTHER KING, JR.

Date: Wednesday, August 28, 1963

Subject: Racial equality. This was King's landmark "I have a dream" speech. In it, he ushers in an era of increased focus on equality among the races in all aspects of modern life (1,413 words). Some memorable excerpts:

★★★

I am happy to join with you today in what will go down in history as the greatest demonstration for freedom in the history of our nation....

In a sense we have come to our Nation's Capital to cash a check. When the architects of our great republic wrote the magnificent words of the Constitution and the Declaration of Independence, they were signing a promissory note to which every American was to fall heir.

This note was a promise that all men, yes, black men as well as white men, would be guaranteed to the inalienable rights of life, liberty, and the pursuit of happiness.

It is obvious today that America has defaulted on this promissory note insofar as her citizens of color are concerned. Instead of honoring this sacred obligation, America has given its colored people a bad check, a check that has come back marked "insufficient funds."

[W]e have come to cash this check, a check that will give us upon demand the riches of freedom and security of justice....

Now is the time to rise from the dark and desolate valley of segregation to the sunlit path of racial justice....

There will be neither rest nor tranquility in America until the colored citizen is granted his citizenship rights....

We cannot be satisfied as long as the colored person's basic mobility is from a smaller ghetto to a larger one....

We cannot be satisfied as long as a colored person in Mississippi cannot vote and a colored person in New York believes he has nothing for which to vote....

I still have a dream. It is a dream deeply rooted in the American dream.

I have a dream that one day this nation will rise up and live out the true meaning of its creed. We hold these truths to be self-evident that all men are created equal.

I have a dream that one day out in the red hills of Georgia the sons of former slaves and the sons of former slave owners will be able to sit down together at the table of brotherhood.

I have a dream that my four little children will one day live in a nation where they will not be judged by the color of their skin but by their character.

I have a dream today....

When we let freedom ring, when we let it ring from every tenement and every hamlet, from every state and every city, we will be able to speed up that day when all of God's children, black men and white men, Jews and Gentiles, Protestants and Catholics, will be able to join hands and sing in the words of the old spiritual, "Free at last, free at last. Thank God Almighty, we are free at last."

2. John F. Kennedy

Date: Friday, January 20, 1961

Subject: Inaugural address. This speech included the legendary exhortation to America's citizens, "Ask not what your country can do for you, ask what you can do for your country" (1,366 words). Some memorable excerpts:

✯✯✯

The world is very different now. For man holds in his mortal hands the power to abolish all forms of human poverty and all forms of human life....

Let the word go forth from this time and place, to friend and foe alike, that the torch has been passed to a new generation of Americans born in this century, tempered by war, disciplined by a hard and bitter peace, proud of our ancient heritage and unwilling to witness or permit the slow undoing of those human rights to which this Nation has always been committed, and to which we are committed today at home and around the world.

Let every nation know, whether it wishes us well or ill, that we shall pay any price, bear any burden, meet any hardship, support any friend, oppose any foe, in order to assure the survival and the success of liberty.

This much we pledge and more....

[T]o those nations who would make themselves our adversary, we offer not a pledge but a request: That both sides begin anew the quest for peace, before the dark powers of destruction unleashed by science engulf all humanity in planned or accidental self-destruction.

We dare not tempt them with weakness. For only when our arms are sufficient beyond doubt can we be certain beyond doubt that they will never be employed.

But neither can two great and powerful groups of nations take comfort from our present course both sides overburdened by the cost of modern weapons, both rightly alarmed by the steady spread of the deadly atom, yet both racing to alter that uncertain balance of terror that stays the hand of mankind's final war.

So let us begin anew remembering on both sides that civility is not a sign of weakness, and sincerity is always subject to proof. Let us never negotiate out of fear. But let us never fear to negotiate....

Let both sides seek to invoke the wonders of science instead of its terrors. Together let us explore the stars, conquer the deserts, eradicate disease, tap the ocean depths, and encourage the arts and commerce....

In the long history of the world, only a few generations have been granted the role of defending freedom in its hour of maximum danger. I do not shrink from this responsibility; I welcome it. I do not believe that any of us would exchange places with any other people or any other generation. The energy, the faith, the devotion which we bring to this endeavor will light our country and all who serve it and the glow from that fire can truly light the world.

And so, my fellow Americans: Ask not what your country can do for you, ask what you can do for your country.

My fellow citizens of the world: Ask not what America will do for you, but what together we can do for the freedom of man.

Finally, whether you are citizens of America or citizens of the world, ask of us the same high standards of strength and sacrifice which we ask of you. With a good conscience our only sure reward, with history the final judge of our deeds, let us go forth to lead the land we love, asking His blessing and His help, but knowing that here on earth God's work must truly be our own.

3. FRANKLIN DELANO ROOSEVELT

Date: Saturday, March 4, 1933

Subject: FDR's first inaugural address, given during the height of the Great Depression, and notable for the affirmation that "the only thing we have to fear is fear itself." FDR's speech provides a more telling and more compelling portrait of recent American history than most history textbooks are capable of doing (1,881 words). Some memorable excerpts:

★★★

I am certain that my fellow Americans expect that on my induction into the presidency I will address them with a candor and a decision which the present situation of our nation impels. This is preeminently the time to speak the truth, the whole truth, frankly and boldly. Nor need we shrink from honestly facing conditions in our country today. This great nation will endure as it has endured, will revive and will prosper. So, first of all, let me assert my firm belief that the only thing we have to fear is fear itself— nameless, unreasoning, unjustified terror which paralyzes needed efforts to convert retreat into advance. In every dark hour of our national life a leadership of frankness and vigor has met with that understanding and support of the people themselves which is essential to victory. I am convinced that you will again give that support to leadership in these critical days.

In such a spirit on my part and on yours we face our common difficulties. They concern, thank God, only material things. Values have shrunken to fantastic levels, taxes have risen, our ability to pay has fallen, government of all kinds is faced by serious curtailment of income, the means of exchange are frozen in the currents of trade, the withered leaves of industrial enterprise lie on every side, farmers find no markets for their produce; the savings of many years in thousands of families are gone.

More important, a host of unemployed citizens face the grim problem of existence, and an equally great number toil with little return. Only a foolish optimist can deny the dark realities of the moment.

Yet our distress comes from no failure of substance. We are stricken by no plague of locusts. Compared with the perils which our forefathers conquered because they believed and were not afraid, we have still much to be thankful for. Nature still offers her bounty and human efforts have multiplied it. Plenty is at our doorstep, but a generous use of it languishes in the very sight of the supply. Primarily this is because the rulers of the exchange of mankind's goods have failed, through their own stubbornness and their own incompetence, have admitted their failure, and abdicated. Practices of the unscrupulous money changers stand indicted in the court of public opinion, rejected by the hearts and minds of men....

Happiness lies not in the mere possession of money; it lies in the joy of achievement, in the thrill of creative effort. The joy and moral stimulation of work no longer must be forgotten in the mad chase of evanescent profits. These dark days will be worth all they cost us if they teach us that our true destiny is not to be ministered unto but to minister to ourselves and to our fellow men....

Restoration calls, however, not for changes in ethics alone. This nation asks for action, and action now.

Our greatest primary task is to put people to work. This is no unsolvable problem if we face it wisely and courageously. It can be accomplished in part by direct recruiting by the government itself, treating the task as we would treat the emergency of a war, but at the same time, through this employment, accomplishing greatly needed projects to stimulate and reorganize the use of our natural resources.

Hand in hand with this we must frankly recognize the overbalance of population in our industrial centers and, by engaging on a national scale in a redistribution, endeavor to provide a better use of the land for those best fitted for the land. The task can be helped by definite efforts to raise the values of agricultural products and with this the power to purchase the output of our cities. It can be helped by preventing realistically the tragedy of the growing loss through foreclosure of our small homes and our farms. It can be helped by insistence that the federal, state, and local governments act forthwith on the demand that their cost be drastically reduced. It can be helped by the unifying of relief activities which today are often scattered, uneconomical, and unequal. It can be helped by national planning for and supervision of all forms of transportation and of communications and other utilities which have a definitely public character. There are many ways in which it can be helped, but it can never be helped merely by talking about it. We must act and act quickly.

Finally, in our progress toward a resumption of work we require two safeguards against a return of the evils of the old order: There must be a strict supervision of all banking and credits and investments, there must be an end to speculation with other people's money, and there must be provision for an adequate but sound currency.

These are the lines of attack. I shall presently urge upon a new Congress in special session detailed measures for their fulfillment, and I shall seek the immediate assistance of the several states.

Through this program of action we address ourselves to putting our own national house in order and making income balance outgo. Our international trade relations, though vastly important, are in point of time and necessity secondary to the establishment of a sound national economy. I favor as a practical policy the putting of first things first. I shall spare no effort to restore world trade by international economic readjustment, but the emergency at home cannot wait on that accomplishment....

In the field of world policy I would dedicate this nation to the policy of the good neighbor—the neighbor who resolutely respects himself and, because he does so, respects the rights of others—the neighbor who respects his obligations and respects the sanctity of his agreements in and with a world of neighbors.

If I read the temper of our people correctly, we now realize as we have never realized before our interdependence on each other; that we cannot merely take but we must give as well; that if we are to go forward, we must move as a trained and loyal army willing to sacrifice for the good of a common discipline, because without such discipline no progress is made, no leadership becomes effective....

Our Constitution is so simple and practical that it is possible always to meet extraordinary needs by changes in emphasis and arrangement without loss of essential form. That is why our constitutional system has proved itself the most superbly enduring political mechanism the modern world has produced. It has met every stress of vast expansion of territory, of foreign wars, of bitter internal strife, of world relations....

I shall ask the Congress for the one remaining instrument to meet the crisis—broad executive power to wage a war against the emergency, as great as the power that would be given to me if we were in fact invaded by a foreign foe.

For the trust reposed in me I will return the courage and the devotion that befit the time. I can do no less.

4. FRANKLIN DELANO ROOSEVELT

Date: Monday, December 8, 1941

Subject: This is FDR's "...a date which will live in infamy..." speech, in which he responded to the Japanese attack on Pearl Harbor and called for a declaration of war against the Japanese Empire (482 words). Here is the complete text:

★★★

Yesterday, December 7, 1941—a date which will live in infamy—the United States of America was suddenly and deliberately attacked by naval and air forces of the Empire of Japan.

The United States was at peace with that nation and, at the solicitation of Japan, was still in conversation with its government and its emperor looking toward the maintenance of peace in the Pacific. Indeed, one hour after Japanese air squadrons had commenced bombing in Oahu, the Japanese ambassador to the United States and his colleague delivered to the Secretary of State a formal reply to a recent American message. While this reply stated that it seemed useless to continue the existing diplomatic negotiations, it contained no threat or hint of war or armed attack.

It will be recorded that the distance of Hawaii from Japan makes it obvious that the attack was deliberately planned many days or even weeks ago. During the intervening time the Japanese Government has deliberately sought to deceive the United States by false statements and expressions of hope for continued peace.

The attack yesterday on the Hawaiian Islands has caused severe damage to American naval and military forces. Very many American lives have been lost. In addition American ships have been reported torpedoed on the high seas between San Francisco and Honolulu.

Yesterday the Japanese Government also launched an attack against Malaya. Last night Japanese forces attacked Hong Kong. Last night Japanese forces attacked Guam. Last night Japanese forces attacked the Philippine Islands. Last night the Japanese attacked Wake Island. This morning the Japanese attacked Midway Island.

Japan has, therefore, undertaken a surprise offensive extending throughout the Pacific area. The facts of yesterday speak for themselves.

The people of the United States have already formed their opinions and well understand the implications to the very life and safety of our nation.

As Commander-in-Chief of the Army and Navy, I have directed that all measures be taken for our defense.

Always will we remember the character of the onslaught against us. No matter how long it may take us to overcome this premeditated invasion, the American people in their righteous might will win through to absolute victory.

I believe I interpret the will of the Congress and of the people when I assert that we will not only defend ourselves to the uttermost but will make very certain that this form of treachery shall never endanger us again.

Hostilities exist. There is no blinking at the fact that our people, our territory, and our interests are in grave danger.

With confidence in our armed forces—with the unbounded determination of our people—we will gain the inevitable triumph, so help us God.

I ask that the Congress declare that since the unprovoked and dastardly attack by Japan on Sunday, December seventh, a state of war has existed between the United States and the Japanese Empire.

5. BARBARA JORDAN

Date: Monday, July 12, 1976

Subject: Barbara Jordan was a Democratic congresswoman from Texas. This was Jordan's elegiac Democratic National Convention keynote speech, a call to arms for a nation that was one community and which put into action the principles of the Democratic Party (1,766 words). Some memorable excerpts:

★★★

One hundred and forty-four years ago, members of the Democratic Party first met in convention to select a presidential candidate. But there is something different about tonight. There is something special about tonight. What is different? What is special? I, Barbara Jordan, am a keynote speaker....

Now that I have this grand distinction what in the world am I supposed to say?

I could easily spend this time praising the accomplishments of this party and attacking the Republicans but I don't choose to do that.

I could list the many problems which Americans have. I could list the problems which cause people to feel cynical, angry, frustrated: problems which include lack of integrity in government, the feeling that the individual no longer counts, the reality of material and spiritual poverty, the feeling that the grand American experiment is failing or has failed. I could recite these problems and then I could sit down and offer no solutions. But I don't choose to do that either.

The citizens of America expect more. They deserve and they want more than a recital of problems....

Throughout our history, when people have looked for new ways to solve their problems, and to uphold the principles of this nation, many times they have turned to political parties. They have often turned to the Democratic Party.

What is it, what is it about the Democratic Party that makes it the instrument that people use when they search for ways to shape their future? Well, I believe the answer to that question lies in our concept of governing. Our concept of governing is derived from our view of people. It is a concept deeply rooted in a set of beliefs firmly etched in the national conscience, of all of us.

Now what are these beliefs?

First, we believe in equality for all and privileges for none....

We believe that the people are the source of all governmental power; that the authority of the people is to be extended, not restricted....

We believe that the government which represents the authority of all the people, not just one interest group, but all the people, has an obligation to actively underscore, actively seek to remove those obstacles which would block individual achievement...obstacles emanating from race, sex, economic condition....

But this is the great danger America faces. That we will cease to be one nation and become instead a collection of interest groups: city against suburb, region against region, individual against individual. Each seeking to satisfy private wants.

If that happens, who then will speak for America?

Who then will speak for the common good?...

For all of its uncertainty, we cannot flee the future. We must not become the new puritans and reject our society. We must address and master the future together....

As a first step, we must restore our belief in ourselves. We are a generous people so why can't we be generous with each other? We need to take to heart the words spoken by Thomas Jefferson:

"Let us restore to social intercourse the harmony and that affection without which liberty and even life are but dreary things."

"A nation is formed by the willingness of each of us to share in the responsibility for upholding the common good."

A government is invigorated when each of us is willing to participate in shaping the future of this nation....

It is hypocritical for the public official to admonish and exhort the people to uphold the common good. More is required of public officials than slogans and handshakes and press releases....

If we promise as public officials, we must deliver. If we as public officials propose, we must produce. If we say to the American people it is time for you to be sacrificial, sacrifice. If the public official says that, we (public officials) must be the first to give....

We cannot improve on the system of government handed down to us by the founders of the Republic, there is no way to improve upon that. But what we can do is to find new ways to implement that system and realize our destiny....

I am going to close my speech by quoting a Republican president and I ask you that as you listen to these words of Abraham Lincoln, relate them to the concept of national community in which every last one of us participates:

"As I would not be a slave, so I would not be a master. This expresses my idea of democracy. Whatever differs from this, to the extent of the difference is no democracy."

6. RICHARD NIXON

Date: Tuesday, September 23, 1952

Subject: In this nationally televised speech, known as the "Checkers" speech, Nixon addressed suspicions about his honesty after allegations of a slush fund surfaced. This speech is one of the more bizarre moments in America's political history, but was ultimately a political triumph for Nixon. Nixon meticulously details his finances, even to the point of revealing a $500 loan from his parents. Molto surreal (4,615 words). Some memorable excerpts:

★★★

My Fellow Americans, I come before you tonight as a candidate for the vice presidency and as a man whose honesty and integrity has been questioned....

I am sure that you have read the charges, and you have heard it, that I, Senator Nixon, took $18,000 from a group of my supporters.

Now, was that wrong? And let me say that it was wrong. I am saying it, incidentally, that it was wrong, just not illegal, because it isn't a question of whether it was legal or illegal, that isn't enough. The question is, was it morally wrong? I say that it was morally wrong if any of that $18,000 went to Senator Nixon, for my personal use. I say that it was morally wrong if it was secretly given and secretly handled....

Let me say this—not a cent of the $18,000 or any other money of that type ever went to me for my personal use. Every penny of it was used to pay for political expenses that I did not think should be charged to the taxpayers of the United States. It was not a secret fund....

The taxpayers should not be required to finance items which are not official business but which are primarily political business.

Well, then the question arises, you say, "Well, how do you pay for these and how can you do it legally?" And there are several ways that it can be done, incidentally, and it is done legally in the United States Senate and in the Congress.

The first way is to be a rich man. So I couldn't use that.

Another way that is used is to put your wife on the payroll. Let me say, incidentally, that my opponent (John J. Sparkman), my opposite number for the vice presidency on the Democratic ticket, does have his wife on the payroll and has had her on his payroll for the past 10 years. Now let me just say this—that is his business, and I am not critical of him for doing that. You will have to pass judgment on that particular point, but I have never done that....

I suggested to Governor Sherman Adams, who is the chief of staff of the Eisenhower campaign, that an independent audit and legal report be obtained, and I have that audit in my hand.

It is an audit made by Price Waterhouse & Co. firm, and the legal opinion by Gibson, Dunn, & Crutcher, lawyers in Los Angeles, the biggest law firm, and incidentally, one of the best ones in Los Angeles....

"It is our conclusion that Senator Nixon did not obtain any financial gain from the collection and disbursement of the funds by Dana Smith, that Senator Nixon did not violate any federal or state law by reason of the operation of the fund, and that neither the portion of the fund paid by Dana Smith directly to third persons, nor the portion paid to Senator Nixon, to reimburse him for office expenses, constituted income in a sense which was either reportable or taxable as income under income tax laws."...

[N]ow, what I am going to do—and incidentally this is unprecedented in the history of American politics—I am going at this time to give to this television and radio audience, a complete financial history, everything I have earned, everything I have spent and everything I own, and I want you to know the facts....

[W]hatever I earned since I went into politics—well, here it is. I jotted it down. Let me read the notes.

First of all, I have had my salary as a Congressman and as a Senator.

Second, I have received a total in this past six years of $1,600 from estates which were in my law firm at the time that I severed my connection with it....

I have made an average of approximately $1,500 a year from nonpolitical speaking engagements and lectures.

And then, unfortunately, we have inherited little money. Pat sold her interest in her father's estate for $3,000, and I inherited $1,500 from my grandfather. We lived rather modestly.

For four years we lived in an apartment in Parkfairfax, Alexandria, Va. The rent was $80 a month. And we saved for a time when we could buy a house. Now that was what we took in....

[W]e've got a house in Washington, which cost $41,000 and on which we owe $20,000. We have a house in Whittier, California which cost $13,000 and on which we owe $3,000. My folks are living there at the present time.

I have just $4,000 in life insurance, plus my GI policy which I have never been able to convert, and which will run out in two years.

I have no life insurance whatever on Pat. I have no life insurance on our two youngsters, Patricia and Julie.

I own a 1950 Oldsmobile car. We have our furniture. We have no stocks and bonds of any type. We have no interest, direct or indirect, in any business. Now that is what we have. What do we owe?

Well, in addition to the mortgages, the $20,000 mortgage on the house in Washington and the $10,000 mortgage on the house in Whittier, I owe $4,000 to the Riggs Bank in Washington D.C. with an interest at 4 percent.

I owe $3,500 to my parents, and the interest on that loan, which I pay regularly, because it is a part of the savings they made through the years they were working so hard—I pay 4 percent interest regularly. And then I have a $500 loan, which I have on my life insurance. Well, that's about it. That's what we have. And that's what we owe. It isn't very much.

But Pat and I have the satisfaction that every dime that we have got is honestly ours.

I should say this, that Pat doesn't have a mink coat. But she does have a respectable Republican cloth coat, and I always tell her she would look good in anything.

One other thing I should probably tell you, because if I don't they will probably be saying this about me, too. We did get something, a gift, after the election.

A man down in Texas heard Pat on the radio mention that our two youngsters would like to have a dog, and, believe it or not, the day we left before this campaign trip we got a message from Union Station in Baltimore, saying they had a package for us. We went down to get it. You know what it was?

It was a little cocker spaniel dog, in a crate that he had sent all the way from Texas, black and white, spotted, and our little girl Tricia, the 6 year old, named it Checkers.

And you know, the kids, like all kids, loved the dog, and I just want to say this, right now, that regardless of what they say about it, we are going to keep it....

I would do nothing that would harm the possibilities of Dwight Eisenhower to become President of the United States. And for that reason I am submitting to the Republican National Committee tonight through this television broadcast the decision which it is theirs to make. Let them decide whether my position on the ticket will help or hurt. And I am going to ask you to help them decide. Wire and write the Republican National Committee whether you think I should stay on or whether I should get off. And whatever their decision, I will abide by it.

But let me just say this last word. Regardless of what happens, I am going to continue this fight. I am going to campaign up and down America until we drive the crooks and the communists and those that defend them out of Washington, and remember folks, Eisenhower is a great man. Folks, he is a great man, and a vote for Eisenhower is a vote for what is good for America.

7. MALCOLM X

Date: April 13, 1964

Subject: "The Ballot or the Bullet." Make no mistake: Malcolm X is angry in this speech and it is a seminal moment in civil rights rhetoric and criticism in America's history. Much of what Malcolm says is true and has merit, but his anger leads him to issue ultimatums that sound as if he is endorsing rioting and violence. Nevertheless, this speech is a landmark moment in the civil rights struggle and it is the perfect introduction to LBJ's 1965 "Voting Rights Act" speech, which could be interpreted as a response to Malcolm's fiery oration (8,647 words).

(*Note:* This speech is difficult to find in its entirety online. However, I found the complete text is at the following URL: *hamp.hampshire.edu/~cmnF93/malcolm.txt.*) Here are the opening paragraphs:

★★★

Mr. Moderator, Brother Lomax, brothers and sisters, friends and enemies: I just can't believe everyone in here is a friend and I don't want to leave anybody out. The question tonight, as I understand it, is "The Negro Revolt, and Where Do We Go From Here?" or, "What Next?" In my little humble way of understanding it, it points toward either the ballot or the bullet.

Before we try and explain what is meant by the ballot or the bullet, I would like to clarify something concerning myself. I'm still a Muslim, my religion is still Islam. That's my personal belief. Just as Adam Clayton Powell is a Christian minister who heads the Abyssinian Baptist Church in New York, but at the same time takes part in the political struggles to try and bring about rights to the black people in this country; and Dr. Martin Luther King is a Christian minister down in Atlanta, Georgia, who heads another organization fighting for the civil rights of black people in this country; and Rev. Galamison, I guess you've heard of him, is another Christian minister in New York who has been deeply involved in the school boycotts to eliminate segregated education. Well, I, myself am a minister, not a Christian minister, but a Muslim minister; and I believe in action on all fronts by whatever means necessary.

Although I'm still a Muslim, I'm not here tonight to discuss my religion. I'm not here to try and change your religion. I'm not here to argue or discuss anything that we differ about, because it's time for us to submerge our differences and realize that it is best for us to first see that we have the same problem, a common problem, a problem that will make you catch hell whether you're a Baptist, or a Methodist, or a Muslim, or a nationalist. Whether you're educated or illiterate, whether you live on the boulevard or in the alley, you're going to catch hell just like I am. We're all in the same boat and we all are going to catch the same hell from the same man. He just happens to be a white man. All of us have suffered here, in this country, political oppression at the hands of the white man, economic exploitation at the hands of the white man, and social degradation at the hands of the white man.

Now in speaking like this, it doesn't mean that we're anti-white, but it does mean we're anti-exploitation, we're anti-degradation, we're anti-oppression. And if the white man doesn't want us to be anti-him, let him stop oppressing and exploiting and degrading us. Whether we are Christians or Muslims or nationalists or agnostics or atheists, we must first learn to forget our differences. If we have differences, let us differ in the closet; when we come out in front, let us not have anything to argue about until we get finished arguing with the man. If the late President Kennedy could get together with Khrushchev and exchange some wheat, we certainly have more in common with each other than Kennedy and Khrushchev had with each other.

If we don't do something real soon, I think you'll have to agree that we're going to be forced either to use the ballot or the bullet. It's one or the other in 1964. It isn't that time is running out—time has run out! 1964 threatens to be the most explosive year America has ever witnessed. The most explosive year. Why? It's also a political year. It's the year when all of the white politicians will be back in the so-called Negro community jiving you and me for some votes. The year when all of the white political crooks will be right back in your and my community with their false promises, building up our hopes for a letdown, with their trickery and their treachery, with their false promises which they don't intend to keep. As they nourish these dissatisfactions, it can only lead to one thing, an explosion; and now we have the type of black man on the scene in America today—I'm sorry, Brother Lomax—who just doesn't intend to turn the other cheek any longer.

Don't let anybody tell you anything about the odds are against you. If they draft you, they send you to Korea and make you face 800 million Chinese. If you can be brave over there, you can be brave right here. These odds aren't as great as those odds. And if you fight here, you will at least know what you're fighting for.

I'm not a politician, not even a student of politics; in fact, I'm not a student of much of anything. I'm not a Democrat, I'm not a Republican, and I don't even consider myself an American. If you and I were Americans, there'd be no problem. Those Hunkies that just got off the boat, they're already Americans; Polacks are already Americans; the Italian refugees are already Americans. Everything that came out of Europe, every blue-eyed thing, is already an American. And as long as you and I have been over here, we aren't Americans yet.

Well, I am one who doesn't believe in deluding myself. I'm not going to sit at your table and watch you eat, with nothing on my plate, and call myself a diner. Sitting at the table doesn't make you a diner, unless you eat some of what's on that plate. Being here in America doesn't make you an American. Being born here in America doesn't make you an American. Why, if birth made you American, you wouldn't need any legislation, you wouldn't need any amendments to the Constitution, you wouldn't be faced with civil-rights filibustering in Washington, D.C., right now. They don't have to pass civil-rights legislation to make a Polack an American.

No, I'm not an American. I'm one of the 22 million black people who are the victims of American-ism. One of the 22 million black people who are the victims of democracy, nothing but disguised hypocrisy. So, I'm not standing here speaking to you as an American, or a patriot, or a flag-saluter, or a flag-waver—no, not I. I'm speaking as a victim of this American system. And I see America through the eyes of the victim. I don't see any American dream; I see an American nightmare.

8. RONALD REAGAN

Date: Tuesday, January 28, 1986

Subject: As often happens in time of national tragedy, Americans turn to the president for an explanation and for comfort. President Reagan was more than up to the task when the Space Shuttle Challenger exploded. In fact, he addressed the nation on national television only a few hours after the explosion. His statement was brief, yet it was one of the most powerful memorial tributes ever offered in response to an unspeakable tragedy. Here is Reagan's complete statement.

One of the most memorable moments in Reagan's statement was his quoting from a poem by American fighter pilot John Gillepsie Magee, killed over England on December 11, 1941. Three months before his death, 19-year-old Magee had written a poem about the transcendent joy of flying titled "High Flight." Magee's poem in its entirety is included with Reagan's statement (453 words). Here is the complete statement:

***

Nineteen years ago, almost to the day, we lost three astronauts in a terrible accident on the ground. But, we've never lost an astronaut in flight; we've never had a tragedy like this. And perhaps we've forgotten the courage it took for the crew of the shuttle; but they, the Challenger Seven, were aware of the dangers, but overcame them and did their jobs brilliantly. We mourn seven heroes: Michael Smith, Dick Scobee, Judith Resnik, Ronald McNair, Ellison Onizuka, Gregory Jarvis, and Christa McAuliffe. We mourn their loss as a nation together.

For the families of the seven, we cannot bear, as you do, the full impact of this tragedy. But we feel the loss, and we're thinking about you so very much. Your loved ones were daring and brave, and they had that special grace, that special spirit that says, "Give me a challenge and I'll meet it with joy." They had a hunger to explore the universe and discover its truths. They wished to serve, and they did. They served all of us.

We've grown used to wonders in this century. It's hard to dazzle us. But for 25 years the United States space program has been doing just that. We've grown used to the idea

HIGH FLIGHT

Oh, I have slipped the surly bonds of earth
And danced the skies on laughter-silvered wings;
Sunward I've climbed, and joined the tumbling mirth
Of sun-split clouds—and done a hundred things
You have not dreamed of—wheeled and soared and swung
High in the sunlit silence. Hov'ring there,
I've chased the shouting wind along, and flung
My eager craft through footless halls of air.
Up, up the long, delirious burning blue,
I've topped the windswept heights with easy grace
Where never lark, or even eagle flew—
And, while with silent, lifting mind I've trod
The high untrespassed sanctity of space,
Put out my hand, and touched the face of God.

—John Gillespie Magee (1922-1941)

of space, and perhaps we forget that we've only just begun. We're still pioneers. They, the members of the Challenger crew, were pioneers.

And I want to say something to the schoolchildren of America who were watching the live coverage of the shuttle's takeoff. I know it is hard to understand, but sometimes painful things like this happen. It's all part of the process of exploration and discovery. It's all part of taking a chance and expanding man's horizons. The future doesn't belong to the fainthearted; it belongs to the brave. The Challenger crew was pulling us into the future, and we'll continue to follow them.

There's a coincidence today. On this day 390 years ago, the great explorer Sir Francis Drake died aboard ship off the coast of Panama. In his lifetime the great frontiers were the oceans, and a historian later said, "He lived by the sea, died on it, and was buried in it." Well, today we can say of the Challenger crew: Their dedication was, like Drake's, complete.

The crew of the space shuttle Challenger honored us by the manner in which they lived their lives. We will never forget them, nor the last time we saw them, this morning, as they prepared for the journey and waved goodbye and "slipped the surly bonds of earth" to "touch the face of God."

9. JOHN F. KENNEDY

Date: Monday, September 12, 1960

Subject: This speech to the Greater Houston Ministerial Association, in which JFK states with certainty, "I do not speak for my church on public matters, and the church does not speak for me." His is one of the most passionate defenses of the separation of church and state ever presented by a politician. Kennedy is brilliant here, and its complete reproduction in this book is warranted so readers can experience what is one of the clearest-cut explications of the principles on which America was founded to date (1,556 words). Here is the complete speech:

★★★

Reverend Meza, Reverend Reck, I'm grateful for your generous invitation to speak my views.

While the so-called religious issue is necessarily and properly the chief topic here tonight, I want to emphasize from the outset that we have far more critical issues to face in the 1960 election: the spread of communist influence, until it now festers 90 miles off the coast of Florida; the humiliating treatment of our president and vice president by those who no longer respect our power; the hungry children I saw in West Virginia, the old people who cannot pay their doctor bills, the families forced to give up their farms; an America with too many slums, with too few schools, and too late to the moon and outer space.

These are the real issues which should decide this campaign. And they are not religious issues—for war and hunger and ignorance and despair know no religious barriers.

But because I am a Catholic, and no Catholic has ever been elected president, the real issues in this campaign have been obscured—perhaps deliberately, in some quarters less responsible than this. So it is apparently necessary for me to state once again—not what kind of church I believe in, for that should be important only to me—but what kind of America I believe in.

I believe in an America where the separation of church and state is absolute; where no Catholic prelate would tell the president (should he be Catholic) how to act, and no Protestant minister would tell his parishioners for whom to vote; where no church or church school is granted any public funds or political preference; and where no man is denied public office merely because his religion differs from the president who might appoint him or the people who might elect him.

I believe in an America that is officially neither Catholic, Protestant, nor Jewish; where no public official either requests or accepts instructions on public policy from the Pope, the National Council of Churches, or any other ecclesiastical source; where no religious body seeks to impose its will directly or indirectly upon the general populace or the public acts of its officials; and where religious liberty is so indivisible that an act against one church is treated as an act against all.

For while this year it may be a Catholic against whom the finger of suspicion is pointed, in other years it has been, and may someday be again, a Jew, or a Quaker, or a Unitarian, or a Baptist. It was Virginia's harassment of Baptist preachers, for example, that helped lead to Jefferson's statute of religious freedom. Today I may be the victim—but tomorrow it may be you—until the whole fabric of our harmonious society is ripped at a time of great national peril.

Finally, I believe in an America where religious intolerance will someday end where all men and all churches are treated as equal; where every man has the same right to attend or not attend the church of his choice; where there is no Catholic vote, no anti-Catholic vote, no bloc voting of any kind; and where Catholics, Protestants and Jews, at both the lay and pastoral level, will refrain from those attitudes of disdain and division which have so often marred their works in the past, and promote instead the American ideal of brotherhood.

That is the kind of America in which I believe. And it represents the kind of presidency in which I believe—a great office that must neither be humbled by making it the instrument of any one religious group nor tarnished by arbitrarily withholding its occupancy from the members of any one religious group. I believe in a president whose religious views are his own private affair, neither imposed by him upon the nation or imposed by the nation upon him as a condition to holding that office.

I would not look with favor upon a president working to subvert the First Amendment's guarantees of religious liberty. Nor would our system of checks and balances permit him to do so—and neither do I look with favor upon those who would work to subvert Article VI of the Constitution by requiring a religious test—even by indirection—for it. If they disagree with that safeguard they should be out openly working to repeal it.

I want a chief executive whose public acts are responsible to all groups and obligated to none; who can attend any ceremony, service, or dinner his office may appropriately require of him; and whose fulfillment of his presidential oath is not limited or conditioned by any religious oath, ritual, or obligation.

This is the kind of America I believe in, and this is the kind I fought for in the South Pacific, and the kind my brother died for in Europe. No one suggested then that we may have a "divided loyalty," that we did "not believe in liberty," or that we belonged to a disloyal group that threatened the "freedoms for which our forefathers died."

And in fact this is the kind of America for which our forefathers died when they fled here to escape religious test oaths that denied office to members of less favored churches; when they fought for the Constitution, the Bill of Rights, and the Virginia Statute of Religious Freedom; and when they fought at the shrine I visited today, the Alamo. For side by side with Bowie and Crockett died McCafferty and Bailey and Carey—but no one knows whether they were Catholic or not. For there was no religious test at the Alamo.

I ask you tonight to follow in that tradition: To judge me on the basis of my record of 14 years in Congress, on my declared stands against an Ambassador to the Vatican, against unconstitutional aid to parochial schools, and against any boycott of the public schools (which I have attended myself), instead of judging me on the basis of these pamphlets and publications we all have seen that carefully select quotations out of context from the statements of Catholic church leaders, usually in other countries, frequently in other centuries, and always omitting, of course, the statement of the American Bishops in 1948 which strongly endorsed church-state separation, and which more nearly reflects the views of almost every American Catholic.

I do not consider these other quotations binding upon my public acts—why should you? But let me say, with respect to other countries, that I am wholly opposed to the state being used by any religious group, Catholic or Protestant, to compel, prohibit, or persecute the free exercise of any other religion.

And I hope that you and I condemn with equal fervor those nations which deny their presidency to Protestants and those which deny it to Catholics. And rather than cite the misdeeds of those who differ, I would cite the record of the Catholic Church in such nations as Ireland and France, and the independence of such statesmen as Adenauer and De Gaulle.

But let me stress again that these are my views, for contrary to common newspaper usage, I am not the Catholic candidate for president. I am the Democratic Party's candidate for president who happens also to be a Catholic. I do not speak for my church on public matters—and the church does not speak for me.

Whatever issue may come before me as president—on birth control, divorce, censorship, gambling, or any other subject—I will make my decision in accordance with these views, in accordance with what my conscience tells me to be the national interest, and without regard to outside religious pressures or dictates. And no power or threat of punishment could cause me to decide otherwise.

But if the time should ever come—and I do not concede any conflict to be even remotely possible—when my office would require me to either violate my conscience or violate the national interest, then I would resign the office, and I hope any conscientious public servant would do the same.

But I do not intend to apologize for these views to my critics of either Catholic or Protestant faith—nor do I intend to disavow either my views or my church in order to win this election.

If I should lose on the real issues, I shall return to my seat in the Senate, satisfied that I had tried my best and was fairly judged. But if this election is decided on the basis that 40 million Americans lost their chance of being president on the day they were baptized, then it is the whole nation that will be the loser, in the eyes of Catholics and non-Catholics around the world, in the eyes of history, and in the eyes of our own people.

But if, on the other hand, I should win the election, then I shall devote every effort of mind and spirit to fulfilling the oath of the presidency—practically identical, I might add, to the oath I have taken for 14 years in the Congress. For without reservation, I can "solemnly swear that I will faithfully execute the office of President of the United States, and will to the best of my ability preserve, protect, and defend the Constitution...so help me God."

10. Lyndon B. Johnson

Date: Monday, March 15, 1965

Subject: This speech, titled "The American Promise," was presented by President Johnson to Congress following the race riots in Selma, Alabama. In it, the president proposed a voting rights act. As unbelievable as it sounds, as recently as the mid-1960s, blacks were being prevented from voting throughout this country. LBJ's outrage is palpable in this powerful speech. With it, he, in essence, responds to Malcolm X's 1964 challenge in the black leader's "Ballot or the Bullet" speech (speech number 7 on page 23). In it, he said, "Lyndon B. Johnson is the head of the Democratic Party. If he's for civil rights, let him go into the Senate...and declare himself....Let him go in there...and take a moral stand—right now, not later" (3,756 words). Here are some memorable excerpts:

Many of the issues of civil rights are very complex and most difficult. But about this there can and should be no argument. Every American citizen must have an equal right to vote. There is no reason which can excuse the denial of that right. There is no duty which weighs more heavily on us than the duty we have to ensure that right.

Yet the harsh fact is that in many places in this country men and women are kept from voting simply because they are Negroes.

Every device of which human ingenuity is capable has been used to deny this right. The Negro citizen may go to register only to be told that the day is wrong, or the hour is late, or the official in charge is absent. And if he persists, and if he manages to present himself to the registrar, he may be disqualified because he did not spell out his middle name or because he abbreviated a word on the application.

And if he manages to fill out an application, he is given a test. The registrar is the sole judge of whether he passes this test. He may be asked to recite the entire Constitution, or explain the most complex provisions of state law. And even a college degree cannot be used to prove that he can read and write.

For the fact is that the only way to pass these barriers is to show a white skin....

Wednesday I will send to Congress a law designed to eliminate illegal barriers to the right to vote....This bill will strike down restrictions to voting in all elections—federal, state, and local—which have been used to deny Negroes the right to vote.

This bill will establish a simple, uniform standard which cannot be used, however ingenious the effort, to flout our Constitution.

It will provide for citizens to be registered by officials of the U.S. Government if the state officials refuse to register them.

It will eliminate tedious, unnecessary lawsuits which delay the right to vote.

Finally, this legislation will ensure that properly registered individuals are not prohibited from voting....

There is no constitutional issue here. The command of the Constitution is plain.

There is no moral issue. It is wrong—deadly wrong—to deny any of your fellow Americans the right to vote in this country.

There is no issue of states rights or national rights. There is only the struggle for human rights....

What happened in Selma is part of a far larger movement which reaches into every section and state of America. It is the effort of American Negroes to secure for themselves the full blessings of American life.

Their cause must be our cause too. Because it is not just Negroes, but really it is all of us, who must overcome the crippling legacy of bigotry and injustice.

And we shall overcome.

As a man whose roots go deeply into Southern soil I know how agonizing racial feelings are. I know how difficult it is to reshape the attitudes and the structure of our society.

---

11 STATES WHERE SCHOOLS WERE SEGREGATED BY LAW UNTIL 1956

Eleven states in the deep South enforced school segregation until 1956, when the Civil Rights Act was passed and the Commission on Civil Rights was created.

President Eisenhower was given the power to enforce school integration and on September 24, 1957, Ike sent 1,000 paratroopers to Little Rock, Ark., to force the schools to allow blacks to attend classes with whites.

There were anti-integration riots from 1957 through 1960 in Clinton, Tenn.; Athens, Ga.; Little Rock, Ark.; New Orleans, La.; and elsewhere. In 1964, in defiance of federal law, the state of Mississippi was still prohibiting blacks from attending schools with whites. In 1965, President Johnson began a systematic enforcement of anti-integration laws and integrated schools slowly spread throughout the South.

1. Virginia.
2. North Carolina.
3. South Carolina.
4. Georgia.
5. Tennessee.
6. Alabama.
7. Mississippi.
8. Florida.
9. Louisiana.
10. Arkansas.
11. Texas.

But a century has passed, more than a hundred years, since the Negro was freed. And he is not fully free tonight.

It was more than a hundred years ago that Abraham Lincoln, a great president of another party, signed the Emancipation Proclamation, but emancipation is a proclamation and not a fact.

A century has passed, more than a hundred years, since equality was promised. And yet the Negro is not equal.

A century has passed since the day of promise. And the promise is unkept.

The time of justice has now come. I tell you that I believe sincerely that no force can hold it back. It is right in the eyes of man and God that it should come. And when it does, I think that day will brighten the lives of every American.

For Negroes are not the only victims. How many white children have gone uneducated, how many white families have lived in stark poverty, how many white lives have been scarred by fear, because we have wasted our energy and our substance to maintain the barriers of hatred and terror?

So I say to all of you here, and to all in the nation tonight, that those who appeal to you to hold on to the past do so at the cost of denying you your future.

This great, rich, restless country can offer opportunity and education and hope to all: black and white, North and South, sharecropper and city dweller. These are the enemies: poverty, ignorance, disease. They are the enemies and not our fellow man, not our neighbor. And these enemies too: poverty, disease, and ignorance, we shall overcome....

The real hero of this struggle is the American Negro. His actions and protests, his courage to risk safety and even to risk his life, have awakened the conscience of this nation. His demonstrations have been designed to call attention to injustice, designed to provoke change, designed to stir reform.

He has called upon us to make good the promise of America. And who among us can say that we would have made the same progress were it not for his persistent bravery, and his faith in American democracy.

For at the real heart of battle for equality is a deep-seated belief in the democratic process. Equality depends not on the force of arms or tear gas but upon the force of moral right; not on recourse to violence but on respect for law and order....

The bill that I am presenting to you will be known as a civil rights bill. But, in a larger sense, most of the program I am recommending is a civil rights program. Its object is to open the city of hope to all people of all races.

Because all Americans just must have the right to vote. And we are going to give them that right.

All Americans must have the privileges of citizenship regardless of race. And they are going to have those privileges of citizenship regardless of race....

My first job after college was as a teacher in Cotulla, Tex., in a small Mexican-American school. Few of them could speak English, and I couldn't speak much Spanish. My students were poor and they often came to class without breakfast, hungry. They knew even in their youth the pain of prejudice. They never seemed to know why people disliked them. But they knew it was so, because I saw it in their eyes. I often walked home late in the afternoon, after the classes were finished, wishing there was more that I could do. But all I knew was to teach them the little that I knew, hoping that it might help them against the hardships that lay ahead.

Somehow you never forget what poverty and hatred can do when you see its scars on the hopeful face of a young child.

I never thought then, in 1928, that I would be standing here in 1965. It never even occurred to me in my fondest dreams that I might have the chance to help the sons and daughters of those students and to help people like them all over this country.

Illustration/New York Historical Society

The Old Senate Chamber, which housed the Supreme Court for 75 years
before moving into their present building.

But now I do have that chance—and I'll let you in on a secret—I mean to use it. And I hope that you will use it with me.

This is the richest and most powerful country which ever occupied the globe. The might of past empires is little compared to ours. But I do not want to be the president who built empires, or sought grandeur, or extended dominion.

I want to be the president who educated young children to the wonders of their world. I want to be the president who helped to feed the hungry and to prepare them to be taxpayers instead of taxeaters.

I want to be the president who helped the poor to find their own way and who protected the right of every citizen to vote in every election.

I want to be the president who helped to end hatred among his fellow men and who promoted love among the people of all races and all regions and all parties.

I want to be the president who helped to end war among the brothers of this earth.

Chapter 4

41 Significant Differences Between 1900 and 2000 in America

"Americans have been conditioned to respect newness, whatever it costs them."
—John Updike,
from *A Month of Sundays*, 1975

"Times don't change. Men do."
—Sam Levenson,
from *You Don't Have To Be in Who's Who To Know What's What*, 1979

On December 27, 1999, *U.S. News & World Report* published a special issue of the magazine in which they named the Man of the 20th Century (it was Uncle Sam...who else?) and also looked at the differences between 1900 and 2000 in several key areas.

These comparisons are incredibly revealing and illustrative of how things have changed in this great land of ours in a hundred years...the interpretation of these figures lies, I guess, in the eyes of the beholder.

1. **Adults completing high school:** 1900: 15 percent; 2000: 83 percent.
2. **Average annual income (in 1999 dollars):** 1900: $8,620; 2000: $23,812.
3. **Average size of household:** 1900: 4.76 persons; 2000: 2.62 persons.
4. **Average work week:** 1900: 60 hours; 2000: 44 hours.
5. **Beer consumption:** 1900: 58.8 gallons per adult; 2000: 31.6 gallons per adult.
6. **Biggest source of immigrants:** 1900: Austria-Hungary; 2000: Mexico.
7. **Birthrate:** 1900: 32.3 births per 1,000; 2000: 14.2 births per 1,000.
8. **Books published:** 1900: 6,356; 2000: 65,800.
9. **Cancer deaths:** 1900: 64 per 100,000; 2000: 200 per 100,000.
10. **Cars produced in the United States:** 1900: 5,000; 2000: 5,500,000.
11. **Cigarettes produced:** 1900: 4 billion; 2000: 720 billion.
12. **City with the most millionaires per capita:** 1900: Buffalo: N.Y.; 2000: Seattle: Wa.
13. **Daily newspapers:** 1900: 2,226; 2000: 1,489.
14. **Deaths in childbirth:** 1900: 9 in 1,000; 2000: 1 in 10,000.

15. **Deaths per year from industrial accidents:** 1900: 35,000; 2000: 6,100.
16. **Defense expenditures (in 1999 dollars):** 1900: $4 billion; 2000: $268 billion.
17. **Divorced men:** 1900: 0.3 percent; 2000: 8.2 percent.
18. **Divorced women:** 1900: 0.5 percent; 2000: 10.3 percent.
19. **Dow Jones Industrial Average:** 1900: 68.13; 2000: 11,000.
20. **Farm population:** 1900: 29,875,000; 2000: 4,600,000.
21. **Federal budget outlay (in 1999 dollars):** 1900: $10.3 billion; 2000: $1.7 trillion.
22. **Highway fatalities:** 1900: 36 per 100 million miles; 2000: 1.64 per 100 million miles.
23. **Homes with electricity:** 1900: 8 percent; 2000: 99.9 percent.
24. **Immigrant population:** 1900: 14.7 percent; 2000: 7.9 percent.
25. **Life expectancy for men:** 1900: 46.3 years; 2000: 73.6 years.
26. **Life expectancy for women:** 1900: 48.3 years; 2000: 79.7 years.
27. **Median age:** 1900: 22.9 years old; 2000: 35.7 years old.
28. **Miles of paved road:** 1900: 10 miles; 2000: 4,000,000 miles.
29. **Most popular song:** 1900: "Good-Bye Dolly Gray" (Harry Macdonough); 2000: "Believe" (Cher).
30. **National debt (in 1999 dollars):** 1900: $24.8 billion; 2000: $5 trillion.
31. **Number of bison:** 1900: 400; 2000: 200,000.
32. **Number of farms:** 1900: 5,740,000; 2000: 2,191,510.
33. **Number of millionaires:** 1900: 3,000; 2000: 3,500,000.
34. **Passenger autos registered in the United States:** 1900: 8,000; 2000: 130,000,000.
35. **Patents granted:** 1900: 24,656; 2000: 147,500.
36. **Per Capita national debt (in 1999 dollars):** 1900: $325; 2000: $23,276.
37. **Population of Los Angeles:** 1900: 102,479; 2000: 3,800,000.
38. **Price of a First Class postage stamp (in 1999 dollars):** 1900: 59 cents; 2000: 33 cents.
39. **United States population:** 1900: 75,994,575; 2000: 273,482,000.
40. **Urban vs. rural populations:** 1900: 40 percent urban: 60 percent rural; 2000: 75 percent urban: 25 percent rural.
41. **Voter turnout:** 1900: 73.7 percent; 2000: 48.9 percent.

(*Source: U.S. News & World Report* [December 27, 1999])

Chapter 5

7 Strange American Car Names

"Except the American woman, nothing interests the eye of the American man more than the automobile, or seems so important to him as an object of aesthetic appreciation."

—A. H. Barr

"The automobile is technically more sophisticated than the bundling board, but the human motives in their uses are sometimes the same."

—Charles M. Allen

THE AMERICAN CHOCOLATE

This car was built for four years, from 1902 through 1906. It got its name from the fact that it was built in a factory that also manufactured chocolate.

THE AVERAGE MAN'S AUTOMOBILE

This was built by a long-forgotten car manufacturer in Kansas that also made vehicles named "Everybody's" and "People's." Obviously, their marketing strategy was to appeal to the "average man." (Guess women weren't buying cars back then, eh?) Since they are but a footnote in automotive history, we can assume their campaign didn't work.

THE BLOOD

The Michigan Automobile Company made this automobile from 1903 through 1908. Looking back, we cannot help but wonder, what were they thinking? Today, with vehicular accidents and road rage ubiquitous facets of modern American life, a car named the "Blood" would be avoided like the plague. Perhaps back then, the connotation was different. However, two years after the Blood was discontinued, the company came out with another "organically-named" model: "The Kidney." Wow.

THE DICTATOR

Studebaker made this car in 1927. It was their lowest-priced model. Its name was meant to play off the moniker of their most expensive Studebaker, then called "The President."

THE LSD

This car was built during the 1920s before those three innocuous letters came to mean something entirely different.

THE NUCLEON

This was Ford Motor Company's early prototype for a nuclear-powered car. It never made it to the market. (Good thing, too, considering how expensive a gallon of plutonium is these days.)

THE ROCKNE

This was a 1932 Studebaker named for Notre Dame football coach Knute Rockne, who had died in a plane crash on 1931. Sentiment for a lost hero was not enough to sell cars, however, and the Rockne was discontinued in 1933. (When it was being manufactured, a Rockne sold for $585.)

Chapter 6

23 Native American Contributions to U.S. Culture

"It is painfully clear that the United States needs its Indians and their culture. A society increasingly homogenized and mechanized—a society headed toward anthill conformity and depersonalized living—desperately needs the lessons of a culture that has a deep reverence for nature, and values the simple, the authentic, and the humane."

—Stewart Udall,
from *American Way*, May, 1971

ative Americans contributed much to American culture: From food to toys. Many of their innovations are still part of daily life in the United States today. Imagine what they would have contributed to America if their race had been allowed to thrive.

1. The potato.
2. The sweet potato.
3. Corn.
4. Tomatoes.
5. Beans.
6. Artichokes.
7. Squash.
8. Turkey.
9. Maple sugar.
10. Vanilla.
11. Coca, used to make novocaine.
12. Quinine, used to treat malaria.
13. Curare, used as a paralyzing agent in surgery.
14. Ipecac, used to induce vomiting.
15. Tents—the military's Sibley tent was directly inspired by the teepee.
16. Igloos.
17. Pueblos.
18. The hammock.
19. The toboggan.
20. The parka.
21. The poncho.
22. Moccasins.
23. Snowshoes.

Chapter 7

28 Retired Hurricane Names

*"And I have asked to be
Where no storms come..."*
—Gerard Manley Hopkins
"Heaven-Haven"

Perhaps it's a superstitious fear of tempting fate, maybe it's a sense of decorum, or maybe it's just clerical convenience. But when a hurricane does major damage to an area, that name is retired from the rotating list of hurricane names used to identify major storms each year.

So, because of this, there will never again be a Hurricane Bob. Or a Hurricane Andrew. Or a Hurricane Gloria.

I guess being able to say that means a lot to the people living in the areas devastated by those storms.

How did this naming business begin? An Australian weatherman started the custom of naming hurricanes early in the 20th century. In 1953, American meteorologists began using this custom. The list in 1953 was as follows: Alice, Barbara, Carol, Dolly, Edna, Florence, Gilda, Hazel, Irene, Jill, Katherine, Lucy, Mabel, Norma, Orpha, Patsy, Queen, Rachel, Susie, Tina, Una, Vickie, and Wallis. (Orpha?)

In 1977, the United States attended a meeting of the World Meteorological Organization and agreed to alternate male and female names for hurricanes.

The following list details the 28 retired hurricane names, with 1992's Hurricane Andrew being the latest retiree.

Year	Hurricane	States Affected
1954	Carol	Northeastern United States.
1954	Hazel	North Carolina and South Carolina (also, the Antilles).
1955	Connie	North Carolina.
1955	Diane	Mid-Atlantic United States and the Northeastern United States.
1955	Ione	North Carolina.
1957	Audrey	Louisiana and Northern Texas.
1960	Donna	Florida and the Eastern United States (also, the Bahamas).
1961	Carla	Texas.
1964	Cleo	Southeastern Florida (also, the Lesser Antilles, Haiti, and Cuba).
1964	Dora	Northeastern Florida.
1964	Hilda	Louisiana.
1965	Betsy	Texas.
1966	Inez	The Florida Keys (also, the Lesser Antilles, Hispañola, and Cuba).
1967	Beulah	Southern Texas (also, the Antilles and Mexico).
1969	Camille	Louisiana, Mississippi, and Alabama.
1970	Celia	Southern Texas.
1972	Agnes	Florida and the Northeastern United States.
1974	Carmen	Central Louisiana (also, Mexico).
1975	Eloise	Northwestern Florida and Alabama (also, the Antilles).
1979	David	Florida and the Eastern United States (also, the Lesser Antilles and Hispañola).
1979	Frederic	Alabama and Mississippi.
1980	Allen	Southern Texas (also, the Antilles and Mexico).
1983	Alicia	Northern Texas.
1985	Elena	Mississippi and Alabama.
1985	Gloria	North Carolina and the Northeastern United States.
1989	Hugo	South Carolina (also, the Antilles).
1991	Bob	North Carolina and the Northeastern United States.
1992	Andrew	Southeastern Florida and Southeastern Louisiana (also, the Bahamas).

Chapter 8

40 UFO Sightings Made by U.S. Military Personnel

I n March 1952, *Project Blue Book* was begun by the U.S. Government to investigate UFO reports.

Project Blue Book's stated goals were as follows: To find an explanation for all the reported sighting(s) of UFOs, to determine if the UFO posed any security threat to the United States, and to determine if UFOs exhibit(ed) any advanced technology that the United States could utilize.

Project Blue Book investigators chronicled and investigated more than 12,000 UFO reports and explained more than 11,000 of these sightings. (Or "explained them away," as many have suggested.) Of the close to 600 that were officially declared as unexplained, 218 were made by the military's own trained personnel: sober-minded, serious, alert, and *observant* men. These are the men the U.S. Government spent millions training and educating in order to be able to make the kind of accurate assessments and reports needed in these cases.

This list looks at 40 especially intriguing UFO sightings in the United States made by military professionals between 1947 and 1967.

ALABAMA

1. Thursday, August 28, 1952 at 9:30 p.m at Chickasaw and Brookley Air Force Base. For 1 hour and 15 minutes, Air Force control tower operators, an officer from the Air Force Office of Special Investigations, and several others saw six objects, varying from fiery red to sparkling diamond appearance, hover and fly erratically up and down.

ALASKA

2. Monday, December 8, 1952 at 8:16 p.m. in the air over Ladd Air Force Base. Pilot First Lieutenant D. Dickman and radar operator First Lieutenant T. Davies in an Air Force F-94 jet interceptor saw one white, oval light (which changed to red at a higher altitude), fly straight and level for two minutes, then climb at phenomenal speed on an erratic flight path for eight minutes more.

ARIZONA

3. Tuesday, October 14, 1947 at 12 noon, 11 miles north-northeast of Cave Creek. For about 45 to 60 seconds, ex-Army Air Force fighter pilot J.L. Clark, civilian pilot Anderson, and a third man saw one 3 foot "flying wing-shaped" object. The object looked black against the white clouds and red against the blue sky. It flew straight at approximately 380 m.p.h., at 8-10,000 feet, from the northwest to the southeast.

ARKANSAS

4. Thursday, June 12, 1952 at 7:30 p.m. at Fort Smith. An Army Major and a Lieutenant Colonel, using binoculars, briefly witnessed one orange ball with a tail fly overhead with a low angular velocity.

CALIFORNIA

5. Thursday, May 1, 1952 at 10:50 a.m. at George Air Force Base. For a total of 15 to 30 seconds, three military personnel on the arms range, along with one Lieutenant Colonel 4 miles away, saw five flat-white discs about the diameter of a C-47's wingspan (95 feet) fly fast, make a 90 degree turn in a formation of three in front and two behind, and then dart around.

COLORADO

6. Friday, November 25, 1955 at 10:30 a.m. in La Veta. For five seconds, Colorado State Senator S.T. Taylor saw a luminous, green-blue, jellylike, dirigible-shaped object in the sky with a fat front that tapered toward the tail. The object dived at a 45 degree angle, and then reduced its angle to a 30 degrees.

FLORIDA

7. Thursday, January 27, 1949 at 10:20 p.m in Cortez-Bradenton. For 25 minutes, Captain Sames, the acting chief of the Aircraft Branch at Elgin Air Force Base, and his wife watched as a cigar-shaped object as long as two Pullman cars and with seven lighted square windows, threw sparks, descended, and then climbed with a bouncing motion at an estimated 400 m.p.h.

GEORGIA

8. Friday, October 31, 1952 at 7:40 p.m. in Fayetteville. Air Force Lieutenant James Allen watched for 1 minute as an orange, blimp-shaped object, 80 feet long and 20 feet high, flew at treetop level, crossed over his car, and then climbed away at a 45-foot altitude and at tremendous speed. When the object passed over Allen's car, his car radio stopped playing.

HAWAII

9. Tuesday, January 4, 1949 at 2 p.m. at Hickam Field. Air Force pilot Captain Paul Storey saw a flat white, elliptical object with a matte top circle overhead, oscillating to the right and left before speeding away.

IDAHO

10. Wednesday, July 9, 1947 at 12:17 p.m. in Meridian. For more than 10 seconds, former Army Air Force B-29 pilot Dave Johnson saw a black disc, which stood out against the clouds and which was seen from an Idaho Air National Guard AT-6, make a half-roll and then a stair-step climb.

ILLINOIS

11. Saturday, May 9, 1964 at 10:20 p.m. in Chicago. U.S. District Court reporter J.R. Betz saw for three seconds three light-green, crescent-shaped objects, about half the apparent size of the moon, fly very fast in tight formation from east to west, oscillating in size and color for the duration of the sighting. (*Note:* Betz was not military personnel but is included here because he was part of the United States court system and, thus, his credibility can reasonably be taken as a given.)

INDIANA

12. Wednesday, July 23, 1952 at 11:35 p.m. in South Bend. For nine minutes, Air Force pilot Captain H.W. Kloth watched as two bright blue-white objects flew together. The rear one veered off at the conclusion of the sighting.

KANSAS

13. Tuesday, July 29, 1952 at 12:35 p.m. in Wichita. For five minutes, Air Force shop employees Douglas and Hess at Municipal Airport watched as one bright white circular object with a flat bottom flew very fast above the airport. It then hovered for 10 to 15 seconds over the Cessna Aircraft plant.

KENTUCKY

14. Sunday, June 15, 1952 at 11:50 p.m. in Louisville. For 15 minutes, ex-Navy radar technician Edward Duke watched as a large, cigar-shaped object with a blunt front, lit sides, and a red stern, maneuvered in a leisurely fashion.

LOUISIANA

15. Friday, February 27, 1953 at 11:58 a.m. in Shreveport. For four minutes, an Air Force airman (who was also a private pilot) watched as five yellow discs made circular turns and fluttered before three of them vanished. The other two discs then flew erratic turns for the remainder of the sighting.

MAINE

16. Monday, September 16, 1952 at 6:22 p.m. in Portland. For 20 minutes, the crew of a Navy P2V Neptune patrol plane watched visually (and by radar) a group of five lights. At the same time, a long, thin blip was being tracked on radar.

MARYLAND

17. Tuesday, June 30, 1959 at 8:23 p.m. at Patuxent River Naval Air Station. For 20 to 30 seconds, Navy Commander D. Connolly watched as a gold, oblate-shaped, metallic object with sharp edges, nine times as wide as it was thick, flew straight and level for the duration of the sighting.

MASSACHUSETTS

18. Sunday, February 5, 1950 at 5:10 p.m. in Teaticket. For five minutes, former Navy fighter pilot Marvin Odom, Air Force Lieutenant Philip Foushee, a pilot from Otis Air Force Base, and two others, watched as two thin, illuminated cylinders (one of which dropped a fireball), maneuvered together. They then disappeared high and fast.

MICHIGAN

19. Sunday, July 27, 1952 from 10:05 a.m. to 10:20 a.m. at Selfridge Air Force Base. Three B-29 bomber crewmen on the ground watched as many round, white objects flew straight and level and very fast. This began with two at 10:05, then one at 10:10, another one at 10:15, and a final one at 10:20.

MINNESOTA

20. Saturday, November 24, 1951 at 3:53 p.m. at Mankato. For five seconds, Air Force or Air National Guard pilots W.H. Fairbrother and D.E. Stewart in P-51 Mustangs watched as a milky white object shaped like a Northrop flying wing flew straight and level. It had a broad, slightly swept-back wing with no fuselage or tail and an estimated 8-foot span.

MISSISSIPPI

21. Wednesday, May 7, 1952 at 12:15 p.m. at Keesler Air Force Base. For five to 10 minutes, Captain Morris, a Master Sergeant, a Staff Sergeant, and an Airman First Class all watched as an aluminum or silver cylindrical object darted in and out of the clouds 10 times.

MISSOURI

22. Saturday, July 26, 1952 at 12:15 a.m. in Kansas City. For one hour, Air Force Captain H.A. Stone and the men in the control towers at Fairfax Field and Municipal Airport watched as a greenish light with red-orange flashes descended in the northwest from 40 degrees elevation to 10 degrees elevation.

MONTANA

23. Thursday, November 13, 1952 at 2:43 a.m. at Glasgow. For 20 seconds, U.S. Weather Bureau observer Earl Oksendahl watched as five oval-shaped objects with lights all around them flew in a V-formation. Each object seemed to change position vertically by climbing or diving as if to hold formation. The formation came from the northwest, made a 90 degree turn overhead, and then flew away to the southwest. (*Note:* As was the case with Court reporter Betz in the Illinois sighting, Oksendahl is not military personnel, but his credibility can likewise be taken for granted.)

NEBRASKA

24. Thursday, June 5, 1952 at 11 p.m. at Offutt Air Force Base in Omaha. For 4.5 minutes, Strategic Air Command top secret control officer and former OSI agent Second Lieutenant W.R. Soper, and two other persons watched as a bright red object remained stationary before speeding away with a visible short tail.

NEVADA

25. Thursday, July 24, 1952 at 3:40 p.m. in the air over Carson Sink. For three to four seconds, Air Force Lieutenant Colonels McGinn and Barton, flying in a B-25 bomber, watched three silver, delta-shaped objects, each with a ridge along the top, cross in front of and above the B-25 at high speed.

New Hampshire

26. Tuesday, July 24, 1951 at approximately 7:10 a.m. in Portsmouth. For 20 seconds, Hanscom Air Force Base Operations Officer Captain Cobb, and Corporal Fein watched as a 100- to 200-foot long tubular object (that was five times long as it was wide), with fins at one end, and with many black and grey spots, flew 800 to 1,000 m.p.h. at an altitude of 1,000 to 2,000 feet, leaving a faint swath behind it.

New Jersey

27. Friday, April 14, 1950 at 2:30 p.m. at Fort Monmouth. For three to four minutes, Army Master Sergeant James watched as four rectangular, amber objects, about three by four feet in size, changed speed and direction rapidly. The group of objects rose and fell during the sighting.

New Mexico

28. Tuesday, October 7, 1952 at 8:30 p.m. in Alamagordo. For four to five seconds, Air Force Lieutenant Bagnell watched as a pale blue oval, with a long vertical axis, flew straight and level, covering 30 degrees during the sighting.

New York

29. Friday, June 1, 1951 at 4:20 a.m. in Niagara Falls. For 30 to 40 seconds, Master Sergeant H.E. Sweeney and two enlisted men watched as a glowing yellow-orange, saucer-shaped object with arc-shaped wings, flew straight up into the sky.

North Carolina

30. Friday, June 20, 1958 at 11:05 p.m. at Fort Bragg. For 10 minutes, Battalion Communication Chief Seaman First Class A. Parsley watched as a silver, circular object hovered, then oscillated slightly, before finally moving away at great speed. The lower portion of the object was seen through a green haze.

Ohio

31. Thursday, July 17, 1952 at 11 a.m. in Lockbourne. For three hours, several Air National Guard employees watched as a light like a big star appeared from nowhere. However, the light disappeared when an aircraft approached it. This object was also seen by Air National Guard personnel on the nights of July 20, 22, and 23 the same year.

Pennsylvania

32. Wednesday, July 23, 1952 at 12:50 p.m. in Altoona. For 20 minutes, the two-man crews of two Air Force F-94 jet interceptors, flying at 35,000 to 46,000 feet altitude, watched as three cylindrical objects in a vertical stack formation flew at an altitude of 50,000 to 80,000 feet.

South Dakota

33. Wednesday, July 9, 1952 at 3:35 p.m. at Rapid City Air Force Base. For five seconds, Staff Sergeant D.P. Foster and three other persons watched as a single white, disc-shaped object sped by three times, flying on a straight and level trajectory.

Tennessee

34. Sunday, November 20, 1955 at 5:20 p.m. in Lake City. For four to 15 minutes, Operations Officer Captain B.G. Denkler and five men of the Air Force 663rd AC&W Squadron (as well as many others in the vicinity) watched as two oblong, bright orange, semi-transparent objects flew erratically at terrific speed toward and away from each other.

Texas

35. Saturday, June 21, 1952 at 12:30 p.m. in the air over Kelly Air Force Base. For only a second or so, B-29 bomber flight Engineer Technical Sergeant Howard Davis, flying at 8,000 feet altitude, saw a flat, white object with a sharply pointed front, rounded rear, dark blue center, and red rim. Its trail sparked as it dove past the B-29 at a distance of 500 feet.

Vermont

36. Thursday, April 24, 1952 at 5 a.m. in the air over Bellevue Hill. For three to four minutes, the crew of an Air Force C-124 transport plane watched as three circular, bluish objects in a loose "fingertip" formation flew parallel to the C-124 twice.

Virginia

37. Monday, April 14 1958 at 1 p.m. in the air over Lynchburg. For four seconds, Air Force Major D.G. Tilley, flying a C-47 transport, observed a gray-black rectangular object rotating very slowly on its horizontal axis.

Washington

38. Sunday, March 23, 1952 at 6:56 p.m. and 7 p.m. in the air over Yakima. For 45 seconds, the pilot and radar operator of an F-94 jet interceptor watched as a stationary red fireball increased in brightness and then faded at both times of the sighting. *Project Blue Book Status Report #7* (May 31, 1952) says the target was also tracked by ground radar at 78 knots (90 m.p.h.) and alternately at 22,500 feet and 25,000 feet in altitude.

West Virginia

39. Tuesday, September 24, 1952 at 3:30 p.m. in the air over Charleston. For 15 minutes, the crew of an Air Force B-29 bomber watched as many bright, metallic particles streamed past the B-29. These particles were up to three feet in length.

Wisconsin

40. Monday, February 20, 1967 at 3:10 a.m. in Oxford. For two minutes, Air Force veteran/ truck driver Stanton Summer watched as an orange-red object flew parallel to his truck.

Chapter 9

64 Sights to See in Washington, D.C.

"I went to Washington as everybody goes there, prepared to see everything done with some furtive intention, but I was disappointed—pleasantly disappointed."
—Walt Whitman, 1888

or information on directions to any of these locales, along with admission prices, hours, and contact details, I recommend *The Rough Guide to Washington D.C.* (distributed by Penguin). Or you can visit the Federal Web Locator Web site (*www.law.vill.edu/Fed-Agency/fedwebloc.html*) for addresses for home pages for almost any governmental branch or agency.

1. The Arlington Memorial Bridge.
2. Arlington National Cemetery (including the Iwo Jima Memorial, the Taft Grave, the Kennedy Gravesites, the Tomb of the Unknowns, the Confederate Memorial, L'Enfant Grave, the USS *Maine* Mast, and Arlington House, the former residence of Robert E. Lee).
3. The Bureau of Engraving and Printing.
4. The Capitol Reflecting Pool.
5. The D.C. War Memorial.
6. The Department of Agriculture.
7. The Department of Commerce.
8. The Department of Education.
9. The Department of Housing and Urban Development.
10. The Department of Justice.
11. The Department of State.
12. The Department of Transportation.
13. The Department of the Interior.
14. The FDR Memorial.
15. The Federal Aviation Administration.
16. The Federal Bureau of Investigation.
17. The Food & Drug Administration.
18. Ford's Theater and the Peterson House.
19. The Francis Scott Key Memorial Bridge.
20. The Frederick Douglass National Historical Site.
21. The Grant Memorial.
22. The Hirshorn Museum.
23. The Internal Revenue Service.
24. The Jefferson Memorial.
25. The John Ericsson Statue.
26. The John Paul Jones Memorial.
27. The Joseph Henry Statue.
28. The Kennedy Center.

29. The Korean War Veterans Memorial.
30. The Library of Congress.
31. The Lincoln Memorial.
32. NASA.
33. The National Academy of Sciences.
34. The National Air and Space Museum.
35. The National Aquarium.
36. The National Archives.
37. The National Gallery of Art.
38. The National Museum of African Art.
39. The National Museum of American Art.
40. The National Museum of American History.
41. The National Museum of Natural History.
42. The National Museum of the American Indian.
43. The National Museum of Women in the Arts.
44. The National Postal Museum.
45. The Navy Memorial.
46. The Navy Museum.
47. The Peace Memorial.
48. The Pentagon.
49. The Reflecting Pool at the Lincoln Memorial.
50. The Sackler Gallery.
51. The Smithsonian Institution.
52. The Supreme Court.
53. The Taft Memorial.
54. The Theodore Roosevelt Memorial Bridge.
55. The United States Holocaust Memorial Museum.
56. The U.S. Capitol.
57. The U.S. Naval Observatory.
58. The Veterans Women's Memorial.
59. The Vietnam Veterans Memorial.
60. The Washington Monument.
61. Washington National Cathedral.
62. The Watergate Complex.
63. The White House.
64. The proposed World War II Memorial.

THE 5 LARGEST AND 6 MOST-VISITED ZOOS IN THE UNITED STATES

THE LARGEST ZOOLOGICAL PARKS IN AMERICA IN 1999

1. **The San Diego Wild Animal Park**, 2,200 acres.
2. **The Minnesota Zoo** in Apple Valley, 500 acres.
3. **The Columbus Zoo and Aquarium** in Powell, Ohio, 404 acres.
4. **The Miami Metrozoo**, 300 acres.
5. **The Bronx Zoo** in New York City, 265 acres.

THE MOST-VISITED ZOOLOGICAL PARKS IN AMERICA IN 1999

1. **The San Diego Zoo**, 3.5 million attendance.
2. **The National Zoo** in Washington, D.C. and the **Lincoln Park Zoological Gardens** in Chicago, both tied at 3 million in attendance.
3. **The St. Louis Zoo**, 2.9 million attendance.
4. **The Bronx Zoo**, 2.2 million attendance.
5. **The Denver Zoo**, 1.7 million attendance.

Chapter 10

197 Nicknames of 39 American Presidents

"Lincoln said in his homely way that he wanted 'to take a bath in public opinion.' I think I have a right to take a bath before I do much talking."

—President James Garfield

ome people get no respect. This truism seems to affect America's presidents as well, as this list of presidential nicknames illustrates.

    Some of these nicknames refer to the manner in which the president assumed office (for example, John Tyler was called "His Accidency," as was Millard Fillmore, Andrew Johnson, Chester A. Arthur, and Grover Cleveland). Some refer to a president's physical appearance (John Adams was "His Rotundity"; Theodore Roosevelt was "Four Eyes"). The 18th century essayist William Hazlitt once wrote, "A nickname is the heaviest stone that the devil can throw at a man." A review of these often unflattering sobriquets would seem to bear him out, wouldn't you say?

GEORGE WASHINGTON

1. The American Fabius.
2. The Farmer President.
3. The Father of His Country.
4. The Old Fox.
5. The Sage of Mount Vernon.
6. The Savior of His Country.
7. The Surveyor President.
8. The Sword of the Revolution.
9. The Stepfather of His Country.

JOHN ADAMS

10. The Atlas of Independence.
11. The Colossus of American Independence.
12. The Duke of Braintree.
13. His Rotundity.

THOMAS JEFFERSON

14. The Father of the Declaration of Independence.
15. Long Tom.
16. The Pen of the Revolution.

17. The Philosopher of Democracy.
18. The Sage of Monticello.

JAMES MONROE

19. The "Era of Good Feelings" President.
20. The Lost Cocked Hat.

JOHN QUINCY ADAMS

21. The Accidental President.
22. Old Man Eloquent.

ANDREW JACKSON

23. The Hero of New Orleans.
24. King Andrew the First.
25. Mischie-Andy.
26. Old Hickory.
27. The Pointed Arrow.
28. The Sage of the Hermitage.
29. The Sharp Knife.

MARTIN VAN BUREN

30. The Albany Regency.
31. The American Tallyrand.
32. The Enchanter.
33. The Fox.
34. Kinderhook Fox.
35. King Martin the First.
36. The Little Magician.
37. Little Van.
38. Machievellian Belshazzar.
39. The Mistletoe Politician.
40. Petticoat Pet.
41. The Red Fox.
42. The Sage of Lindenwald.
43. Whiskey Van.

WILLIAM HENRY HARRISON

44. The Farmer President.
45. The Log Cabin Candidate.
46. Old Granny.
47. Tippecanoe.
48. The Washington of the West.

JOHN TYLER

49. The Accidental President.
50. His Accidency.

JAMES K. POLK

51. The First Dark Horse.
52. The Napoleon of the Stump.
53. Young Hickory.

ZACHARY TAYLOR

54. Old Rough and Ready.
55. Zach.

MILLARD FILLMORE

56. The American Louis Philippe.
57. His Accidency.

JAMES BUCHANAN

58. The Bachelor President.
59. Old Buck.
60. The Old Public Functionary.
61. The Sage of Wheatland.
62. Ten-Cent Jimmy.
63. The Squire.

ABRAHAM LINCOLN

64. The Ancient.
65. The Emancipation President.
66. Father Abraham.
67. The Great Emancipator.
68. Greatheart.
69. Honest Abe.
70. The Illinois Baboon.
71. Old Abe.
72. The Railsplitter.
73. The Sage of Springfield.
74. The Sectional President.

ANDREW JOHNSON

75. The Daddy of the Baby.
76. The Father of the Homestead.

77. His Accidency.
78. King Andy.
79. The Veto.

ULYSSES S. GRANT

80. The Butcher from Galena.
81. The Great Hammerer.
82. The Hero of Appomattox.
83. Hug Grant.
84. Lyss.
85. The Man on Horseback.
86. Old Three Stars.
87. Texas.
88. Uncle Sam.
89. Unconditional Surrender.
90. The Uniformed Soldier.
91. United States.
92. Useless.

RUTHERFORD B. HAYES

93. The Dark Horse.
94. Granny Hayes.
95. His Fraudulency.
96. Old Eight-to-Seven.
97. President De Facto.

JAMES A. GARFIELD

98. The Canal Boy.
99. The Martyr President.
100. The Preacher.
101. The Teacher President.

CHESTER A. ARTHUR

102. Arthur the Gentleman.
103. The Dude.
104. The First Gentleman of the Land.
105. His Accidency.
106. Our Chet.
107. Prince Arthur.

GROVER CLEVELAND

108. Big Beefhead.
109. The Buffalo Hangman.
110. The Claimant.

111. The Dumb Prophet.
112. His Accidency.
113. The Man of Destiny.
114. Old Grover.
115. Old Veto.
116. The People's President.
117. The Perpetual Candidate.
118. The Pretender.
119. The Sage of Princeton.
120. The Stuffed Prophet.
121. Uncle Jumbo.

BENJAMIN HARRISON

122. Baby McKee's Grandfather.
123. Chinese Harrison.
124. The Grandfather's Hat.
125. Kid Gloves.
126. Little Ben.

WILLIAM McKINLEY

127. The Idol of Ohio.
128. The Napoleon of Protection.
129. Prosperity's Advance Agent.
130. The Stocking-Foot Orator.
131. Wobbly Willie.

THEODORE ROOSEVELT

132. The Bull Moose.
133. The Driving Force.
134. The Dynamo of Power.
135. Four Eyes.
136. The Great White Chief.
137. The Happy Warrior.
138. Haroun-al-Roosevelt.
139. The Hero of San Juan Hill.
140. The Man on Horseback.
141. The Old Lion.
142. Old Rough and Ready.
143. The Roughrider.
144. Telescope Teddy.
145. Theodore the Meddler.
146. TR.
147. The Trust-Buster.
148. The Typical American.
149. The Wielder of the Big Stick.

WILLIAM HOWARD TAFT

150. Big Bill.

WOODROW WILSON

151. The Big One of the Peace Conference.
152. The Phrasemaker.
153. The Schoolmaster.
154. Woody.

WARREN G. HARDING

155. The Shadow of Blooming Grove.

CALVIN COOLIDGE

156. Silent Cal.

HERBERT C. HOOVER

157. The Chief.

FRANKLIN D. ROOSEVELT

158. The Boss.
159. Deficit.
160. FDR.
161. The Featherduster of Dutchess County.
162. The Gallant Leader.
163. Houdini in the White House.
164. The Kangaroosevelt.
165. The Man in the White House.
166. Mr. Big.
167. The New Dealer.
168. The Raw Dealocrat.
169. Roosocrat.
170. The Sphinx.
171. The Squire of Hyde Park.
172. A Traitor to His Class.

HARRY S TRUMAN

173. Give 'Em Hell Harry.
174. The Haberdasher.
175. High Tax Harry.

DWIGHT D. EISENHOWER

176. Ike.

JOHN F. KENNEDY

177. Jack.
178. JFK.

LYNDON B. JOHNSON

179. Big Daddy.
180. Landslide Lyndon.
181. LBJ.

RICHARD M. NIXON

182. Gloomy Gus.
183. The Iron Butt.
184. The New Nixon.
185. Tricky Dick.

GERALD R. FORD

186. Jerry.

JAMES E. CARTER, JR.

187. Jimmy.

RONALD W. REAGAN

188. The Defender.
189. Dutch.
190. The Gipper.
191. The Great Communicator.
192. The Oldest and the Wisest.
193. The Teflon President.

GEORGE H. W. BUSH

194. Poppie.

WILLIAM J. CLINTON

195. Bill.
196. Bubba.
197. Slick Willie.

Chapter 11

5 Really Big American Deserts

1. **The Chihuahuan Desert**: 140,000 square miles, covering parts of Texas, New Mexico, Arizona (and Mexico).
2. **The Sonoran Desert**: 70,000 square miles, covering parts of southwestern Arizona and southeastern California (extending into northwest Mexico).
3. **The Mojave Desert**: 15,000 square miles, covering part of southern California.
4. **Death Valley**: 3,300 square miles covering parts of California and Nevada.
5. **The Painted Desert**: A 150-mile section of high plateau in northern Arizona.

(*Note:* The world's largest desert is the Sahara desert, which covers 3.5 million square miles in North Africa and extends westward to the Atlantic Ocean.)

Chapter 12

The Alma Maters of 19 U.S. Presidents

*"The use of university is to make young gentlemen
as unlike their fathers as possible."*
—**Woodrow Wilson**, Princeton, Class of 1879.

*"A muttonhead, after an education at West Point—
or Harvard—is a muttonhead still."*
—**Theodore Roosevelt**, Harvard, Class of 1880.

This chapter looks at where 29 of our chief executives went to college. The list of schools runs the gamut from the most prestigious institutions of higher learning to humble local colleges.

☆ **John Adams (second president)**: Harvard (Class of 1755).

☆ **Thomas Jefferson (third president)**: College of William and Mary (Class of 1762).

☆ **James Madison (fourth president)**: College of New Jersey (now Princeton) (Class of 1771).

☆ **John Quincy Adams (sixth president)**: Harvard (Class of 1787).

☆ **John Tyler (10th president)**: College of William and Mary (Class of 1807).

☆ **James K. Polk (11th president)**: University of North Carolina (Class of 1818).

☆ **Franklin Pierce (14th president)**: Bowdoin College (Class of 1824).

☆ **James Buchanan (15th president)**: Dickinson College (Class of 1809).

☆ **Ulysses S. Grant (18th president)**: U.S. Military Academy (at West Point, NY) (Class of 1843).

☆ **Rutherford B. Hayes (19th president)**: Kenyon College (Class of 1842); Harvard Law School (Class of 1845).

☆ **James A. Garfield (20th president)**: Williams College (Class of 1856).

☆ **Chester A. Arthur (21st president)**: Union College (Class of 1848).

☆ **Benjamin Harrison (23rd president)**: Miami University (in Oxford, Ohio) (Class of 1852).

* **Theodore Roosevelt (26th president)**: Harvard (Class of 1880).
* **William Howard Taft (27th president)**: Yale (Class of 1878).
* **Woodrow Wilson (28th president)**: Princeton (Class of 1879).
* **Warren G. Harding (29th president)**: Ohio Central College (Class of 1882).
* **Calvin Coolidge (30th president)**: Amherst College (Class of 1895).
* **Herbert C. Hoover (31st president)**: Stanford (Class of 1895).
* **Franklin D. Roosevelt (32nd president)**: Harvard (Class of 1903), Columbia University Law School (Class of 1907).
* **Dwight D. Eisenhower (34th president)**: U.S. Military Academy (at West Point, NY) (Class of 1915).
* **John F. Kennedy (35th president)**: Harvard (Class of 1940).
* **Lyndon B. Johnson (36th president)**: Southwest Texas State Teachers College (Class of 1930).
* **Richard M. Nixon (37th president)**: Whittier College (Class of 1934); Duke University Law School (Class of 1937).
* **Gerald R. Ford (38th president)**: University of Michigan (Class of 1935), Yale Law School (Class of 1941).
* **Jimmy Carter (39th president)**: U.S. Naval Academy (Class of 1946).
* **Ronald Reagan (40th president)**: Eureka College (Class of 1932).
* **George Bush (41st president)**: Yale (Class of 1948).
* **Bill Clinton (42nd president)**: Georgetown University (Class of 1968); Oxford University, England (Rhodes Scholar, 1968-1970); Yale Law School (Class of 1973).

The following American presidents never graduated from college. (Some of them did attend college and then dropped out for a variety of reasons, including illness and entering the military.):

George Washington (first president), James Monroe (fifth president), Andrew Jackson (seventh president), Martin Van Buren (eighth president), William Henry Harrison (ninth president), Zachary Taylor (12th president), Millard Fillmore (13th president), Abraham Lincoln (16th president), Andrew Johnson (17th president), Grover Cleveland (22nd, 24th president), William McKinley (25th president), and Harry S Truman (33rd president).

The following are schools that have educated more than one president:

* **Harvard** (5): John Adams, John Quincy Adams, Theodore Roosevelt, Franklin D. Roosevelt, John F. Kennedy.
* **Yale** (4): William Howard Taft, Gerald Ford, George Bush, Bill Clinton.
* **College of William and Mary** (2): Thomas Jefferson, John Tyler.
* **Princeton** (2): James Madison, Woodrow Wilson.
* **U.S. Military Academy** (at West Point, NY) (2): Ulysses S. Grant, Dwight D. Eisenhower.

Chapter 13

2 Formerly "Gay" U.S. Locales

Sometimes, a word's meaning changes over the years. And there is probably no word for which this is truer than the word "gay." Nowadays, it is downright odd to watch an old black-and-white movie and hear a tuxedoed dancer sing about how "gay" he is to a lovely woman because she is his true love.

Two locales in America were less than thrilled with the word's new meaning and took steps to distance themselves from the "revised context," so to speak, of the word.

GAY COURT, LA VERNE, CALIF.

The residents of this street went to their city council and requested an official name change because of the new meaning of the word. The city council agreed and Gay Court officially became Bayberry Court.

GAY MOUNTAIN, N.C.

The landowners on this mountain had the same complaint as the residents of Gay Court. Civic authorities again agreed and the mountain's name was officially changed to Misty Mountain.

OTHER GAY LOCALES

Interesting enough, the following U.S. cities have *not* changed their name (even though some town residents have tried).

★	Dike, Tex.	★	Gay, Ky.
★	Dyke, Va.	★	Gay, Mich.
★	Ferrysburg, Mich.	★	Gays Creek, Ky.
★	Fort Gay, Wyo.	★	Gays Mills, Wis.
★	Fruitland, Md.	★	Gays, Il.
★	Fruitvale, Idaho.	★	Gaysville, Vt.
★	Gay, Ga.	★	Gayville, S.D.

(*Source: Lavender Lists* by Lynne Yamaguchi Fletcher and Adrien Saks. Alyson Publications, 1990.)

Chapter 14

10 American Nobel Prize Winners for Literature

The Nobel Prize for Literature is, in many ways, a superior accolade to the Pulitzer Prize, since the Nobel is awarded for a body of work instead of a single book. Ten Americans have won this august honor since 1930. Following the Nobel winner is a brief list of some of the writer's most notable and recommended works.

1930: SINCLAIR LEWIS

Babbitt (1922, novel), *Arrowsmith* (1925, novel), *Elmer Gantry* (1927, novel), *Dodsworth* (1929, novel).

1936: EUGENE O'NEILL

Anna Christie (1922, play), *The Hairy Ape* (1923, play), *Desire Under the Elms* (1925, play), *Mourning Becomes Electra* (1931, play), *Ah, Wilderness!* (1933, play), *The Iceman Cometh* (1946, play), *A Long Day's Journey Into Night* (1956, play).

1938: PEARL BUCK

The Good Earth (1931, novel), *Sons* (1932, novel), *A House Divided* (1935, novel), *Dragon Seed* (1942, novel), *My Several Worlds* (1954, autobiography), *Imperial Woman* (1956, novel).

1949: WILLIAM FAULKNER

The Sound and the Fury (1929, novel), *As I Lay Dying* (1930, novel), *Sanctuary* (1931, novel), *Light in August* (1932, novel), *Absalom, Absalom!* (1936, novel), *Intruder in the Dust* (1948, novel), *Collected Stories* (1950, short story collection—National Book Award), *Requiem for a Nun* (1951, play), *A Fable* (1954, novel), *The Town* (1957, novel), *The Mansion* (1959, novel).

1954: ERNEST HEMINGWAY

In Our Time (1925, short story collection), *The Sun Also Rises* (1926, novel), *Men Without Women* (1927, short story collection), *A Farewell To Arms* (1929, novel), *Death in the Afternoon* (1932, nonfiction), *Winner Take Nothing* (1933, short story collection), *Green Hills of Africa* (1935, nonfiction), *To Have and Have Not* (1937, novel), *The Fifth Column and the First Forty-Nine Stories* (1938, play and short story collection), *For Whom the Bell Tolls* (1940, novel), *The Old Man and the Sea* (1952, novel—Pulitzer Prize), *A Moveable Feast* (1964, memoir), *Islands in the Stream* (1970, novella collection).

1962: JOHN STEINBECK

Tortilla Flat (1935, novel), *In Dubious Battle* (1936, novel), *Of Mice and Men* (1937, novella), *The Grapes of Wrath* (1939, novel), *The Red Pony* (1937, short story collection), *The Moon is Down* (1942, novel), *Cannery Row* (1945, novel), *The Pearl* (1947, novel), *East of Eden* (1952, novel), *The Winter of Our Discontent* (1961, novel).

1976: SAUL BELLOW

The Adventures of Augie March (1953, novel), *Henderson the Rain King* (1959, novel), *Seize the Day* (1956, novella), *Mosby's Memoirs* (1968, short story collection), *Herzog* (1964, novel—National Book Award), *Mr. Sammler's Planet* (1970, novel—National Book Award), *Humboldt's Gift* (1975, novel—Pulitzer Prize), *To Jerusalem and Back* (1976, nonfiction).

1980: CZESLAW MILOSZ

The Captive Mind (1953, essays), *The Seizure of Power* (1955, novel), *The Issa Valley* (1955, novel), *The Poetic Treatise* (1957, history), *Native Realm* (1959, autobiography), *Bells of Winter* (1978, poetry), *The Witness of Poetry* (1983, lectures).

1987: JOSEPH BRODSKY

Selected Poems (1973, poetry), *A Part of Speech* (1980, poetry), *History of the Twentieth Century* (1986, poetry), *To Urania* (1988, poetry), *Less Than One* (1986, essays).

1993: TONI MORRISON

The Bluest Eye (1970, novel), *Sula* (1973, novel), *Song of Solomon* (1977, novel), *Tar Baby* (1981, novel), *Beloved* (1987, novel—Pulitzer Prize), *Jazz* (1992, novel), *Playing in the Dark: Whiteness and the Literary Imagination* (1992, literary criticism).

Chapter 15

The 9 Most Devastating American Earthquakes

"All things have second birth;
The earthquake is not satisfied at once."
—William Wordsworth, *The Prelude*

Seven of nine earthquakes in America in the past 115 years ranking 6.2 or higher on the Richter Scale have taken place in California. In these seven quakes, close to 1,000 people died along with billions of dollars in property damage and lost business. (These facts, however, do not seem to bother many California residents.)

The intensity of the earthquakes is expressed in magnitude using the Richter Scale which indicates the severity of the quake and its subsequent damage. The scale uses numbers varying from 1.5 to 10. The Richter Scale was developed in 1935 by American seismologist Charles Richter. It was designed to be logarithmic in nature, meaning that each successive whole number represents a 10-fold increase in power and intensity. It is still used today by seismologists to express an earthquake's magnitude.

Another system used to describe earthquake intensity is the Mercalli Earthquake Intensity scale, which was developed in 1902 by Italian seismologist Giuseppe Mercalli. Although now obsolete, the descriptions of the 12 levels of earthquake effects in populated areas as codified by Mercalli accurately portray the damage at varying levels of intensity.

The Mercalli scale is as follows:

Level I: Generally not felt by people, but detectable by seismologists.

Level II: Felt by a few people. Some objects, such as hanging baskets or lamps, may swing if suspended.

Level III: Felt by a few people, but mostly indoors. This level has been described as feeling like the vibrations of a passing truck.

Level IV: Felt by many people indoors, but very few people outdoors. Windows, dishes, and doors rattle.

Level V: Felt by nearly everyone both indoors and outdoors. Sleepers awaken, small unstable objects may fall and break, and doors move.

Level VI: Felt by everyone. Some heavy furniture may move, people walk unsteadily, windows break, dishes fall and break, books fall off shelves, and bushes and trees visibly shake.

Level VII: It is difficult to stand and there is moderate to heavy damage to poorly constructed buildings. Plaster, tiles, loose bricks, and stones fall. There are small landslides along slopes. Water becomes opaque as sediment is stirred up.

Level VIII: It is difficult to steer cars. There is damage to chimneys, monuments, and towers. Elevated tanks fall, tree branches crack, and steep slopes crack.

Level IX: There is extensive damage to buildings, masonry is seriously damaged, foundations crack, there is serious damage to reservoirs, and underground pipes break.

Level X: Most masonry, frame structures, and foundations are destroyed. There are numerous large landslides, water is hurled onto the banks of rivers and lakes, and railroad tracks bend in some places.

Level XI: Few buildings made of brick are left standing. Railroad tracks bend severely, many bridges are destroyed, and underground pipelines are completely inoperative.

Level XII: Nearly total destruction. Large rock masses are displaced, as objects are thrown violently into the air.

In Chronological Order

Date	Location	Magnitude (Richter Scale)
August 31, 1886	Charleston, S.C.	6.6
April 18-19, 1906	San Francisco, Calif.	8.3
March 10, 1933	Long Beach, Calif.	6.2
March 27, 1964	Alaska	9.2
February 9, 1971	San Fernando Valley, Calif.	6.6
October 17, 1989	San Francisco Bay area, Calif.	7.1
June 28, 1992	Southern California	7.5 & 6.6
January 17, 1994	Northridge, Calif.	6.8
October 16, 1999	Southern California	7.0

In Order of Intensity

Date	Location	Magnitude (Richter Scale)
March 27, 1964	Alaska	9.2
April 18-19, 1906	San Francisco, Calif.	8.3
June 28, 1992	Southern California	7.5 & 6.6
October 17, 1989	San Francisco Bay area, Calif.	7.1
October 16, 1999	Southern California	7.0
January 17, 1994	Northridge, Calif.	6.8
August 31, 1886	Charleston, S.C.	6.6
February 9, 1971	San Fernando Valley, Calif.	6.6
March 10, 1933	Long Beach, Calif.	6.2

Chapter 16

14 Important Supreme Court Decisions Concerning Religion

"Congress shall make no law respecting an establishment of religion, or prohibiting the free exercise thereof; or abridging the freedom of speech, or of the press; or of the right of the people peaceably to assemble, and to petition the government for a redress of grievances."
—Article I, *The Constitution of the United States of America*

Over the years, the Supreme Court has had to tackle many thorny religious issues. These 14 cases are some of their more important landmark rulings—rulings on religion that changed America.

Of these 14, one of the most significant (and most controversial) was the 1962 ruling that banned prayer in public schools. Now, more than three decades later, this issue still rankles the faithful and there is constant debate about the ruling and repeated legal challenges to overturn it. So far, none of these efforts have succeeded.

1879: REYNOLDS V. UNITED STATES

With this decision, the Supreme Court ruled that polygamy (having more than one spouse at any one time) was illegal. This stood in conflict with the Church of Jesus Christ of Latter-Day Saints (the Mormons), who claimed that God commanded men to engage in multiple marriage. The Court ruled that criminal or offensive behavior, even if a part of a person's religious beliefs—is not protected by the First Amendment. (Eventually, the Mormons rejected multiple marriage, punishing polygamists with excommunication. However, some Mormon fundamentalist break-off churches still engage in the practice illegally.)

1948: McCollum v. Board of Education

The Court ruled that public money and public schools cannot be used to teach religion. Prior to this ruling, students in public schools were dismissed from regular classes to attend religious classes taught by public school teachers.

1952: ZORACH V. CLAUSON

With this ruling, the Supreme Court cleared the way for students to receive religious education during their normal school day, as long as the classes took place off public school property.

1962: ENGEL V. VITALE

This is the ruling that restricted prayer in public school. The Court found that both denominational and nondenominational prayer in public school violated the church/state separation intent of the First Amendment.

1963: SCHOOL DISTRICT OF ABINGTON V. SCHEMPP

This ruling expanded the 1962 ban on school prayer to include a ban on teacher-led Bible reading in public school. The decision came following a lawsuit mounted by parents in the Abingdon School District in protest against a 1959 Pennsylvania law requiring teachers to read at least 10 Bible passages to their students at the start of each school day.

1968: BOARD OF EDUCATION
OF CENTRAL SCHOOL DISTRICT NO. 1 V. ALLEN

With this decision, the Court ruled that public monies could be used to pay for textbooks for students in parochial schools. Their reasoning was that the availability of the books benefited the students, not the church. Thus, spending taxpayer dollars for school books for parochial school students did not violate the church/state separation guaranteed in the First Amendment.

1970: WALZ V. TAX COMMISSION

This ruling reaffirmed that all church property was not taxable by cities, states, or the federal government.

1972: CRUZ V. BETO

The Court ruled that prisoners have a right to practice their religion even while they are "guests" of the government.

1981: THOMAS V. REVIEW BOARD
OF THE INDIANA EMPLOYMENT SECURITY DIVISION

This case went to the Supreme Court when a Seventh-Day Adventist was turned down for unemployment benefits after she was fired for refusing to work on Saturdays due to her religious beliefs. The Court ruled that she was entitled to benefits, affirming the right of the courts to protect individual religious rights.

1984: LYNCH V. DONNELLY

This ruling cleared the way for cities to display Christmas Nativity scenes and pay for their maintenance, even if other religious displays were not part of the cities' holiday pageantry. The Court ruled that a city was not showing preference for one religion over another by allowing a particular display.

1985: WALLACE V. JAFFREE

The Court ruled that Alabama's "moment of silence" (inaugurated to get around the "no school prayer" ruling of 1962) was a violation of the First Amendment.

1987: EDWARDS V. AGUILLARD

The Court ruled that the Louisiana statute that required schools that taught evolution to also teach creationism was a violation of the First Amendment. Creationists believe in the Biblical version of creation and of late have taken to calling their doctrine "creation science" in an attempt to give their belief more academic credence.

1992: LEE V. WEISMAN

The Court ruled that officially sanctioned prayer at public school graduation ceremonies was a violation of the First Amendment.

1993: CHURCH OF THE LUKUMI BABALU AYE V. CITY OF HIALEAH

The Court overruled a Florida law that forbade the use of animals in religious ceremonies, affirming the right of people to use animals in ceremonies as part of their religious beliefs.

Chapter 17

 34 Civil War Firsts

1. The first black field officer (Harvard Medical School graduate Martin Delany).
2. The first Congressional Medal of Honor (awarded to Private Jacob Parott).
3. The first ever "General of the Army" (Ulysses S. Grant).
4. The first military attack on an oil installation (at Burning Springs, Va.).
5. The first Native American military secretary (Colonel Ely Parker, secretary to Ulysses S. Grant).
6. The first time "dog tags" were used for military identification by U.S. troops. (They were handwritten pieces of paper or handkerchiefs that were pinned to the soldier's uniform.)
7. The first time a Civil War monument was erected. (A monument was raised on the Shiloh battlefield in the winter of 1863. The battle of Shiloh, which involved at least 100,000 men, is now considered the first modern battle.)
8. The first time a federal warship blockaded a Southern port. (The *Sabine* blockaded Pensacola, Fla., in April, 1861.)
9. The first time a gun was fired in defense of the Union. (This occurred in Pensacola, Fla. on January 8, 1861 when Florida troops occupied federal forts and were fired upon.)
10. The first time a naval battle took place between ironclad vessels. (The battle occurred at Hampton Roads, Va., on March 8, 1862.)
11. The first time a news service was created specifically to compete with the Associated Press in the gathering and dissemination of war news. (The Independent News Room out of Washington, D.C., was created for this purpose. The service no longer exists.)
12. The first time a railroad was used for strategic military mobility. (Confederate General Joseph Johnston moved his troops for the battle of First Bull Run, July 18, 1861.)
13. The first time a Republican was elected President of the United States. (Abraham Lincoln, elected in 1860. The previous 15 presidents had been either Federalist, Democrat, Democrat-Republican, or Whig.)
14. The first time a severe epileptic prone to ferocious seizures served as a brigadier general during wartime. (Rufus King of New York was a Union Brigadier General who aggravated his epilepsy by indulging in periods of excessive drinking.)
15. The first time a sitting Vice President of the United States volunteered for military service—and served—during wartime (James Buchanan's VP, Hannibal Hamlin).

16. The first time a slave trader was executed under federal law. (Nathaniel Gordon of Portland, Maine, was hung in the summer of 1862 after President Lincoln refused to commute his sentence.)

17. The first time a United States Army officer refused an offer to be promoted to Commanding General. (Colonel Robert E. Lee rejected his country's offer and instead joined the Confederate Army.)

18. The first time a war decoration was presented to black soldiers (The Butler Medal).

19. The first time an American female civilian was killed during a major battle. (Judith Henry was hit by a shell on July 21, 1861.)

20. The first time an amphibious landing under enemy fire was carried out. (Union vessels attacked Confederate troops on Roanoke Island, N.C., on February 8, 1862.)

21. The first time an enormous amount of gunpowder was used as an explosive. It occurred at the Crater in Petersburg, Va., when four tons of gunpowder were detonated in a tunnel beneath Confederate defenses on July 30, 1864. Unfortunately, due to a lack of leadership, union troops were left to their own judgment and 4,000 men crowded into the resulting crater in an attempt to finish off the surviving Confederate troops. Instead, they became targets for Robert E. Lee's men. Confederate troops positioned themselves on the rim of the Crater and turned all 4,000 into war statistics.

22. The first time an Indian tribe declared allegiance to the Confederacy. (The Choctaw tribe passed a resolution on February 7, 1861 declaring loyalty to the Confederate States of America.)

23. The first time an iron-clad gunboat was commissioned for U.S. military use. (The USS St. Louis was launched on October 12, 1861 at Carondelet, Miss.)

24. The first time an underwater vessel sank a ship during wartime. (The *CSS H. L. Hunley* rammed and sank the the *USS Housatonic* on February 17, 1864 in Charleston harbor.)

25. The first time black troops fought on the side of the Union in a major battle. (The Battle of Port Hudson, La., on May 27, 1863.)

26. The first time canned rations were given to U.S. military troops. (Canned beef, called "embalmed beef" by the soldiers.)

27. The first time the "Rebel yell" was ever used in battle (at First Bull Run, July 21, 1861).

THE 8 BIGGEST U.S. BATTLESHIPS IN WORLD WAR II

The biggest battleships in World War II were Japanese, the *Yamato* and the *Musashi* (both 72,809 tons and 862 feet). This list consists of the eight biggest American battleships used during the war.

1. The *Iowa*
Weight: 55,710 tons
Length: 887 feet

2. The *New Jersey*
Weight: 55,710 tons
Length: 887 feet

3. The *Missouri*
Weight: 55,710 tons
Length: 887 feet

4. The *Wisconsin*
Weight: 55,710 tons
Length: 887 feet

5. The *North Carolina*
Weight: 44,800 tons
Length: 729 feet

6. The *Washington*
Weight: 44,800 tons
Length: 729 feet

7. The *Tennessee*
Weight: 40,500 tons
Length: 624 feet

8. The *California*
Weight: 40,500 tons
Length: 624 feet

(*Note:* There were 22 enormous battleships deployed during World War II [each was more than 40,000 tons and longer than 600 feet]. Eight were American, six were British, four were Japanese, two were French, and two were German.)

The bloody aftermath of Gettysburg.

photo/Library of Congress

28. The first time the Congressional Medal of Honor was awarded twice to the same person. (It was awarded two times to George A. Custer's brother, Lieutenant Thomas Custer.)

29. The first time the Fourth of July was celebrated with a 21-gun salute (July, 1862).

30. The first time the Gatling machine gun was purchased and used in battle. (Major General Benjamin Butler bought a dozen for the Union for $1,000 each.)

31. The first time the Congressional Medal of Honor was authorized for men of the United States Navy and Marine Corps. (Congress authorized it on December 21, 1861.)

32. The first time the term "The Lost Cause" was used to describe the South's futile attempt to leave the Union. (The phrase was used by journalist Edward Pollard as the title of his 1866 book.)

33. The first time the U.S. Government passed legislation allowing the United States to "draft" men into military service. (The law was called the National Conscription Act and it was passed on March 3, 1863. Prior to this Act, the Union's military had been comprised of state militias and volunteers.)

34. The first time the writ of habeas corpus was legally suspended in the United States. (The suspension of this important right against unlawful restraint was made legal by an act of Congress in March, 1863. President Lincoln had suspended the writ by presidential decree two years earlier.)

Chapter 18

31 Peculiar American Tourist Attractions

There's a very funny moment in the Chevy Chase movie *National Lampoon's Vacation* that flawlessly illustrates America's fascination with strange tourist attractions. In the scene I'm referring to, Chevy's character, the astonishingly inept but enthusiastic Clark Griswold, tells his family to hurry up so that they can get the Family Truckster back on the road. If they wait much longer, he frets, they won't have enough time to visit the world's largest House of Mud on their way to Wally World.

America has some truly unusual tourist attractions. The stranger the site, it seems, the more popular its appeal.

One of the best guidebooks to the "weird and the wacky" is *The New Roadside America*, by Mike Wilkins, Ken Smith, and Doug Kirby. These guys actually visited hundreds and hundreds of these odd tourist sites. They wallowed in the kitsch and the camp of these places, but they also took the whole thing quite seriously in an attempt to document the quintessential American road trip.

They cataloged hundreds of places that are so strange, my first reaction was, "Aw, you're makin' that up." But, no, Virginia, there actually is a Bra Museum (see No. 6) as well as a Pet Casket Company that offers guided tours (No. 10). Not to mention the World's Largest "Anything-You-Can-Imagine" and the annual Clinton, Montana Testicle Festival (No. 21).

Here is a sampling of 31 of America's most peculiar roadside attractions:

1. **The Atomic Bomb Crater** (Mars Bluff, S.C.): In 1958, a B-47 pilot accidentally dropped a bomb on a guy's farm. It exploded. The result was, not unexpectedly, a huge hole. This hole is now a tourist attraction.

2. **The Dan Blocker Memorial Head** (O'Donnell, Tex.): This is a big granite head of Hoss (from Blocker's character in the TV show *Bonanza*) in the O'Donnell town square. (O'Donnell was his hometown.)

3. **The Donner Party Museum** (Truckee, Calif.): This is a museum commemorating the mountain excursion that culminated in members of the Donner Party eating other (dead) Party members in order to survive. Bring the kids.

4. **The Five-Story-Tall Chicken** (Marietta, Ga.): This 55-foot-tall chicken is made of sheet metal. Not much else to say, is there?

5. **Flintstone Bedrock City** (Vail, Ariz.): Visit a replica of the town the modern Stone-Age family calls home.

6. **Fredrick's Bra Museum** (Hollywood, Calif.): Bras, bras, and more bras!

7. **The Hair Museum** (Independence, Miss.): This museum boasts weird objects made out of human hair. A haircut is included in the admission price. Really.

8. **The Hall of Mosses** (Port Angeles, Wash.): Admit it: You've always dreamed that one day all the various types of mosses would be gathered in one place. Well, dream no more!

9. **Hobbiton, U.S.A.** (Phillipsville, Calif.): This is a life-size replica of Bilbo Baggins' hometown (from J.R.R. Tolkien's cult classic *Lord of the Rings* trilogy).

10. **The Hoegh Pet Casket Company** (Gladstone, Mich.): The tour includes the casket showroom and factory, as well as a look at a prototype pet cemetery.

11. **Holy Land, U.S.A.** (Waterbury, Conn.): Religious shrines, dioramas, and statues galore. Sort of like a religious Disneyland.

12. **The House of Telephones** (Coffeyville, Kans.): It's a house that has 1,000 phones in it.

13. **Jimi Hendrix Viewpoint** (Seattle, Wash.): Jimi's View overlooks a zoo and is surrounded by purple bushes.

14. **The Liberace Museum** (Las Vegas, Nev.): This shrine is in a shopping center and serves as the ultimate tribute to the Keyboard King of Kitsch.

15. **The Museum of Questionable Medical Devices** (Minneapolis, Minn.): This museum (also in a shopping center) is a must see. Don't miss the interesting exhibit on prostate warmers!

16. **The Nut Museum** (Old Lyme, Conn.): The Nut Museum is run by Elizabeth Tashjian, who has been on *Late Night with David Letterman*. Twice. Elizabeth loves nuts and has even composed a "Nut Anthem."

17. **Philip Morris Cigarette Tours** (Richmond, Va.): At the cigarette tour, you can see how cigarettes are made. They make a point of bragging about their factory's ventilation system. Hmmm.

18. **The Soup Tureen Museum** (Camden, N.J.): This museum, located near Campbell's headquarters, is dedicated to the noble soup tureen. (One wonders if the Spatula Museum is next.)

19. **The Spam Museum** (Austin, Minn.): Everything you've always wanted to know about Spam, Spam, Spam, glorious Spam (including things you probably wish you had never been told).

20. **Spongeorama** (Tarpon Springs, Fla.): Sponges, sponges, and more sponges! (One need not be spongeworthy to visit, though.)

21. **The Testicle Festival** (Clinton, Montana): No,

FAMILYFUN MAGAZINE'S 12 MOST POPULAR U.S. TOURIST ATTRACTIONS

1. Yosemite National Park.
2. Walt Disney World.
3. SeaWorld Orlando.
4. Washington, D.C.
5. Yellowstone National Park.
6. SeaWorld San Diego.
7. Pacific Science Center in Seattle.
8. Glacier National Park.
9. The Children's Museum of Indianapolis.
10. Disneyland.
11. Acadia National Park.
12. Mount Rushmore.

it's not a gathering of male porn stars. It's a banquet. Of testicles. Really. And regarding the name of the host city...let's just leave it alone, okay?

22. **Toilet Rock** (City of Rocks, N. Mex.): It's a giant rock formation that looks like a flush toilet. People come from miles.

23. **The Tupperware Awareness Center** (Kissimmee, Fla.): Better ways to burp the tops of Tupperware containers so as to get all the air out, plus a wondrous display of *all* the Tupperware products known to man.

24. **The Urinal Used by JFK** (Salem, Ohio): It's clearly marked in the men's room in Reilly Stadium. "C'mon in and take my picture standing next to it, honey. The guys won't mind."

25. **The Wonderful World of Tiny Horses** (Eureka Springs, Ark.): The title says it all. The world's smallest horse lives there: a little stallion measuring all of 20 inches in height.

26. **The World's Largest Artichoke** (Castroville, Calif.): A commonly heard comment at this attraction is, "That's a big artichoke."

27. **The World's Largest Chest of Drawers** (High Point, N.C.): It has four drawers and sleeps six.

28. **The World's Largest Crucifix** (Bardstown, Ky.): A 60-foot-high reminder of Jesus' sacrifice by mankind's more vicious forms of execution.

29. **The World's Largest Office Chair** (Anniston, Ala.): It's 33 feet tall. If you want to put your feet up while sitting in it, rest them on the apartment building across the street.

30. **The World's Largest Stump** (Kokomo, Ind.): It's 57 feet around and 12 feet high. The tree didn't mind being cut down: It *wanted* to be a dead landmark.

31. **The World's Largest Twine Ball** (Darwin, Minn.): It is 12 feet around and weighs 21,140 pounds. Do you think the guy who built it had just a *wee* bit too much time on his hands?

(*Note:* A slightly different version of this chapter originally appeared in *The Odd Index* by Stephen J. Spignesi, [Plume, 1994].)

Chapter 19

65 Ridiculous American Sex Laws

hat is it with legislators? The ludicrous failure of prohibition should have taught all lawmakers a lesson: You cannot legislate morality, no matter how badly the government would like to. If laws are passed that citizens feel intrude upon their privacy and pertain to activities that are none of the government's business, they will simply ignore them. Sort of like repeal by apathy, you know?

America is a sexually repressed nation and nowhere is that more evident than in our body of laws. People in countries around the world laugh at America's preoccupation with controlling the sexual behavior of its citizens. It's true. Ask anyone who has ever been in another country. Topless and nude beaches are a yawn in France or Italy. In the United States, "clothing optional" beaches are often raided by the police. In some cases, there have been marches, pickets, press conferences by religious and civic leaders, and amateur shutterbugs clamoring for shots they can post on the Internet. All this would be funny if it were not so sad.

Some of our sex laws are so convoluted and incident-specific, one cannot help but wonder if a lewd act was committed and the lawmakers passed a law forbidding that specific act from occurring again.

This list of surreal American laws is perhaps the most dramatic example of how the United States government would like to be a presence in the bedrooms of every citizen, no matter how unwelcome a guest it might be. (*Note:* If no town is mentioned, the law is a statewide law.)

1. **Alabama (Anniston)**: If a woman loses a game of pool, it is illegal for her to settle her tab with sex.
2. **Alabama**: It is illegal to hire a girl between 10 and 18 years of age for prostitution.
3. **Arizona (Cottonwood)**: It is illegal for a couple to have sex in a vehicle with flat wheels. The fine is doubled if the sex occurs in the back seat.
4. **Arizona**: It is illegal for a man to cause his wife to become a prostitute.
5. **Arizona**: It is illegal for unmarried persons to have sex. The penalty is three years in prison.
6. **Arkansas**: Adultery is punishable by a $20 to $100 fine.
7. **Arkansas**: It is illegal for a husband to place his wife in a brothel.
8. **Arkansas**: Only physicians and other medical personnel may legally sell condoms.
9. **California**: Adultery is punishable by a $1,000 fine and/or one year in prison.
10. **California**: Husbands and wives are prohibited from having oral sex.

11. **California**: It is illegal to import an Asian woman and make her a prostitute.
12. **Colorado (Castle Creek)**: It is illegal for a married couple to have sex in a river, lake, or stream. (Single couples: inquire.)
13. **Connecticut**: "Private sexual behavior between consenting adults" is still illegal in Connecticut. (Mull *that* one over.)
14. **Delaware**: Only physicians and wholesale druggists may legally sell condoms.
15. **Florida**: Oral sex is punishable by a 20-year prison term.
16. **Illinois (Oblong)**: It is illegal for a husband and wife to have sex while out hunting or fishing on their wedding day.
17. **Indiana**: It is illegal to entice someone under 21 to masturbate.
18. **Indiana**: Male skating instructors are prohibited from having sex with their female students. However, there is no parallel law preventing female skating instructors from having sex with their male students.
19. **Kansas:** Anal sex is punishable by a maximum six-month prison term.
20. **Kentucky**: Only physicians and other medical personnel may legally sell condoms. However, their "condom selling" license may not be publicly displayed.
21. **Louisiana**: Streaking is illegal, but only if the streaker intended on arousing anyone who saw him or her. (One must ask how this is proven.)
22. **Maine (Buckfield)**: It is illegal for a cab driver to charge a passenger a fare if the passenger had sex with the driver while on their way home from any place that sold liquor.
23. **Maine**: Condom sellers must obtain a license from the state and display their license at all times.
24. **Maine**: It is illegal for a husband to place his wife in a brothel.
25. **Maryland**: Anal sex is punishable by a one- to 10-year prison sentence.
26. **Maryland**: Condom vending machines may only be installed in places where alcohol is served.
27. **Maryland**: It is illegal to have oral sex with a person or an animal.
28. **Michigan**: It is illegal for a husband to place his wife in a brothel.
29. **Michigan**: It is illegal to masturbate. The penalty is five years in prison.
30. **Michigan**: Sex between unmarried consenting adults is punishable by a fine up to $5,000 and/or up to five years in prison.
31. **Minnesota (Alexandria)**: It is illegal for a man to have sex with his wife if his breath stinks of garlic, onions, or sardines. By law, the husband must brush his teeth if asked to by his wife.
32. **Missouri**: It is illegal for a husband to force his wife to work as a hooker on the streets.
33. **Montana (Bozeman)**: Sex is illegal between two people who are naked on their front lawns after sundown.
34. **Nebraska (Hastings)**: It is illegal for a man and woman to sleep together in a hotel when both are naked. Also, a couple may not have sex in the hotel unless they are both wearing plain white cotton nightshirts, which, by law, must be provided to them by the hotel.
35. **Nebraska**: Anal sex is illegal and punishable by a $5,000 fine and 10 years in prison.
36. **Nebraska**: Only physicians may legally sell condoms.
37. **Nevada**: Condoms are mandatory for sex with a (legal) prostitute.

38. **New Jersey**: It is illegal for two men to masturbate in the presence of each other or to masturbate each other. The penalty is three years in prison.

39. **New Mexico (Carlsbad)**: It is illegal for couples to have sex in a parked car or van while on their lunch break if they can be seen by passersby.

40. **New Mexico**: Oral sex is punishable by a two- to 10-year prison term and a $5,000 fine.

41. **North Carolina**: It is illegal for a man to spy on a woman through a window. The same law restriction does not apply to women watching men or men watching men.

42. **Ohio**: Male skating instructors are prohibited from having sex with their female students. As in Indiana, this law does not apply to female skating instructors.

43. **Oklahoma (Clinton)**: It is illegal to masturbate while watching a couple have sex in the backseat of a car at a drive-in theater.

44. **Oregon (Willowdale)**: A husband may not use profanity while making love to his wife. (The same is not true for his wife, who may cuss to her heart's content when she's with her loving husband.)

45. **Pennsylvania (Harrisburg)**: Female toll booth workers cannot have sex with male truck drivers in the confines of their toll booth.

46. **Rhode Island**: It is illegal for unmarried persons to have sex. The fine is $10.

47. **Rhode Island**: Oral sex is punishable by a seven- to 10-year prison term.

48. **South Carolina (Branchville)**: It is illegal for a couple to "lewdly or lasciviously romp" either in private, or in public. The fine is $500 and a possible six-month prison term. (Can you imagine this one going to court?! "Your honor, my clients were most assuredly not romping—they were engaging in a prurient roll…")

49. **South Carolina**: Anal sex is punishable by a $500 fine and a five-year prison sentence.

50. **South Dakota (Sioux Falls)**: It is illegal for a couple to have sex on the floor between two single beds in a hotel.

51. **South Dakota**: It is illegal for prostitutes to solicit customers from a covered wagon.

52. **South Dakota**: Oral sex is punishable by a 10-year prison term.

53. **Tennessee (Skullbone)**: It is illegal for a woman to masturbate a man or perform oral sex on him while he is driving a car.

54. **Texas**: Only a "registered pharmacist" may legally sell condoms. Anyone else will be prosecuted for illegally practicing medicine.

55. **Texas**: Sex between unmarried consenting adults is punishable by a $500 fine.

56. **Utah (Tremonton)**: It is illegal to have sex in an ambulance. (Just wait until you get to the E.R. Duh.)

57. **Utah**: Oral sex is punishable by a six-month prison term and a $299 fine.

58. **Vermont (Beanville)**: It is illegal for massage parlors to advertise on road maps.

59. **Virginia (Norfolk)**: It is illegal to have sex while riding in the sidecar of a motorcycle.

60. **Virginia**: Adultery is punishable by a $20 to $100 fine.

61. **Washington, D.C.**: It is illegal for a man to cause his wife to become a prostitute.

62. **Washington**: It is illegal to have sex with a virgin. (Think about *that* one for a moment.)

63. **Wisconsin (Connorsville)**: It is illegal for a man to fire off a gun when his partner has an orgasm.

64. **Wyoming (Newcastle)**: It is illegal for a couple to have sex while standing up in a market's walk-in meat freezer.

65. **Wyoming**: It is illegal to entice or help someone under 21 to masturbate.

(*Source: Loony Sex Laws* by Robert Wayne Pelton [Walker and Company, 1992].)

Chapter 20

132 Notable American Writers

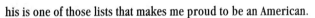

This is one of those lists that makes me proud to be an American.

This list of 131 American writers is a testament to the rich and glorious body of work produced by scribes born in the good old U.S. of A.

Everyone is here: playwrights (Edward Albee and Eugene O'Neill), essayists (Thomas Paine and James Thurber), novelists (too many to mention!), poets (Emily Dickinson, e. e. cummings, and Lawrence Ferlinghetti) and science fiction writers (Harlan Ellison, Richard Matheson, Robert Heinlein and Isaac Asimov).

I have not included representative titles for these 131 writers because part of the joy of discovering a new writer is working through their body of work and finding things you enjoy.

Many of these wonderful writers have authored classics that you have probably already read (T. S. Eliot, Ernest Hemingway, Henry James, Jack London, and Herman Melville).

Many of the names from this list are writers we've all read in school (Mark Twain, J. D. Salinger, Thomas Wolfe, F. Scott Fitzgerald, Edgar Allan Poe, and John Steinbeck). Others are incredibly popular writers whose books regularly sell in the millions (Stephen King, Dean Koontz, John Grisham, and Tom Clancy).

If there is anything this list says about the state of American letters, it's that it is alive and thriving..and is an important source for entertainment, enlightenment, and education around the world.

So, pick a writer...any writer, and read away.

1.	James Agee.	13.	Pearl S. Buck.
2.	Edward Albee.	14.	Edgar Rice Burroughs.
3.	Louisa May Alcott.	15.	William Burroughs.
4.	Sherwood Anderson.	16.	Erskine Caldwell.
5.	Isaac Asimov.	17.	Truman Capote.
6.	Richard Bachman.	18.	Willa Cather.
7.	James Baldwin.	19.	Raymond Chandler.
8.	John Barth.	20.	John Cheever.
9.	Saul Bellow.	21.	Tom Clancy.
10.	Ray Bradbury.	22.	Mary Higgins Clark.
11.	Anne Bradstreet.	23.	Pat Conroy.
12.	Richard Brautigan.	24.	James Fenimore Cooper.

25. Stephen Crane.
26. Michael Crichton.
27. e.e. cummings.
28. Philip K. Dick.
29. Emily Dickinson.
30. E.L. Doctorow.
31. Theodore Dreiser.
32. Richard Eberhart.
33. Jonathan Edwards.
34. T.S. Eliot.
35. Harlan Ellison.
36. Ralph Ellison.
37. Ralph Waldo Emerson.
38. Philip Jose Farmer.
39. James Farrell.
40. William Faulkner.
41. Edna Ferber.
42. Lawrence Ferlinghetti.
43. F. Scott Fitzgerald.
44. Benjamin Franklin.
45. Robert Frost.
46. John Gardner.
47. John Grisham.
48. Dashiell Hammett.
49. Bret Harte.
50. Nathaniel Hawthorne.
51. Robert Heinlein.
52. Joseph Heller.
53. Ernest Hemingway.
54. O. Henry.
55. Frank Herbert.
56. L. Ron Hubbard.
57. Langston Hughes.
58. Zora Neale Hurston.
59. John Irving.
60. Washington Irving.
61. Shirley Jackson.
62. Henry James.
63. Robinson Jeffers.
64. LeRoi Jones.
65. Erica Jong.
66. Jack Kerouac.
67. Ken Kesey.
68. Stephen King.
69. John Knowles.
70. Dean Koontz.

71. Harper Lee.
72. Ursula K. Le Guin.
73. Ira Levin.
74. Sinclair Lewis.
75. Henry Wadsworth Longfellow.
76. Jack London.
77. Robert Lowell.
78. Ed McBain.
79. Carson McCullers.
80. John D. MacDonald.
81. Norman Mailer.
82. Bernard Malamud.
83. Richard Matheson.
84. Herman Melville.
85. H.L. Mencken.
86. Edna St. Vincent Millay.
87. Henry Miller.
88. Marianne Moore.
89. Toni Morrison.
90. Frank Norris.
91. Flannery O'Connor.
92. John O'Hara.
93. Eugene O'Neill.
94. Thomas Paine.
95. John Dos Passos.
96. Sylvia Plath.
97. Edgar Allan Poe.
98. Frederick Pohl.

THE 10 MOST-READ NEWSPAPERS IN AMERICA (RANKED ACCORDING TO CIRCULATION)

1. *The Wall Street Journal.*
2. *USA Today.*
3. *The Los Angeles Times.*
4. *The New York Times.*
5. *The Washington Post.*
6. *The New York Daily News.*
7. *The Chicago Tribune.*
8. *Newsday* (Long Island, N.Y.).
9. *The Houston Chronicle.*
10. *The Chicago Sun-Times.*

(*Source: 1999 Editor & Publisher International Yearbook*)

photo/Bettmann Archive

Edgar Allan Poe

99. Katherine Anne Porter.
100. Ezra Pound.
101. Thomas Pynchon.
102. Edward Arlington Robinson.
103. Theodore Roethke.
104. Philip Roth.
105. Muriel Rukeyser.
106. Carl Sagan.
107. J.D. Salinger.
108. Carl Sandburg.
109. Rod Serling.
110. Anne Sexton.
111. Gertrude Stein.
112. John Steinbeck.
113. Wallace Stevens.
114. Harriet Beecher Stowe.
115. Theodore Sturgeon.

116. William Styron.
117. Henry David Thoreau.
118. James Thurber.
119. Mark Twain.
120. John Updike.
121. Gore Vidal.
122. Kurt Vonnegut, Jr.
123. Robert Penn Warren.
124. Eudora Welty.
125. Nathanael West.
126. Edith Wharton.
127. Walt Whitman.
128. Richard Wilbur.
129. William Carlos Williams.
130. Thomas Wolfe.
131. Herman Wouk.
132. Richard Wright.

Chapter 21

The Vietnam War by the Numbers

T he Center for Electronic Records of the National Archives and Records Administration (NARA) has computerized files with records of casualties of the Vietnam conflict. NARA used statistical software to analyze the contents of these records and the results (a sampling of the lists follows) are quite illuminating. They serve to debunk many myths about the Vietnam War and its aftermath. When read in conjunction with Gary Roush's chapter "13 Myths About the Vietnam War," the result is to paint a picture of the war not usually seen.

Vietnam War deaths by year

This list includes all deaths attributed to the Vietnam War, as compiled by the U.S. National Archives and Records Administration, from information provided to them by the U.S. Department of Defense. These figures are complete through the year 1998.

The second part of this list provides the same information, but is organized by year, allowing us to see how war casualties rose and fell as the years went by.

Breakdown by fatalities

Year	Deaths	Year	Deaths
1968	16,592	1975	161
1969	11,616	1979	148
1967	11,153	1963	118
1966	6,143	1977	96
1970	6,081	1976	77
1971	2,357	1962	52
1965	1,863	1980	26
1972	641	1961	16
1978	447	1981-1990	34
1964	206	1991-1998	11
1974	178	1956-1960	9
1973	168	**Total**	**58,193**

CHRONOLOGICAL BREAKDOWN

1956-1960	9	1972	641
1961	16	1973	168
1962	52	1974	178
1963	118	1975	161
1964	206	1976	77
1965	1,863	1977	96
1966	6,143	1978	447
1967	11,153	1979	148
1968	16,592	1980	26
1969	11,616	1981-1990	34
1970	6,081	1991-1998	11
1971	2,357	**Total**	**58,193**

THE 23 CAUSES OF DEATH IN THE VIETNAM WAR

This list, compiled from information from the U.S. National Archives and Records Administration, lists the official causes of death during, or as a result of, the Vietnam War.

The total deaths (58,193) is higher than the number of battle deaths (47,355) because the NARA figures are complete through the year 1998. They account for all deaths that were a result of the Vietnam War.

Gun, small arms fire	18,518	Other causes	754
Multiple fragmentary wounds	8,456	Air loss, crash in sea	577
Air loss, crash on land	7,992	Burns	530
Other explosive devices	7,450	Illness, disease	482
Artillery, rocket, or mortar	4,914	Suicide	382
Other accident	1,371	Heart attack	273
Misadventure (friendly fire)	1,326	Intentional homicide	234
Drowned, suffocated	1,207	Malaria	118
Vehicle loss, crash	1,187	Bomb explosion	52
Accidental homicide (death caused by someone else's accident)	944	Stroke	42
Accidental self-destruction	842	Hepatitis	22
		Unknown, not reported	520
		Total	**58,193**

NUMBER OF VIETNAM WAR DEATHS

BY BRANCH OF THE MILITARY

Army	38,209
Marine Corps	14,838
Air Force	2,584
Navy	2,555
Coast Guard	7
Total	**58,193**

VIETNAM WAR DEATHS BY RACE

Caucasian	50,120
African-American	7,264
Malayan	252
American Indian	226
Unknown, Not Reported	215
Mongolian	116
Total	**58,193**

NUMBER OF VIETNAM WAR DEATHS BY STATE (IN ORDER OF HIGHEST CASUALTIES PER STATE)

This list, also compiled from information from the U.S. National Archives and Records Administration, lists the home states of record of the men and women who died during, or as a result of, the Vietnam War.

California	5,573	Massachusetts	1,323
New York	4,121	Virginia	1,304
Texas	3,415	Tennessee	1,291
Pennsylvania	3,144	Alabama	1,207
Ohio	3,096	Wisconsin	1,161
Illinois	2,934	Minnesota	1,072
Michigan	2,654	Kentucky	1,055
Florida	1,952	Washington	1,050
North Carolina	1,609	Maryland	1,014
Indiana	1,532	Oklahoma	988
New Jersey	1,484	South Carolina	896
Missouri	1,413	Louisiana	882

Iowa	853	Montana	268
West Virginia	732	District of Columbia	242
Oregon	709	New Hampshire	227
Mississippi	637	Idaho	217
Kansas	627	Rhode Island	207
Arizona	623	North Dakota	198
Colorado	620	South Dakota	193
Connecticut	611	Nevada	151
Arkansas	588	Delaware	122
New Mexico	399	Other (non-U.S. home)	121
Nebraska	395	Wyoming	120
Utah	366	Vermont	100
Puerto Rico	345	Guam	70
Maine	343	Alaska	57
Georigia	276	Virgin Islands	15
Hawaii	276	Canal Zone	2
		Total	**56,880**

THE 5 FASTEST U.S. FIGHTER PLANES IN WORLD WAR II

The fastest fighter planes in World War II were all German, the Messerschmitt ME-263 (596 m.p.h.) and ME-262 (560 m.p.h.); and the Heinkel HE-162A (553 m.p.h.). This list consists of the five American planes capable of speeds in excess of 400 m.p.h. There were 19 fighter planes deployed during World War II capable of speeds in excess of 400 m.p.h. Six were Russian, five were American, five were German, and three were British.

1. The P-51-H
  ✯ Maximum Speed: 487 m.p.h.
  ✯ Maximum Range: 850 mi.

2. The P-51-D Mustang
  ✯ Maximum Speed: 440 m.p.h.
  ✯ Maximum Range: 2,300 mi.

3. The P-47-D Thunderbolt
  ✯ Maximum Speed: 428 m.p.h.
  ✯ Maximum Range: 1,000 mi.

4. The F4U Corsair
  ✯ Maximum Speed: 417 m.p.h.
  ✯ Maximum Range: 1,015 mi.

5. The P-38-L Lightning
  ✯ Maximum Speed: 414 m.p.h.
  ✯ Maximum Range: 460 mi.

Chapter 22

The 4 Most Performed Plastic Surgeries in the United States

BREAST AUGMENTATION

This surgery involves adding implants under a woman's breasts in order to make them larger. Silicone was once the implant material of favor, but a yet-to-be-proved link between silicone and connective tissue disease forced a move in the 1970s to saline implants. Many women actually had their silicone implants removed and replaced with saline after patients started coming forward and blaming their silicone implants for their lupus and rheumatoid arthritis, among other diseases.

RHINOPLASTY

This surgery involves reconstruction of the nose to enhance one's appearance. Many patients, though, will claim they went in for a *septoplasty*, which is the surgical correction of deformities of the septum, which is the wall that separates the two nostrils. The scenario usually consists of the following: "Oh, you got a nose job!" "No, I had a deviated septum and they had to change my nose to repair it."

FACELIFT

This surgery consists of the removal of excess skin, fat, and tissue from the face. It is performed when the patient desires a more youthful look as the surgery usually eliminates wrinkles and gives the patient's skin a smoother look.

BLEPHAROPLASTY

A blepharoplasty consists of the removal of excess fat and skin from around the eyelids. It is often performed in conjunction with a facelift, but can also be done independently if the patient doesn't like the look of his or her eyelids.

Chapter 23

The 9 Worst Aircraft Disasters in the United States

These nine aircraft disasters are the worst to have occurred on American soil or in American airspace since 1937.

While the worst American aircraft disaster is a horrible tragedy, the single worst aircraft disaster worldwide occurred on Sunday, March 27, 1977. It was a collision between a KLM 747 and a Pan American 747 on the runway at the Tenerife airport in the Canary Islands. This collision resulted in 582 dead, including many Americans.

1. **Date**: Friday, May 25, 1979.
   Number of Dead: 275, including two on the ground.
   Aircraft: American Airlines DC-10.
   What Happened: The DC-10 crashed after takeoff at O'Hare International Airport in Chicago, Ill. This disaster resulted in the single highest death toll in American aviation history.

2. **Date**: Wednesday, July 17, 1996.
   Number of Dead: 230.
   Aircraft: Trans World Airlines Boeing 747.
   What Happened: The Boeing 747 exploded and crashed into the Atlantic Ocean off Long Island, N.Y. According to the National Transportation Safety Board, the accident was caused by "…an explosion of the center wing tank resulting from ignition of the flammable fuel/air mixture in the tank." Many witnesses, however, insist that they saw a missile launch from the ground and strike the doomed airliner, causing the crash.

3. **Date**: Sunday, August 16, 1987.
   Number of Dead: 156.
   Aircraft: Northwest Airlines MD-82.
   What Happened: The MD-82 crashed after takeoff in Romulus, Mich.

4. **Date**: Friday, July 9, 1982.
   Number of Dead: 153, including eight on the ground.
   Aircraft: Pan Am Boeing 727.
   What Happened: The Boeing 727 crashed after takeoff in Kenner, La.

5. **Date**: Monday, September 25, 1978.
   Number of Dead: 150.
   Aircraft: A Boeing 727 and a Cessna 172.
   What Happened: The Boeing and the Cessna collided in midair over San Diego, Calif.

6. **Date**: Friday, August 2, 1985.
   Number of Dead: 137.
   Aircraft: Delta Air Lines L-1101.
   What Happened: The L-1101 crashed at Dallas-Ft. Worth International Airport while approaching for a landing.

7. **Date**: Friday, December 16, 1960.
   Number of Dead: 134, including six on the ground.
   Aircraft: A United DC-8 jet and a TWA Super-Constellation.
   What Happened: The two planes collided in midair over New York City.

8. **Date**: Thursday, September 8, 1994.
   Number of Dead: 132.
   Aircraft: USAir Boeing 737-300.
   What Happened: The plane crashed in Aliquippa, Pa., near Pittsburgh International Airport.

9. **Date**: Saturday, June 30, 1956.
   Number of Dead: 128.
   Aircraft: Venezuelan Super-Constellation.
   What Happened: The plane crashed in the Atlantic off the coast of Asbury Park, N.J.

THE 10 LEADING CAUSES OF DEATH
IN THE UNITED STATES

In 1998 (the latest year for which final figures were available), one out of three Americans died from either heart disease, cancer, or stroke. Interestingly, suicide also made the top 10 causes of death, showing up at number eight, above kidney disease and liver disease.

1. Heart disease.
2. Cancer, all types.
3. Stroke.
4. Chronic obstructive lung disease and allied conditions.
5. Pneumonia and influenza.
6. Accidents and adverse effects of accidents.
7. Diabetes mellitus.
8. Suicide.
9. Kidney disease.
10. Chronic liver disease and cirrhosis.

Chapter 24

2 Different Rankings of America's Presidents

"History, in general, only informs us what bad government is."
—Thomas Jefferson, June 14, 1807

THE INTERCOLLEGIATE STUDIES INSTITUTE

The Intercollegiate Studies Institute's (ISI) panel of judges includes some of the most prestigious and august historians, politicians, writers, educators, and researchers working today. (See the end of this chapter for their names.) They assigned numerical values to the accomplishments of all the U.S. presidents, which resulted in their ranking. The presidents are ranked from the best on down. (The numerical grades have been deleted for this feature.)

GREAT PRESIDENTS

- ✯ George Washington.
- ✯ Abraham Lincoln.

NEAR-GREAT PRESIDENTS

- ✯ Ronald Reagan.
- ✯ Thomas Jefferson.
- ✯ Theodore Roosevelt.
- ✯ Andrew Jackson.
- ✯ Franklin D. Roosevelt.
- ✯ Dwight D. Eisenhower.

HIGH-AVERAGE PRESIDENTS

- ✯ James K. Polk.
- ✯ Harry S Truman.
- ✯ John Adams.
- ✯ Calvin Coolidge.
- ✯ Grover Cleveland.
- ✯ James Monroe.
- ✯ John Quincy Adams.
- ✯ William McKinley.
- ✯ William Howard Taft.

LOW-AVERAGE PRESIDENTS

★ Martin Van Buren.
★ Benjamin Harrison.
★ James Madison.
★ Rutherford B. Hayes.
★ George H.W. Bush.
★ Chester A. Arthur.
★ James Garfield.
★ Gerald R. Ford.

BELOW-AVERAGE PRESIDENTS

★ Woodrow Wilson.
★ John F. Kennedy.
★ Herbert Hoover.
★ John Tyler.

BELOW-AVERAGE PRESIDENTS (CONT.)

★ Richard M. Nixon.
★ Millard Fillmore.

FAILURES AS PRESIDENT

★ Franklin Pierce.
★ Ulysses S. Grant.
★ Warren G. Harding.
★ Andrew Johnson.
★ Bill Clinton.
★ Lyndon B. Johnson.
★ Jimmy Carter.
★ James Buchanan.

THE 1994 SIENA COLLEGE RESEARCH INSTITUTE SURVEY OF U.S. HISTORIANS

As you'll see, this ranking is somewhat different from the ISI ranking. ISI's top president, George Washington, drops to number four on this list. ISI's number three man, Ronald Reagan, only rises to number 20 here. And these two rankings also disagree on the worst president: The ISI judges choose James Buchanan; the Siena College historians pick Warren Harding. And look at how high the Siena historians place John F. Kennedy, compared to the ISI judges. Comparing the two lists, if it does anything, guarantees a stimulating debate.

1. Franklin D. Roosevelt.
2. Abraham Lincoln.
3. Theodore Roosevelt.
4. George Washington.
5. Thomas Jefferson.
6. Woodrow Wilson.
7. Harry S Truman.
8. Dwight D. Eisenhower.
9. James Madison.
10. John F. Kennedy.
11. Andrew Jackson.
12. John Adams.
13. Lyndon B. Johnson.
14. James Polk.
15. James Monroe.
16. Bill Clinton.
17. John Quincy Adams.
18. William McKinley.
19. Grover Cleveland.
20. Ronald Reagan.
21. William H. Taft.
22. Martin Van Buren.
23. Richard Nixon.
24. Rutherford B. Hayes.
25. Jimmy Carter.
26. James Garfield.
27. Chester Arthur.
28. William Henry Harrison.
29. Herbert Hoover.
30. Benjamin Harrison.

31. George Bush.
32. Gerald Ford.
33. Zachary Taylor.
34. John Tyler.
35. Millard Fillmore.
36. Calvin Coolidge.

37. Franklin Pierce.
38. Ulysses S. Grant.
39. James Buchanan.
40. Andrew Johnson.
41. Warren Harding.

Chapter 25

99 Books Written by U.S. Presidents

Jimmy Carter credits his 1976 autobiography *Why Not the Best?* as the single most important factor in getting him elected president. (He handed out free books at campaign rallies.)

Dwight D. Eisenhower's 1948 autobiography *Crusade in Europe* was a huge success. The book outsold everything but *Dr. Spock's Baby and Child Care* and the Bible, and played an important role in winning him the presidency.

Grover Cleveland wrote books about fishing and good citizenship. Teddy Roosevelt wrote about ranching, hunting, the Rough Riders, and the life of Thomas Hart Benton. Woodrow Wilson wrote a monumental five-volume history of the American people. Herbert Hoover wrote about mining. Jimmy Carter wrote a book of poetry and a children's book. Bill Clinton used his best-seller *Putting People First* as a book-length campaign ad that helped win him the presidency.

All told, since the days of John Adams, 26 U.S. presidents have been published authors, with a presidential total of 99 volumes.

These books have ranged from political analyses to heartfelt reminiscences. In their totality they comprise a unique library of important American works that have never before been looked at as a group.

Presidential speeches and State of the Union addresses provide and chronicle a presidential point-of-view relative to his administration and his long-term agenda. These texts originate from one very specific forum available to the president to speak to the American people.

Books by the presidents, on the other hand, show us another side of our chief executives, allowing us more insights into their characters, their other interests, and their secret passions. Books by the presidents may very well be one of the most important treasure troves of psychological and biographical information available to us, all the more important because they are from the pens of the presidents themselves. (*Note:* Posthumous collections of a president's papers are not considered books for the purposes of this list.)

JOHN ADAMS (1797-1801)

- ★ *A Defense of the Constitutions of Government of the United States of America* (3 volumes, 1787-1788).
- ★ *Discourses on Davila* (1805).
- ★ *Diary and Autobiography of John Adams* (4 volumes, 1961).

THOMAS JEFFERSON (1801-09)

★ *Notes on the State of Virginia* (1785).

JAMES MONROE (1817-25)

★ *A View of the Conduct of the Executive in the Foreign Affairs of the United States* (1797).

JOHN QUINCY ADAMS (1825-29)

★ *Dermot MacMorrogh or, The Conquest of Ireland: An Historical Tale of the Twelfth Century* (poetry, 1832).
★ *The Lives of James Madison and James Monroe* (1850).

JAMES K. POLK (1845-49)

★ *The Diary of James K. Polk during His Presidency, 1845 to 1849* (4 volumes, 1910).

JAMES BUCHANAN (1857-61)

★ *Mr. Buchanan's Administration on the Eve of the Rebellion* (1866).

ULYSSES S. GRANT (1869-77)

★ *Personal Memoirs of U.S. Grant* (2 volumes, 1885-1886).

BENJAMIN HARRISON (1889-93)

★ *This Country of Ours* (1897).
★ *Views of an Ex-President* (1901).

GROVER CLEVELAND (1893-97)

★ *Presidential Problems* (1904).
★ *Fishing and Shooting Sketches* (1904).
★ *Good Citizenship* (1908).

WILLIAM McKINLEY (1897-1901)

★ *The Tariff in the Days of Henry Clay and Since* (1896).

THEODORE ROOSEVELT (1901-09)

★ *The Naval War of 1812* (1882).
★ *Hunting Trip of a Ranchman* (1885).
★ *Life of Thomas Hart Benton* (1887).
★ *Gouverneur Morris* (1888).

* *Ranch Life and the Hunting Trail* (1888).
* *The Winning of the West 1769-1807* (4 volumes, 1889-1896).
* *New York* (1891).
* *Hero Tales from American History* (1895).
* *Rough Riders* (1899).
* *African Game Trails* (1910).
* *The New Nationalism* (1910).
* *History as Literature, and Other Essays* (1913).
* *Theodore Roosevelt, An Autobiography* (1913).
* *Through the Brazilian Wilderness* (1914).
* *Life Histories of African Game Animals* (1914).
* *America and the World War* (1915).
* *Fear God and Take Your Own Part* (1916).
* *The Foes of Our Own Household* (1917).
* *National Strength and International Duty* (1917).

WILLIAM HOWARD TAFT (1909-13)

* *Four Aspects of Civic Duty* (1906).
* *Our Chief Magistrate and His Powers* (1916).

WOODROW WILSON (1913-21)

* *Congressional Government: A Study in American Politics* (1885).
* *The State: Elements of Historical and Practical Politics* (1889).
* *George Washington* (1893).
* *An Old Master and Other Political Essays* (1893).
* *More Literature and Other Essays* (1896).
* *A History of the American People* (5 volumes, 1902).
* *President Wilson's Case for the League of Nations* (1923).

CALVIN COOLIDGE (1923-29)

* *The Autobiography of Calvin Coolidge* (1929).

HERBERT C. HOOVER (1929-33)

* *Principles of Mining* (1909).
* *American Individualism* (1922).
* *The New Day* (1929).
* *The Challenge to Liberty* (1934).
* *America's First Crusade* (1943).
* *The Problems of Lasting Peace* (with Hugh Gibson, 1943).
* *The Basis of Lasting Peace* (with Hugh Gibson, 1944).
* *The Memoirs of Herbert Hoover* (3 volumes, 1951-1952).
* *The Ordeal of Wilson* (1958).
* *An American Epic* (3 volumes, 1959-1961).

★ *On Growing Up* (1962).
★ *Fishing for Fun* (1963).

FRANKLIN D. ROOSEVELT (1933-45)

★ *The Happy Warrior Alfred E. Smith* (1928).

HARRY S TRUMAN (1945-53)

★ *Year of Decisions* (1955).
★ *Years of Trial and Hope* (1956).
★ *Mr. Citizen* (1960).

DWIGHT D. EISENHOWER (1953-61)

★ *Crusade in Europe* (1948).
★ *The White House Years* (2 volumes, 1965-1966).
  - *Mandate for Change, 1953-1956* (1965).
  - *Waging Peace, 1956-1961* (1966).
★ *At Ease: Stories I Tell to Friends* (1967).

JOHN F. KENNEDY (1961-63)

★ *Why England Slept* (1940).
★ *Profiles in Courage* (1956).

LYNDON B. JOHNSON (1963-69)

★ *The Vantage Point: Perspectives of the Presidency, 1963-1969* (1971).

RICHARD M. NIXON (1969-74)

★ *Six Crises* (1962).
★ *The Memoirs of Richard Nixon* (1978).
★ *The Real War* (1980).
★ *Leaders* (1982).
★ *Real Peace: Strategy for the West* (1984).
★ *No More Vietnams* (1985).
★ *Victory Without War* (1988).
★ *Beyond Peace* (1994).

GERALD R. FORD (1974-77)

★ *Portrait of an Assassin* (with John R. Stiles, 1976).
★ *A Time to Heal* (1979).

JIMMY CARTER (1977-81)

★ *Why Not the Best?* (1976).
★ *Turning Point: A Candidate, a State, and a Nation Come Of Age* (1980).

* *Keeping Faith: Memoirs of a President* (1982).
* *Everything to Gain: Making the Most Out of the Rest of Your Life* (with Rosalynn Carter, 1987).
* *An Outdoor Journal: Adventures and Reflections* (1988).
* *America on My Mind: The Best of America in Words and Photographs* (1991).
* *Always a Reckoning and Other Poems* (1994).
* *The Little Baby Snoogle-Fleejer* (children's book, with Amy Carter, 1995).
* *Talking Peace: A Vision for the Next Generation* (1996).
* *Living Faith* (1996).
* *The Virtues of Aging* (1998).
* *Sources of Strength: Meditations on Scripture for a Living Faith* (1999).

Ronald W. Reagan (1981-89)

* *Where's the Rest of Me? The Ronald Reagan Story* (with Richard G. Huble, 1965).
* *An American Life: The Autobiography* (1990).

George H.W. Bush (1989-93)

* *Looking Forward: An Autobiography* (with Victor Gold, 1987).
* *Man of Integrity* (with Doug Wead, 1988).
* *A World Transformed* (with Brent Scowcroft, 1998).
* *A Charge to Keep* (1999).
* *Building a Better America* (1999).
* *All the Best, George Bush: My Life in Letters and Other Writings* (1999).

Bill Clinton (1993-2001)

* *Putting People First* (with Al Gore, 1992).
* *Between Hope and History: Meeting America's Challenges for the 21st Century* (1996).

Chapter 26

18 Historic Assassinations and Assination Attempts in America

"Why put up the bars when the fence is all around? If they kill me, the next man will be just as bad for them. And in a country like this, where habits are simple, and must be, assassination is always possible, and will come if they are determined upon it."
—Abraham Lincoln, in a comment to Harriet Beecher Stowe during the winter of 1862-1863

hese 18 tragic assassinations and assassination attempts are in chronological order, beginning with what might be the most notorious assassination in American history, the murder of President Abraham Lincoln.

1.   **Assassination**, April 14, 1865 (Friday): U.S. President Abraham Lincoln is shot and mortally wounded by John Wilkes Booth in a theater in Washington, D.C. Lincoln died the following day.

2.   **Assassination**, July 2, 1881 (Saturday): President James A. Garfield is shot and mortally wounded by Charles J. Guiteau in the Baltimore and Potomac railroad station in Washington, D.C. Garfield died from his wounds on Monday, September 19, 1881.

3.   **Assassination**, September 6, 1901 (Friday): President William McKinley is shot and mortally wounded by Leon F. Czolgosz at the Temple of Music on the grounds of the Pan American Exposition in Buffalo, N.Y. McKinley died from his wounds on Saturday, September 14, 1901.

4.   **Assassination attempt**, October 14, 1912 (Monday): Former president Theodore Roosevelt is shot and wounded by John Schrank, a German immigrant bartender later judged insane and institutionalized. Roosevelt recovered completely. (Roosevelt himself had become president due to the assassination of President McKinley.)

5.   **Assassination attempt/assassination**, February 15, 1933 (Wednesday): President-elect Franklin D. Roosevelt is shot at by Joseph Zangara, an anarchist. The bullet intended for Roosevelt instead hits Chicago, Ill., Mayor Anton Cermak, who died of his wounds Wednesday, March 6, 1933.

6. **Assassination**, September 8, 1935 (Sunday): U.S. Senator Huey P. Long is shot and mortally wounded in Baton Rouge, La. by Dr. Carl Austin Weiss. Long died from his wounds Tuesday, September 19, 1935. Weiss was killed by Long's bodyguards at the scene.

7. **Assassination attempt**, November 1, 1950 (Wednesday): Two Puerto Rican nationalists, Griselio Torresola and Oscar Collazo, try to shoot their way into Blair House (the vice president's residence) in an attempt to assassinate President Harry S Truman. Torresola was shot and killed. A White House policeman, Private Leslie Coffelt, was shot and later died from his wounds.

8. **Assassination**, June 12, 1963 (Wednesday): Medgar Evers, the NAACP's Mississippi field secretary is shot and killed by Byron De La Beckwith in Jackson, Miss.

9. **Assassination**, November 22, 1963 (Friday): U.S. President John F. Kennedy is shot and killed while traveling in an open vehicle in a motorcade in Dallas, Texas. Lee Harvey Oswald is arrested and accused of the murder but Oswald is murdered by Jack Ruby while being transported to the county jail. To this day, conspiracy theorists believe that Oswald did not act alone and that there may have been other gunmen involved in the assassination.

10. **Assassination**, February 21, 1965 (Sunday): Malcolm X, a black nationalist leader, is shot and killed in New York City.

11. **Assassination**, April 4, 1968 (Thursday): Civil rights leader, the Reverend Dr. Martin Luther King, is shot and killed in Memphis, Tenn. James Earl Ray is arrested and convicted of the crime, although he denied culpability then and continued to assert his innocence until his death in 1998. (King's family also believes that Ray was innocent.)

12. **Assassination**, June 5, 1968 (Wednesday): U.S. Senator Robert F. Kennedy, brother of the slain president, is shot and killed in Los Angeles while campaigning for his own run for the presidency. Sirhan Sirhan is arrested and convicted of the crime.

13. **Assassination attempt**, May 15, 1972 (Monday): Alabama Governor George Wallace is shot and crippled by Arthur Bremer in Laurel, Md.

14. **Assassination attempt**, September 5, 1975 (Friday): Charles Manson follower Lynette "Squeaky" Fromme aims a pistol at President Gerald Ford. A Secret Service agent grabs the gun, and Ford is unharmed. Fromme is apprehended, charged with attempted assassination, and convicted of the crime.

15. **Assassination attempt**, September 22, 1975 (Monday): Sara Jane Moore fires a revolver at President Gerald Ford, but misses. President Ford is unharmed and Moore is apprehended, charged with attempted assassination, and convicted of the crime.

16. **Assassination attempt**, May 29, 1980 (Thursday): Civil rights leader Vernon Jordan is shot and wounded in Fort Wayne, Ind.

17. **Assassination attempt**, March 30, 1981 (Monday): President Ronald Reagan is shot and seriously wounded by John Hinckley Jr. in Washington, D.C. Press Secretary Jim Brady, Secret Service agent Timothy McCarthy, and D.C. police officer Thomas Delahanty are also seriously wounded in the assassination attempt. Hinckley shot Reagan to impress actress Jodie Foster, was found not guilty by reason of insanity, and was committed to a mental institution.

Chapter 27

The Presidential Chain of Succession

During each year's State of the Union address, one of the people on this list always remains in another location in case the president, the Senate, and the House of Representatives are killed in a terrorist attack. It's allegedly an honor to be barred from the Capitol Building during the State of the Union Address.

In any case, if the president dies, becomes incapacitated, or incapable of fulfilling his constitutional duties, the following is the order in which the office of the presidency will be filled.

1. Vice President.
2. Speaker of the House.
3. President Pro Tempore of the Senate.
4. Secretary of State.
5. Secretary of the Treasury.
6. Secretary of Defense.
7. Attorney General.
8. Secretary of the Interior.
9. Secretary of Agriculture.
10. Secretary of Commerce.
11. Secretary of Labor.
12. Secretary of Health and Human Services.
13. Secretary of Housing and Urban Development.
14. Secretary of Transportation.
15. Secretary of Energy.
16. Secretary of Education.

Chapter 28

The 46 Wives of U.S. Presidents

he first year listed is when the First Lady married her presidential hubby; the second year is when she died.

1. **George Washington**: Martha Dandridge Custis (1759, 1802).
2. **John Adams**: Abigail Smith (1764, 1818).
3. **Thomas Jefferson**: Martha Wayles Skelton (1772, 1782).
4. **James Madison**: Dorothy "Dolly" Payne Todd (1794, 1849).
5. **James Monroe**: Elizabeth "Eliza" Kortright (1786, 1830).
6. **John Quincy Adams**: Louisa Catherine Johnson (1797, 1852).
7. **Andrew Jackson**: Rachel Donelson Robards (1791, 1828).
8. **Martin Van Buren**: Hannah Hoes (1807, 1819).
9. **William Henry Harrison**: Anna Symmes (1795, 1864).
10. **John Tyler**: Letitia Christian (1813, 1842), Julia Gardiner (1844, 1889).
11. **James K. Polk**: Sarah Childress (1824, 1891).
12. **Zachary Taylor**: Margaret Smith (1819, 1852).
13. **Millard Fillmore**: Abigail Powers (1826, 1853), Caroline Carmichael McIntosh (1858, 1881).
14. **Franklin Pierce**: Jane Means Appleton (1834, 1863).
15. **James Buchanan**: Unmarried.
16. **Abraham Lincoln**: Mary Todd (1842, 1882).
17. **Andrew Johnson**: Eliza McCardle (1827, 1876).
18. **Ulysses S. Grant**: Julia Dent (1848, 1902).
19. **Rutherford B. Hayes**: Lucy Ware Webb (1852, 1889).
20. **James A. Garfield**: Lucretia Rudolph (1858, 1918).
21. **Chester A. Arthur**: Ellen Lewis Herndon (1859, 1880).
22. **Grover Cleveland**: Frances Folsom (1886, 1947).

Rembrant Peale's famous portrait of Dolly Madison.

23. **Benjamin Harrison**: Caroline Lavinia Scott (1853, 1892), Mary Scott Lord Dimmick (1896, 1948).
24. **Grover Cleveland**: Frances Folsom (1886, 1947).
25. **William McKinley**: Ida Saxton (1871, 1907).
26. **Theodore Roosevelt**: Alice Hathaway Lee (1880, 1884), Edith Kermit Carow (1886, 1948).
27. **William Howard Taft**: Helen Herron (1886, 1943).
28. **Woodrow Wilson**: Ellen Louise Axson (1885, 1914), Edith Bolling Galt (1915, 1961).
29. **Warren G. Harding**: Florence Kling DeWolfe (1891, 1924).
30. **Calvin Coolidge**: Grace Anna Goodhue (1905, 1957).
31. **Herbert C. Hoover**: Lou Henry (1899, 1944).
32. **Franklin Delano Roosevelt**: Anna Eleanor Roosevelt (1905, 1962).
33. **Harry S Truman**: Bess Wallace (1919, 1982).
34. **Dwight D. Eisenhower**: Mamie Geneva Doud (1916, 1979).
35. **John F. Kennedy**: Jacqueline Lee Bouvier (1953, 1994).
36. **Lyndon B. Johnson**: Claudia Alta "Lady Bird" Taylor (1934, —).
37. **Richard M. Nixon**: Thelma Catherine "Pat" Ryan (1940, 1993).
38. **Gerald R. Ford**: Elizabeth "Betty" Bloomer Warren (1948, —).
39. **Jimmy Carter**: Rosalynn Smith (1946, —).
40. **Ronald Reagan**: Jane Wyman (1940, —), Nancy Davis (1952, —).
41. **George Bush**: Barbara Pierce (1945, —).
42. **Bill Clinton**: Hillary Rodham (1975, —).

Chapter 29

The 132 Children of Presidents

 any Americans hold the offspring of presidents in high regard: We have a protective, proprietary attitude towards the sons and daughters of our presidents, even if the kids exhibit questionable behavior. (Amy Carter's arrest for protesting comes to mind; as does Patti Davis's decision to pose naked for *Playboy*). Nevertheless, we are fascinated by these presidential progeny and want to know more about them.

Being in the spotlight can be an unbearable burden. Many children of presidents couldn't handle the overwhelming attention and the expectations of the country.

To wit:

★ Two of President John Adams' sons became alcoholics.

★ President Van Buren's son once spent 24 hours in jail for getting into a fistfight with a lawyer in a courtroom.

★ President Harrison's son John Cleves Symmes was charged with embezzlement and was fired for it.

★ President Harrison's other son William died a penniless alcoholic (as did President Andrew Johnson's son Robert).

★ President Arthur's son took full advantage of his fame by deciding to live the life of a playboy.

★ Teddy Roosevelt Jr. was involved in the Teapot Dome Scandal.

★ President Taft's son Robert supported McCarthyism and blacklisting.

★ President Wilson's daughter Margaret joined the cult of an Indian guru and lived her life as a recluse.

★ FDR's son Elliot married and divorced an astonishing five times.

★ Amy Carter, in addition to being arrested for protesting, was thrown out of Brown University for poor grades.

★ President Bush's son Neil was involved in a savings and loan scandal that ultimately cost the American taxpayers $1 billion.

★★★

But for every presidential child who acts out and embarrasses the nation, there are 10 White House children that make us all proud.

Dozens of sons of presidents served their country in every war we've been involved in, and many have been awarded Purple Hearts, Distinguished Service Medals, Congressional Medals of Honor, and other commendations and accolades. Many presidential children have started businesses that became incredibly successful, including Union Carbide (started by Rutherford B. Hayes' son James); as well as the New York, New Haven and Hartford Railroad Company (Calvin Coolidge's son John was an executive with the company in its earliest days). Many presidential children have written bestselling books. And it would literally be impossible to compile a list of the charitable work all these people have been involved in.

The following list details all 130 of the children of U.S. presidents and provides a capsule overview of their lives and accomplishments.

(*Note:* Direct blood offspring of the U.S. presidents who lived to maturity are indicated by a round bullet [•]; adopted children are indicated by an asterisk [*]. Children of the presidents who died during childbirth or during early infancy are not included in this list.)

1. GEORGE WASHINGTON

George Washington had no natural children, but he adopted his wife Martha's two children from a previous marriage. There are no direct blood descendants of George Washington.

* **John Parke "Jacky" Custis** (1755-1781): His granddaughter, Mary Custis, married Robert E. Lee.
* **Martha Parke Custis** (1756-1783): Patsy died at the age of 17 due to complications from epilepsy.

2. JOHN ADAMS

* **Abigail "Nabby" Adams** (1765-1813): Married her father's secretary William Smith.
* **John Quincy Adams** (1767-1848): J.Q. was elected the sixth President of the United States.
* **Charles Adams** (1770-1800): A lawyer, he died an alcoholic at age 30.
* **Thomas Boylston Adams** (1772-1832): As a lawyer, he once defended owners of a brothel. Thomas was an alcoholic like his brother Charles.

3. THOMAS JEFFERSON

* **Martha "Patsy" Jefferson** (1772-1836): Served as White House hostess when her widowed father was in office.
* **Mary "Polly" Jefferson** (1778-1804): Died at 25 during childbirth.

4. JAMES MADISON

James Madison had no children and, therefore, no direct blood descendants.

5. JAMES MONROE

* **Eliza Monroe** (1787-?): Converted to Roman Catholicism.
* **Maria Hester Monroe** (1803-1850): Was married in the first wedding ever performed in the White House. Maria, however, didn't get along with her sister.

6. JOHN QUINCY ADAMS

- **George Washington Adams** (1801-1829): A lawyer. He was born in Germany. He died by drowning when he either fell off a steamer or jumped off of it. George Adams' behavior has led scholars to believe he was probably paranoid schizophrenic.
- **John Adams II** (1803-1834): Served as a presidential aide. He also served as private secretary to his father during his administration. He later ran his father's flour mill for a time but died suddenly at the age of 31.
- **Charles Francis Adams** (1807-1886): Diplomat, legislator, author, and editor. In 1872, he lost the Republican presidential nomination to Horace Greeley.

7. ANDREW JACKSON

Andrew Jackson had no natural children, but he adopted his wife's infant nephew—a twin originally born to his wife's cousins, Mr. and Mrs. Severn Donelson.

- * **Andrew Jackson Jr.**

8. MARTIN VAN BUREN

- **Abraham Van Buren** (1807-1873): A Mexican War hero, he also served as his father's secretary during his administration.
- **John Van Buren** (1810-1866): A lawyer, he was a Democratic Congressman who opposed slavery. He once spent a day in jail for getting into a fistfight with an attorney in court.
- **Martin Van Buren Jr.** (1812-1855): As a political aide to his father, he compiled the materials the president used to write his memoirs. He died suddenly in Europe at the age of 43.
- **Smith Thompson Van Buren** (1817-1876): Also a political aide to his father, he wrote some of his father's speeches and edited the *Van Buren Papers*. He married one of Washington Irving's nieces.

9. WILLIAM HENRY HARRISON

- **Elizabeth "Betsy" Bassett Harrison** (1796-1846): Married a judge and lived on a farm given to them by her father.
- **John Cleves Symmes Harrison** (1798-1830): Public official, he was charged with embezzlement and was subsequently fired by President Jackson. He died at age 32 from typhoid fever and his father assumed responsibility for his debts, his widow, and his six children.
- **Lucy Singleton Harrison** (1800-1826): Married a lawyer, died at the age of 26.
- **William Henry Harrison, Jr.** (1802-1838): A lawyer, became an alcoholic, and gave up his practice to become a farmer. He died at age 50 from drinking. His father assumed responsibility for his debts and his widow and children.
- **John Scott Harrison** (1804-1878): The only man ever to be the *son* of a president and the *father* of a president (the 23rd president, Benjamin Harrison).
- **Benjamin Harrison** (1806-1840): A doctor, he died at age 34 after starting his medical practice.
- **Mary Symmes Harrison** (1809-1842): Married a doctor, she died at age 33.

- **Carter Bassett Harrison** (1811-1839): An attache to Colombia, a lawyer. He died at 27.
- **Anna Tuthill Harrison** (1813-1845): Married her cousin William Henry Harrison Taylor, she died at 32.

10. John Tyler

- **Mary Tyler** (1815-1848): Married a planter, died at age 33.
- **Robert Tyler** (1816-1877): Lawyer, sheriff's solicitor, served as his father's private secretary, chief clerk of the Pennsylvania supreme court, and married an actress.
- **John Tyler Jr.** (1819-1896): Lawyer, served as private secretary to his father, assistant secretary of war for the Confederacy during the Civil War, and ended up working for the Internal Revenue Bureau in Florida.
- **Letitia Tyler** (1821-1907): An educator, opened a school in Baltimore called The Eclectic Institute.
- **Elizabeth Tyler** (1823-1850): Died during childbirth at 27.
- **Alice Tyler** (1827-1854): Married an Episcopalian priest, died suddenly of colic at 27.
- **Tazewell Tyler** (1830-1874): A doctor, served as a surgeon in the Confederate Army during the Civil War.
- **David Gardiner "Gardie" Tyler** (1846-1927): A lawyer, served in the Confederate Army; was also a senator, a congressman, and a judge.
- **John Alexander "Alex" Tyler** (1848-1883): An engineer, served in the Confederate Army, served in the Saxon Army during the Franco-Prussian War, became a mining engineer, served as a surveyor of the U.S. Department of the Interior. He died at age 35 from drinking contaminated water.
- **Julia Gardiner Tyler** (1849-1871): Married a poor farmer and died during childbirth at age 22.
- **Lachlan Tyler** (1851-1902): A doctor and U.S. Navy surgeon.
- **Lyon Gardiner Tyler** (1853-1935): Lawyer, Educator, Professor of Literature at the College of William and Mary, President of the college from 1888-1919, and a prolific writer of treatises defending his father's administration.
- **Robert Fitzwater "Fitz" Tyler** (1856-1927): Became a farmer.
- **Pearl Tyler** (1860-1947): Pearl was born when John Tyler was 70 years old. John Tyler died when she was only 2 and she never truly knew him. She converted to Roman Catholicism at the age of 12. She married William Ellis, a member of the Virginia House of Delegates, whom she claimed to have seen in a dream before they met.

11. James K. Polk

James Polk had no children and, therefore, no direct blood descendants.

12. Zachary Taylor

- **Ann Mackall Taylor** (1811-1875): Married an Army surgeon.
- **Sarah Knox Taylor** (1814-1835): Married Jefferson Davis, future president of the Confederate States. She died of malaria that same year at the age of 21.
- **Mary Elizabeth "Betty" Taylor** (1824-1909): Served as White House hostess during her father's administration because of her mother's chronic illnesses.
- **Richard "Dick" Taylor** (1826-1879): Served as military aide to his father during the Mexican War, served as his father's private secretary during his administration, ran a

sugar plantation, was elected Louisiana state senator, and served in the Confederate Army during the Civil War. Later, he wrote a book titled *Destruction and Reconstruction* about the impact of the Civil War on the South.

13. MILLARD FILLMORE

- **Millard Powers Fillmore** (1828-1889): A lawyer, served as private secretary for his father during his administration. He was later appointed a federal court clerk.
- **Mary Abigail Fillmore** (1832-1854): An educator, spoke five languages, she was also an accomplished musician. She died of cholera at age 22.

14. FRANKLIN PIERCE

- **Benjamin Pierce** (1841-1853): Died at age 12 in a train accident.

15. JAMES BUCHANAN

James Buchanan had no children and, therefore, no direct blood descendants.

16. ABRAHAM LINCOLN

- **Robert Todd Lincoln** (1843-1926): Lawyer, served as a captain under General Ulysses S. Grant in the Union Army during the Civil War, served as War Secretary from 1881 to 1885, served as minister to Great Britain from 1889 to 1893, was the president of the Pullman Company from 1897 to 1911, and decreed that his father's personal papers could not be made public until 1947.
- **Edward "Eddie" Lincoln** (1846-1850): Died of tuberculosis at the age of 3. His death devastated Mary Lincoln, who did not have her husband's Christian faith to turn to for solace.
- **William "Willie" Wallace Lincoln** (1850-1862): A studious young man who was close to his father. He was the only president's child to die in the White House.
- **Thomas "Tad" Lincoln** (1853-1871): Born with a cleft palate and a lisp speech impediment, Tad comforted his father following his brother Willie's death. He studied in England and Germany and died at the age of 18.

17. ANDREW JOHNSON

- **Martha Johnson** (1828-1891): Served as White House hostess during her father's administration (First Lady Eliza Johnson was an invalid). She married a U.S. senator and they ran a farm outside Greeneville, Tenn.
- **Charles Johnson** (1830-1863): A doctor and a pharmacist, he served as assistant surgeon in the Middle Tennessee Union Infantry during the Civil War. He died at the age of 33 when he was thrown from his horse and killed.
- **Mary Johnson** (1832-1883): Married a Union Infantry Colonel, ran a farm after the Civil War, and remarried following the death of her first husband.
- **Robert Johnson** (1834-1869): A lawyer, served in the Tennessee State Legislature, served as a colonel for the First Tennessee Union Cavalry during the Civil War, and served as private secretary to his father during his administration. He died at age 35 from complications from alcoholism.
- **Andrew Johnson Jr.** (1852-1879): A journalist, founded the weekly newspaper the *Greeneville Intelligencer*. He died at the age of 27 not long after the paper's failure.

18. ULYSSES S. GRANT

- **Frederick Dent Grant** (1850-1912): Accompanied his father during the Civil War, was president of a utility company following the war, served as U.S. minister to Austria-Hungary under President Harrison, served on the New York City of Board of Police Commissioners, was appointed police commissioner in 1897 (succeeding Theodore Roosevelt), served as assistant war secretary under President McKinley, and fought in the Spanish-American War.
- **Ulysses S. "Buck" Grant** (1852-1929): A lawyer, served as personal secretary to his father, was an assistant district attorney in New York, and formed with a brokerage house his father in New York. He was also a delegate to the 1896 Republican National Convention and ran unsuccessfully for U.S. Senator to California in 1899.
- **Ellen "Nellie" Wrenshall Grant** (1855-1922): Married a wealthy English actor who died young, leaving Ellen a wealthy young widow.
- **Jesse Root Grant** (1858-1934): An engineer, he eventually switched to the Democratic Party. He was a candidate for the Democratic presidential nomination in 1908. In 1925 he published the book *In the Days of My Father General Grant*.

19. RUTHERFORD B. HAYES

- **Sardis Birchard "Birchard Austin" Hayes** (1853-1926): A lawyer, he was very successful as a real estate and tax attorney.
- **James Webb "Webb Cook" Hayes** (1856-1934): Served as secretary to his father during his administration, founded Union Carbide. He served as a major during the Spanish-American War, and won the Congressional Medal of Honor.
- **Rutherford Platt Hayes** (1858-1931): Library official, served as a bank clerk, and promoted libraries. He helped develop Asheville, N.C., into a tourist resort.
- **Frances "Fanny" Hayes** (1867-1950): Educated at a private girls' school and married a U.S. Naval Academy instructor.
- **Scott Russell Hayes** (1871-1923): He was an executive with railroad service companies in New York.

20. JAMES A. GARFIELD

- **Harry Augustus Garfield** (1863-1942): A lawyer, law professor, and first professor of politics at Princeton. He served as Chairman of the Price Commission of the U.S. Food Administration during World War I (responsible for "gasless Sundays" and "heatless days" conservation programs). He was awarded the Distinguished Service Medal in 1921 and eventually created the Institute of Politics at Williams College.
- **James Rudolph Garfield** (1865-1950): Lawyer, served as Ohio state senator from 1896 to 1900, served on the U.S. Civil Service Commission, and was appointed Secretary of the Interior in 1907.
- **Mary "Molly" Garfield** (1867-1947): Educated at private schools and married her father's presidential secretary.
- **Irving McDowell Garfield** (1879-1951): Lawyer, served on the board of directors of several corporations.
- **Abram Garfield** (1872-1958): Architect, graduated from the Massachusetts Institute of Technology, served as Chairman of the Cleveland Planning Commission from 1929 to 1942.

21. Chester A. Arthur

- **Chester Alan Arthur Jr.** (1864-1937): A lawyer, but never practiced. He decided to live as a playboy and succeeded quite admirably at it. (His father reportedly warned him early on not to go into politics.)
- **Ellen "Nell" Herndon Arthur** (1871-1915): Was kept away from the media as a child. She married and lived in New York until her death at the age of 44.

22. Grover Cleveland

- **Ruth Cleveland** (1891-1904): Given the nickname "Baby Ruth" by the press shortly after her birth. She died suddenly at age 12 from diphtheria.
- **Esther Cleveland** (1893-1980): The only child of a president actually born in the White House. She did volunteer work in England during World War II, married a British captain, and lived in England for a time.
- **Marion Cleveland** (1895-1977): Attended Columbia University Teachers College, married twice, and served as community relations adviser for the Girl Scouts of America from 1943 to 1960.
- **Richard Folsom Cleveland** (1897-1974): A lawyer, served as General Counsel for the Public Service Commission in Baltimore from 1934 to 1935, and was active in the American Liberty League.
- **Francis Grover Cleveland** (1903-1995): An actor, he founded the summer stock company, The Barnstormers.

23. Benjamin Harrison

- **Russell Benjamin Harrison** (1854-1936): Mechanical engineer, assistant assayer at the U.S. Mint in New Orleans. He raised livestock, and was the publisher of the *Helena Daily Journal*. He served as private secretary to his father during his administration. He was also the president of a streetcar company. He was reprimanded for raising the U.S. flag prematurely in Cuba at the conclusion of the Spanish-American War. He became a lawyer after the war, and was Mexico's lawyer in the United States for many years. He later served as both congressman and senator in the Indiana legislature.
- **Mary Scott "Mamie" Harrison** (1858-1930): Served as White House hostess during her father's administration.
- **Elizabeth Harrison** (1897-1955): A lawyer, founded and published an investment newsletter for women called *Cues on the News*.

24. Grover Cleveland

See number 22.

25. William McKinley

McKinley had two daughters who both died in infancy. Therefore, no direct blood descendants of President McKinley survived.

26. Theodore Roosevelt

- **Alice Roosevelt** (1884-1980): Nicknamed "Princess Alice" by the press; she was outspoken and feisty all her long life.

- **Theodore Roosevelt Jr.** (1887-1944): Graduated from Harvard, was commissioned a major and wounded during World War I. He was awarded the Purple Heart, the Distinguished Service Medal, and the Distinguished Service Cross. He served in 1919 in the New York State Assembly and was appointed Assistant Secretary of the Navy from 1921 to 1925. He was involved in the Teapot Dome Scandal (albeit unwittingly), lost the New York governor's election in 1924, was governor of Puerto Rico from 1929 to 1932, served as a brigadier general during World War II, and landed at Normandy on D-Day. He died of natural causes and was posthumously awarded the Congressional Medal of Honor.
- **Kermit Roosevelt** (1889-1943): Kermit accompanied his father on safaris. He was a Captain in the British Army during World War I, served as a major in the British Army during World War II and later joined the U.S. Army. He died in Alaska while on duty.
- **Ethel Carow Roosevelt** (1891-1977): Served as a nurse in Paris during World War I.
- **Archibald Bulloch Roosevelt** (1894-1979): Served as a captain in the U.S. Army during World War I and was wounded in France. After the war he made a fortune as a Wall Street investor. He later served as a lieutenant colonel in the Army during World War II but was discharged because of injuries sustained during combat.
- **Quentin Roosevelt** (1897-1918): An Army Air Corps pilot during World War I. He was shot down by German fighters over France. He didn't survive.

27. WILLIAM HOWARD TAFT

- **Robert Alphonso Taft** (1889-1953): A lawyer, elected congressman and senator in Ohio and then elected to the U.S. Senate from 1939 to 1953. He was a severe critic of President Franklin Roosevelt's "New Deal" program, President Taft's "Fair Deal" program, U.S. participation in NATO, U.S. participation in the United Nations, and the Nuremberg Trials. He sponsored the Taft-Hartley Act and he endorsed Senator Joseph McCarthy's anti-communist attacks along with the subsequent blacklisting of suspected communists. He lost the Republican presidential nomination to Dwight D. Eisenhower and served until his death as Republican Senate majority leader.
- **Helen Herron Taft Manning** (1891-1987): Earned a doctorate in history and became dean of Bryn Mawr college as well as head of their history department.
- **Charles Phelps Taft** (1897-1983): Served in World War I as a first lieutenant. He was a lawyer, a prosecutor, and served in Franklin Roosevelt's administration. He was the Director of Economic Affairs at the State Department. He was later named president of the Federal Council of Churches in America from 1947 to 1948 (even though he was not ordained ministry). He ran for governor in Ohio and later wrote the books *City Management: The Cincinatti Experiment* (1933) and *You and I and Roosevelt* (1936).

28. WOODROW WILSON

- **Margaret Woodrow Wilson** (1886-1944): Margaret was a trained professional singer and performed with the Chicago Symphony Orchestra as well as at army camps for the Red Cross. She worked as a writer for an advertising agency and became an investor and stock speculator. In 1940, she became a follower of the Indian spiritual and mystic leader Sri Aurobondo and changed her name to Dishta. She lived in spiritual retreat until her death from uremia at age 58.

- **Jessie Woodrow Wilson** (1887-1933): Active in the League of Women Voters and was secretary of the Massachusetts Democratic Committee. She died at age 46 from complications following appendix surgery.
- **Eleanor Randolph Wilson** (1889-1967): Wrote the book *The Woodrow Wilsons* (1937), and was said to be most like her father.

29. WARREN G. HARDING

- **Elizabeth Ann Christian** (1919-?): The president's illegitimate daughter from his extramarital affair with Nan Briton. Harding paid child support, but the Harding estate refused to establish a trust fund for the child following the President and First Lady's deaths. The angry Briton went on to write a best-seller called *The President's Daughter*. The last known whereabouts (1964) of Elizabeth Ann Christian was Glendale, Calif.

30. CALVIN COOLIDGE

- **John Coolidge** (1906-): Executive with the New York, New Haven, and Hartford Railroad until 1941, and then was president of a printing company in Hartford until his retirement.
- **Calvin Coolidge Jr.** (1908-1924): Died at 16 when a blister on his toe became terminally infected. His father was campaigning for president when Calvin Jr. died.

31. HERBERT C. HOOVER

- **Herbert Hoover Jr.** (1903-1969): An aircraft engineer and educator, he founded United Geophysical Company in 1935. He helped develop equipment to discover oil, acted as mediator between Britain and Iran during their 1953-1954 oil dispute, and was appointed under-Secretary of State for Middle Eastern Affairs from 1954 to 1957.
- **Allan Hoover** (1907-1993): Mining engineer who has shunned the media his entire life.

32. FRANKLIN D. ROOSEVELT

- **Anna Eleanor Roosevelt** (1906-1975): Attended Cornell University, and was an editor for the *Seattle Post Intelligencer* from 1936-1943. She co-hosted a radio show with her mother, attended the Yalta Conference with her father, worked as a public relations liaison for hospitals from 1952 to 1958, and she worked to start a medical school in Iran from 1958 to 1960.
- **James Roosevelt** (1907-1991): Insurance executive, served as secretary for his father during his administration, and served in the Marines during World War II. He was elected to the U.S. House of Representatives and served from 1955 to 1966. He wrote the books *Affectionately, FDR* (1959) and *My Parents* (1976).
- **Elliott Roosevelt** (1910-1990): Radio company executive, served in the Army Air Corps during World War II and was awarded the Distinguished Flying Cross. He ran an import-export business and was mayor of Miami Beach, Fla. in the 1960s. He was married five times (including once to actress Faye Emerson) and edited his father's letters (1947-1950). He later wrote the book *An Untold Story: The Roosevelts of Hyde Park* (1974).
- **Franklin D. Roosevelt Jr.** (1914-1988): A lawyer, he served as a ship commander in the U.S. Navy during World War II. He was elected a Democratic congressman from 1949-1954, was under-Secretary of Commerce from 1963-1965, chairman of the Equal

Opportunity Commission from 1965 to 1966, and eventually became a distributor for Fiat automobiles in the United States.

- **John Aspinwall Roosevelt** (1916-1981): Served in the Navy as a logistics officer during World War II, ran a department store in Los Angeles after the war, became a partner in Bache and Company on Wall Street. He ultimately switched loyalties and became a Republican.

33. HARRY S TRUMAN

- **(Mary) Margaret Truman** (1924-): Made her debut as a coloratura soprano in 1947. She eventually became a well-known writer specializing in murder mysteries set in Washington, D.C., using politics and politicians elements and characters in her stories.

34. DWIGHT D. EISENHOWER

- **John Sheldon Doud Eisenhower** (1922-): Graduated from West Point, and earned a master's degree in English literature. He served in the Korean War and later became a General in the Army reserve. He was appointed Ambassador to Belgium from 1969 to 1971. He was the author of several books, including *The Bitter Woods* (1969) and *Strictly Personal* (1974).

35. JOHN F. KENNEDY

- **Caroline Kennedy** (1957-): Lawyer and author of books about privacy. She once worked as film curator for the Metropolitan Museum of Art.
- **John F. Kennedy Jr.** (1960-1999): Lawyer and founder and editor of *George* magazine. He died in a small plane crash on July 16, 1999.

36. LYNDON B. JOHNSON

- **Lynda Bird Johnson** (1944-): Attended George Washington University. She was, for a time, a contributing editor for *Ladies Home Journal*. President Carter appointed her chairperson of the National Advisory Committee for Women from 1982 to 1986.
- **Luci Baines Johnson** (1947): Converted to Roman Catholicism, divorced once, married an investment banker, and settled in Toronto.

37. RICHARD M. NIXON

- **Patricia "Tricia" Nixon** (1946-): Graduated from Finch College and married in the White House Rose Garden. She has deliberately stayed out of the spotlight her entire life.
- **Julie Nixon** (1948-): Married David Eisenhower, the grandson of President Eisenhower. She authored the book *Special People* as well as a 1986 biography of her mother, Pat Nixon.

38. GERALD R. FORD

- **Michael Gerald Ford** (1950-): An ordained minister, he is often at odds with his father's political views.
- **John "Jack" Gardener Ford** (1952-): A journalist, he brought George Harrison to the White House. He once worked as editorial assistant for *Outside* magazine and co-published

the weekly newspaper *Del-Mar News Press* from 1978 to 1980. He is rumored to be considering a move into the political arena.

- **Steven Meigs Ford** (1956-): An actor, he is a regular on *The Young and the Restless*.
- **Susan Elizabeth Ford** (1957-): Professional photographer, she worked on *Jaws II*.

39. JAMES E. "JIMMY" CARTER, JR.

- **John William "Jack" Carter** (1947-): Lawyer, has a degree in nuclear physics, and works for the Chicago Board of Trade.
- **James Earl "Chip" Carter III** (1950-): Ran the Carter peanut business for a time. He now runs Carter/Smith & Associates, a corporate consulting firm.
- **(Donnell) Jeffrey Carter** (1952-): Computer cartographer and founder of Computer Mapping Consultants.
- **Amy Lynn Carter** (1968-): A student activist, she has been arrested for being involved in illegal protests, was thrown out of Brown University for poor grades, has kept a low profile ever since.

40. RONALD W. REAGAN

- **Maureen Reagan** (1941-): Worked in show business for many years; founded the magazine *Showcase, USA*, claims to have seen Lincoln's ghost in the White House, and wrote the book *First Father, First Daughter* (1989).
- * **Michael Reagan** (1945-): The adopted son of President Reagan and his first wife Jane Wyman. He has worked as a boat salesman, as the vice president of a defense contract plant, as an actor, a TV talk show host, as a speedboat racer. He wrote the book *On the Outside Looking In* (1988).
- **Patti Reagan Davis** (1952-): Actress and novelist, she was the author of the bestselling book *Home Front* (1986).
- **Ronald Prescott Reagan** (1958-): Ballet dancer; danced for a time with the Joffrey Ballet; also worked as an on-air correspondent for *Good Morning, America*.

41. GEORGE H.W. BUSH

- **George W. Bush** (1946-): Governor of Texas; 2000 Republican presidential candidate, oil and gas executive, co-owned the Texas Rangers.
- **John E. "Jeb" Bush** (1953-): Banker, real estate developer, politician, headed his father's reelection campaign in Florida in 1992.
- **Neil M. Bush** (1955-): Oil company executive, involved with a failed savings and loan scandal in 1988 that cost the American taxpayers $1 billion.
- **Marvin P. Bush** (1956-): Investment consultant; worked with Shearson, Lehman; had a colostomy in 1986 and has been active with the United Ostomy Association since.
- **Dorothy W. "Doro" Bush** (1959-): Works for the National Rehabilitation Hospital in Washington, D.C., has also worked as a travel agent, a caterer, and a bookkeeper.

42. WILLIAM J. "BILL" CLINTON

- **Chelsea Victoria Clinton** (1980-): Named for the Joni Mitchell song "Chelsea Morning." Chelsea handled herself with dignity and grace during her father's Monica Lewinsky scandal and impeachment trial. In 1998, she entered college with thoughts of becoming an astronautical engineer or a doctor (or both?).

Chapter 30

18 Cases of Miraculous Religious Phenomena

"The miracles of the church seem to me to rest not so much upon faces or voices or healing power coming suddenly near to us from afar off, but upon our perceptions being made finer, so that for a moment our eyes can see and our ears can hear what is there about us always."
—Willa Cather, *Death Comes for the Archbishop*

"I think it pisses God off if you walk by the color purple in a field somewhere and don't notice it."
—Alice Walker, *The Color Purple*

theists do not believe that there is anything to existence other than this world and this life. Their ideology states that there is no God, that miracles are impossible, and that the purpose of organized religions is to keep the masses intellectually and emotionally sedated. Nonbelievers dismiss religious experiences such as sightings of the Virgin Mary or other unexplainable spiritual phenomena as mass hallucinations—a form of global delusional thinking.

The bottom line of their philosophy is that belief in God is a crutch, and that until mankind as a species outgrows the need to depend on mythos, we will never solve the very real problems of real people in our very real world.

Now admittedly, there is much to be said for "faith" in science. And yet science is not infallible, nor is it static. A mere few centuries ago, science "knew" that the earth was the center of the universe. And before that, science also "knew" that the earth was flat. As has often been asked, what does science "know" now that will be shown to be false 100 years from now?

Atheists are entitled to believe what they wish. But what about the occurrence of what appear to be *real* miracles? What about the documented cases of seemingly impossible events?

The atheists dismiss these events as hallucinations or natural phenomena that we cannot yet understand. The faithful, however, look to them as signs that there is indeed a supernatural power beyond this plane of existence and that life does, indeed, go on after our brief stint here on earth.

For your consideration: If our human mind can affect our physical bodies (and it has been proven that it can), then isn't it possible that there is a universal mind—what Apollo 14 astronaut Edgar Mitchell described to me as an "intelligent and creative force"—that can affect the physical universe, including our world and the beings on it?

At the dawn of a new millennium, then, it is critical to realize that the specific meanings of miracles and divine apparitions, is in the eyes, heart, and soul of the beholder.

The following unusual events are all documented and witnessed by oridnary people. Their credibility and trustworthiness were accepted as a given in their varied communities. In many of the following cases, more than one person witnessed the phenomena and corroborated the original report. As an exercise, try explaining them without falling back on the possibility that there may be a supernatural component to their occurrence.

ARKANSAS

★ **October 17, 1987,** Wynne: A cross appears on a glass door after a woman prays for her dead husband.

CALIFORNIA

★ **December 24, 1984,** Bakersfield: Our Lady of Guadeloupe appears to the faithful in a La Loma barrio.

★ **1981,** Thornton: A statue of the Virgin Mary weeps oil and is seen to move 30 feet.

CONNECTICUT

★ **1992,** New Haven: A figure of the crucified Christ appears in the configuration of the trunk and limbs of a tree in the Wooster Square park. The apparition becomes known locally as "The Jesus Tree."

FLORIDA

★ **December 1969,** Tarpon Springs: An icon of St. Nicholas weeps.

★ **December 1973,** Tarpon Springs: The icon of St. Nicholas that wept here in December 1969 weeps again.

★ **June 1999,** Jacksonville Beach: A 34-year-old woman does not commit suicide after a visit from a being she believes was Jesus Christ.

ILLINOIS

★ **May 1970,** Chicago: Human blood oozes from the 1,700-year-old remains of St. Maximina.

★ **May 1984,** Chicago: A statue of the Virgin Mary weeps in front of witnesses.

★ **December 6, 1986,** Chicago: A painting of the Virgin Mary weeps in front of witnesses.

★ **April 30, 1999,** Chicago: A 50-year-old man dying of an inoperable brain tumor has a vision of Jesus. Within 24 hours, he recovers completely with no sign of the brain tumor that was killing him.

NEVADA

★ **May 1999,** Reno: A young boy is saved from being killed by a marauding bear when a being his father believes was Jesus appears between the boy and the bear.

NEW JERSEY

★ **1992-present,** Marlboro Township: The Virgin Mary appears to Joseph Januskiewicz in his backyard on the first Sunday of every month. Hundreds of followers flock to his home for messages from Mary.

NEW MEXICO

★ **May 26, 1976,** Roswell: A portrait of Christ bleeds. The bleeding is witnessed by many and is photographed.

NEW YORK

★ **1975-present,** Queens: The Virgin Mary regularly appears and speaks through a Long Island grandmother. As in the case of Joseph Januskiewicz of New Jersey, hordes of the faithful make a pilgrimage to the woman's home, hoping for a message from the Virgin.

PENNSYLVANIA

★ **April 1975,** Boothwyn: A statue of Christ bleeds at the hands in front of witnesses.
★ **Good Friday, 1989,** Ambridge: A statue of Jesus closes its eyes.

TEXAS

★ **August 1988,** Lubbock: The Virgin Mary appears in the sky above a church before many witnesses. The Blessed Mother's image is photographed during her appearance.

Chapter 31

42 Interesting Things You May Not Have Known About America's Presidents

"No pessimist ever did anything for the welfare of the world."
—Harry S Truman

1.   **George Washington** was the only president who never lived in the White House. The building was not completed until after his death.
2.   In an attempt to curb his appetite, **John Adams** always insisted that boiled cornmeal pudding be served first before his meal. (Behind his back, Adams was often referred to as "Mr. Rotundity.")
3.   **Thomas Jefferson**'s personal library of 10,000 volumes was of such importance that after the British burned the Library of Congress in 1814, Jefferson offered his own collection of books as a replacement for what was lost in the fire. Congress accepted Jefferson's books. They are still a part of the archives of the Library of Congress today.
4.   Between the years 1780 and 1826, best friends **James Madison** and **Thomas Jefferson** exchanged an average of a letter every two weeks. Over a period of 46 years, their correspondence totaled more than 1,200 letters.
5.   When **James Monroe** left the White House following his presidency, his political debts were so high, he was forced to sell off his slaves along with all of his property to fend off bankruptcy.
6.   **John Quincy Adams** considered his four years as president "the four most miserable years of my life."
7.   **Andrew Jackson** sometimes coughed up blood due to a bullet painfully lodged near his heart from an early duel. To alleviate the pain from the bullet, he sometimes resorted to slitting open his own veins with a pocketknife and "bleeding" himself.
8.   **Martin Van Buren** was the first president who was born as an American citizen.
9.   **William Henry Harrison**'s inaugural address, which lasted close to two hours, was the longest in U.S. history. His presidency, a mere 30 days, was, and still is, the shortest term in U.S. history. Harrison delivered his meandering inaugural address hatless in bitter

cold weather. He eventually caught a cold from the exposure, which turned to pneumonia, which killed him a month later.

10. **John Tyler** was the first president to ascend to the office due to the death of a president (Tyler was William Henry Harrison's vice president.) This was such a unique and unprecedented event in American history that many refused to consider Tyler a "real" president. (Some even referred to him as "His Accidency.")

11. During his presidency, **James K. Polk** kept a detailed diary that eventually numbered 25 volumes of between 100 and 250 pages each. Polk's complete diaries were published in book form in 1910 within four volumes.

12. When **Zachary Taylor** was elected president in 1849, the 64-year-old cavalry general had never voted.

13. In what might be the only instance of a prenuptial agreement ever being signed by a former president, in 1858, widower **Millard Fillmore** signed a prenup before marrying Caroline McIntosh (13-years younger than Fillmore), the wealthy widow of a railroad magnate.

14. **Franklin Pierce**, was devastated by the death of his 11-year-old son Bennie in a train accident two moths before Pierce's inauguration. Pierce witnessed his son's death, almost completely losing his religious faith. Because of this, Pierce was the only president to refuse to say "I solemnly swear" when he was sworn in as president. (In its stead, he said "I solemnly affirm.")

15. **James Buchanan** is the only president to remain a bachelor his entire life. Buchanan's charming and vivacious niece Harriet Lane (his sister Jane's daughter) served as his official White House hostess during his presidency.

16. **Abraham Lincoln** loved to read. One of his favorite writers was William Shakespeare. There are stories of Abe reciting entire soliloquies from *Hamlet* and *Macbeth* flawlessly from memory to visitors of the White House. Lincoln was so good that there are reports that some who were privileged to witness one of the president's "performances" felt he had missed his calling and would have made a superb actor.

17. **Andrew Johnson**, the only U.S. president other than Bill Clinton to be impeached, was an avowed racist and a confirmed white supremacist. After his elevation to president following Lincoln's assassination, Johnson said, "This is a country for white men, and by God, as long as I am president, it shall be a government for white men." He was also a slave owner and is on record as saying, "If you liberate the negro what will be the next step? It would place every splay-footed, bandy-shanked, humpbacked negro in the country upon an equality with the poor white man....You can't get rid of the negro except by holding him in slavery."

18. **Ulysses S. Grant** smoked up to 20 cigars a day from a young age. The habit eventually killed him after he developed cancer of the throat in 1884. However, he refused to succumb to the disease until he completed the writing of his autobiography, *Personal Memoirs of U.S. Grant* (2 volumes, 1885-1886), a tome that is now considered a literary masterpiece.

19. **Rutherford B. Hayes** accepted the Republican nomination for president with a condition attached: If elected, he would serve one term and one term only. True to his word, he happily retired from the presidency after four years and attended the inauguration of his successor, the Republican James Garfield.

20. **James A. Garfield** was the only ordained preacher ever to be elected President of the United States. Garfield was a minister in the Church of the Disciples of Christ when he was elected in 1881.

21. **Chester A. Arthur**, lying on his death bed and worried about his place in American history, had all his papers and correspondence placed into a trash can and burned as he watched. He was then able to die in peace.

22. In 1893, heavy smoker **Grover Cleveland** was diagnosed with a malignant tumor of the mouth. Fearing a financial panic that would make the Depression (or "the panic of 1893") worse, Cleveland's condition was not revealed to the public. Cleveland was secretly operated on on a yacht on the East River in New York on July 1, 1893, by five doctors and a dentist. They removed his left upper jaw along with a large tumor. The president was fitted with a rubber jaw and spent months learning how to speak naturally again. Cleveland's surgery was not revealed to the American public until 1917, 24 years after his operation.

23. In **Benjamin Harrison**'s time in the 19th century, the White House grounds were open to the public. (President Harrison—grandson of President William Henry Harrison—often complained about the lack of privacy.) When Harrison strolled the grounds, he would always stare up at the sky so that he would not have to make eye contact with tourists nor converse with well-wishers.

24. **Grover Cleveland** was elected to the presidency twice, in 1885 and 1893. In the four years between his first and second term (the years 1889 through 1893), Cleveland moved his family back to New York where they lived on Madison Avenue. Cleveland took a position with the law firm Bangs, Stetson, Tracy, and McVeagh, and went to work every day on the streetcar.

25. Ida McKinley, **William McKinley**'s First Lady, was an epileptic who was frequently bedridden and prone to depression. However, McKinley adored her. There is a story of the rare times Ida accompanied the president to a public dinner. (He always insisted that she sat next to him instead of at the other end of the table.) During one dinner, the First Lady suffered an epileptic seizure. McKinley gently placed his napkin over his wife's face to save her the embarrassment of the other attendees witnessing the grimacing and contortions of her face. When the seizure stopped, McKinley removed the napkin. Without acknowledging what had happened in any way, he continued on with his conversation.

26. **Theodore Roosevelt** loved being president. But toward the end of his administration, it began to bother him that his time in office had been an era of total peace. Wanting to leave some kind of military legacy, Teddy doubled the size of the U.S. Navy. And, in his final year in office, he sent the American naval fleet around the world (for no apparent military gain).

27. **William Howard Taft** weighed as much as 332 pounds during his life. Yet, no matter what his girth, he was always an astonishingly good dancer. Taft was also the last president to keep a dairy cow tethered on the White House lawn, but he was the first president to throw out the first ball at the opening of baseball season.

28. **Woodrow Wilson**, who had an amazingly photographic memory, drank herbal tea instead of coffee. He also gave new meaning to the term "three-minute egg": Wilson insisted that his eggs be boiled for *30* minutes.

29. **Warren G. Harding** was a regular card player. Once, thanks to a bad hand of poker, he lost a complete set of china dating back to president Benjamin Harrison's stay in the White House.

30. **Calvin Coolidge** was known for being a tad on the abrupt side, and was often perceived as taciturn and cold. The story is told of the time that the hostess of a dinner Coolidge attended wagered him that she could break down his barriers and talk with him for a full five minutes, certain that she could get more than two words out of him. Coolidge looked at the woman and responded, "You lose."

31. Before becoming president, **Herbert Hoover** used his degree in geology to identify bountiful gold mines around the globe as a freelance mining consultant. He bought stakes in many of these gold mines and was a multimillionaire by the time he was 40

years old. He once remarked that if a man "has not made a million dollars by the time he is 40, he is not worth much."

32. **Franklin D. Roosevelt** and his wife, Eleanor, were fifth cousins. FDR was also a fourth cousin of President Ulysses S. Grant, a fourth cousin of President Zachary Taylor, a fifth cousin of President Theodore Roosevelt, and a seventh cousin of Winston Churchill.

33. As President, **Harry S Truman** stuck to the same routine every morning: Up at five, a two-mile walk around Washington, a shot of bourbon, a massage, a light breakfast, and then off to the Oval Office. Truman was at his desk every morning by 7 a.m.

34. **Dwight D. Eisenhower** was a skilled chef. His best dishes were cornmeal pancakes, vegetable soup, and charcoal-broiled steaks.

35. **John F. Kennedy** suffered from excruciating back pain all his life and wore a back brace for support every day. Kennedy was wearing the brace when he was shot in Dallas. There is speculation today that if he had not been wearing it, he may have survived the shooting. The brace kept his body in an upright position following the first shot—the one that penetrated his neck. If he had not been wearing the stiff canvas corset, he probably would have slumped forward. The second shot—the fatal bullet that resulted in his death—would not have struck him in the head.

36. **Lyndon Johnson** could sometimes be a bit "crude" (to put it nicely). Once, during a trip to Thailand, the president needed to use the men's room. As he exited the bathroom, he ran into a group of reporters, many of whom were from foreign countries. Johnson stopped in his tracks, unzipped his fly, and said, "Don't see 'em this big out here, do they?"

37. **Richard Nixon** once asked an injured police officer waiting for an ambulance, "How do you like your job?" (In a totally unrelated note, Nixon claimed he had never had a headache his entire life.)

38. In what must have been a security nightmare for the Secret Service, **Gerald Ford** lived at his home in Alexandria, Va., and commuted to the White House to go to work for several days *after* his swearing in as president following Richard Nixon's resignation.

39. **Jimmy Carter** grew up playing with black kids but witnessed racial discrimination when he was forced to attend segregated schools. Back in the 1960s, he was invited to join a blatantly racist organization called the "White Citizens Council." Carter's response? "I've got five dollars but I'd flush it down the toilet before I'd give it to you."

40. Have you ever heard of U.S. President Tracy Malone? Malone was a fictitious 62-year-old white female and "she" was president in 1985. However, that Tracy Malone was really **Ronald Reagan**. To prevent news leaks, a piece of suspicious tissue removed from President Reagan's nose was sent for biopsy under the name of Ms. Malone. The tissue turned out to be a basal cell carcinoma, a malignancy that was probably caused by excessive sun exposure. The White House subsequently issued a statement that "a small area of irritated skin" had been "submitted for routine studies for infection and it was determined no further treatment is necessary."

41. When **George H.W. Bush** returned to Washington following the shooting of President Reagan in 1981, his aides urged him to take a helicopter to the White House after landing in D.C. Bush refused, saying, "Only the president lands on the South Lawn." Bush's helicopter landed near the vice-presidential residence and he then drove to the White House.

42. Shortly after Jackie and JFK moved into the White House, the First Lady found a magnificent desk in storage. It had been made from wood from the sailing ship *Resolute*. Jackie had it installed in the Oval Office for JFK. (One of the most famous and memorable photographs from that period shows John Jr. crawling around underneath the desk.) **Bill Clinton** used the same desk in his Oval Office.

Chapter 32

13 Myths About the Vietnam War

"No event in American history is more misunderstood than the Vietnam War. It was misreported then, and it is misremembered now. Rarely have so many people been so wrong about so much. Never have the consequences of their misunderstanding been so tragic."

—Richard Nixon

This chapter is derived largely from material provided by Gary Roush, a former Vietnam helicopter pilot, who maintains a Web site devoted to telling the truth about the Vietnam War. (Visit Gary's site at *www.vhfcn.org/stats.htm*.)

I would like to express my sincerest appreciation to Gary for his generous assistance and immediate willingness to participate in *The U.S.A. Book of Lists*.

The sources for Gary's facts are in parentheses following each "myth/truth" discussion. At the end of this chapter you will find specific details for each. It will be up to each of you as individuals to decide how much the ideologies of the sources slanted their perceptions of events. Aside from personal spin, however, facts are facts and as the cited numbers prove, a great deal of what is considered gospel truth about the Vietnam War is simply incorrect.

THE MYTH:

Most American soldiers were addicted to drugs, guilt-ridden about their role in the war, and deliberately used cruel and inhumane tactics.

THE TRUTH:

- ✮ 91 percent of Vietnam veterans say they are glad they served. (Westmoreland)
- ✮ 74 percent said they would serve again even knowing the outcome. (Westmoreland)
- ✮ There is no difference in drug usage between Vietnam veterans and non-veterans of the same age group. (This is from a Veterans Administration study). (Westmoreland)

★ Isolated atrocities committed by American soldiers produced torrents of outrage from antiwar critics and the news media. Communist atrocities were so common that they received hardly any attention at all. The United States sought to minimize and prevent attacks on civilians, while North Vietnam made attacks on civilians a centerpiece of its strategy. Americans who deliberately killed civilians received prison sentences. Communists who did so received commendations. From 1957 to 1973, the National Liberation Front assassinated 36,725 South Vietnamese and abducted another 58,499. The death squads focused on leaders at the village level or anyone who assisted peasants (such as medical personnel, social workers, and schoolteachers.) (Nixon)

★ Vietnam veterans are less likely to be in prison—only one-half of one percent of Vietnam veterans have been jailed for crimes. (Westmoreland)

★ 97 percent were discharged under honorable conditions, the same percentage of honorable discharges as 10 years prior to Vietnam. (Westmoreland)

★ 85 percent of Vietnam veterans made a successful transition to civilian life. (McCaffrey)

★ Vietnam veterans' personal income exceeds that of any non-veteran age group by more than 18 percent. (McCaffrey)

★ Vietnam veterans have a lower unemployment rate than any non-veteran age group. (McCaffrey)

★ 87 percent of the American people hold Vietnam veterans in high esteem. (McCaffrey)

The Myth:

Most Vietnam veterans were drafted.

The Truth:

Two-thirds of the men who served in Vietnam were volunteers. Two-thirds of the men who served in World War II were drafted. (Westmoreland) Approximately 70 percent of those killed were volunteers. (McCaffrey)

The Myth:

The media have reported that suicides among Vietnam veterans range from 50,000 to 100,000—six- to 11-times the non-Vietnam veteran population.

The Truth:

Mortality studies show that 9,000 is a better estimate. "The CDC Vietnam Experience Study Mortality Assessment showed that during the first five years after discharge, deaths from suicide were 1.7-times more likely among Vietnam veterans than non-Vietnam veterans. After that initial post-service period, Vietnam veterans were no more likely to die from suicide than non-Vietnam veterans. In fact, after the five-year post-service period, the rate of suicides is less in the Vietnam veterans' group." (Houk)

The Myth:

A disproportionate number of African-Americans were killed in the Vietnam War.

The Truth:

86 percent of the men who died in Vietnam were caucasians, 12.5 percent were African-Americans, 1.2 percent were of other racial descent. (CACF and Westmoreland) Sociologists Charles C. Moskos and John Sibley Butler, in their recently published book, *All That We Can Be*, analyzed the claim that blacks were used like cannon fodder during Vietnam. Their conclusion: "and (we) can report definitely that this charge is untrue. Black fatalities amounted to 12 percent of all Americans killed in Southeast Asia—a figure proportional to the number of blacks in the U.S. population at the time and slightly lower than the proportion of blacks in the Army at the close of the war." (*All That We Can Be*)

The Myth:

The war was fought largely by the poor and uneducated.

The Truth:

Servicemen who went to Vietnam from well-to-do areas had a slightly elevated risk of dying because they were more likely to be pilots or infantry officers. Vietnam veterans were the best-educated forces our nation had ever sent into combat. 79 percent had a high school education or better. (McCaffrey)

The Myth:

The average age of an infantryman fighting in Vietnam was 19.

The Truth:

Based on statistics from the Combat Area Casualty File (CACF) as of November 1993, the average age of 58,148 killed in Vietnam was 23.11 years

The Myth:

The domino theory was proved to be false.

The Truth:

The domino theory was accurate. The Association of Southeast Asian Nations (ASEAN) countries— the Philippines, Indonesia, Malaysia, Singapore, and Thailand—stayed free of communism because of the U.S. commitment to Vietnam. The Indonesians threw the Soviets out in 1966 because of America's presence. Without that commitment, communism would have swept all the way to the Malacca Straits (south of Singapore and of great strategic importance to the free world). If you ask people who live in these countries that won the war in Vietnam, they'll have a different opinion from the American news media. The Vietnam War was the turning point in the spread of communism. (Westmoreland)

The Myth:

The fighting in Vietnam was not as intense as in World War II.

The Truth:

The average infantryman in the South Pacific during World War II saw about 40 days of combat in four years. The average infantryman in Vietnam saw about 240 days of combat in one year…thanks to the mobility of the helicopter. One out of every 10 Americans who served in Vietnam was a casualty. 58,169 were killed and 304,000 wounded out of 2.59 million who served. Although the percent who died is similar to other wars, amputations or crippling wounds were 300 percent higher than in World War II. 75,000 Vietnam veterans are severely disabled. (McCaffrey) MedEvac helicopters flew nearly 500,000 missions. More than 900,000 patients were airlifted (nearly half were American). The average time lapse between wounding to hospitalization was less than one hour. As a result, less than one percent of all Americans wounded died in the first 24 hours of their battle wounds. (VHPA 1993) The helicopter provided unprecedented mobility. Without the helicopter, it would have taken three-times as many troops to secure the 800-mile border of Vietnam with Cambodia and Laos (the politicians thought the Geneva Conventions of 1954 and the Geneva Accords or 1962 would secure the border). (Westmoreland)

THE MYTH:

Air America (the airline operated by the CIA in Southeast Asia) and its pilots were involved in drug trafficking.

THE TRUTH:

The unsuccessful movie *Air America* (1990) helped to establish the myth of a connection between Air America, the CIA, and the Laotian drug trade. The movie and a book the movie was based on contend that the CIA condoned a drug trade conducted by a Laotian client. Both agree that Air America provided the essential transportation for the trade. And both view the pilots with sympathetic understanding. American-owned airlines never knowingly transported opium in or out of Laos, nor did their American pilots ever profit from its transport. Yet undoubtedly, every plane in Laos carried opium at some time, unknown to the pilot and his superiors. For more information take a look at *www.air-america.org*.

THE MYTH:

The American military was running for their lives during the fall of Saigon in April 1975.

THE TRUTH:

Almost everyone has seen the picture of a helicopter evacuating people from the top of what was billed as the U.S. Embassy in Saigon. It was taken the last week of April 1975 during the fall of Saigon. This famous picture is the property of Corbus-Bettman Archives. It was originally a UPI photograph that was taken by an Englishman, Mr. Hugh Van Ess.

Here are some facts to clear up that poor job of reporting by the news media:

★ It was a "civilian" (Air America) Huey, not one from the Army or the Marines.
★ It was *not* the U.S. Embassy. The building is the Pittman Apartments. The U.S. Embassy and its helipad were much larger.
★ The evacuees were Vietnamese, not American military.
★ The person that can be seen aiding the refugees is Mr. O.B. Harnage. He was a CIA case officer and is now retired in Arizona.

THE MYTH:

Kim Phuc, the little 9-year-old Vietnamese girl running naked from the napalm strike near Trang Bang on June 8, 1972, was burned by Americans bombing Trang Bang.

The Truth:

No American had involvement in this incident near Trang Bang that burned Phan Thi Kim Phuc. The planes doing the bombing near the village were VNAF (Vietnam Air Force) and were being flown by Vietnamese pilots supporting South Vietnamese troops on the ground. (The Vietnamese pilot who dropped the napalm in error is currently living in the United States.) Even the AP photographer, Nick Ut, who took the picture was Vietnamese. The incident in the photo took place on the second day of a three-day battle between the North Vietnamese Army (NVA) who occupied the village of Trang Bang, and the ARVN (Army of the Republic of Vietnam), who were trying to force the NVA out of the village.

Recent reports in the news media that an American commander ordered the air strike that burned Kim Phuc have been proven as being incorrect. There were no Americans involved in any capacity. "We (Americans) had nothing to do with controlling VNAF," according to Lieutenant General (Ret.) James F. Hollingsworth, the Commanding General of TRAC at that time. Also, it has been incorrectly reported that two of Kim Phuc's brothers were killed in this incident. They were Kim's cousins, not her brothers.

The Myth:

The United States lost the war in Vietnam.

The Truth:

The American military was not defeated in Vietnam. The American military did not lose a battle of any consequence. From a military standpoint, it was almost an unprecedented performance. (Westmoreland quoting Douglas Pike, a professor at the University of California, Berkley a renowned expert on the Vietnam War.) This included Tet 68, which was a major military defeat for the VC and NVA. The United States did not lose the war in Vietnam…the South Vietnamese did.

The Myth:

Agent Orange poisoned millions of Vietnam veterans.

The Truth:

Over the 10 years of U.S. involvement in the war, Operation Ranch Hand sprayed about 11-million gallons of Agent Orange on the South Vietnamese landscape. (The herbicide was called "orange" in Vietnam, not Agent Orange. That sinister-sounding term was coined after the war.) Orange was sprayed at three gallons per acre, equivalent to 0.009 of an ounce per square foot. When sprayed on dense jungle foliage, less than 6 percent ever reached the ground. Ground troops typically did not enter a sprayed area until four to six weeks after being sprayed. Most Agent Orange contained 0.0002 of 1 percent of dioxin. Scientific research has shown that dioxin degrades in sunlight after 48 to 72 hours. In this way, troops' exposure to dioxin was infinitesimal. (Burkett)

Facts about the End of the War

★ The fall of Saigon happened April 30, 1975, two years *after* the American military left Vietnam. The last American troops departed in their entirety March 29, 1973. How could we lose a war we had already stopped fighting? We fought to an agreed stalemate. The peace settlement was signed in Paris on January 27, 1973. It called for release of all U.S. prisoners, withdrawal of U.S. forces, limitation of both sides' forces inside South

Vietnam, and a commitment to peaceful reunification. (*1996 Information Please Almanac*)

★ The 140,000 evacuees in April 1975 during the fall of Saigon consisted almost entirely of civilians and Vietnamese military, *not* American military running for their lives. (*1996 Information Please Atlas & Yearbook*)

★ There were almost twice as many casualties in Southeast Asia (primarily Cambodia) the first two years after the fall of Saigon in 1975 then there were during the 10 years the United States was involved in Vietnam. (*1996 Information Please Almanac*)

SOURCES

★ **Nixon**: *No More Vietnams* (1985) by Richard Nixon. Also, *Parade* magazine, August 18, 1996, page 10.

★ **CACF** (Combat Area Casualty File) November 1993. (The CACF is the basis for the Vietnam Veterans Memorial [The Wall]), Center for Electronic Records, National Archives, Washington, D.C.

★ *All That We Can Be* (Basic Books, 1997) by Charles C. Moskos and John Sibley Butler.

★ **Westmoreland**: Speech by General William C. Westmoreland before the Third Annual Reunion of the Vietnam Helicopter Pilots Association (VHPA) at the Washington, D.C. Hilton on July 5th, 1986 (reproduced in a *Vietnam Helicopter Pilots Association Historical Reference Directory* Volume 2A).

★ **McCaffrey**: Speech by Lt. Gen. Barry R. McCaffrey, (reproduced in the *Pentagram*, June 4, 1993) assistant to the Chairman of the Joint Chiefs of Staff, to Vietnam veterans and visitors gathered at "The Wall," Memorial Day, 1993.

★ **Houk**: Testimony by Dr. Houk, Oversight on Post-Traumatic Stress Disorder, 14 July 1988 page 17. Hearing before the Committee on Veterans' Affairs, United States Senate One Hundredth Congress, second session. Also "Estimating the Number of Suicides Among Vietnam Veterans" (*American Journal of Psychiatry* 147, June 6, 1990, pages 772-776).

★ *The Wall Street Journal*, June 1, 1996, page A15.

★ **VHPA 1993**: *Vietnam Helicopter Pilots Association 1993 Membership Directory*, page 130.

★ **VHPA Databases**: Vietnam Helicopter Pilots Association Databases.

★ *1996 Information Please Atlas & Yearbook*, 49th edition, Houghton Mifflin Company, Boston & New York, 1996, pages 117, 161, and 292.

★ **Burkett**: *Stolen Valor: How the Vietnam Generation was Robbed of its Heroes and its History* (Verity Press, 1998) by B.G. Burkett and Glenna Whitley. Book review.

Chapter 33

9 Bearded or Mustachioed U.S. Presidents

"With eyes severe, and beard of formal cut,
Full of wise saws and modern instances;
And so he plays his part."
—William Shakespeare,
As You Like It, Act II, Scene vii

Presidential facial hair seems to have fallen out of favor. Since President Taft and his whiskers, an American President hasn't even worn a mustache, let alone a full beard. Why is that? A full beard adds gravity and suggests a distinguished air of dignity...why else do so many writers and professors wear beards? Of course, some in the mental health field suggest that perhaps beard wearers are hiding something, but that's just one profession's spin on a man's choice to shave, or not to shave. Here is a look at our more hirsute chief executives.

1. **Abraham Lincoln** (16th president): Thick black beard with no mustache.
2. **Ulysses S. Grant** (18th president): Thick brown beard with grey at the chin.
3. **Rutherford B. Hayes** (19th president): Thick, long white "ZZ Top" beard.
4. **James Garfield** (20th president): Light brown and grey scraggly long beard.
5. **Chester A. Arthur** (21st president): Thick mutton-chop sideburns and neatly trimmed mustache.
6. **Grover Cleveland** (22nd and 24th president): Thick mustache extending below the lower lip.
7. **Benjamin Harrison** (23rd president): Full, light brown beard with reddish tints.
8. **Theodore Roosevelt** (26th president): Neatly trimmed mustache.
9. **William Howard Taft** (27th president): Thick chestnut brown handlebar mustache.

Chapter 34

The 11 Busiest U.S. Airports

"If man were meant to fly, God would have lowered the fares."
—American Coach Lines
(advertising slogan)

1. **Hartsfield International Airport** in Atlanta, Ga: 73,474,298 arrivals and departures in 1998 (201,300 per day).
2. **O'Hare Airport** in Chicago, Ill: 72,485,228 arrivals and departures (198,590 per day).
3. **Los Angeles Airport** in Los Angeles, Calif.: 61,215,712 arrivals and departures in 1998 (167,714 per day).
4. **Dallas/Ft. Worth International Airport** in Dallas, Tex.: 60,482,700 arrivals and departures in 1998 (165,706 per day).
5. **San Francisco Airport** in San Francisco, Calif.: 40,060,326 arrivals and departures in 1998 (109,754 per day).
6. **Denver Airport** in Denver, Col.: 36,831,400 arrivals and departures in 1998 (100,907 per day).
7. **Miami Airport** in Miami, Fla.: 33,935,491 arrivals and departures in 1998 (92,973 per day).
8. **Newark Airport** in Newark, N.J.: 32,512,106 arrivals and departures in 1998 (89,074 per day).
9. **Sky Harbor International Airport** in Phoenix, Ariz.: 31,769,113 arrivals and departures in 1998 (87,038 per day).
10. **Detroit Metropolitan Airport** in Detroit, Mich.: 31,544,426 arrivals and departures in 1998 (86,423 per day).
11. **John F. Kennedy International Airport** in New York, N.Y.: 31,436,478 arrivals and departures in 1998 (86,127 per day).

(*Source:* Airports Council International—North America.)

Chapter 35

The 11 Things Americans Spend Most of Their Money On

Every year, the U.S. Department of Commerce's Bureau of Economic Analysis tracks what we Americans spend our money on.

The latest complete figures available, from fiscal year 1997, paint an intriguing portrait of our country. What do you think we spend most of our money on? Food? Housing? Clothing?

The answer to all of the above is no.

The number one expenditure of personal income in this country is for medical care...as it has been for the past six years.

Does this mean we're a sickly nation, or that we just spend more money taking care of ourselves than we do on anything else? It's open to interpretation, but it does explain why America's healthcare system—with all its wonders and problems—is often the number one topic on the evening news.

(By the way, the total spent for these 11 personal consumption expenditure categories is a whopping $5.494 *trillion*.)

1. MEDICAL CARE: $957.3 BILLION

This category includes money spent for prescription and over-the-counter drugs and supplies, payments to physicians and dentists, payments to hospitals and nursing homes, and health insurance premiums.

2. FOOD AND TOBACCO: $832.3 BILLION

This category includes food purchased for off-premises consumption (such as groceries); restaurant, bar food, and beverage purchases; and all tobacco products.

3. HOUSING: $829.8 BILLION

This category includes owner-occupied nonfarm dwellings (such as mortgage payments for a home), tenant-occupied nonfarm dwellings (such as, house or apartment rent payments), and the rental value of farm dwellings.

4. TRANSPORTATION: $636.4 BILLION

This category includes expenditures for new cars, used cars, car repairs, car washes, parking, storage, payments for renting and leasing, gasoline, tolls, and auto insurance premiums (less claims paid). It also includes expenditures for local mass transit such as subways, buses, and taxicabs; and expenditures for intercity transportation (such as trains, buses, and airline flights).

5. HOUSEHOLD OPERATIONS: $620.7 BILLION

This category includes furniture, bedding, kitchen appliances, china, glassware, tableware, utensils, miscellaneous durable household furnishings; miscellaneous semidurable household furnishings and other household appliances. It also includes expenditures for all household utilities and expenditures for household telephone expenses.

6. RECREATION: $462.9 BILLION

This category includes books, maps, magazines, newspapers, sheet music; toys and sport supplies and sports equipments; photographic equipment and supplies; boats; pleasure aircraft; video and audio products; computers, computer software and peripherals; musical instruments; flowers, seeds, potted plants; expenditures for motion picture theaters; expenditures for theater and opera; admission to spectator sports events; and dues and membership fees for clubs and fraternal organizations.

7. PERSONAL BUSINESS: $459.1 BILLION

This category includes brokerage charges, fees for investment counseling, bank service charges, fees for trust services, bank safe deposit fees, all legal services, and expenditures for funerals and burial expenses.

THE 12 RICHEST AMERICANS

According to *Forbes* magazine, on July 1, 2000, these 12 people were the wealthiest Americans. *Forbes* defines wealth by net worth, including cash, stock, real estate holdings, and other assets. The person's name is followed by their net worth, which is followed by how they made their money. Combined, these 12 people are worth a staggering $319.5 billion. To put this in context, their collective wealth is $58.1 billion more than the entire U.S. military budget for fiscal year 1999.

1. Bill Gates, $60 billion (Microsoft).
2. Lawrence Ellison, $47 billion (Oracle Corporation).
3. Paul Allen, $28 billion (Microsoft).
4. Warren Buffet, $28 billion (Berkshire Hathaway).
5. Gordon Moore, $21 billion (Intel Corporation).
6. Alice Walton, $20 billion [Inheritance (Wal-Mart Stores)].
7. Helen Walton, $20 billion [Inheritance (Wal-Mart Stores)].
8. Jim C. Walton, $20 billion [Inheritance (Wal-Mart Stores)].
9. John T. Walton, $20 billion [Inheritance (Wal-Mart Stores)].
10. S. Robson Walton, $20 billion (Wal-Mart Stores).
11. Michael Dell, $20 billion (Dell Computer Corporation).
12. Philip Anschultz, $15.5 billion (Anschutz Corporation).

8. CLOTHING, ACCESSORIES, AND JEWELRY: $353.3 BILLION

This category includes shoes, clothing, accessories, and jewelry and watches.

9. RELIGIOUS AND CHARITABLE EXPENSES: $157.6 BILLION

This category includes cash donations to organized religious groups and charitable organizations.

10. EDUCATION AND RESEARCH: $129.4 BILLION

This category includes expenditures for higher education, along with expenditures for nursery, elementary, and secondary schools.

11. PERSONAL CARE: $79.4 BILLION

This category includes all expenditures for toiletries and expenditures for barber shops, beauty parlors, and health clubs.

Chapter 36

51 State Mottoes

Some state mottoes are a little strange. Maryland's, for instance, boasts about "manly deeds" and "womanly words." And North Carolina's is "To be rather than seem." (Say what?) Washington's motto is the cryptic "By and by."

Some mottoes are blunt and honest: What does Montana want you to envision when you think of Montana? "Gold and silver." What about Maine? "I direct." West Virginia? "Mountaineers are always free."

These 51 state mottoes (the District of Columbia is included) are an eclectic representation of the rich panoply of peoples, attitudes, and beliefs so much a part of the cultural fabric of the United States.

1. **Alabama**: We dare to defend our rights.
2. **Alaska**: North to the future.
3. **Arizona**: God enriches.
4. **Arkansas**: Let the people rule.
5. **California**: I have found it.
6. **Colorado**: Nothing without providence.
7. **Connecticut**: He who transplanted sustains.
8. **Delaware**: Liberty and independence.
9. **District of Columbia**: Justice to all.
10. **Florida**: In God we trust.
11. **Georgia**: Wisdom, justice, moderation.
12. **Hawaii**: The life of the land is perpetuated by righteousness.
13. **Idaho**: May she endure forever.
14. **Illinois**: State sovereignty—national union.
15. **Indiana**: The crossroads of America.
16. **Iowa**: Our liberties we prize and our rights we will maintain.
17. **Kansas**: To the stars through difficulties.
18. **Kentucky**: United we stand, divided we fall.
19. **Louisiana**: Union, justice, and confidence.
20. **Maine**: I direct.
21. **Maryland**: Manly deeds, womanly words.
22. **Massachusetts**: By the sword we seek peace, but peace only under liberty.
23. **Michigan**: If you seek a pleasant peninsula, look around you.
24. **Minnesota**: The star of the north.
25. **Mississippi**: By valor and arms.

26. **Missouri**: The welfare of the people shall be the supreme law.
27. **Montana**: Gold and silver.
28. **Nebraska**: Equality before the law.
29. **Nevada**: All for Our country.
30. **New Hampshire**: Live free or die.
31. **New Jersey**: Liberty and prosperity.
32. **New Mexico**: It grows as it goes.
33. **New York**: Ever upward.
34. **North Carolina**: To be rather than seem.
35. **North Dakota**: Liberty and union, now and forever, one and inseparable.
36. **Ohio**: With God, all things are possible.
37. **Oklahoma**: Work conquers all things.
38. **Oregon**: The Union.
39. **Pennsylvania**: Virtue, liberty, and independence.
40. **Rhode Island**: Hope.
41. **South Carolina**: Prepared in mind and resources.
42. **South Dakota**: Under God the people rule.
43. **Tennessee**: America at its best.
44. **Texas**: Friendship.
45. **Utah**: Industry.
46. **Vermont**: Freedom and unity.
47. **Virginia**: Thus always to tyrants.
48. **Washington**: By and by.
49. **West Virginia**: Mountaineers are always free.
50. **Wisconsin**: Forward.
51. **Wyoming**: Equal rights.

THE 10 MOST POPULATED STATES

These figures, taken from the U.S. Census Bureau as of July 1, 1999, show the dynamic growth of population in the United States. Of these 10 states, Texas saw an 18-percent increase from 1990 through July 1999—the largest increase in population in the United States. None of these states saw their population decrease in the decade, but New York and Pennsylvania were on the bottom of the growth list with only a one percent increase during the 10-year period.

1. **California**: 33,145,121.
2. **Texas**: 20,044,141.
3. **New York**: 18,196,601.
4. **Florida**: 15,111,244.
5. **Illinois**: 12,128,370.
6. **Pennsylvania**: 11,994,016.
7. **Ohio**: 11,256,654.
8. **Michigan**: 9,863,775.
9. **New Jersey**: 8,143,412.
10. **Georgia**: 7,788,240.

Chapter 37

63 State Nicknames

State nicknames often represent what a state is most famous for. Connecticut is the Constitution State. Florida is the Sunshine State. Rhode Island is the Ocean State…and so on. My personal favorite nickname? For historic reasons, I love the simplicity of Delaware calling itself the "First State" (because it was). No other state can claim that distinction. (To point out the obvious, this chapter proclaims 63 state nicknames because twelve states have two nicknames.)

1. **Alabama:** Heart of Dixie; Camellia State.
2. **Alaska:** The Last Frontier.
3. **Arizona:** Grand Canyon State.
4. **Arkansas:** Land of Opportunity.
5. **California:** Golden State.
6. **Colorado:** Centennial State.
7. **Connecticut:** Constitution State; Nutmeg State.
8. **Delaware:** First State; Diamond State.
9. **District of Columbia:** Capital City.
10. **Florida:** Sunshine State.
11. **Georgia:** Empire State of the South, Peach State.
12. **Hawaii:** Aloha State.
13. **Idaho:** Gem State.
14. **Illinois:** Prairie State, Land of Lincoln.
15. **Indiana:** Hoosier State.
16. **Iowa:** Hawkeye State.
17. **Kansas:** Sunflower State.
18. **Kentucky:** Bluegrass State.
19. **Louisiana:** Pelican State.
20. **Maine:** Pine Tree State.
21. **Maryland:** Old Line State; Free State.
22. **Massachusetts:** Bay State; Colony State.
23. **Michigan:** Great Lake State; Wolverine State.
24. **Minnesota:** North Star State.
25. **Mississippi:** Magnolia State.
26. **Missouri:** Show-Me State.
27. **Montana:** Treasure State.
28. **Nebraska:** Cornhusker State.
29. **Nevada:** Sagebrush State; Battle-Born State.
30. **New Hampshire:** Granite State.
31. **New Jersey:** Garden State.
32. **New Mexico:** Land of Enchantment.
33. **New York:** Empire State.
34. **North Carolina:** Tar Heel State; Old North State.

35. **North Dakota:** Peace Garden State.
36. **Ohio:** Buckeye State.
37. **Oklahoma:** Sooner State.
38. **Oregon:** Beaver State.
39. **Pennsylvania:** Keystone State.
40. **Rhode Island:** Little Rhody; Ocean State.
41. **South Carolina:** Palmetto State.
42. **South Dakota:** Coyote State; Sunshine State.
43. **Tennessee:** Volunteer State.
44. **Texas:** Lone Star State.
45. **Utah:** Beehive State.
46. **Vermont:** Green Mountain State.
47. **Virginia:** Old Dominion.
48. **Washington:** Evergreen State.
49. **West Virginia:** Mountain State.
50. **Wisconsin:** Badger State.
51. **Wyoming:** Equality State.

The 10 Least Populated States

These figures are as of July 1, 1999 and are from the U.S. Census Bureau. (As always, for purposes of this book, I count the District of Columbia as a state, even though it is not officially.) Of these 10 states, Alaska and Delaware saw the largest increase in population—13 percent—from 1990 through July 1999. The District of Columbia saw the largest decrease—15 percent—in the decade.

1. **Wyoming:** 479,602.
2. **District of Columbia:** 519,000.
3. **Vermont:** 593,470.
4. **Alaska:** 619,500.
5. **North Dakota:** 633,666.
6. **South Dakota:** 733,133.
7. **Delaware:** 753,538.
8. **Montana:** 882,779.
9. **Rhode Island:** 990,819.
10. **Hawaii:** 1,185,497.

Chapter 38

The **13** Intolerable Acts the British Parliament Passed that Drove the American Colonists to Revolt

"There seems to be a direct and formal design on foot [by Great Britain] to enslave all America....The first step that is intended seems to an entire system of subversion of the whole system of our fathers, by the introduction of feudal and canon law into America."

—John Adams, "Dissertation on the Canon and the Feudal Law" (1775)

I know it was a different time, but you had to wonder what the "veddy proper" boys in the British Parliament were thinking when they passed these 13 acts. (These were known collectively as the Intolerable Acts—and for good reason.) As is often the case when extremism rears its ugly head, they were undoubtedly acting out of fear—the fear of losing control, of losing revenue, or of losing influence. For a centuries-old monarchy, the thought of ceding power to her colonies was monumentally unacceptable.

In any case, these 13 acts were the figurative straws that broke the Colonists' backs. Two years after the 1774 Quartering Act, the British Parliament was presented with a document from the colonists titled the Declaration of Independence. As we know, the Brits were not pleased. (Although they seem to have gotten over it.)

1. **The Royal Proclamation of 1763**: This proclamation put a buffer zone between the American territories and the Indians and forbade colonists from crossing the Appalachians. This did work to placate the Indians and avert war, but prevented the settlers from acquiring new land to settle. The settlers ignored the proclamation and crossed King George's line carved in the mountains.

2. **The Currency Act (1764)**: This act declared all American money null and void and forbade the colonists from issuing new currency.

3. **The Sugar Act (1764)**: This act applied heavy taxes on coffee, sugar, wine, and other sundries and necessities imported into the American colonies.

4. **The Quartering Act (1765)**: This act required colonists to house British soldiers in their homes if there wasn't enough room in public military housing. This did not go over too well with colonists who had very little living space to begin with.

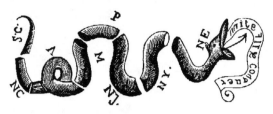

JOIN or DIE

Benjamin Franklin's famous battlecry to the American colonists.

5. **The Stamp Act (1765)**: This act applied burdensome taxes on essentially *every* written document produced in the colonies, including land deeds, wills, bills of lading, bills of sale, advertisements, and many more.

6. **The Declaratory Act (1766)**: This act repealed the loathed Stamp Act of 1765, but also arrogantly declared the colonies utterly subservient to the British Crown.

7. **The Townshend Act (1767)**: This act applied more taxes on goods imported into the Colonies from Great Britain, including all types of paper, ink, paint, tea, and other materials.

8. **The Tea Act (1773)**: This act applied more burdensome taxes on the colonists, this time on all types of imported tea.

9. **The Administration of Justice Act (1774)**: This act reasserted Britain's legal authority over the colonists and threatened to put on trial in Britain those colonial legal authorities who did not enforce British law in the colonies.

10. **The Boston Port Act (1774)**: This devastating act blocked all imports into the Boston port. It was legislated following the Boston Tea Party of December 16, 1773. In the famous "party," colonists destroyed imported tea worth a staggering 9,000 pounds. To give you the scope of this amount of wasted tea, the average annual income of a colonist in 1773 was 100 pounds.

11. **The Massachusetts Government Act (1774):** This act declared that all elected officials in Massachusetts were no longer legally in power and that subsequently, all Massachusetts authorities were only to be appointed by the British Parliament.

12. **The Quebec Act (1774):** This act gave land west of the Appalachians and south of the Ohio River to Quebec, essentially nullifying the relevant colonial charters.

13. **The Quartering Act (1774):** This act strengthened the 1765 **Quartering Act**.

Chapter 39

16 Connecticut Blue Laws

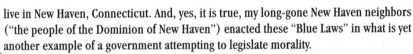

I live in New Haven, Connecticut. And, yes, it is true, my long-gone New Haven neighbors ("the people of the Dominion of New Haven") enacted these "Blue Laws" in what is yet another example of a government attempting to legislate morality.

These "blue laws," first implemented in 1650 are so-named for the color of the paper they were initially printed on.

1. The governor and magistrates convened in general assembly are the supreme power, under God, of the independent dominion.
2. From the determination of the assembly no appeal shall be made.
3. No one shall be a freeman or have a vote unless he is converted and a member of one of the churches allowed in the dominion.
4. Each freeman shall swear by the blessed God to bear true allegiance to this dominion and that Jesus is the only king.
5. No dissenter from the essential worship of this dominion shall be allowed to give a vote for electing of magistrates or any officer.
6. No food or lodging shall be offered to a heretic.
7. No one shall cross a river on the Sabbath but authorized clergymen.
8. No one shall travel, cook victuals, make beds, sweep houses, cut hair, or shave on the Sabbath Day.
9. No one shall kiss his or her children on the Sabbath or feasting days.
10. The Sabbath Day shall begin at sunset Saturday.
11. Whoever wears clothes trimmed with gold, silver, or bone lace above one shilling per yard shall be presented by the grand jurors and the selectmen shall tax the estate 300 pounds.
12. Whoever brings cards or dice into the dominion shall pay a fine of five pounds.
13. No one shall eat mince pies, dance, play cards, or play any instrument of music except the drum, trumpet, or jewsharp.
14. A man who strikes his wife shall be fined 10 pounds.
15. A woman who strikes her husband shall be punished as the law directs.
16. No man shall court a maid in person or by letter without obtaining the consent of her parents—five pounds penalty for the first offense, 10 pounds for the second, and for the third imprisonment during the pleasure of the court.

Chapter 40

The First Person Born in America

The first person born of English parents in America was Virginia Dare.

Virginia Dare was born on Tuesday, August 18, 1587 on Roanoke Island, off the coast of present-day North Carolina. Her parents were Ananias and Eleanor Dare. She was born a few days after the colonists had arrived on the island. Virginia's mother was the daughter of Roanoke's Governor John White.

Virginia was baptized the following Sunday, August 23, 1587. Her baptism was the second recorded Christian baptism in the New World. (The first recorded Christian baptism had been performed a few days earlier on an Indian chief named Manteo.)

Nine days after Virginia was born, on Thursday, August 27, 1587, Governor White was forced to return to England for supplies. Before he left, he worked out a secret code system for the colonists to use if they were forced to leave the island. They were to carve the name of their new destination on a clearly visible tree or post. As part of the code, Governor White instructed them to carve a Maltese Cross over the name of the place if they were being forced to leave because of Indian attack or because of an assault by the Spaniards.

Four years to the month after he left, Governor White returned to Roanoke Island to find it completely deserted. Carved into a tree was the lone word "Croatoan." There was no Maltese Cross above the word.

Croatoan was the name of an Indian tribe living on Roanoke Island when the colonists made landfall. It was also the name of an island about 50 miles off of Virginia's coast. There is speculation that the colonists went off with the Croatoan Indians (a highly likely possibility) but no evidence has ever been found of their whereabouts. It is assumed that the child Virginia Dare was among their company when they departed the island.

Virginia Dare and everyone else that was part of the Roanoke Island New World contingent are now known as the Lost Colony.

Chapter 41

The 31 Ethnic Origins of 248 Million Americans

The 1990 Census reported a grand total of 248 million people in the good old United States. Along with the grand totals, the census takers also tried to ascertain the ethnic origin of everyone in the country. The results dramatically illustrate the diverse essence of America. It proves the old adage that tells us that, in America, everyone you meet is from somewhere else.

This list is comprised of the 31 ethnic ancestries claimed by groups larger than 300,000 Americans. There are more immigrants in America from Germany than from anywhere else, followed by the Irish, the English, and the 30,000,000 Americans whose ancestors were brought here from sub-Sahara Africa as slaves. (Approximately 1.5 million African-Americans claimed the West Indies as their ancestral home.)

57,000,000	German.	1,600,000	Czech.
39,000,000	Irish.	1,600,000	Danish.
33,000,000	English.	1,500,000	West Indian.
28,506,000	African.	1,200,000	Portuguese.
15,000,000	Italian.	1,100,000	Greek.
10,000,000	French.	1,000,000	Swiss.
9,300,000	Polish.	870,000	Arab.
6,200,000	Dutch.	870,000	Austrian.
5,400,000	Scottish.	812,000	Lithuanian.
4,700,000	Swedish.	741,000	Ukrainian.
3,900,000	Norwegian.	659,000	Finnish.
2,900,000	Russian.	561,000	Canadian.
2,800,000	French Canadian.	498,000	Yugoslavian.
2,000,000	Welsh.	395,000	Belgian.
1,900,000	Slovak.	366,000	Rumanian.
1,600,000	Hungarian.		

For more information, visit the Ellis Island Web site (*www.ellisisland.org*). One of the site's most valuable resources is its "Wall of Honor" search engine. You can search for family names and countries of origin.

Chapter 42

The 30 States With a Coastline

1. **Alaska** (Beaufort Sea, Bering Sea, Pacific Ocean).
2. **Hawaii** (Pacific Ocean).
3. **Washington** (Pacific Ocean).
4. **Oregon** (Pacific Ocean).
5. **California** (Pacific Ocean).
6. **Texas** (Gulf of Mexico).
7. **Louisiana** (Gulf of Mexico).
8. **Mississippi** (Gulf of Mexico).
9. **Alabama** (Gulf of Mexico).
10. **Florida** (Gulf of Mexico, Atlantic Ocean).
11. **Georgia** (Atlantic Ocean).
12. **South Carolina** (Atlantic Ocean).
13. **North Carolina** (Atlantic Ocean).
14. **Virginia** (Atlantic Ocean).
15. **Maryland** (Atlantic Ocean).
16. **Delaware** (Atlantic Ocean).
17. **New Jersey** (Atlantic Ocean).
18. **New York** (Atlantic Ocean, Lake Ontario, Lake Erie).
19. **Connecticut** (Long Island Sound [Atlantic Ocean]).
20. **Rhode Island** (Atlantic Ocean).
21. **Massachusetts** (Atlantic Ocean).
22. **New Hampshire** (Atlantic Ocean).
23. **Maine** (Atlantic Ocean).
24. **Pennsylvania** (Lake Erie).
25. **Ohio** (Lake Erie).
26. **Michigan** (Lake Erie, Lake Huron, Lake Superior, Lake Michigan).
27. **Indiana** (Lake Michigan).
28. **Illinois** (Lake Michigan).
29. **Wisconsin** (Lake Michigan, Lake Superior).
30. **Minnesota** (Lake Superior).

Chapter 43

The 50 Greatest American TV Characters According to *TV Guide*

I don't agree with this list, especially the number one choice, but felt I should include it because, well, because *TV Guide* is a popular culture *institution* in this country and the views of its editors are definitely worth considering. Even if they are wrong about the number one choice. (It should have been either Barney Fife or Ed Norton.)

And while we're on the subject, where are Fred Mertz, Aunt Bea, Dr. Smith, Dr. Peter Benton, Dr. Doogie Howser, Dr. Kildare, Dr. Hawkeye Pierce, Dr. Ben Casey, Dr. Marcus Welby, Dr. Joel Fleischman, Ally McBeal, Latka Graves, Edith Bunker, Chandler Bing, Phoebe Buffay, Rob Petrie, Gilligan, The Professor (too), Jeannie, Samantha Stevens, Perry Mason, Tattoo, Rhoda Morgenstern, John-Boy Walton, Mannix, Chrissy Snow, Mr. Kotter, George *and* Weezy Jefferson, Corporal Agarn, Napoleon Solo, Hoss Cartwright, Ozzie Nelson, Barney Miller, Herman Munster, Grandpa Munster, Marcia Brady, Nurse Hathaway, Cagney *and* Lacey, Nurse Colleen McMurphy, Murphy Brown, Maude, Matlock, Max Headroom, Kate *and* Allie, Jessica Fletcher, Quincy, Fred Flintstone, Maggie O'Connell, Larry Sanders, Tony Soprano, Uncle Junior, and Mr. Ed and Lassie—as well as a slew of other memorable American TV characters?!

Ah, American television, the great and glorious font of entertainment for the world. Is this a great country or what? (Just for fun, characters in **bold** are my personal favorites.)

50. Buddy Sorrell
    (*The Dick Van Dyke Show*).
49. Elliot Carlin
    (*The Bob Newhart Show*).
48. Miles Drentell (*thirtysomething*).
47. Douglas Wambaugh
    (*Picket Fences*).
46. **Xena** (*Xena: Warrior Princess*).
45. Jane Tennison (*Prime Suspect*).
44. David Addison (*Moonlighting*).
43. **Adam** (*Northern Exposure*).
42. Bill Bittinger (*Buffalo Bill*).
41. Dr. Mark Craig (*St. Elsewhere*).
40. Alexis Carrington (*Dynasty*).

39. **Artie** (*The Larry Sanders Show*).
38. Jane Hathaway
    (*The Beverly Hillbillies*).
37. Hawk (*Spenser: For Hire*).
36. **Fred Sanford** (*Sanford and Son*).
35. **Kramer** (*Seinfeld*).
34. **Mork** (*Mork & Mindy*).
33. Diane Chambers (*Cheers*).
32. **Jim Ignatowski** (*Taxi*).
31. **Niles Crane** (*Frasier*).
30. Frank Pembleton
    (*Homicide: Life on the Street*).
29. Ted Baxter
    (*The Mary Tyler Moore Show*).

28. Edina Monsoon (*Absolutely Fabulous*).
27. Steve Urkel (*Family Matters*).
26. Roseanne (*Roseanne*).
25. Jim Rockford (*The Rockford Files*).
24. Paladin (*Have Gun Will Travel*).
23. **Andy Sipowicz** (*NYPD Blue*).
22. Maynard G. Krebs (*The Many Loves of Dobie Gillis*).
21. **Mary Richards** (*The Mary Tyler Moore Show*).
20. Eddie Haskell (*Leave It To Beaver*).
19. Maxwell Smart (*Get Smart*).
18. Theo Kojak (*Kojak*).
17. Alex P. Keaton (*Family Ties*).
16. Sgt. Bilko (*The Phil Silvers Show*).
15. Lilli Harper (*I'll Fly Away*).

14. Homer Simpson (*The Simpsons*).
13. **Ralph Kramden** (*The Honeymooners*).
12. **Felix Unger and Oscar Madison** (*The Odd Couple*).
11. J.R. Ewing (*Dallas*).
10. **George Costanza** (*Seinfeld*).
9. **Barney Fife** (*The Andy Griffith Show*).
8. Emma Peel (*The Avengers*).
7. Lt. Columbo (*Columbo*).
6. **Mr. Spock** (*Star Trek*).
5. **Archie Bunker** (*All in the Family*).
4. Fonzie (*Happy Days*).
3. **Lucy Ricardo** (*I Love Lucy*).
2. **Ed Norton** (*The Honeymooners*).
1. Louis De Palma (*Taxi*).

For the record, three shows had two characters on this list: *The Honeymooners*, *Seinfeld*, and *Taxi*. Also, *The Odd Couple*'s Oscar Madison and Felix Unger both made the list, but they share a single spot. (Felix was probably upset about that!)

Chapter 44

The 56 Major Religious Denominations in America

This is a list of the 56 most prevalent religious denominations in America. The combined total membership of these 56 sects is 164,919,732, or approximately two-thirds of the American population.

1. Roman Catholic: 61,207,914.
2. Baptist: 33,064,341.
3. Methodist: 13,463,552.
4. Pentecostal: 10,396,628.
5. Lutheran: 8,312,036.
6. Islamic: 5,500,000.
7. Church of Jesus Christ of Latter-day Saints: 5,171,623.
8. Eastern Orthodoxy: 5,058,998.
9. Presbyterian: 4,145,932.
10. Jewish: 4,075,000.
11. Episcopal: 2,339,113.
12. Reformed Churches: 1,965,148.
13. United Church of Christ: 1,800,000.
14. Hindi: 1,285,000.
15. Jehovah's Witnesses: 974,719.
16. Disciples of Christ: 879,436.
17. Adventist: 857,513.
18. Church of the Nazarene: 619,576.
19. Salvation Army: 453,150.
20. Mennonite: 350,844.
21. Christian and Missionary Alliance: 328,078.
22. Churches of God: 285,234.
23. International Council of Community Churches: 250,000.
24. Evangelical Free Church of America: 242,619.
25. Unitarian-Universalist Association of North America: 214,000.
26. Full Gospel Fellowship of Churches and Ministers International: 195,000.
27. German Baptists Brethren: 191,459.
28. Friends (Quakers): 176,666.
29. Bahá'i Faith: 133,000.
30. Christian Congregation Inc.: 115,881.
31. Plymouth Brethren: 100,000.
32. Evangelical Covenant Church: 93,414.
33. Independent Fundamental Churches of America: 69,857.

34. National Association of Congregational Christian Churches: 68,510.
35. Grace Gospel Fellowship: 60,000.
36. Polish National Catholic Church: 50,000.
37. Missionary Church: 47,550.
38. Universal Fellowship of Metropolitan Comunity Churches: 46,000.
39. National Organization of the New Apostolic Church of North America: 41,863.
40. Conservative Congregational Christian Conference: 38,956.
41. Christian Church of North America General Council: 31,558.
42. Moravian Church: 30,371.
43. American Catholic Church: 25,000.
44. Church of the United Brethren in Christ: 23,585.
45. Evangelical Congregational Church: 22,957.
46. Brethren in Christ: 18,424.
47. Buddhist Churches of America: 15,750.
48. Apostolic Christian Church of America: 12,538.
49. Evangelical Church: 12,430.
50. Churches of Christ in Christian Union: 10,400.
51. Holiness Church of Christ U.S.A.: 10,243.
52. American Rescue Workers: 10,000.
53. Church Christ in Christian Union: 9,858.
54. Liberal Catholic Church—Province of the U.S.A.: 6,500.
55. Reformed Episcopal Church: 6,084.
56. General Church of the New Jerusalem: 5,424.

(*Source: The 1999 Yearbook of American & Canadian Churches*, published by the National Councils of Churches of Christ in the U.S.A.; *The World Alamanac and Book of Facts*, 2000 edition.)

Chapter 45

51 State Birds

The Cardinal (7 states), Meadowlark (6 states), Mockingbird (5 states), and Robin (3 states) seem to be America's most popular feathered friends. And yes, all those cartoons were true: There really is a Roadrunner (meep, meep) and he is New Mexico's official state bird.

1. **Alabama:** Yellowhammer.
2. **Alaska:** Willow ptarmigan.
3. **Arizona:** Cactus wren.
4. **Arkansas:** Mockingbird.
5. **California:** California valley quail.
6. **Colorado:** Lark bunting.
7. **Connecticut:** American robin.
8. **Delaware:** Blue hen chicken.
9. **District of Columbia:** Wood thrush.
10. **Florida:** Mockingbird.
11. **Georgia:** Brown thrasher.
12. **Hawaii:** Hawaiian goose.
13. **Idaho:** Mountain bluebird.
14. **Illinois:** Cardinal.
15. **Indiana:** Cardinal.
16. **Iowa:** Goldfinch.
17. **Kansas:** Western meadowlark.
18. **Kentucky:** Kentucky cardinal.
19. **Louisiana:** Eastern brown pelican.
20. **Maine:** Chickadee.
21. **Maryland:** Baltimore oriole.
22. **Massachusetts:** Chickadee.
23. **Michigan:** Robin.
24. **Minnesota:** Common loon.
25. **Mississippi:** Mockingbird.
26. **Missouri:** Bluebird.
27. **Montana:** Western meadowlark.
28. **Nebraska:** Meadowlark.
29. **Nevada:** Mountain bluebird.
30. **New Hampshire:** Purple finch.
31. **New Jersey:** Eastern goldfinch.
32. **New Mexico:** Roadrunner.
33. **New York:** Bluebird.
34. **North Carolina:** Cardinal.
35. **North Dakota:** Western meadowlark.
36. **Ohio:** Cardinal.
37. **Oklahoma:** Scissor-tailed flycatcher.
38. **Oregon:** Western meadowlark.
39. **Pennsylvania:** Ruffed grouse.
40. **Rhode Island:** Rhode Island hen.
41. **South Carolina:** Carolina wren.
42. **South Dakota:** Pheasant.
43. **Tennessee:** Mockingbird.
44. **Texas:** Mockingbird.
45. **Utah:** Seagull.
46. **Vermont:** Thrush.
47. **Virginia:** Cardinal.
48. **Washington:** Willow goldfinch.
49. **West Virginia:** Cardinal.
50. **Wisconsin:** Robin.
51. **Wyoming:** Meadowlark.

Chapter 46

The Occupations of the 56 Signers of the Declaration of Independence

"We must be unanimous—we must all hang together."
—John Hancock, at the signing of the Declaration of Independence

"Or most assuredly we will all hang separately."
—Benjamin Franklin, responding to Hancock

The signers of the Declaration of Independence—visionaries of the highest order—were in actuality ordinary men. They ranged from "professional" men, such as doctors, lawyers, educators, and judges; to what we might describe today as "blue-collar" men: farmers, merchants, and even an ironmaster.

This list looks at how the Founding Fathers were earning their daily bread that hot summer of 1776 when they, in unison, created the greatest nation ever to exist on earth. They had no idea how they would change the course of human existence for all who would come afterwards.

(*Note:* There were only 56 signers of the Declaration of Independence, but the total men listed here number 63, because some of the Founders had two or more occupations. They are listed individually.

JUDGE (15)

Josiah Bartlett (N.H.).
Samuel Chase (Md.).
Stephen Hopkins (R.I.).
Frances Hopkinson (N.J.).
Samuel Huntington (Conn.).
John Morton (Pa.).
William Paca (Md.).
Robert Treat Paine[1] (Mass.).
George Read (Del.).
Caesar Rodney (Del.).
George Ross (Pa.).
George Walton (Ga.).
William Whipple (N.H.).
James Wilson (Pa.).
Oliver Wolcott (Conn.).

LAWYER (14)

John Adams (Mass.).
Charles Carroll (Md.).
William Ellery (R.I.).
Thomas Heyward, Jr. (S.C.).
William Hooper (N.C.).
Thomas Jefferson (Va.).

Thomas McKean (Del.).
John Penn (N.C.).
Edward Rutledge (S.C.).
Roger Sherman (Conn.).
James Smith (Pa.).
Richard Stockton (N.J.).
Thomas Stone (Md.).
George Wythe (Va.).

FARMER (10)

Carter Braxton (Va.).
Benjamin Harrison (Va.).
John Hart (N.J.).
Thomas Heyward, Jr. (S.C.).
Francis Lightfoot Lee (Va.).
Henry Richard Lee (Va.).
Thomas Lynch, Jr. (S.C.).
Arthur Middleton (S.C.).
Lewis Morris (N.Y.).
Thomas Nelson, Jr. (Va.).

MERCHANT (10)

George Clymer (Pa.).
Elbridge Gerry (Mass.).
Button Gwinnett (Ga.).
John Hancock (Mass.).
Joseph Hewes (N.C.).
Francis Lewis (N.Y.).
Philip Livingston (N.Y.).
Robert Morris (Pa.).
William Whipple (N.H.).
William Williams (Conn.).

PHYSICIAN (4)

Josiah Bartlett (N.H.).
Lyman Hall (Ga.).

Benjamin Rush (Pa.).
Matthew Thornton (N.H.).

EDUCATOR (2)

Stephen Hopkins (R.I.).
John Witherspoon (N.J.).

AUTHOR (1)

Frances Hopkinson (N.J.).

CLERGYMAN (1)

John Witherspoon (N.J.).

IRONMASTER (1)

George Taylor (Pa.).

POLITICAL LEADER (1)

Samuel Adams (Mass.).

PRINTER (1)

Benjamin Franklin (Pa.).

PUBLISHER (1)

Benjamin Franklin (Pa.).

SURVEYOR (1)

Abraham Clark (N.J.).

SOLDIER (1)

William Floyd (N.Y.).

[1] The actor Treat Williams, whose actual name is Robert Williams, took his nickname "Treat" from this Massachusetts judge and Declaration of Independence signer. Paine is an ancestor of Treat Williams's on his mother's side.

Chapter 47

Special Guest Contributor:

Paul Revere's Own Account of His Midnight Ride

I am delighted to have as a Guest Contributor *to The U.S.A. Book of Lists* the esteemed patriot Paul Revere (1735-1818). He was a silversmith from Charlestown, Mass., a member of the Sons of Liberty, and a participant in the Boston Tea Party.

Mr. Revere is most remembered, though, for his famous "Midnight Ride" on the night of April 18, 1775. In it, he rode from Charlestown to Lexington to alert the colonists of the approach of British troops.

In this essay, Mr. Revere gives his own account of his memorable ride. However, you won't find him shouting "The British are coming! The British are coming!" This is probably because he never said it. Historians suspect that this is a folk legend that cannot be proven or disproven.

I, Paul Revere, of Boston, in the colony of the Massachusetts Bay in New England; of lawful age, do testify and say; that I was sent for by Dr. Joseph Warren, of said Boston, on the evening of the 18th of April, about 10 o'clock; when he desired me, "to go to Lexington, and inform Mr. Samuel Adams, and the Hon. John Hancock Esq. that there was a number of soldiers, composed of light troops, and grenadiers, marching to the bottom of the common, where there was a number of boats to receive them; it was supposed that they were going to Lexington, by the way of Cambridge River, to take them, or go to Concord, to destroy the colony stores."

I proceeded immediately, and was put across Charles River and landed near Charlestown Battery; went in town, and there got a horse. While in Charlestown, I was informed by Richard Devens Esq., that he met that evening, after sunset, nine officers of the ministerial army, mounted on good horses, and armed, going towards Concord.

I set off, it was then about 11 o'clock, the moon shone bright. I had got almost over Charlestown Common, towards Cambridge, when I saw two officers on horse-back, standing under the shade of a tree, in a narrow part of the road. I was near enough to see their holsters and cockades. One of them started his horse towards me, the other up the road, as I supposed, to head me, should I escape the first. I turned my horse short about, and rode upon a full gallop for Mistick Road. He followed me about 300 yards, and finding he could not catch me, returned. I proceeded to Lexington, through Mistick, and alarmed Mr. Adams and Col. Hancock.

After I had been there about half an hour Mr. Daws arrived, who came from Boston, over the Neck.

We set off for Concord, and were overtaken by a young gentleman named Prescot, who belonged to Concord, and was going home. When we had got about half way from Lexington to Concord, the other two stopped at a house to awake the men, I kept along. When I had got about 200 yards ahead of them, I saw two officers as before. I called to my company to come up, saying here was two of them, (for I had told them what Mr. Devens told me, and of my being stopped). In an instant I saw four of them, who rode up to me with their pistols in their bands, said "G-d d—n you, stop. If you go an inch further, you are a dead man." Immediately Mr. Prescot came up. We attempted to get through them, but they kept before us, and swore if we did not turn in to that pasture, they would blow our brains out, (they had placed themselves opposite to a pair of bars, and had taken the bars down). They forced us in. When we had got in, Mr. Prescot said "Put on!" He took to the left, I to the right towards a wood at the bottom of the pasture,

intending, when I gained that, to jump my horse and run afoot. Just as I reached it, out started six officers, seized my bridle, put their pistols to my breast, ordered me to dismount, which I did. One of them, who appeared to have the command there, and much of a gentleman, asked me where I came from; I told him. He asked what time I left. I told him, he seemed surprised, said "Sir, may I crave your name?" I answered "My name is Revere. "What" said he, "Paul Revere"? I answered "Yes." The others abused much; but he told me not to be afraid, no one should hurt me. I told him they would miss their aim. He said they should not, they were only waiting for some deserters they expected down the road. I told him I knew better, I knew what they were after; that I had alarmed the country all the way up, that their boats were caught aground, and I should have 500 men there soon. One of them said they had 1,500 coming; he seemed surprised and rode off into the road, and informed them who took me, they came down immediately on a full gallop. One of them (whom I since learned was Major Mitchel of the 5th Reg.) clapped his pistol to my head, and said he was going to ask me some questions, and if I did not tell the truth, he would blow my brains out. I told him I esteemed myself a man of truth, that he had stopped me on the high-

illustration/Bettmann Archive

The Ride of Paul Revere

way, and made me a prisoner, I knew not by what right; I would tell him the truth; I was not afraid. He then asked me the same questions that the other did, and many more, but was more particular; I gave him much the same answers. He then ordered me to mount my horse, they first searched me for pistols. When I was mounted, the Major took the reins out of my hand, and said "By G-d Sir, you are not to ride with reins I assure you"; and gave them to an officer on my right, to lead me. He then ordered 4 men out of the bushes, and to mount their horses; they were country men which they had stopped who were going home; then ordered us to march. He said to me, "We are now going towards your friends, and if you attempt to run, or we are insulted, we will blow your brains out." When we had got into the road they formed a circle, and ordered the prisoners in the center, and to lead me in the front. We rode towards Lexington at a quick pace; they very often insulted me calling me rebel, etc., etc. After we had got about a mile, I was given to the sergeant to lead, he was ordered to take out his pistol, (he rode with a hanger), and if I ran, to execute the Major's sentence.

When we got within about half a mile of the Meeting House we heard a gun fired. The Major asked me what it was for, I told him to alarm the country; he ordered the four prisoners to dismount, they did, then one of the officers dismounted and cut the bridles and saddles off the horses, and drove them away, and told the men they might go about their business. I asked the Major to dismiss me, he said he would carry me, let the consequence be what it will. He then ordered us to march.

When we got within sight of the Meeting House, we heard a volley of guns fired, as I supposed at the tavern, as an alarm; the Major ordered us to halt, he asked me how far it was to Cambridge, and many more questions, which I answered. He then asked the sergeant, if his horse was tired, he said yes; he ordered him to take my horse. I dismounted, and the sergeant mounted my horse; they cut the bridle and saddle of the sergeant's horse, and rode off down the road. I then went to the house were I left Messrs. Adams and Hancock, and told them what had happened; their friends advised them to go out of the way; I went with them, about two miles across road.

After resting myself, I set off with another man to go back to the tavern, to inquire the news; when we got there, we were told the troops were within two miles. We went into the tavern to get a trunk of papers belonging to Col. Hancock. Before we left the house, I saw the ministerial troops from the chamber window. We made haste, and had to pass through our militia, who were on a green behind the Meeting House, to the number as I supposed, about 50 or 60, I went through them; as I passed I heard the commanding officer speak to his men to this purpose; "Let the troops pass by, and don't molest them, without they begin first." I had to go across road; but had not got half gunshot off, when the ministerial troops appeared in sight, behind the Meeting House. They made a short halt, when one gun was fired. I heard the report, turned my head, and saw the smoke in front of the troops. They immediately gave a great shout, ran a few paces, and then the whole fired. I could first distinguish irregular firing, which I supposed was the advance guard, and then platoons; at this time I could not see our militia, for they were covered from me by a house at the bottom of the street.

–Paul Revere

(*Note*: Special thanks to Rick Gardiner, who maintains the American History Source Document Web site where I found this incredible essay. This site offers complete texts of important documents related to American history, from 500 B.C. through 1800 A.D. You can find it at *personal.pitnet.net/ primarysources.*)

Chapter 48

The 75 Most Expensive 4-Year Colleges and Universities in America

This list is scary. It's scary for students who get accepted to an expensive college but who are terrified of being saddled with six-figure student loans when they graduate. It's scary for parents who want to help their kids but don't want to still be carrying a mortgage when they're collecting Social Security.

But I guess this list perfectly illustrates the American way, eh? You get what you pay for (usually). And a degree from one of these schools almost guarantees an extremely well-paying job right out of school.

Unless, of course, the grad decides to go for a master's degree...or a Ph. D.

Of the more than 1,300 accredited four-year colleges or universities in the United States with an enrollment of 1,000 or more, these are the 75 most expensive.

The amount given for each school is for the annual tuition and fees required for all full-time students for the 1998-1999 academic year. Middlebury College of Vermont leads the way at $29,340 per year ($117,360 for a four-year degree). The number in parenthesis is the founding date of the school.

And by the way, none of these fees include room and board and books. Those fees are extra.

1. Middlebury College (1800) Middlebury, Vt.: $29,340.
2. Colby College (1813) Waterville, Maine: $29,190.
3. Bates College (1855) Lewiston, Maine: $28,650.
4. Connecticut College (1911) New London, Conn.: $28,475.
5. Princeton University (1746) Princeton, N.J.: $23,820[1].
6. Hampshire College (1965) Amherst, Mass.: $23,780.
7. Boston University (1839) Boston, Mass.: $23,148.
8. Brown University (1764) Providence, R.I.: $23,124.
9. Massachusetts Institute of Technology (1861) Cambridge, Mass.: $23,100.
10. Yale University (1701) New Haven, Conn.: $23,100[2].
11. Sarah Lawrence College (1926) Bronxville, N.Y.: $23,076.
12. Dartmouth College (1769) Hanover, N.H.: $23,012.
13. Williams College (1793) Williamston, Mass.: $22,990.
14. Wesleyan University (1831) Middletown, Conn.: $22,980.
15. Bowdoin College (1794) Brunswick, Maine: $22,905.

16. Brandeis University (1948) Waltham, Mass.: $22,851.
17. Kenyon College (1824) Gambier, Ohio: $22,850.
18. Tufts University (1852) Medford, Mass.: $22,811.
19. Harvard University (1636) Cambridge, Mass.: $22,802.
20. Colgate University (1819) Hamilton, N.Y.: $22,770.
21. Hamilton College (1812) Clinton, N.Y.: $22,700.
22. Franklin & Marshall College (1787) Lancaster, Pa.: $22,664.
23. Columbia College (1754) New York, N.Y.: $22,650.
24. University of Chicago (1891) Chicago, Il.: $22,476.
25. Trinity College (1823) Hartford, Conn.: $22,470.
26. Northwestern University (1851) Evanston, Il.: $22,458.
27. Oberlin College (1833) Oberlin, Ohio: $22,438.
28. Gettysburg College (1832) Gettysburg, Pa.: $22,430.
29. Hobart & William Smith Colleges (1822) Geneva, N.Y.: $22,380.
30. Mount Holyoke College (1837) South Haldey, Mass.: $22,340.
31. Reed College (1908) Portland, Ore.: $22,340.
32. Union College (1795) Schnectady, N.Y.: $22,315.
33. University of Pennsylvania (1740) Philadelphia, Pa.: $22,250.
34. Hartwick College (1797) Oneonta, N.Y.: $22,235.
35. Bard College (1860) Annandale-on-Hudson, N.Y.: $22,220.
36. Duke University (1838) Durham, N.C.: $22,173.
37. Vassar College (1861) Poughkeepsie, N.Y.: $22,090.
38. Tulane University (1834) New Orleans, La.: $22,066.
39. Swarthmore College (1864) Swarthmore, Pa.: $22,000.
40. Skidmore College (1903) Saratoga Springs, N.Y.: $21,988.
41. Carleton College (1866) Northfield, Minn.: $21,885.
42. Haverford College (1833) Haverford, Pa.: $21,740.
43. New York University (1831) New York, N.Y.: $21,730.
44. Johns Hopkins University (1867) Baltimore, Md.: $21,675.
45. Wellesley College (1870) Wellesley, Mass.: $21,660.
46. Dickinson College (1773) Carlisle, Pa.: $21,600.
47. Smith College (1871) Northampton, Mass.: $21,512.
48. Vanderbilt University (1873) Nashville, TN: $21,478.
49. Bryn Mawr College (1885) Bryn Mawr, Pa.: $21,430.
50. Georgetown University (1789) Washington, D.C.: $21,405.
51. Drew University (1867) Madison, N.J.: $21,396.
52. Stanford University (1891) Stanford, Calif.: $21,389.
53. The George Washington University (1821) Washington, D.C.: $21,360.
54. Lehigh University (1865) Bethlehem, Pa.: $21,350.
55. St. Lawrence University (1856) Canton, N.Y.: $21,345.
56. Bucknell University (1846) Lewisburg, Pa.: $21,210.
57. Lafayette College (1826) Easton, Pa.: $21,202.
58. Emory University (1836) Atlanta, Ga.: $21,120.
59. College of the Holy Cross (1843) Worcester, Mass.: $21,080.
60. University of Rochester (1850) Rochester, N.Y.: $21,020.
61. Barnard College (1889) New York, N.Y.: $20,976.

62. Clark University (1887) Worcester, Mass.: $20,940.
63. Wheaton College (1834) Norton, Mass.: $20,820.
64. Pomona College (1887) Claremont, Calif.: $20,680.
65. Rensselaer Polytechnic Institute (1824) Troy, N.Y.: $20,604.
66. Davidson College (1837) Davidson, N.C.: $20,595.
67. University of Southern California (1880) Los Angeles, Calif.: $20,480.
68. Carnegie Mellon University (1900) Pittsburgh, Pa.: $20,375.
69. Babson College (1919) Babson Park, Mass.: $20,365.
70. Boston College (1863) Chestnut Hill, Mass.: $20,292.
71. Willamette University (1842) Salem, Ore.: $20,290.
72. Elmira College (1855) Elmira, N.Y.: $20,276.
73. Denison University (1831) Granville, Ohio: $20,250.
74. Ohio Wesleyan University (1842) Delaware, Ohio: $20,040.
75. Rollins College (1885) Winter Park, FL: $20,010.

[1] In February 2000, Princeton announced that its 2000-2001 tuition would go up to $25,430.

[2] In February 2000, Yale announced that its 2000-2001 tuition would go up to $25,220.

It isn't often that I recommend one Web site as the only site you will need for a research project. But in the case of *anystudent.com*, the praise is justified. This amazing Web site is a portal to thousands of colleges and universities in the United States, organized by name or state. For example, I clicked on Connecticut, and a list of every college and university appeared almost instantly. And every name contained a hyperlink that took me right to the site of the school with a single click. If you want to research institutions of higher learning on the Internet, give *anystudent.com* a shot.

Chapter 49

The Capital Cities of the 50 United States

1.	Alabama	Montgomery.	26.	Montana	Helena.
2.	Alaska	Juneau.	27.	Nebraska	Lincoln.
3.	Arizona	Phoenix.	28.	Nevada	Carson City.
4.	Arkansas	Little Rock.	29.	New Hampshire	Concord.
5.	California	Sacramento.	30.	New Jersey	Trenton.
6.	Colorado	Denver.	31.	New Mexico	Santa Fe.
7.	Connecticut	Hartford.	32.	New York	Albany.
8.	Delaware	Dover.	33.	North Carolina	Raleigh.
9.	Florida	Tallahassee.	34.	North Dakota	Bismarck.
10.	Georgia	Atlanta.	35.	Ohio	Columbus.
11.	Hawaii	Honolulu.	36.	Oklahoma	Oklahoma City.
12.	Idaho	Boise.	37.	Oregon	Salem.
13.	Illinois	Springfield.	38.	Pennsylvania	Harrisburg.
14.	Indiana	Indianapolis.	39.	Rhode Island	Providence.
15.	Iowa	Des Moines.	40.	South Carolina	Columbia.
16.	Kansas	Topeka.	41.	South Dakota	Pierre.
17.	Kentucky	Frankfort.	42.	Tennessee	Nashville.
18.	Louisiana	Baton Rouge.	43.	Texas	Austin.
19.	Maine	Augusta.	44.	Utah	Salt Lake City.
20.	Maryland	Annapolis.	45.	Vermont	Montpelier.
21.	Massachusetts	Boston.	46.	Virginia	Richmond.
22.	Michigan	Lansing.	47.	Washington	Olympia.
23.	Minnesota	St. Paul.	48.	West Virginia	Charleston.
24.	Mississippi	Jackson.	49.	Wisconsin	Madison.
25.	Missouri	Jefferson City.	50.	Wyoming	Cheyenne.

Chapter 50

45 Major Conflicts of the Civil War

hese are the 45 Civil War battles (out of a total of 2,258 during the War) that cost the most lives, and the ones that were the major turning points in the war.

1861

April 12-14	Bombardment of Fort Sumter, S.C.
June 10	Battle of Big Bethel, Va.
July 21	First Bull Run, (First Manassas, Va.).
August 10	Battle of Wilson's Creek, Miss.

1862

February 12-16	Battle of Fort Donelson, Tenn.
March 7-8	Battle of Pea Ridge, Ark.
March 26-28	Battle at Glorietta Pass, N.Mex.
April 6-7	Battle of Shiloh (Pittsburgh Landing), Tenn.
April 10-12	Attack on Fort Pulaski, Ga.
May 8	Battle of McDowell, Va.
June 8	Battle of Cross Keys, Va.
June 9	Battle of Port Republic, Va.
June 27	Battle at Gaines' Mill, Va.
July 1	Battle at Malvern Hill, Va.
August 9	Battle of Cedar Mountain, Va.

1862 (CONT.)

August 28-30	Second Bull Run (Second Manassas, Va.).
September 13-15	Battle of Harper's Ferry. Va.
September 17	Battle of Antietam (Sharpsburg), Md.
October 3-4	Battle of Corinth, Miss.
October 8	Battle of Perryville, Ky.
December 11-13	Battle of Fredericksburg, Va.
December 31	Battle at Stones River (Murfreesboro), Tenn. (beginning).

1863

January 1	Battle at Stones River (Murfreesboro), Tenn. (conclusion).
May 1-3	Battle of Chancellorsville, Va.
May 16	Battle of Champion Hill, Miss.
May 18-July 4	Siege of Vicksburg, Miss.
May 22-July 9	Battle of Port Hudson, La.
June 9	Battle at Brandy Station, Va.
July 1-3	Battle of Gettysburg, Pa.
September 18-20	Battle of Chickamauga, Ga.
November 23-25	Battle of Chattanooga, Tenn.

1864

May 5-6	Battle of The Wilderness, Va.
May 8-21	Battle of Spotsylvania Court House, Va.
May 15	Battle of New Market, Va.
May 23-26	Battle of the North Anna River, Va.
May 31-June 3	Battle of Cold Harbor, Va.
June 10	Battle of Brice's Cross Roads, Miss.
June 27	Battle of Kennesaw Mountains, Ga.
July 14-15	Battle of Tupelo, Miss.
June 15-April 1, 1865	Siege of Petersburg, Va.
July 9	Battle of Monocacy, Md.
August 5-23	Battle of Mobile Bay, Ala.

1865

January 6-15	Battle of Fort Fisher, N.C.
April 1	Battle at Five Forks, Va.
April 6	Battle of Sayler's Creek, Va.

Major Civil War battles by state

Virginia	21 battles	Kentucky	1 battle
Mississippi	5 battles	Louisiana	1 battle
Tennessee	5 battles	Missouri	1 battle
Georgia	3 battles	New Mexico	1 battle
Maryland	2 battles	North Carolina	1 battle
Alabama	1 battle	Pennsylvania	1 battle
Arkansas	1 battle	South Carolina	1 battle

Total of all Civil War battles by state (in descending order)

Virginia	519	Dakota Territory	11
Tennessee	298	Pennsylvania	9
Missouri	244	Kansas	7
Mississippi	186	California	6
Arkansas	167	Minnesota	6
Kentucky	138	Arizona	4
Louisiana	118	Colorado	4
Georgia	108	Indiana	4
North Carolina	85	Oregon	4
West Virginia	80	Nebraska	2
Alabama	78	Nevada	2
South Carolina	60	District of Columbia	1
Florida	32	Idaho	1
Maryland	30	Illinois	1
New Mexico	19	New York	1
Indian Territory	17	Utah	1
Texas	14	Washington	1
		Total	2,258

Chapter 51

Heinz's **57** Varieties

I n 1896, Henry John Heinz, entrepreneur and founder of the H.J. Heinz food company, saw a billboard for a company that offered 21 varieties of shoes. Heinz was so captivated by the idea of informing the consumer of the number of products sold by a company that he decided to do the same thing with his own company. One must wonder if it occurred to Heinz to actually count the products his company sold…and then use that number in his advertising

Perhaps, but the truth is that Henry wanted a number he felt customers would remember, regardless of whether or not it was an accurate tally of the Heinz Company's products.

He eventually came up with the magic number "57." Then, he picked from his company's roster of products to come up with the following list, as published in one of the company's 1923 newspaper ads. The ad copy read, "56 is just a number—58 is just a number—but 57 means good things to eat."

You'll notice that Heinz gave 14 slots to preserves and jellies alone, and 13 slots to pickles and olives. Arbitrary or not, the slogan worked and the company still boasts of "Heinz's 57 Varieties," even though they sell many more products than that. But who am I to argue with success? (And who doesn't just love their ketchup?)

1. Heinz Baked Beans with Pork and Tomato Sauce.
2. Heinz Baked Beans without Tomato Sauce, with Pork-*Boston Style*.
3. Heinz Baked Beans in Tomato Sauce without Meat-*Vegetarian*.
4. Heinz Baked Red Kidney Beans.
5. Heinz Peanut Butter.
6. Heinz Cream of Tomato Soup.
7. Heinz Cream of Pea Soup.
8. Heinz Cream of Celery Soup.
9. Heinz Cooked Spaghetti.
10. Heinz Cooked Macaroni.
11. Heinz Mince Meat.
12. Heinz Plum Pudding.
13. Heinz Fig Pudding.
14. Heinz Cherry Preserves.
15. Heinz Red Raspberry Preserves.
16. Heinz Peach Preserves.
17. Heinz Damson Plum Preserves.
18. Heinz Strawberry Preserves.
19. Heinz Pineapple Preserves.
20. Heinz Black Raspberry Preserves.
21. Heinz Blackberry Preserves.
22. Heinz Apple Butter.
23. Heinz Crab-apple Jelly.
24. Heinz Currant Jelly.

25. Heinz Grape Jelly.
26. Heinz Quince Jelly.
27. Heinz Apple Jelly.
28. Heinz Dill Pickles.
29. Heinz Sweet Midget Gherkins.
30. Heinz Preserved Sweet Gherkins.
31. Heinz Preserved Sweet Mixed Pickles.
32. Heinz Sour Spiced Gherkins.
33. Heinz Sour Midget Gherkins.
34. Heinz Sour Mixed Pickles.
35. Heinz Chow Chow Pickles.
36. Heinz Sweet Mustard Pickles.
37. Heinz Queen Olives.
38. Heinz Manzanilla Olives.
39. Heinz Stuffed Olives.
40. Heinz Ripe Olives.
41. Heinz Pure Olive Oil.
42. Heinz Sour Pickled Onions.
43. Heinz Worcestershire Sauce.
44. Heinz Chili Sauce.
45. Heinz Beefsteak Sauce.
46. Heinz Red Pepper Sauce.
47. Heinz Green Pepper Sauce.
48. **Heinz Tomato Ketchup.**
49. Heinz Prepared Mustard.
50. Heinz India Relish.
51. Heinz Evaporated Horseradish.
52. Heinz Salad Dressing.
53. Heinz Mayonnaise.
54. Heinz Pure Malt Vinegar.
55. Heinz Pure Cider Vinegar.
56. Heinz Distilled White Vinegar.
57. Heinz Tarragon Vinegar.

Chapter 52

30 Outrageous Things Presidents Have Said About Each Other

1. **Thomas Jefferson on John Adams**: "He is vain, irritable, and a bad calculator of the force and probable effect of the motives which govern men."

2. **James Buchanan on John Quincy Adams**: "His disposition is as perverse and mulish as that of his father."

3. **Woodrow Wilson on Chester A. Arthur**: "(Arthur is) a nonentity with side whiskers."

4. **Ulysses S. Grant on James Buchanan**: "(Buchanan is) our present granny executive."

5. **Gerald Ford on Jimmy Carter**: "Teddy Roosevelt...once said 'Speak softly and carry a big stick.' Jimmy Carter wants to speak loudly and carry a fly swatter."

6. **Harry S Truman on Dwight Eisenhower**: "The general doesn't know any more about politics than a pig knows about Sunday."

7. **Harry S Truman on Millard Fillmore**: "(W)hen we needed a strong man, what we got was a man that swayed with the slightest breeze."

8. **Ulysses S. Grant on James Garfield**: "Garfield has shown that he does not even possess the backbone of an angleworm."

9. **Woodrow Wilson on Warren Harding**: "He has a bungalow mind."

10. **Martin Van Buren on William Henry Harrison**: "He does not seem to realize the vast importance of his elevation...He is as tickled with the presidency as a young man with a new bonnet."

11. **Calvin Coolidge on Herbert Hoover**: "That man has offered me unsolicited advice for six years, all of it bad."

12. **John Quincy Adams on Andrew Jackson**: "(Andrew Jackson is) a barbarian who cannot write a sentence of grammar and can hardly spell his own name."

13. **John Quincy Adams on Thomas Jefferson**: "His genius is of the old French school. It conceives better than it combines."

14. **Ulysses S. Grant on Andrew Johnson**: "I would impeach him because he is such an infernal liar."

15. **Richard Nixon on Lyndon Johnson**: "Johnson...seemed unable to carry on a conversation without nudging or poking or even shaking the other person."

16. **Richard Nixon on John F. Kennedy**: "Kennedy had two principal political liabilities. In my judgment one was only apparent—his Catholicism. The other was real—his lack of experience."

17. **Theodore Roosevelt on Abraham Lincoln**: "(W)hile I may not share any other quality with Abraham Lincoln, I do share his lack of intimate acquaintance with finance."

18. **Theodore Roosevelt on William McKinley**: "McKinley has no more backbone than a chocolate eclair." (This was said a year after McKinley became president, and three years before Roosevelt became McKinley's vice president. At the time Roosevelt uttered this insult, Garret Hobart was veep.)

19. **Thomas Jefferson on James Monroe**: "He is a man whose soul might be turned wrong side outwards, without discovering a blemish to the world."

20. **John F. Kennedy on Richard Nixon**: "Do you realize the responsibility I carry? I'm the only person standing between Nixon and the White House."

21. **Theodore Roosevelt on Franklin Pierce**: "A small politician, of low capacity and mean surroundings, proud to act as the servile tool of men worse than himself, but also stronger and abler. He was ever ready to do any work the slavery leaders set to him...."

22. **Andrew Jackson on James Polk**: "Polk's appointments all in all are the most damnable set that was ever made by any president since the government was organized."

23. **Jimmy Carter on Ronald Reagan**: "Reagan was, 'Aw, shucks, this and that. I'm a grandfather, and...I love peace,' etc."

24. **Herbert Hoover on Franklin D. Roosevelt**: "(FDR was a) chameleon on plaid."

25. **Woodrow Wilson on Theodore Roosevelt**: "He is the most dangerous of the age."

26. **Theodore Roosevelt on William Howard Taft**: "A flub-dub with a streak of the second-rate and the common in him."

27. **James Polk on Zachary Taylor**: "He is evidently a weak man and has been made giddy with the idea of the presidency."

28. **James Buchanan on John Tyler**: "A manifesto...will appear tomorrow from the Whigs in Congress reading John Tyler out of the Whig Church and delivering him over to Satan to be buffeted."

29. **John Quincy Adams on Martin Van Buren**: "His principles are all subordinate to his ambitions."

30. **Theodore Roosevelt on Woodrow Wilson**: "Byzantine logothete...(that) infernal skunk in the White House."

(Source: The World Almanac of Presidential Quotations [Pharos Books, 1988]).

Chapter 53

The 167 Patents of Thomas Edison

In Edison, one deals with a central figure of the great age that saw the invention and introduction in practical form of the telegraph, the submarine cable, the telephone, the electric light, the electric railway, the electric trolley-car, the storage battery, the electric motor, the phonograph, (and) the wireless telegraph...the influence of these on the world's affairs has not been excelled at any time by that of any other corresponding advances in the arts and sciences."

—from *Edison: His Life and Inventions* (1910) by Frank Lewis Dyer

There are more than 1,000 patents recorded in the name of Thomas Alva Edison (1847-1931) in the U.S. Patent Office. When you read through the entire list, it paints a portrait of the sheer genius of the man. Edison was a man of enterprise, creativity, and astonishing discipline. (Edison had more than 1,200 foreign patents in his name in addition to the ones here in the United States.)

Edison is responsible for the mimeograph, the phonograph, bringing electricity into homes, the incandescent light bulb, the phonograph, motion picture equipment, and for inventing the devices that made Alexander Graham Bell's invention of the telephone commercially practical. One can only dream about what a genius such as Edison might have accomplished if he had been born into the computer age and had access to the vast resources of the Internet.

This list looks at 167 of Edison's most groundbreaking and innovative patents. Some of these are quite intriguing—many are quite a revelation. For example, number 28 is a patent for "preserving fruit," number 56 is a patent for "treating products derived from vegetable fibres," number 73 is a patent for "extracting gold from sulphide ores," number 162 is for "automobiles," and number 165 is for "flying machines."

Thomas Edison's laboratory complex in West Orange, N.J. (a part of the Edison National Historic Site, consisting of Thomas Edison's research and development laboratory and his home, Glenmont) is open to the public year-round. (Call for a schedule of hours.) The site is about 15 miles west of New York City.

Thomas Edison died in West Orange, N.J., on October 18, 1931 at the age of 84. However, his contributions to science were extraordinary and live on far past his own life. He will also be remembered for his observation that genius is "one percent inspiration and 99 percent perspiration." His achievements and incredible work ethic dramatically illustrate that he wasn't kidding.

	Patent No.	Title of patent	Date executed
1.	90,646	Electrographic Vote Recorder (his first patent)	October 13, 1868
2.	91,527	Printing Telegraph	January 25, 1869
3.	121,601	Machinery for Perforating Paper for Telegraph Purposes	August 16, 1871
4.	133,841	Typewriting Machine	November 13, 1871
5.	132,455	Improvement in Paper for Chemical Telegraphs	April 10, 1872
6.	133,019	Electrical Printing Machine	April 18, 1872
7.	142,999	Galvanic Batteries	October 31, 1872
8.	198,087	Telephonic Telegraphs	May 9, 1876
9.	205,370	Pneumatic Stencil Pens	February 3, 1877
10.	474,230	Speaking Telegraph	April 18, 1877
11.	230,621	Addressing Machine	May 8, 1877
12.	203,017	Telephone Call Signals	February 28, 1878
13.	214,636	Electric Lights	October 5, 1878
14.	218,866	Electric Lighting Apparatus	December 3, 1878
15.	295,990	Typewriter	December 4, 1878
16.	224,665	Autographic Stencils for Printing	March 10, 1879
17.	227,679	Phonograph	March 19, 1879
18.	221,957	Telephone	March 24, 1879
19.	223,898	Electric Lamp	November 1, 1879
20.	228,617	Brake for Electro-Magnetic Motors	March 10, 1880
21.	251,545	Electric Meter	March 10, 1880
22.	228,329	Magnetic Ore Separator	April 3, 1880
23.	248,430	Electro-Magnetic Brake	July 2, 1880
24.	265,778	Electro-Magnetic Railway Engine	July 3, 1880
25.	239,147	System of Electric Lighting	July 31, 1880
26.	248,435	Utilizing Electricity as Motive Power	August 12, 1880
27.	239,149	Incandescing Electric Lamp	December 3, 1880
28.	248,431	Preserving Fruit	December 11, 1880
29.	248,433	Vacuum Apparatus	January 19, 1881
30.	482,549	Means for Controlling Electric Generation	March 2, 1881
31.	251,553	Electric Chandeliers	March 7, 1881
32.	251,554	Electric Lamp and Socket or Holder	March 7, 1881
33.	248,424	Fitting and Fixtures for Electric Lamps	March 8, 1881
34.	251,552	Underground Conductors	April 22, 1881
35.	251,549	Electric Lamp and the Manufacture thereof	May 20, 1881
36.	263,131	Magnetic Ore Separator	June 4, 1881
37.	435,687	Means for Charging and Using Secondary Batteries	June 21, 1881
38.	404,902	Electrical Distribution System	August 24, 1881

	Patent No.	Title of patent	Date executed
39.	257,677	Telephone	September 7, 1881
40.	273,715	Malleableizing Iron	October 4, 1881
41.	446,667	Locomotives for Electric Railways	October 11, 1881
42.	251,559	Electrical Drop Light	October 25, 1881
43.	266,588	Vacuum Apparatus	November 25, 1881
44.	251,536	Vacuum Pump	December 5, 1881
45.	439,391	Junction Box for Electric Wires	December 5, 1881
46.	274,576	Transmitting Telephone	March 30, 1882
47.	273,492	Secondary Battery	May 19, 1882
48.	460,122	Process of and Apparatus for Generating Electricity	May 19, 1882
49.	265,786	Apparatus for Electrical Transmission of Power	May 22, 1882
50.	273,828	System of Underground Conductors of Electric Distribution	May 22, 1882
51.	365,509	Filament for Incandescent Electric Lamps	June 3, 1882
52.	446,668	Electric Arc Light	June 3, 1882
53.	273,489	Turn-Table for Electric Railway	June 9, 1882
54.	273,490	Electro-Magnetic Railway System	June 9, 1882
55.	273,494	Electrical Railroad	July 7, 1882
56.	543,986	Process for Treating Products Derived from Vegetable Fibres	October 17, 1882
57.	281,351	Electrical Generator	March 5, 1883
58.	370,125	Electrical Transmission of Power	June 1, 1883
59.	526,147	Plating One Material with Another	January 22, 1884
60.	314,115	Chemical Stock Quotation Telegraph	February 9, 1884
61.	436,968	Method and Apparatus for Drawing Wire	June 2, 1884
62.	350,234	System of Railway Signaling	March 27, 1885
63.	506,215	Making Plate Glass	November 9, 1887
64.	382,414	Burnishing Attachments for Phonographs	November 22, 1887
65.	386,974	Phonograph	November 22, 1887
66.	382,416	Feed and Return Mechanism for Phonographs	November 29, 1887
67.	394,105	Phonograph Recorder	February 20, 1888
68.	476,991	Method of and Apparatus for Separating Ores	May 9, 1888
69.	393,465	Preparing Phonograph Recording Surfaces	June 30, 1888
70.	448,780	Device for Turning Off Phonogram Blanks	June 30, 1888
71.	393,966	Recording and Reproducing Sounds	July 14, 1888
72.	448,781	Turning-Off Device for Phonographs	July 16, 1888
73.	474,591	Extracting Gold from Sulphide Ores	September 12, 1888
74.	406,572	Automatic Determining Device for Phonographs	February 1, 1889

	Patent No.	Title of patent	Date executed
75.	438,309	Insulating Electrical Conductors	April 25, 1889
76.	423,039	Phonograph Doll or Other Toys	June 15, 1889
77.	430,279	Voltaic Battery	June 15, 1889
78.	506,216	Apparatus for Making Glass	June 29, 1889
79.	465,250	Extracting Copper Pyrites	February 8, 1890
80.	434,589	Propelling Mechanism for Electric Vehicles	February 14, 1890
81.	438,310	Lamp Base	April 25, 1890
82.	437,428	Propelling Device for Electric Cars	April 29, 1890
83.	436,127	Electric Motor	May 17, 1890
84.	476,984	Expansible Pulley	August 9, 1890
85.	476 985	Trolley for Electric Railways	October 27, 1890
86.	500,281	Phonograph	November 17, 1890
87.	493,425	Electric Locomotive	December 20, 1890
88.	476,986	Means for Propelling Electric Cars	February 24, 1891
89.	463,251	Bricking Fine Ores	July 31, 1891
90.	470,928	Alternating Current Generator	July 31, 1891
91.	476,988	Lightning Arrester	July 31, 1891
92.	476,989	Conductor for Electric Railways	July 31, 1891
93.	485,840	Bricking Fine Iron Ores	July 31, 1891
94.	493,426	Apparatus for Exhibiting Photographs of Moving Objects	July 31, 1891
95.	589,168	Kinetographic Camera	July 31, 1891
96.	471,268	Ore Conveyor and Method of Arranging Ore Thereon	August 28, 1891
97.	472,288	Dust-Proof Bearings for Shafts	August 28, 1891
98.	472,752	Dust-Proof Journal Bearings	August 28, 1891
99.	472,753	Ore-Screening Apparatus	August 28, 1891
100.	474,592	Ore-Conveying Apparatus	August 28, 1891
101.	474,593	Dust-Proof Swivel Shaft Bearing	August 28, 1891
102.	498,385	Rollers for Ore-Crushing or Other Material	August 28, 1891
103.	564,423	Separating Ores	June 2, 1892
104.	485,842	Magnetic Ore Separation	July 9, 1892
105.	485,841	Mechanically Separating Ores	July 9, 1892
106.	602,064	Conveyor	December 13, 1893
107.	643,764	Reheating Compressed Air for Industrial Purposes	February 24, 1899
108.	641,281	Expanding Pulley	March 28, 1899
109.	727,116	Grinding Rolls	June 15, 1899
110.	685,911	Apparatus for Reheating Compressed Air for Industrial Purposes	November 24, 1899
111.	759,356	Burning Portland Cement	April 10, 1900
112.	657,527	Making Metallic Phonograph Records	April 30, 1900

photo/Library of Congress

Quintessential American inventor
Thomas Edison with phonograph

	Patent No.	Title of patent	Date executed
113.	667,202	Duplicating Phonograph Records	April 30, 1900
114.	713,863	Coating Phonograph Records	May 15, 1900
115.	672,617	Apparatus for Breaking Rock	August 1, 1900
116.	684,204	Reversible Galvanic Battery	October 15, 1900
117.	831,606	Sound Recording Apparatus	October 24, 1901
118.	827,089	Calcining Furnaces	December 24, 1901
119.	734,522	Process of Nickel-Plating	February 11, 1902
120.	727,118	Manufacturing Electrolytically Active Finely Divided Iron	October 13, 1902
121.	721,870	Funnel for Filling Storage Battery Jars	November 13, 1902
122.	723,449	Electrode for Storage Batteries	November 13, 1902
123.	754,755	Compressing Dies	November 13, 1902
124.	754,858	Storage Battery Tray	November 13, 1902
125.	764,183	Separating Mechanically Entrained Globules from Gases	November 13, 1902
126.	852,424	Secondary Batteries	November 13, 1902
127.	722,502	Handling Cable-Drawn Cars on Inclines	December 18, 1902
128.	724,089	Operating Motors in Dust-Laden Atmospheres	December 18, 1902
129.	750,102	Electrical Automobile	December 18, 1902
130.	873,219	Feed Regulators for Grinding Machines	December 18, 1902
131.	832,046	Automatic Weighing and Mixing Apparatus	December 18, 1902

Patent No.		Title of patent	Date executed
132.	772,647	Photographic Film for Moving Picture Machine	January 13, 1903
133.	831,269	Storage Battery Electrode Plate	January 30, 1903
134.	775,600	Rotary Cement Kilns	July 20, 1903
135.	796,629	Lamp Guard	July 30, 1903
136.	850,912	Making Articles by Electro-Plating	October 3, 1903
137.	857,041	Can or Receptacle for Storage Batteries	October 3, 1903
138.	766,815	Primary Battery	November 16, 1903
139.	767,554	Rendering Storage Battery Gases Non-Explosive	June 8, 1904
140.	861,241	Portland Cement and Manufacturing Same	June 20, 1904
141.	821,622	Cleaning Metallic Surfaces	June 24, 1904
142.	879,612	Alkaline Storage Batteries	June 24, 1904
143.	880,484	Process of Producing Very Thin Sheet Metal	June 24, 1904
144.	827,297	Alkaline Batteries	July 12, 1904
145.	797,845	Sheet Metal for Perforated Pockets of Storage Batteries	July 12, 1904
146.	847,746	Electrical Welding Apparatus	July 12, 1904
147.	970,615	Methods and Apparatus for Making Sound Records	August 23, 1904
148.	813,490	Cement Kiln	October 29, 1904
149.	879,859	Apparatus for Producing Very Thin Sheet Metal	February 16, 1905
150.	804,799	Apparatus for Perforating Sheet Metal	March 17, 1905
151.	870,024	Apparatus for Producing Perforated Strips	March 23, 1905
152.	862,145	Process of Making Seamless Tubular Pockets or Receptacles for Storage Battery Electrodes	April 26, 1905
153.	943,663	Horns for Talking Machines	May 20, 1905
154.	898 404	Making Articles by Electro-Plating	November 2, 1906
155.	890,625	Apparatus for Grinding Coal	November 27, 1906
156.	855,562	Diaphragm for Talking Machines	February 23, 1907
157.	876,445	Electrolyte for Alkaline Storage Batteries	May 8, 1907
158.	861,819	Discharging Apparatus for Belt Conveyors	June 11, 1907
159.	954,789	Sprocket Chain Drives	June 11, 1907
160.	909,167	Water-Proofing Paint for Portland Cement Buildings	February 4, 1908
161.	944,481	Processes and Apparatus for Artificially Aging or Seasoning Portland Cement	March 13, 1908
162.	947,806	Automobiles	March 13, 1908
163.	909,168	Water-Proofing Fibres and Fabrics	May 27, 1908
164.	909,169	Water-Proofing Paint for Portland Cement Structures	May 27, 1908
165.	970,616	Flying Machines	August 20, 1908
166.	930,947	Gas Purifier	February 15, 1909
167.	40,527	Design Patent for Phonograph Cabinet (his last patent)	September 13, 1909

Chapter 54

12 Strange Patented American Inventions

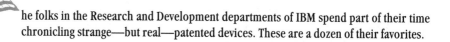

he folks in the Research and Development departments of IBM spend part of their time chronicling strange—but real—patented devices. These are a dozen of their favorites.

1. **A Drinking Vessel with Sound Effects** (U.S. Patent No. 5,536,196). This is a beer mug that makes burping sounds when you drink from it.

2. **A Device for Making Artificial Egg Yolk in the Shape of a (floppy) Disk** (U.S. Patent No. 5,547,358). Obviously, *someone* felt that there was need to be able to do this.

3. **A Hat Simulating a Fried Egg** (U.S. Patent No. 5,457,821). This is a hat that looks like a fried egg. What else can we say? (Evidentially, there is a niche for odd egg devices in the market.)

4. **A Fly Swatter with Sound Effects** (U.S. Patent No. 5,351,436). This is a fly swatter that makes a sound or plays a tune when you hit a skeeter, bee, human, or any other object.

5. **Bird Trap and Cat Feeder** (U.S. Patent No. 4,150,505). This is an outdoor trap designed to capture birds…and then feed them to a cat. The inventor thoughtfully built in a feature that allows really small birds like wrens and swallows to escape without being eaten.

6. **The Greenhouse Helmet** (U.S. Patent No. 4,605,000). We all know that it's a fact that the oxygen given off by plants is beneficial to humans. (This is why having many plants in the home is encouraged.) This invention goes one step further—it is a helmet with plants growing in it. The helmet fits over a person's head and allows him or her to breathe in the beneficial oxygen…without having to share it with anyone else in the house.

7. **A Necktie Tying Aid Gauge** (U.S. Patent No. 5,505,002). This is a device for men who can never get the two ends of their tie to hang at the right length. It also allows the user to choose the size of the knot. (What's next? A template to make sure the buttons of your shirt are all lined up correctly?)

8. **Pneumatic Shoe Lacing Apparatus** (U.S. Patent No. 5,205,055). Power laces?! POWER LACES?! Didn't I see this in one of the *Back to the Future* movies?

9. **Earthquake Sensor and Nightlight** (U.S. Patent No. 4,978,948). This is a nightlight that registers the vibrations of earthquake. (It would seem to me that if you feel an earthquake, you're going to be out of bed before your nightlight will have a chance to tell you about it.)

10. **Graffiti Prevention Apparatus** (U.S. Patent No. 5,675,18). This device repels spray paint and makes it fly back at the graffiti artist. Fleeing is recommended following its application, unless you're a performance artist.

11. **A Gravity-Powered Shoe Air Conditioner** (U.S. Patent No. 5,375,430). This is a shoe with a compressor-type cooling system in its heel.

12. **Flushable Vehicle Spittoon** (U.S. Patent No. 4,989,275). This device allows you to spit while driving and have it drain out at the back of the car.

Chapter 55

The Religious Affiliations of U.S. Presidents

merica has, to date, never had an atheist for president. Some of our presidents were somewhat "casual" about officially joining (or even attending) any one church. However, all our chief executives professed a faith in a higher power...and most manifested a spiritual side. Here is a list of the religious denominations attributed to the presidents.

1. **George Washington**: Episcopalian.
2. **John Adams**: Unitarian Congregationalist.
3. **Thomas Jefferson**: Deist, but grew up Episcopalian.
4. **James Madison**: Episcopalian.
5. **James Monroe**: Episcopalian.
6. **John Quincy Adams**: Unitarian Congregationalist.
7. **Andrew Jackson**: Presbyterian.
8. **Martin Van Buren**: Dutch Reformed.
9. **William Henry Harrison**: Episcopalian.
10. **John Tyler**: Episcopalian.
11. **James K. Polk**: Presbyterian and Methodist.
12. **Zachary Taylor**: Episcopalian.
13. **Millard Fillmore**: Unitarian.
14. **Franklin Pierce**: Episcopalian.
15. **James Buchanan**: Presbyterian.
16. **Abraham Lincoln**: Baptist (although never baptized) and Presbyterian (he unofficially attended services).
17. **Andrew Johnson**: Methodist, Baptist, and Roman Catholic (all unofficial attendance of services—Johnson did not belong to any one church).
18. **Ulysses S. Grant**: Methodist.
19. **Rutherford B. Hayes**: Presbyterian (baptized), Episcopal (attended services), and Methodist (attended services after marriage).
20. **James A. Garfield**: Disciples of Christ.

photo/Washington National Cathedral

The Washington National Cathedral (Episcopal) in Washington D.C.

21. **Chester A. Arthur**: Episcopalian.
22. **Grover Cleveland**: Presbyterian.
23. **Benjamin Harrison**: Presbyterian.
24. **Grover Cleveland**: Presbyterian.
25. **William McKinley**: Methodist.
26. **Theodore Roosevelt**: Dutch Reformed.
27. **William Howard Taft**: Unitarian.
28. **Woodrow Wilson**: Presbyterian.
29. **Warren G. Harding**: Baptist.
30. **Calvin Coolidge**: Congregationalist.
31. **Herbert Hoover**: Quaker.
32. **Franklin D. Roosevelt**: Episcopalian.
33. **Harry S Truman**: Baptist.
34. **Dwight D. Eisenhower**: Presbyterian.
35. **John F. Kennedy**: Roman Catholic.
36. **Lyndon B. Johnson**: Disciples of Christ.
37. **Richard M. Nixon**: Quaker.
38. **Gerald R. Ford**: Episcopalian.
39. **Jimmy Carter**: Baptist.
40. **Ronald Reagan**: Disciples of Christ and Presbyterian.
41. **George Bush**: Episcopalian.
42. **Bill Clinton**: Southern Baptist.

Chapter 56

The Last Words of **20** U.S. Presidents

ometimes the last words of a dying president were not recorded. Or in some cases, the president was in a coma or otherwise unconscious and did not utter a final declaration before expiring. This chapter looks at the witnessed and recorded last words of 20 U.S. presidents. If a president does not appear on this list, there were no final words recorded.

There is a simple, yet profound poetry in some of these final words. (Footnotes explain some of the more cryptic utterances.)

* **George Washington** (first president): "I am just going. Have me decently buried and do not let my body be put into a vault in less than two days after I am dead. Do you understand me? 'Tis well." December 14, 1799, sometime after 10 p.m.

* **John Adams** (second president): "Thomas Jefferson still survives."[1] July 4, 1826, around 6 p.m.

* **Thomas Jefferson** (third president): "Is it the Fourth?" July 4, 1826, 12:50 p.m.

* **James Madison** (fourth president): "Nothing more than a change of *mind*, my dear." June 28, 1836, sometime after 6 a.m.

* **John Quincy Adams** (sixth president): "This is the end of earth," followed by either, "but I am composed" or "I am content." February 23, 1848, 7:20 p.m.

* **Andrew Jackson** (seventh president): "Oh, do not cry. Be good children, and we shall all meet in Heaven." June 8, 1845, around 6 p.m.

* **William Henry Harrison** (ninth president): "I wish you to understand the true principles of the government. I wish them carried out. I ask nothing more." April 4, 1841, 12:30 a.m.

* **John Tyler** (10th president): "Doctor, I am going. Perhaps it is best." January 18, 1862, 12:15 a.m.

* **Zachary Taylor** (12th president): "I am about to die. I expect the summons very soon. I have tried to discharge my duties faithfully. I regret nothing, but I am sorry that I am about to leave my friends." July 9, 1850, 10:35 a.m.

* **Abraham Lincoln** (16th president): Mary Lincoln was apparently uncertain about her husband's last words, spoken just before Booth's fatal shot rang out 10:13 p.m. on April

14, 1865. One account has her asking him, "What will Miss Harris think of my hanging on to you so?" to which Lincoln replied, "She won't think anything about it." (Clara Harris, along with her fiancé, Major Henry Rathbone, were the Lincoln's guests in the presidential box that fateful night.) Another account has Lincoln saying to his wife, "How I should like to visit Jerusalem sometime." It is likely that one of these accounts are true, although it is a pity that Mrs. Lincoln could not remember what the president's final words actually were. The mortally wounded Lincoln did not utter another word and died at 7:22 a.m.

⭑ **Ulysses S. Grant** (18th president): "Water." July 23, 1885, approximately 8 a.m.

⭑ **Rutherford B. Hayes** (19th president): "I know that I am going where Lucy is."[2] January 17, 1893, 11 p.m.

⭑ **James A. Garfield** (20th president): "Swaim, can't you stop this? Oh, Swaim!"[3] July 2, 1881, 9:30 a.m. (assassinated).

⭑ **Grover Cleveland** (22nd and 24th president): "I have tried so hard to do right." June 24, 1908, 8:40 p.m.

⭑ **William McKinley** (25th president): "Goodbye. Goodbye to all. It is God's will. His will, not ours, be done." September 6, 1901, 4:07 p.m.

⭑ **Theodore Roosevelt** (26th president): "Please put out the light." January 6, 1919, shortly after 4 a.m.

⭑ **Woodrow Wilson** (28th president): "I am a broken piece of machinery. When the machinery is broken...I am ready." February 3, 1924, 11:15 a.m.

⭑ **Warren G. Harding** (29th president): "That's good. Go on, read some more."[4] August 2, 1923, 7:23 p.m.

⭑ **Franklin D. Roosevelt** (32nd president): "I have a terrific headache."[5] April 12, 1945, 3:35 p.m.

⭑ **Dwight D. Eisenhower** (34th president): "I want to go, God take me." March 28, 1969, 12:35 p.m.

⭑ **John F. Kennedy** (35th president): "That is very obvious."[6] November 22, 1963, 12:30 p.m. (assassinated).

[1]In one of most astonishing coincidences of American history, John Adams and Thomas Jefferson, the two signers of the Declaration of Independence to become U.S. presidents, both died on the same day, July 4, 1826. This was the 50th anniversary of the signing of the Declaration of Independence. Ironically, when Adams uttered his final declaration, he did not know that Jefferson had died about five hours earlier.

[2]Lucy was President Hayes' deceased wife.

[3]Swaim was President Garfield's physician. Garfield was asking him if he could stop the pain he was suffering.

[4]Mrs. Harding was reading aloud an article to the president titled "A Calm View of a Calm Man" from *The Saturday Evening Post*. The article was very positive and complimentary toward Harding.

[5]When he uttered this, FDR had suffered what would ultimately be a fatal cerebral hemorrhage.

[6]JFK said this in response to a comment Mrs. Connally (the Texas governor's wife) said to the president. "Mr. President," she remarked, "you can't say Dallas doesn't love you."

Chapter 57

The Causes of Death of 36 U.S. Presidents

"Only those are fit to live who do not fear to die; and none are fit to die who have shrunk from the joy of life and the duty of life. Both life and death are parts of the same Great Adventure."

—Theodore Roosevelt, 1918

"Everybody is headed for the same place...on the same train, and under the same engineer."

—Harry S Truman

1. GEORGE WASHINGTON (FIRST PRESIDENT)

Died December 14, 1799; pneumonia.

Washington had gone horseback riding in cold, snowy weather and the following day he complained of a sore throat. This was the beginning of his demise. He was initially diagnosed as suffering from inflammatory quinsy, an inflammation of the tonsils often marked by abscesses. His condition was gravely aggravated by his doctors' "treatments": They bled him with leeches four separate times and raised blisters on his throat and legs as a counterirritant.

2. JOHN ADAMS (SECOND PRESIDENT)

Died July 4, 1826; heart failure and pneumonia.

Adams's death culminated a period of deterioration that confined him to his home. His death prevented him from attending the celebration marking the 50th anniversary of the formation of the United States.

3. THOMAS JEFFERSON (THIRD PRESIDENT)

Died July 4, 1826; complications (probably heart failure) from rheumatism, an enlarged prostate (possibly cancerous), and chronic diarrhea.

Jefferson's final days were spent bedridden and in tremendous pain. To alleviate some of the pain, he took the opium-based drug laudanum. Like Adams, Jefferson was too sick to attend the nation's 50th birthday party in Washington.

4. JAMES MADISON (FOURTH PRESIDENT)

Died June 28, 1836; heart failure, with complications from rheumatism and liver problems and/or gall bladder attacks.

Madison was so sick in 1836 that he spent the six months of the last year of his life suffering in bed. He was not able to survive to the Fourth of July.

5. JAMES MONROE (FIFTH PRESIDENT)

Died July 4, 1831; heart failure with possible tuberculosis.

In one of those incredible historical coincidences, Monroe was the third of the first five U.S. presidents to die on the Fourth of July.

6. JOHN QUINCY ADAMS (SIXTH PRESIDENT)

Died February 23, 1848; stroke.

Adams had survived one stroke in 1846. But a second stroke, suffered in February 1848 while Adams was working during a session of Congress, put him into a coma and ultimately killed him two days later.

7. ANDREW JACKSON (SEVENTH PRESIDENT)

Died June 8, 1845; Heart failure caused by tuberculosis, dropsy (a pathological accumulation of diluted lymph in body tissues and cavities), and chronic diarrhea.

Jackson died six days after doctors performed an operation to drain fluid from his abdomen.

8. MARTIN VAN BUREN (EIGHTH PRESIDENT)

Died July 24, 1862; heart failure caused by complications from chronic bronchial asthma.

Van Buren's funeral procession consisted of 80 carriages, yet no bells tolled for the departed president. Van Buren had left specific instructions that he did not want any bells to chime at his funeral.

9. WILLIAM HENRY HARRISON (NINTH PRESIDENT)*

Died April 4, 1841; heart failure caused by complications from pneumonia, initially diagnosed by his doctors as "bilious pleurisy."

The president insisted on giving his one hour and 40-minute inaugural address outside in poor weather without wearing a coat or hat. Following this, he was caught in a cold downpour and caught a cold. The cold progressively worsened and ultimately killed him. Harrison's administration – all 32 days of it—was the shortest in U.S. history.

10. JOHN TYLER (10TH PRESIDENT)

Died January 18, 1862; heart failure from gall bladder and/or liver problems and bronchitis.

At the time of his death, Tyler had recently been elected to the Confederate House of Representatives (16 years after his presidential administration ended) but died before taking his seat in the legislature.

11. James K. Polk (11th President)

Died June 5, 1849; cholera (An acute, infectious, often epidemic disease characterized by watery diarrhea, vomiting, cramps, and suppression of urine).

Polk died a mere three months after retiring from the presidency.

12. Zachary Taylor (12th President)

Died July 9, 1850; systemic failure and complications caused by heat stroke.

A heavily dressed Taylor attended Fourth of July festivities under a blazing sun, followed by a walk in the direct sun. Upon his return to the White House, he consumed a large bowl of cherries and iced milk, both of which were dangerous to eat in Washington during the summer, due to the city's inadequate food sanitation capabilities. Taylor developed terrible cramps and over the next few days suffered from severe diarrhea, vomiting, and coughing up of green bile. His doctors' diagnoses included cholera morbus, bilious fever, and typhoid fever. Taylor's body could not take the repeated and relentless assault on his bodily systems and he died on the 9th, five days after his day in the sun.

In 1991, Taylor's body was exhumed and examined because there was always the suspicion among some historians that Taylor had been poisoned. Scientists examined Taylor's corpse for higher-than-normal traces of arsenic. The arsenic levels in his body, while consistent with the amount sometimes found in cherries, were hundreds of times smaller than they would have been if he was poisoned.

13. Millard Fillmore (13th President)

Died March 8, 1874; stroke.

Fillmore suffered a stroke on February 13, 1874 that left his left side paralyzed but which he survived. However, a second stroke two weeks later paralyzed his throat muscles and ultimately killed him.

14. Franklin Pierce (14th President)

Died October 8, 1869; complications and heart failure caused by chronic, severe inflammation of the stomach from years of alcohol abuse, compounded by dropsy.

15. James Buchanan (15th President)

Died June 1, 1868; pneumonia and pericarditis (inflammation of the lining of the heart) caused by chronic rheumatic gout, and chronic dysentery, both of which severely compromised his immune system.

16. Abraham Lincoln (16th President)*

Died April 15, 1865; assassinated.

Lincoln was shot in the head on April 14, 1865 and never regained consciousness. He died the following day.

17. Andrew Johnson (17th President)

Died July 31, 1875; two strokes, possibly complicated by contracting cholera a couple of years earlier.

When Johnson suffered the first of the two strokes that eventually killed him, he refused to allow doctors or clergy to be called.

18. ULYSSES S. GRANT (18TH PRESIDENT)

Died July 23, 1885; cancer of the tongue and throat.

Grant's lifelong smoking habit caused the tongue and throat cancer that ultimately killed him. In his final days, the retired president became addicted to the cocaine that doctors were using to swab his throat. Eventually, he needed regular morphine injections for the intractable pain.

19. RUTHERFORD B. HAYES (19TH PRESIDENT)

Died January 17, 1893; heart failure.

As was the case with President Harrison, Hayes's death may have been hastened by catching a cold and refusing to rest.

20. JAMES A. GARFIELD (20TH PRESIDENT)*

Died September 19, 1881; assassinated.

Garfield was shot on July 2, 1881. Following several surgeries (involving physicians using bare hands and unsterilized instruments) he died of blood poisoning a little over two months after being shot.

21. CHESTER A. ARTHUR (21ST PRESIDENT)

Died November 18, 1886; a stroke, probably caused by renal failure from Bright's disease, a fatal kidney ailment.

When Arthur knew that he was dying, he ordered his personal papers burned. (See Richard Nixon.)

22. GROVER CLEVELAND (22ND AND 24TH PRESIDENT)

Died June 24, 1908; heart failure caused by complications from severe rheumatism, chronic nephritis, and chronic gastritis.

In his final months, Cleveland used a pump on himself to drain his stomach in an attempt to get some relief from his crippling abdominal pains.

23. BENJAMIN HARRISON (23RD PRESIDENT)

Died March 13, 1901; pneumonia, caused by the flu.

Harrison's doctors tried treating the retired president with inhalation therapy but he deteriorated and died a few weeks after contracting the flu.

24. WILLIAM McKINLEY (25TH PRESIDENT)*

Died September 14, 1901; assassinated.

McKinley was shot in the pancreas on September 6, 1901. He died eight days later from systemic failure caused by gangrene from the infected bullet holes and bullet path.

25. THEODORE ROOSEVELT (26TH PRESIDENT)

Died January 6, 1919; coronary embolism, complicated by chronic inflammatory rheumatism, and recurring infections, including leg and ear.

Roosevelt suffered the embolism in his sleep and died without awakening.

26. WILLIAM HOWARD TAFT (27TH PRESIDENT)

Died March 8, 1930; heart failure caused by arteriosclerotic heart disease, high blood pressure, and chronic bladder inflammation.

Taft was serving as Chief Justice of the Supreme Court at the time of his death. (Taft was the only U.S. president to also serve as chief justice.)

27. WOODROW WILSON (28TH PRESIDENT)

Died February 3, 1924; stroke, complicated by acute asthma.

It is believed that Wilson's asthma was caused by the influenza he contracted during the devastating 1918 flu epidemic in America.

28. WARREN HARDING (29TH PRESIDENT)*

Died August 2, 1923; stroke, caused by high blood pressure and an enlarged heart, and complicated by pneumonia.

Harding was on an arduous tour of America dubbed the "Voyage of Understanding" (a trip to explain his policies to the masses) when he suffered his fatal stroke.

29. CALVIN COOLIDGE (30TH PRESIDENT)

Died January 5, 1933; coronary thrombosis (heart failure caused by a blood clot in the heart).

For months before his death, Coolidge had complained of the classic symptoms of heart disease (such as breathlessness, fatigue, weakness, and abdominal symptoms). They were attributed to indigestion, but they were probably angina pains.

30. HERBERT HOOVER (31ST PRESIDENT)

Died October 20, 1964; massive internal bleeding caused by gastrointestinal hemorrhages secondary to intestinal cancer.

Hoover was 90 years old when he died. He was 84-years-old when he underwent a surgical procedure for the first time ever (an operation to remove a diseased gall bladder).

THE 10 LIKELIEST REASONS AN AMERICAN WILL VISIT AN EMERGENCY ROOM

1. Stomach and abdominal pain, stomach cramps, stomach spasms.
2. Chest pain and related symptoms.
3. Fever.
4. Headache, pain in the head.
5. Injury of an upper extremity (collar bone, shoulder, arm, elbow, wrist, etc.).
6. Shortness of breath.
7. Cough.
8. Back symptoms.
9. Pain (site not specific).
10. Throat symptoms.

(*Source:* U.S. Department of Health and Human Services)

photo/Library of Congress

JFK's coffin lying in state in the Capitol Rotunda.

31. FRANKLIN D. ROOSEVELT (32ND PRESIDENT)*

Died April 12, 1945; cerebral hemorrhage caused by high blood pressure and arteriosclerosis.

Roosevelt's arteries were so clogged that his morticians had a great deal of trouble embalming his body. The embalming fluid would not flow through FDR's heavily blocked arteries.

32. HARRY S TRUMAN (33RD PRESIDENT)

Died December 26, 1972; systemic failure caused by heart failure complicated by lung congestion and kidney malfunction.

Truman was one of the few presidents to die in a hospital.

33. DWIGHT D. EISENHOWER (34TH PRESIDENT)

Died March 28, 1969; congestive heart failure.

Eisenhower suffered a heart attack while president, and many more attacks during his retirement. As you may know, each heart attack kills a section of the heart muscle, resulting in the heart growing less efficient following each subsequent attack. Eisenhower's heart could not handle the pneumonia he developed following a minor operation in early 1969, which is what ultimately killed him.

34. JOHN F. KENNEDY (35TH PRESIDENT)*

Died November 22, 1963; assassinated.

Kennedy was shot through the throat and in the head while riding in a motorcade in Dallas. He never regained consciousness and died from his wounds shortly after the shooting.

35. LYNDON B. JOHNSON (36TH PRESIDENT)

Died January 22, 1973; Cardiac arrest caused by arteriosclerosis.

The heart attack that killed LBJ woke him from a nap. He managed to call one of his Secret Service agents for help, but he died on the way to the hospital.

36. RICHARD M. NIXON (37TH PRESIDENT)

Died April 22, 1994; Stroke.

As he was the only U. S president to resign his office, Nixon left very specific instructions regarding the disposition of his personal papers. In his will he wrote:

> "I direct my executors to collect and destroy my 'personal diaries.' (T)he property consti-
> tuting my 'personal diaries' shall be subject to the following restrictions: At no time shall my
> executors be allowed to make public, publish, sell, or make available to any individual
> other than my executor...the contents or any part or all of my 'personal diaries' and,
> provided further, that my executors shall...destroy all of my 'personal diaries.' My 'personal
> diaries' shall be defined as any notes, tapes, transcribed notes, folders, binders, or books
> that are owned by me or to which I may be entitled under a judgment of law including, but
> not limited to, folders, binders, or books labeled as Richard Nixon's Diaries, Diary Notes, or
> labeled just by dates, that may contain my daily, weekly or monthly activities, thoughts, or
> plans. The determination of my executors as to what property is included in this bequest
> shall be conclusive and binding upon all parties interested in my estate; however, it is my
> wish that my executors consult with my surviving daughters and/or my office staff in making
> this determination."

*Died in office

Chapter 58

51 State Flowers

It seems that states are not picky when it comes to flower exclusivity. The District of Columbia, Georgia, Iowa, New York, and North Dakota all have a rose as their state flower. North Carolina and Virginia use the dogwood. Wisconsin, Illinois, New Jersey, and Rhode Island all use the violet. Kentucky and Nebraska both have the goldenrod as their state flower. Washington and West Virginia both use rhododendron. Connecticut and Pennsylvania both use the mountain laurel.

1. **Alabama:** Camellia.
2. **Alaska:** Forget-me-not.
3. **Arizona:** Saguaro Cactus.
4. **Arkansas:** Apple Blossom.
5. **California:** Golden Poppy.
6. **Colorado:** Columbine.
7. **Connecticut:** Mountain Laurel.
8. **Delaware:** Peach Blossom.
9. **District of Columbia:** American Beauty Rose.
10. **Florida:** Orange Blossom.
11. **Georgia:** Cherokee Rose.
12. **Hawaii:** Yellow Hibiscus.
13. **Idaho:** Syringa.
14. **Illinois:** Native Violet.
15. **Indiana:** Peony.
16. **Iowa:** Wild Rose.
17. **Kansas:** Native Sunflower.
18. **Kentucky:** Goldenrod.
19. **Louisiana:** Magnolia.
20. **Maine:** White Pine Cone and Tassel.
21. **Maryland:** Black-eyed Susan.
22. **Massachusetts:** Mayflower.
23. **Michigan:** Apple Blossom.
24. **Minnesota:** Showy Lady's Slipper.
25. **Mississippi:** Magnolia.
26. **Missouri:** Hawthorn.
27. **Montana:** Bitteroot.
28. **Nebraska:** Goldenrod.
29. **Nevada:** Sagebrush.
30. **New Hampshire:** Purple Lilac.
31. **New Jersey:** Purple Violet.
32. **New Mexico:** Yucca.
33. **New York:** Rose.
34. **North Carolina:** Dogwood.
35. **North Dakota:** Wild Prairie Rose.
36. **Ohio:** Scarlet Carnation.
37. **Oklahoma:** Mistletoe.
38. **Oregon:** Oregon Grape.
39. **Pennsylvania:** Mountain Laurel.
40. **Rhode Island:** Violet.
41. **South Carolina:** Yellow Jessamine.
42. **South Dakota:** Pasque Flower.
43. **Tennessee:** Iris.
44. **Texas:** Bluebonnet.
45. **Utah:** Sego Lily.
46. **Vermont:** Red Clover.
47. **Virginia:** Dogwood.
48. **Washington:** Rhododendron.
49. **West Virginia:** Big Rhododendron.
50. **Wisconsin:** Wood Violet.
51. **Wyoming:** Indian Paintbrush.

Chapter 59

36 Presidential Burial Places

Only two presidents are buried in Arlington National Cemetery: John F. Kennedy and William Howard Taft. Seven presidents are buried in New York, five are buried in Ohio, four are buried in Virginia, and three are buried in Tennessee. Woodrow Wilson is the only president interred in Washington National Cathedral.

* **George Washington**: Mt. Vernon, Va.
* **John Adams**: Quincy, Mass.
* **Thomas Jefferson**: Charlottesville, Va.
* **James Madison**: Montpelier Station, Vt.
* **James Monroe**: Richmond, Va.
* **John Quincy Adams**: Quincy, Mass.
* **Andrew Jackson**: Nashville, Tenn.
* **Martin Van Buren**: Kinderhook, N.Y.
* **William Henry Harrison**: North Bend, Ohio.
* **John Tyler**: Richmond, Va.
* **James K. Polk**: Nashville, Tenn.
* **Zachary Taylor**: Louisville, Ky.
* **Millard Fillmore**: Buffalo, N.Y.
* **Franklin Pierce**: Concord, N.H.
* **James Buchanan**: Lancaster, Penn.
* **Abraham Lincoln**: Springfield, Ill.
* **Andrew Johnson**: Greeneville, Tenn.
* **Ulysses S. Grant**: New York, N.Y.
* **Rutherford B. Hayes**: Fremont, Ohio.
* **James A. Garfield**: Cleveland, Ohio.
* **Chester A. Arthur**: Albany, N.Y.

* **Grover Cleveland**: Princeton, N.J.
* **Benjamin Harrison**: Indianapolis, Ind.
* **William McKinley**: Canton, Ohio.
* **Theodore Roosevelt**: Oyster Bay, N.Y.
* **William Howard Taft**: Arlington National Cemetery.
* **Woodrow Wilson**: Washington National Cathedral.
* **Warren G. Harding**: Marion, Ohio.
* **Calvin Coolidge**: Plymouth, Vt.
* **Herbert C. Hoover**: West Branch, Iowa.
* **Franklin D. Roosevelt**: Hyde Park, N.Y.
* **Harry S Truman**: Independence, Miss.
* **Dwight D. Eisenhower**: Abilene, Kans.
* **John F. Kennedy**: Arlington National Cemetery.
* **Lyndon B. Johnson**: Johnson City, Tex.
* **Richard M. Nixon**: Yorba Linda, Calif.

Chapter 60

14 Vice Presidents Who Became President

"My God, this is a hell of a job!"

—President Warren Harding, said to William Allen White when Harding was in office.

When John Adams was vice president to George Washington, he confided in a letter to a friend that he believed that "My country has in its wisdom contrived for me the most insignificant office that ever the invention of man contrived or his imagination conceived."

The vice president of the United States has an odd job: He is, as the Constitution has decreed and history has proven, a heartbeat away from the Presidency. Yet, the vice president really doesn't have all that much to do when he is in office.

But a handful of vice presidents—six, in fact—have actually been elected president on their own. In these cases, the office of the vice president was viewed as an excellent training ground for becoming president. But in nine cases, the vice president was elevated to president because the president died in office, was assassinated, or in one ignoble case, resigned.

This list looks at those 15 men who served both as vice president and as president.

1. JOHN ADAMS

★ **Vice president to:** George Washington.
★ **Means of advancement:** Elected.

2. THOMAS JEFFERSON

★ **Vice president to:** John Adams.
★ **Means of advancement:** Elected.

3. MARTIN VAN BUREN

★ **Vice president to:** Andrew Jackson.
★ **Means of advancement:** Elected.

4. JOHN TYLER

★ **Vice president to:** William Henry Harrison.
★ **Means of advancement:** Harrison died in office.

5. MILLARD FILLMORE

★ **Vice president to:** Zachary Taylor.
★ **Means of advancement:** Taylor died in office.

6. ANDREW JOHNSON

★ **Vice president to:** Abraham Lincoln.
★ **Means of advancement:** Lincoln was assassinated.

7. CHESTER A. ARTHUR

★ **Vice president to:** James Garfield.
★ **Means of advancement:** Garfield was assassinated.

8. THEODORE ROOSEVELT

★ **Vice president to:** William McKinley.
★ **Means of advancement:** McKinley was assassinated.

9. CALVIN COOLIDGE

★ **Vice president to:** Warren Harding.
★ **Means of advancement:** Harding died in office.

10. HARRY S TRUMAN

★ **Vice president to:** Franklin D. Roosevelt.
★ **Means of advancement:** Roosevelt died in office.

11. RICHARD NIXON

★ **Vice president to:** Dwight D. Eisenhower.
★ **Means of advancement:** Elected[1].

12. LYNDON B. JOHNSON

★ **Vice president to:** John F. Kennedy.
★ **Means of advancement:** Kennedy was assassinated.

13. GERALD FORD

★ **Vice president to:** Richard Nixon.
★ **Means of advancement:** Nixon resigned the presidency.

14. GEORGE BUSH

★ **Vice president to:** Ronald Reagan.
★ **Means of advancement:** Elected.

---

[1]Nixon was vice president to Eisenhower from 1953-1961, but was not elected president until 1968.

Chapter 61

Presidential Libraries, Museums, and National Archives

The presidential library system is made up of 10 libraries, each of which also contains a museum. (The Nixon Library is privately funded.) President Clinton's library and museum are in the planning stages and will open sometime after his Administration ends in 2001.

The presidential libraries and museums are vast repositories of papers and other historical materials from the administrations and lives of 10 presidents. They are gold mines of information for American citizens and people from all over the world who want to learn more about our chief executives, along with their terms in the White House.

The combined holdings of these 10 libraries are more than 300 million pages of textual materials; 7 million photographs; 14.5 million feet of motion picture films; 83,000 hours of disc, audiotape, and videotape recordings; and 350,000 museum objects.

This chapter looks at these unique institutions and provides some useful information about what each has to offer, plus contact details and other relevant information.

1. THE HERBERT HOOVER LIBRARY AND MUSEUM

211 Parkside Drive
P.O. Box 488
West Branch, IA 52358-0488
Phone: 319-643-5301
Fax: 319-643-5825
E-mail: *library@hoover.nara.gov*
Web site: *www.hoover.nara.gov*
Presidency: 1929-1933.
Library Dedication Date: August 1962.
Nearby: Hoover's birthplace and gravesite.

From the Library's Web site: "The Herbert Hoover Presidential Library and Museum was opened to the public on August 10, 1962, Mr. Hoover's 88th birthday. In the years since, nearly 3 million visitors have toured the museum and more than 2,200 researchers from every state in the union and a dozen foreign countries have utilized the library's 7 million pages of documentary holdings."

The library has extensive holdings of President Hoover's papers and other materials from his presidency. The museum has several permanent gallery exhibits chronicling Herbert Hoover's life, with such titles as: "Years of Adventure," "The Humanitarian Years," "The Roaring Twenties," "The Wonder Boy," "The Logical Candidate," "The Great Depression," "From Hero to Scapegoat," "An Uncommon Woman," and "Counselor to the Republic."

2. THE FRANKLIN D. ROOSEVELT LIBRARY AND MUSEUM

511 Albany Post Road
Hyde Park, NY 12538-1999
Phone: 914-229-8114
          800-FDR-VISIT
Fax: 914-229-0872
E-mail: *library@roosevelt.nara.gov*
Web site: *www.academic.marist.edu/fdr*
Presidency: 1933-1945.
Library Dedication Date: June 1941.
Nearby: Roosevelt's birthplace, home, and gravesite.

FDR's library is the only presidential library to actually have been used by a sitting president. FDR personally planned his library while he was in his second term (of an unprecedented and never repeated four terms as president). He actually personally designed the stone Dutch colonial building. FDR placed some of the initial exhibits in the library. During his third and fourth terms he used the library as an office away from the White House. He held conferences with world leaders at the library and even gave four of his fireside chats from there. The library's holdings include 44,000 of FDR's books, large collections of manuscripts, photographs, prints, recordings, and films.

3. THE HARRY S TRUMAN LIBRARY AND MUSEUM

500 West U.S. Highway 24
Independence, MO 64050-1798
Phone: 1-800-833-1225, 816-833-1400
Fax: 816-833-4368
E-mail: *library@truman.nara.gov*
Web site: *www.trumanlibrary.org*
Presidency: 1945-1953.
Library Dedication Date: July 1957.
Nearby: Truman's home and gravesite.

The Truman library has a great many holdings on a wide range of 20th century subjects, including: the Korean War, Jewish refugees, the recognition of Israel and United States/Israeli relations, the North Atlantic Treaty Organization (NATO), Saudi Arabia, desegregation of the armed forces, the four point program of technical assistance to the developing nations of the world, World War II, the decision to drop the atomic bomb, the Marshall Plan, and the Truman Doctrine.

The popular Truman museum is equally impressive with a fascinating range of exhibits and galleries, including such recent highlights as: "The Truman Chryslers," "NATO at 50," "Dear Bess: Love Letters from the President," "Looking Back at the American Century," and "First Families: An Intimate Portrait from the Kennedys to the Clintons." The Truman Library and Museum's Web site is one of the best on the Internet. It has won many awards and receives an astonishing 500,000 hits each month.

4. THE DWIGHT D. EISENHOWER LIBRARY AND EISENHOWER CENTER

200 SE 4th Street
Abilene, KS 67410-2900
Phone: 785-263-4751
Fax: 785-263-4218
E-mail: *library@eisenhower.nara.gov*
Web site: *www.eisenhower.utexas.edu*
Presidency: 1953-1961.
Library Dedication Date: May 1962.
Nearby: Eisenhower's boyhood home and gravesite.

The Eisenhower Library and Center consists of five buildings on 22 acres. It includes the Eisenhower family home, the Eisenhower Museum, the Eisenhower Library, the Eisenhower Place of Meditation (which is the final resting place of Dwight D. Eisenhower, Mamie Eisenhower, and their son Dwight Doud Eisenhower), the visitors center, as well as the 11-foot tall "Ike Statue."

5. THE JOHN FITZGERALD KENNEDY LIBRARY

Columbia Point
Boston, MA 02125-3398
Phone: 617-929-4500
Group Tour Info: 617-929-4523
Fax: 617-929-4538
E-mail: *library@kennedy.nara.gov*
Web site: *www.cs.umb.edu/jfklibrary/museum.htm*
Presidency: 1961-1963.
Library Dedication Date: October 1979.
Nearby: Kennedy's birthplace.

The JFK Library, designed by I.M. Pei, presents "25 dramatic exhibits drawing on rare film and television footage, personal family keepsakes and treasures from the White House." The library also has three theaters for video presentations. An exhibit in honor of John F. Kennedy Jr. was added following John Jr.'s death in July 1999. There is a museum store and a museum cafe on the premises as well.

6. THE LYNDON BAINES JOHNSON LIBRARY AND MUSEUM

2313 Red River Street
Austin, TX 78705-5702
Phone: 512-482-5279
Fax: 512-478-9104
E-mail: *library@johnson.nara.gov*
Web site: *www.lbjlib/utexas.edu*
Presidency: 1963-1969.
Library Dedication Date: May 1971.
Nearby: Johnson's birthplace and ranch.

The LBJ Library is located on the campus of the University of Texas at Austin. It consists of the library itself, which houses 35,000,000 pages of historical documents (utilized today primarily by scholars, researchers, writers, and students), as well as the museum, which is open to the public year-round. It provides many historical and cultural exhibits. Some recent exhibits include: "The Early Years," "Road to the Presidency," "Presidential Limousine," "Family Album," "Foreign Affairs," "To the Moon and Beyond," "The Humor of LBJ," "The Johnson Style," "American Political Memorabilia," and "The First Lady Theater." The library provides a 122-page trade paperback catalog listing many of the library's holdings. The museum store also publishes a full-color catalog of Johnson memorabilia available for sale, including mugs, postcards, books, models, tote bags, medallions, sculptures, CDs, bookends, and jigsaw puzzles.

7. THE RICHARD NIXON LIBRARY AND BIRTHPLACE

18011 Yorba Linda Boulevard
Yorba Linda, CA 92886-3949
Phone: 714-993-3393
Fax: 714-528-9554
Web site: *www.nixonfoundation.org*
Presidency: 1969-1974.
Library Dedication Date: July 1990.

The Richard Nixon Library and Birthplace is described as "the most active, innovative, and visited presidential center in America." His is the only presidential center built and operated entirely without federal funds. On their Web site, they tell us that the center "is a privately supported, nonprofit institution dedicated to educating the public about the life and times of the 37th president and encouraging interest in history, government, and public affairs." Also, "the nine acre library and birthplace is a three-dimensional walk-through memoir featuring a 52,000 square foot museum, 22 high-tech galleries, movie and interactive video theaters, the spectacular First Lady's Garden, the president's faithfully restored 1910's birthplace, and the flower-ringed memorial sites of President and Mrs. Nixon." Some of the library's permanent exhibits include a world leaders presentation, the Structure of Peace Gallery, the Berlin Wall Freedom Presentation, the Lincoln Sitting Room, the Gowns Gallery, a domestic affairs gallery, The Watergate Gallery, and President Nixon's private study.

Also worth noting...
The Nixon Presidential Materials Staff
National Archives at College Park
8601 Adelphi Road
College Park, MD 20740-6001
Phone: 301-713-6950
Fax: 301-713-6916
E-mail: *nixon@arch2.nara.gov*
Web site: *www.nara.gov*

8A. THE GERALD R. FORD LIBRARY

1000 Beal Avenue
Ann Arbor, MI 48109-2114
Phone: 734-741-2218
Fax: 734-741-2341
E-mail: *library@fordlib.nara.gov*

Web site: *www.ford.utexas.edu*
Presidency: 1974-1977.
Library Dedication Date: April 1981.

The Ford Library holds "20 million pages of letters, memoirs, minutes, cables, plans, and reports, plus historic film, video, audio, and photo records." The library is user-friendly and is open to researchers, students, and scholars from around the world. The library's holdings are extensive and, admirably, quite balanced. Letters from schoolchildren blasting Ford for pardoning President Nixon are included in the archives and are accessible to the public.

8B. THE GERALD R. FORD MUSEUM

303 Pearl Street NW
Grand Rapids, MI 49504-5353
Phone: 616-451-9263
Fax: 616-451-9570
E-mail: *information.museum@fordmus.nara.gov*
Web site: *www.ford.utexas.edu*

The Ford Museum boasts more than 8,000 historical artifacts and items for viewing. The permanent exhibits include gifts from foreign leaders (all of which belong to the American people) including a diamond-crested gold falcon from the Sultan of Oman and a three-foot-high Waterford crystal vase from the Prime Minister of Ireland.

Other memorable exhibits include: a holographic presentation of 11 "off-limits" White House rooms; a gallery of The Ford Paint and Varnish Company from Ford's youth; a recreation of President Ford's Oval Office; an actual Vietnam-era helicopter; a State Dinner Table video exhibit, which allows you to be a guest at six different White House dinner events; a part of the original White House switchboard; an exhibit of the original Watergate burglary tools; and a Betty Ford exhibit.

9. THE JIMMY CARTER LIBRARY AND MUSEUM

441 Freedom Parkway
Atlanta, GA 30307-1406
Phone: 404-331-3942
Fax: 404-730-2215
E-mail: *library@carter.nara.gov*
Web site: *www.carterlibrary.galileo.peachnet.edu*
Presidency: 1977-1981.
Library Dedication Date: October 1986.

The library and the museum are known collectively as the Carter Presidential Center (the archives of the Jimmy Carter Library are open by appointment only). However, the museum offers a wide range of exhibits that are open to the public. These exhibits include: a reproduction of Carter's Oval Office, gifts presented to the Carters by world leaders, an interactive video "Town Meeting," a video presentation on the evolution of the presidency, a formal dinner setting from the White House, and memorabilia from President Carter's 1976 campaign. The Carter Center also houses the offices of President and Mrs. Carter's Task Force for Child Survival, the offices of Global 2000, and the Carter Center of Emory University.

For further information...

The Carter Center
Office of Public Information
One Copenhill
453 Freedom Parkway
Atlanta, GA 30307
Phone: 404-420-5117
Web site: *www.emory.edu/CARTER_CENTER*

10. THE RONALD REAGAN LIBRARY AND MUSEUM

40 Presidential Drive
Simi Valley, CA 93065-0666
Phone: 805-522-8444
Fax: 805-522-9621
E-mail: *library@reagan.nara.gov*
Web site: *www.reagan.utexas.edu*
Presidency: 1981-1989.
Library Dedication Date: November 1991.

The Reagan Library has the largest volume of holdings of all the presidential libraries—a staggering 50,000,000 pages of documents. All of the holdings are in the process of being opened and made available to the public for research. Early in 2000, I was told that approximately 3,500,000 pages—7 percent of the library's holdings—had been processed for public access. The library's staff is very helpful with in-person, phone, and mail requests for research assistance. My e-mail request for assistance was responded to with a huge packet of information, including a four-page pamphlet containing facts about Ronald Reagan, a four-page chronology of Reagan's post-presidential activities, a comprehensive Reagan timeline and presidency timeline, a Reagan bibliography, and more, (including a list of "Things Named in Honor of Ronald Reagan"). The Reagan Museum boasts a full-scale replica of Reagan's Oval Office, an interactive cabinet room, an exhibit featuring an actual piece of the Berlin Wall, as well as many exhibits that change every few months.

11. THE GEORGE BUSH LIBRARY AND MUSEUM

1000 George Bush Drive, West
College Station, TX 77482-0410
Phone: 409-260-9552
Fax: 409-260-9557
E-mail: *library@bush.nara.gov*
Web site: *www.csdl.tamu.edu/bushlib*
Presidency: 1989-1993.
Library Dedication Date: November 1997.

The Bush Library's collections include: 38,000,000 pages of official and personal papers from George Bush's life and presidency, 1,000,000 photographs, 2,500 hours of videotape, and 50,000 museum objects. The Bush Museum is 17,000 square feet of exhibits and galleries, including: films, memorabilia, a special section all about Barbara Bush, and a computer-equipped classroom for students from kindergarten through high school. Some of the larger museum exhibits include a World War II

Avenger Torpedo Bomber, a slab of the Berlin Wall, and full-scale replicas of President Bush's Camp David and Air Force One offices.

FOR FURTHER INFORMATION...

The Office of Presidential Libraries
National Archives and Records Administration
8601 Adelphi Road
College Park, MD 20740-6001
Phone: 301-713-6050
Fax: 301-713-6045

Presidential Materials Staff
National Archives and Records Administration
700 Pennsylvania Avenue NW, Room 104
Washington, DC 20408
Phone: 202-501-5700
Fax: 202-501-5709

Chapter 62

The 20 Most Prescribed Drugs in the United States

I guess you could say that how a country medicates itself paints an exceptionally vivid portrait of its people...or at least their ailments. Based on this list, it seems that the average American is nervous, depressed, in pain, has stomach and heart problems, has high cholesterol, and is hormonally out of whack. This list looks at the 20 most prescribed drugs in America in 1999.

1. **Premarin** (Estrogen): Prescribed for menopausal symptoms and postmenopausal osteoporosis.
2. **Synthroid** (Thyroid hormone replacement): Prescribed for an underactive thyroid gland.
3. **Lipitor** (Atorvastatin): Prescribed to lower total blood cholesterol levels.
4. **Prilosec** (Omeprazole): Prescribed to stop the production of stomach acid and to aid in the healing of gastrointestinal ulcers.
5. **Hydrocodone with APAP** (Narcotic-analgesic combination): Prescribed for mild to moderate pain. The hydrocodone is the narcotic ingredient in this medication and it is often combined with either acetaminophen (Vicodin, Lortab) or aspirin.
6. **Albuterol** (Bronchdilator): Prescribed for asthma and bronchospasm.
7. **Norvasc** (Amlodipine): Calcium channel blocker prescribed for angina pectoris and high blood pressure.
8. **Claritin** (Loratidine): An antihistamine prescribed for seasonal allergy relief.
9. **Trimox** (Penicillin antibiotic): Prescribed for bacterial and other types of infections.
10. **Prozac** (Fluoxetine): Prescribed for depression, bulimia, obsessive-compulsive disorder, attention-deficit disorder, anorexia, and other psychological disorders.
11. **Zoloft** (Antidepressant).
12. **Glucophage** (Diabetes drug).
13. **Lanoxin** (Heart drug).
14. **Prempro** (Synthetic hormone).
15. **Paxil** (Antidepressant).
16. **Zithromax** (Antibiotic).
17. **Zestril** (Blood-pressure lowering agent).
18. **Zocor** (Cholesterol-lowering drug).
19. **Prevacid** (Stomach-acid inhibitor)
20. **Augmentin** (Antibiotic).

(*Source:* The pharmaceutical Web site *rxlist.com*, based on more than 2.8 billion U.S. prescriptions.)

Chapter 63

153 State Web Sites and Phone Numbers

his list provides each state's toll-free tourism information phone number, its official Web site, and its tourism Web Site. Happy trails!

1. Alabama
Tourism Info: 1-800-ALABAMA
State Web site: *alaweb.asc.edu*
Tourism Web site: *www.touralabama.org*

2. Alaska
Tourism Info: 1-907-465-2010
State Web site: *www.state.ak.us*
Tourism Web site: *www.commerce.state.ak.us/ tourism*

3. Arizona
Tourism Info: 1-602-224-9896
State Web site: *www.state.az.us*
Tourism Web site: *www.arizonaguide.com*

4. Arkansas
Tourism Info: 1-800-NATURAl
State Web site: *www.state.ar.us*
Tourism Web site: *www.arkansas.com*

5. California
Tourism Info: 1-800-862-2543
State Web site: *www.stateca.us/s*
Tourism Web site: *www.gocalif.ca.gov*

6. Colorado
Tourism Info: 1-800-COLORADO
State Web site: *www.state.co.us*
Tourism Web site: *www.colorado.com*

7. Connecticut
Tourism Info: 1-800-CTBOUND
State Web site: *www.state.ct.us*
Tourism Web site: *www.state.ct.us/tourism*

8. Delaware
Tourism Info: 1-800-441-8846
State Web site: *www.state.de.us*
Tourism Web site: *www.state.de.us/tourism/ intro.htm*

9. District of Columbia
Tourism Info: 1-202-789-7000
District Web site: *www.dcpages.ari.net*
Tourism Web site: *www.washington.org*

10. Florida
Tourism Info: 1-888-7FLA-USA
State Web site: *www.state/fl.us*
Tourism Web site: *www.flausa.com*

11. Georgia
Tourism Info: 1-800-VISITGA
State Web site: *www.state.ga.us*
Tourism Web site: *www.georgia.org*

12. Hawaii
Tourism Info: 1-800-464-2924
State Web site: *www.hawaii.gov*
Tourism Web site: *www.gohawaii.com*

13. Idaho
Tourism Info: 1-800-VISIT-ID
State Web site: *www.state.id.us*
Tourism Web site: *www.visitid.org*

14. Illinois
Tourism Info: 1-800-2-CONNECT
State Web site: *www.state.il.us*
Tourism Web site: *www.enjoyillinois.com*

15. Indiana
Tourism Info: 1-800-289-6646
State Web site: *www.ai.org*
Tourism Web site: *www.state.in.us/tourism*

16. Iowa
Tourism Info: 1-800-345-IOWA
State Web site: *www.state.ia.us*
Tourism Web site: *www.state.ia.us/tourism/index.html*

17. Kansas
Tourism Info: 1-800-2KANSAS
State Web site: *www.ink.org*
Tourism Web site: *www.kansascommerce.com*

18. Kentucky
Tourism Info: 1-800-225-TRIP
State Web site: *www.state.ky.us*
Tourism Web site: *www.kentuckytourism.com*

19. Louisiana
Tourism Info: 1-800-677-4082
State Web site: *www.state.la.us*
Tourism Web site: *www.louisianatravel.com*

20. Maine
Tourism Info: 1-888-624-6345
State Web site: *www.state.me.us*
Tourism Web site: *www.visitmaine.com*

21. Maryland
Tourism Info: 1-800-543-1036
State Web site: *www.state.md.us*
Tourism Web site: *www.mdisfun.org*

22. Massachusetts
Tourism Info: 1-800-227-6277
State Web site: *www.state.ma.us*
Tourism Web site: *www.mass-vacation.com*

23. Michigan
Tourism Info: 1-888-784-7328
State Web site: *www.migove.state.mi.us*
Tourism Web site: *www.michigan.org*

24. Minnesota
Tourism Info: 1-800-657-3700
State Web site: *www.state.mn.us*
Tourism Web site: *www.dted.state.mn.us/explore/explore.html*

25. Mississippi
Tourism Info: 1-800-WARMEST
State Web site: *www.state.ms/us*
Tourism Web site: *www.decd.state.ms.us/tourism.htm*

26. Missouri
Tourism Info: 1-888-925-3875, ext.124
State Web site: *www.state.mo.us*
Tourism Web site: *www.missouritourism.org*

27. Montana
Tourism Info: 1-800-VISITMT
State Web site: *www.mt.gov*
Tourism Web site: *www.travel.mt.gov*

28. Nebraska
Tourism Info: 1-800-228-4307
State Web site: *www.state.ne.us*
Tourism Web site: *www.visitnebraska.org*

29. Nevada
Tourism Info: 1-800-638-23282
State Web site: *www.state.nv.us*
Tourism Web site: *www.travelnevada.com*

30. New Hampshire
Tourism Info: 1-800-386-4664
State Web site: *www.state.nh.us*
Tourism Web site: *www.visitnh.gov*

31. New Jersey
Tourism Info: 1-800-JERSEY7
State Web site: *www.state.nj.us*
Tourism Web site: *www.state.nj.us/travel*

32. New Mexico
Tourism Info: 1-800-545-2040 ext. 751
State Web site: *www.state.nm.us*
Tourism Web site: *www.newmexico.org*

33. New York
Tourism Info: 1-800-CALLNYS
State Web site: *www.empire.state.us*
Tourism Web site: *www.iloveny.state.ny.us*

34. North Carolina
Tourism Info: 1-800-VISITNC
State Web site: *www.state.nc.us*
Tourism Web site: *www.visitnc.com*

35. North Dakota
Tourism Info: 1-800-HELLO-ND
State Web site: *www.state.nd.us*
Tourism Web site: *www.glness.com/tourism*

36. Ohio
Tourism Info: 1-800-BUCKEYE
State Web site: *www.state.oh.us*
Tourism Web site: *www.ohiotourism.com*

37. Oklahoma
Tourism Info: 1-800-652-6552
State Web site: *www.state.ok.us*
Tourism Web site: *www.otrd.state.ok.us*

38. Oregon
Tourism Info: 1-800-547-7842
State Web site: *www.state.or.us*
Tourism Web site: *www.traveloregon.com*

39. Pennsylvania
Tourism Info: 1-800-VISITPA
State Web site: *www.state.pa.us*
Tourism Web site: *www.state.pa.us/visit*

40. Rhode Island
Tourism Info: 1-800-556-2484
State Web site: *www.state.ri.us*
Tourism Web site: *www.visitrhodeisland.com*

41. South Carolina
Tourism Info: 1-800-346-3634
State Web site: *www.state.sc.us*
Tourism Web site: *www.sccsi.com/sc*

42. South Dakota
Tourism Info: 1-800-SDAKOTA
State Web site: *www.state.sd.us*
Tourism Web site: *www.state.sd.us/tourism*

43. Tennessee
Tourism Info: 1-800-TENN200
State Web site: *www.state.tn.us*
Tourism Web site: *www.state.tn.us/tourdev*

44. Texas
Tourism Info: 1-800-8888TEX
State Web site: *www.state.tx.us*
Tourism Web site: *www.traveltex.com*

45. Utah
Tourism Info: 1-800-200-1160
State Web site: *www.state.ut.us*
Tourism Web site: *www.utah.com*

46. Vermont
Tourism Info: 1-800-VERMONT
State Web site: *www.state.vt.us*
Tourism Web site: *www.travel-vermont.com*

47. Virginia
Tourism Info: 1-800-VISITVA
State Web site: *www.state.va.us*
Tourism Web site: *www.virginia.org*

48. Washington
Tourism Info: 1-800-544-1800, ext. 101
State Web site: *access.wa.gov*
Tourism Web site: *www.tourism.wa.gov*

49. West Virginia
Tourism Info: 1-800-CALLWVA
State Web site: *www.state.wv.us*
Tourism Web site: *www.wvweb.com/www/travel_recreation*

50. Wisconsin
Tourism Info: 1-800-432-8747
State Web site: *www.state.wi.us*
Tourism Web site: *tourism.state.wi.us*

51. Wyoming
Tourism Info: 1-800-CALLWYO
State Web site: *www.state.wy.us*
Tourism Web site: *www.state.wy.us/state/tourism/tourism/html*

Chapter 64

Internet Research Web Sites

he site suggestions listed here are for learning more. Listed here are several United States government sites (Library of Congress, the White House, the Smithsonian, the Hubble Telescope, etc.), which are some of the most user-friendly and exhaustively comprehensive sites on the Web.

GENERAL U.S. INFORMATION PORTALS

FedWorld

www.fedworld.gov

This site will help you locate federal government servers, documents, and other resources.

The Federal Web Locator

www.law.vill.edu/Fed-Agency/fedwebloc.html

An extremely useful site that can help you find government Web sites, including the home pages of the Supreme Court, the Senate, and so forth.

GPO Gate

www.gpo.ucop.edu

GPO Gate is a service of the libraries of the University of California as members of the Federal Depository Library Program. The gateway provides access to the full-text databases made available by the GPO Access service of the Government Printing Office in Washington, D.C. This essential Web site can give you access to millions of pages of government documents. Some of the links accessible through GPO Gate include: The 1999 Budget of the U.S. Government, the Congressional Bills Database for the 103rd through 106th Congresses, The Congressional Directory, congressional documents, the Congressional Record, congressional Reports, The Constitution of the United States of America, and on and on.

U.S. GOVERNMENT SITES

The Library of Congress

lcweb.loc.gov/loc/libserv

The gold standard for information and research resources.

Thomas

thomas.loc.gov

Named after Thomas Jefferson, this site allows you to search congressional bills, track bills as they move through the legislative process, search for keywords in bills, monitor roll call votes, and much more. Thomas and GPO Gate put almost everything the government publishes at your fingertips.

The Library of Congress Photo Catalog

lcweb.loc.gov/rr/print/catalog.html

A searchable database of millions of images in the Library of Congress's photo archives. Many have digitial images to view; and the search engine is fast and very easy to use. A caution: Don't start browsing, you may never stop.

The White House

www.whitehouse.gov

A virtual tour and history lesson about America's most famous residence. (It can't seem to keep a tenant, though.)

The White House Briefing Room

www.whitehouse.gov/WH/html/briefroom.html

Everything released by the White House, including complete transcripts of every presidential and presidential press secretary news conference, presidential statements, press releases, and more. The site is updated constantly.

The United States Senate

www.senate.gov

The United States House of Representatives

www.house.gov

The Internal Revenue Service

www.irs.ustreas.gov

The U.S. Postal Service

www.usps.gov

The Social Security Administration

www.ssa.gov

Social Security Death Index Interactive Search

ssdi.genealogy.rootsweb.com/cgi-bin/ssdi.cgi

Allows a search of close to 65 million deaths recorded by the Social Security Administration. More names are constantly being added and each result provides the Social Security number of the deceased, their last known place of residence and, when available, date of birth and date of death.

The Federal Bureau of Investigation

www.fbi.gov

"The 10 Most Wanted" list, ongoing investigations, the history of the agency, and more.

The Central Intelligence Agency

www.odci.gov/cia

The Peace Corps

www.peacecorps.gov

U.S. Census Bureau

www.census.gov

NASA

www.nasa.gov

An excellent site—it is paradise for science junkies.

National Air and Space Museum

nasm.si.edu

A fascinating branch of the Smithsonian.

National Archives and Records Administration

www.nara.gov

Mountains of government documents.

Smithsonian Museum of American History

www.si.edu

***Smithsonian* Magazine**

www.smithsonianmag.si.edu

The online edition of the Smithsonian's official publication.

U.S. Patent and Trademark Office

www.uspto.gov

The Hubble Telescope

oposite.stsci.edu/pubinfo/pr/1999/45/index.html

Public pictures from the Hubble space telescope.

Miscellaneous Sites of Great Value

Mr. Smith E-Mails Washington
Mr. Smith E-Mails the Media

www.mrsmith.com

These sites allow direct e-mail contact with, respectively, all the members of Congress and many media outlets, including magazines, TV and radio outlets, and newspapers.

The Democratic Party Online

www.democrats.org

The official Web site of the Democratic Party.

The Republican National Committee Online

www.rnc.org

The official Web site of the Republican Party.

The Libertarian Party

www.lp.org

The official Web site of the Libertarian Party.

The Reform Party

www.reformparty.org

The official Web site of the Reform Party.

C-SPAN

www.c-span.org

Nirvana for political junkies.

The SETI Institute

www.seti.org/Welcome-page.html

Everything you could possibly want to know about the search for extraterrestrial intelligence...short of finding out if there is any.

American Memory

memory.loc.gov

A virtual, interactive Internet archive of American history and other valuable information. A Library of Congress production. Essential.

American History Source Documents

personal.pitnet.net/primarysources

Complete texts of important documents related to American history—from 500 B.C. through 1800 A.D. A gold mine of information.

Archiving Early America

www.earlyamerica.com

A virtual tour of early America, including complete text reproductions and JPEGs of early American texts and historical sites.

The American President

www.americanpresident.org

A site based on the Kundhardts' amazing book *The American President* (it's listed in the Bibliography).

SUGGESTED SEARCH ENGINES

www.google.com

A simple search box with no bells and whistles and incredibly fast results makes this one of the first search engines you should try.)

www.four11.com

Four11.com is a search engine for finding e-mail addresses.

Other search engines:

www.altavista.com

www.ask.com

www.dogpile.com

www.excite.com

www.hotbot.com

www.infoseek.com

www.lycos.com

www.snap.com

www.yahoo.com

Chapter 65

192 Really Smart Things Said by U.S. Presidents

GEORGE WASHINGTON

★ "Labor to keep alive in your breast that little spark of celestial fire called conscience." (1746)

★ "Few men have virtue to withstand the highest bidder." (August 17, 1779)

JOHN ADAMS

★ "I have lived in this old and frail tenement a great many years. It is very much dilapidated, and, from all that I can learn, my landlord doesn't intend to repair it."

★ "Did you ever see a portrait of a great man without perceiving strong traits of pain and anxiety?" (May 6, 1816)

★ "I have accepted a seat in the House of Representatives, and thereby have consented to my own ruin, to your ruin, and the ruin of our children." (May 1770)

★ "The business of the Congress is tedious beyond expression...Every man in it is a great man, an orator, a critic, a statesman. And therefore every man upon every question must show his oratory, his criticism, and his political abilities." (October 9, 1774)

★ "In a word, let every sluice of knowledge be opened and set a-flowing." (August 1765)

THOMAS JEFFERSON

★ "Of all the faculties of the human mind, that of memory is the first which suffers decay with age." (1812)

★ "No man has a natural right to commit aggression on the equal rights of another; and this is all from which the laws ought to restrain him." (1816)

★ "I had rather be shut up in a very modest cottage, with my books, my family, and a few old friends, dining on simple bacon, and letting the world roll on as it liked, than to occupy the most splendid post which any human power can give." (1789)

☆ "Its soul, its climate, its equality, liberty, laws, people, and manners. My God! how little do my countrymen know what precious blessing they are in possession of, and which no other people on earth enjoy!" (June 17, 1785)

☆ "Establish the eternal truth that acquiescence under insult is not the way to escape war."

☆ "Whenever a man has cast a longing eye on offices, a rottenness begins in his conduct." (1820)

☆ "The accounts of the United States ought to be, and may be made, as simple as those of a common farmer, and capable of being understood by common farmers." (1796)

☆ "I think we have more machinery of government than is necessary, too many parasites living on the labor of the industrious." (1816)

☆ "The earth belongs to the living, not the dead." (June 24, 1813)

☆ "He is happiest of whom the world says least, good or bad." (August 27, 1786)

☆ "The Constitution...is unquestionably the wisest ever yet presented to men." (March 1789)

☆ "The time to guard against corruption and tyranny is before they shall have gotten hold of us. It is better to keep the wolf out of the fold than to trust to drawing his teeth and talons after he shall have entered." (1782)

☆ "Knowledge is power...knowledge is safety...knowledge is happiness." (November 25, 1817)

☆ "Books constitute capital. A library book lasts as long as a house, for hundreds of years. It is not, then, an article of mere consumption but fairly of capital, and often in the case of professional men, setting out in life, it is their only capital." (September 16, 1821)

☆ "An injured friend is the bitterest of foes." (April 28, 1793)

☆ "Delay is preferable to error." (May 16, 1792)

☆ "It is more honorable to repair a wrong than to persist in it." (January 10, 1806)

☆ "It is neither wealth nor splendor, but tranquillity and occupation, which give happiness." (1788)

☆ "Life is the art of avoiding pain." (October 12, 1786)

JAMES MADISON

☆ "Conscience is the most sacred of all property." (March 29, 1792)

☆ "If men were angels, no government would be necessary." (1788)

JAMES MONROE

☆ "In this great nation there is but one order, that of the people." (March 4, 1821)

☆ "A little flattery will support a man through great fatigue." (January 24, 1818)

JOHN QUINCY ADAMS

☆ "Our Constitution professedly rests upon the good sense and attachment of the people. This basis, weak as it may appear, has not yet been found to fail." (January 27, 1801)

☆ "To believe all men honest would be folly. To believe none so, is something worse." (June 22, 1809)

ANDREW JACKSON

☆ "If you have a job in your department that can't be done by a Democrat, then abolish the job."

☆ "Good officers will make good soldiers." (January 18, 1815)

★ "One man with courage makes a majority." (July 10, 1832)
★ "I hope and trust to meet you in Heaven, both white and black—both white and black." (June 8, 1845)

MARTIN VAN BUREN

★ "Most men are not scolded out of their opinion." (1803)

WILLIAM HENRY HARRISON

★ "But I contend that the strongest of all governments is that which is most free." (September 27, 1829)

JOHN TYLER

★ "I deem it of the most essential importance that a complete separation should take place between the sword and the purse." (April 9, 1841)

JAMES K. POLK

★ "The president's power is negative merely, and not affirmative." (December 5, 1848)

ZACHARY TAYLOR

★ "It would be judicious to act with magnanimity towards a prostrate foe." (September 28, 1846)

MILLARD FILLMORE

★ "It is better to wear out than rust out." (March 19, 1855)

FRANKLIN PIERCE

★ "In a body where there are more than 100 talking lawyers, you can make no calculation upon the termination of any debate. And frequently, the more trifling the subject, the more animated and protracted the discussion."

JAMES BUCHANAN

★ "Capital and capitalists...are proverbially timid." (1854)
★ "There is nothing stable but Heaven and the Constitution." (May 13, 1856)

ABRAHAM LINCOLN

★ "As a nation of free men, we must live through all time, or die by suicide." (January 27, 1838)
★ "A nation may be said to consist of its territory, its people, and its laws. The territory is the only part which is of certain durability. Laws change, people die; the land remains." (December 1, 1862)
★ "A fellow once came to me to ask for an appointment as a minister abroad. Finding he could not get that, he came down to some more modest position. Finally, he asked to be

made a tide-waiter. When he saw he could not get that, he asked me for an old pair of trousers. It is sometimes well to be humble." (1865)

★ "Stand with anybody that stands right, stand with him while he is right and part with him when he goes wrong." (October 16, 1854)

★ "Those who deny freedom to others deserve it not for themselves. And, under a just God, cannot long retain it." (April 6, 1859)

★ "I have always found that mercy bears richer fruits than strict justice." (1865)

ANDREW JOHNSON

★ "Slavery is dead, and you must pardon me if I do not mourn over its dead body." (1864)

ULYSSES S. GRANT

★ "I am more of a farmer than a soldier. I take little or no interest in military affairs." (1879)

RUTHERFORD B. HAYES

★ "We do not want a united North, nor a united South. We want a united country." (February 25, 1877)

JAMES A. GARFIELD

★ "Assassination can no more be guarded against than death by lightning, and it is best not to worry about either."

★ "We may divide the whole struggle of the human race into two chapters: First, the fight to get leisure, and then the second fight of civilization—what shall we do with our leisure when we get it." (1880)

CHESTER A. ARTHUR

★ "The extravagant expenditure of public money is an evil, not to be measured by the value of that money to the people who are taxed for it." (August 1, 1882)

GROVER CLEVELAND

★ "This dreadful damnable office-seeking hangs over me, and surrounds me—and makes me feel like resigning."

★ "A man is known by the company he keeps, and also by the company from which he is kept out."

BENJAMIN HARRISON

★ "Have you not learned that not stocks or bonds or stately homes or products of mill or field are our country? It is the splendid thought that is in our minds."

★ "Unlike many other people less happy, we give our devotion to a government, to its Constitution, to its flag, and not to men." (April 30, 1891)

WILLIAM McKINLEY

* "That's all a man can hope for during his lifetime—to set an example. And when he is dead, to be an inspiration for history." (December 29, 1899)

THEODORE ROOSEVELT

* "Get action. Do things; be sane, don't fritter away your time; create, act, take a place wherever you are and be somebody; get action." (1900)
* "Actions speak louder than words."
* "The American people are slow to wrath, but when their wrath is once kindled, it burns like a consuming flame." (December 3, 1901)
* "The things that will destroy America are prosperity-at-any-price, peace-at-any-price, safety-first instead of duty-first, the love of soft living and the get-rich-quick theory of life." (January 10, 1917)
* "We must insist that when anyone engaged in big business honestly endeavors to do right, he himself shall be given a square deal." (1913)
* "No people is wholly civilized where the distinction is drawn between stealing an office and stealing a purse." (June 22, 1912)
* "It was my good fortune at Santiago to serve besides colored troops. A man who is good enough to shed his blood for the country is good enough to be given a square deal afterward. More than that no man is entitled to, and less than that no man shall have." (July 4, 1903)
* "I wish that all Americans would realize that American politics is world politics." (1908)
* "Congress does from a third to a half of what I think is the minimum that it ought to do, and I am profoundly grateful that I get as much." (December 1904)
* "The Constitution was made for the people and not the people for the Constitution." (1902)
* "No man is justified in doing evil on the ground of expedience." (1899)

WILLIAM HOWARD TAFT

* "There is a well-known aphorism that men are different, but all husbands are alike. The same idea may be paraphrased with respect to Congressmen. Congressmen are different, but when in opposition to an administration they are very much alike in their attitude and in their speeches." (1916)

WOODROW WILSON

* "Life does not consist in thinking, it consists in acting." (September 28, 1912)
* "Some people call me an idealist. Well, that is the way I know I am an American. America is the only idealist nation in the world." (September 8, 1919)
* "I have sometimes heard men say politics have nothing to do with business, and I have often wished that business had nothing to do with politics." (1904)
* "The truth is, we are all caught in a great economic system which is heartless." (1912-1913)
* "Never murder a man who is committing suicide."
* "A presidential campaign may easily degenerate into a mere personal contest, and so lose its real dignity. There is no indispensable man." (August 7, 1912)

* "If you want to make enemies, try to change something." (July 10, 1916)
* "There is here a great melting pot in which we must compound a precious metal. That metal is the metal of nationality." (April 19, 1915)
* "The Constitution was not made to fit us like a straitjacket. In its elasticity lies its chief greatness." (November 19, 1904)
* "The Constitution of the United States is not a mere lawyer's document; it is a vehicle of life, and its spirit is always the spirit of the age." (1908)
* "You must act in your friend's interest whether it please him or not; the object of love is to serve, not to win." (May 9, 1907)

WARREN G. HARDING

* "Let the black man vote when he is fit to vote; prohibit the white man voting when he is unfit to vote." (August 1921)
* "Our most dangerous tendency is to expect too much of government, and at the same time do for it too little." (March 4, 1921)

CALVIN COOLIDGE

* "I have to appoint human beings to office." (1925)
* "No nation ever had an army large enough to guarantee it against attack in time of peace, or insure it victory in time of war." (1925)
* "The business of America is business." (January 1925)
* "Character is the only secure foundation of the state." (February 12, 1924)
* "Civilization and profits go hand in hand." (November 27, 1920)
* "If you see 10 troubles coming down the road, you can be sure that nine will run into the ditch before they reach you and you have to battle with only one of them."
* "The more I study [the Constitution] the more I have come to admire it, realizing that no other document devised by the hand of man ever brought so much progress and happiness to humanity." (1929)
* "The spiritual nature of men has a power of its own that is manifest in every great emergency from Runnymede to Marston Moor, from the Declaration of Independence to the abolition of slavery." (1929)

HERBERT C. HOOVER

* "The course of unbalanced budgets is the road to ruin." (May 31, 1932)
* "Free speech does not live many hours after free industry and free commerce die." (October 22, 1928)
* "We do not need to burn down the house to kill the rats." (1934)

FRANKLIN D. ROOSEVELT

* "The overwhelming majority of Americans are possessed of two great qualities—a sense of humor and a sense of proportion." (November 18, 1945)
* "We would rather die on our feet than live on our knees." (January 20, 1941)
* "We can afford all that we need; but we cannot afford all we want." (May 22, 1935)
* "Private enterprise is ceasing to be free enterprise." (1938)

* "The United States Constitution has proved itself the most marvelously elastic compilation of rules of government ever written." (March 2, 1930)
* "Our Constitution is so simple and practical that it is possible always to meet extraordinary needs by changes in emphasis and arrangement without loss of essential form." (March 4, 1933)
* "There is nothing mysterious about the foundations of a healthy and strong democracy....They are: equality of opportunity for youth and for others, jobs for those who can work, security for those who need it, the ending of special privilege for the few, the preservation of civil liberties for all, the enjoyment of the fruits of scientific progress in a wider and constantly rising standard of living." (January 6, 1941)
* "No man can tame a tiger by stroking it." (December 29, 1940)
* "The only thing we have to fear is fear itself—nameless, unreasoning, unjustified terror." (March 4, 1933)
* "We believe that the only whole man is a free man." (October 2, 1940)

HARRY S TRUMAN

* "As you get older, you get tired of doing the same things over and over again, so you think Christmas has changed. It hasn't. It's you who has changed." (December 1955)
* "America was not built on fear. America was built on courage, on imagination and an unbeatable determination to do the job at hand." (January 8, 1947)
* "You know that being an American is more than a matter of where your parents came from. It is a belief that all men are created free and equal and that everyone deserves an even break. It is respect for the dignity of men and women without regard to race, creed, or color. That is our creed." (October 26, 1948)
* "The atomic bomb was no 'great decision.' It was merely another powerful weapon in the arsenal of righteousness." (April 28, 1959.)
* "It isn't important who is ahead at one time or another in either an election or a horse race. It's the horse that comes in first at the finish that counts." (October 17, 1948)
* "A man cannot have character unless he lives within a fundamental system of morals that creates character." (1950)
* "If you tell Congress everything about the world situation, they get hysterical. If you tell them nothing, they go fishing." (July 17, 1950)
* "About the meanest thing you can say about a man is that he means well." (May 10, 1950)
* "It's a recession when your neighbor loses his job. It's a depression when you lose your own." (April 6, 1958)
* "You know that education is one thing that can't be taken away from you. Nobody can rob you of your education, because that is in your head; that is, if you have any head and are capable of holding it. Most of us are capable of holding an education, if we try to get it." (June 11, 1948)
* "You don't set a fox to watching the chickens just because he has a lot of experience in the hen house." (October 30, 1960)
* "Children and dogs are as necessary to the welfare of this country as Wall Street and the railroads." (May 6, 1948)

DWIGHT D. EISENHOWER

* "Accomplishment will prove to be a journey, not a destination." (December 16. 1957)
* "We cannot live alone, and we've got to find some way for our allies to earn a living, because we do not want to carry them on our backs." (March 29, 1954)

★ "Whatever America hopes to bring to pass in this world must first come to pass in the heart of America." (January 20, 1953)

★ "No one should be appointed to political office if he is a seeker after it." (January 1, 1953)

★ "Destruction is not a good police force." (March 11, 1959)

★ "Whatever America hopes to bring to pass in the world must first come to pass in the heart of America." (January 20, 1953)

★ "Neither a wise man nor a brave man lies down on the tracks of history to wait for the train of the future to run over him." (October 6, 1952)

★ "Don't join the book-burners. Don't think you are going to conceal faults by concealing evidence that they ever existed. Don't be afraid to go in your library and read every book." (June 14, 1953)

★ "You do not lead by hitting people over the head—that's assault, not leadership."

JOHN F. KENNEDY

★ "The American, by nature, is optimistic. He is experimental, an inventor and a builder who builds best when called upon to build greatly." (January 1, 1960)

★ "The path we have chosen for the present is full of hazards, as all paths are. But it is the one most consistent with our character and courage as a nation and our commitments around the world. The cost of freedom is always high, but Americans have always paid it. And there is one path we shall never choose, and that is the path of surrender or submission." (October 22, 1962)

★ "The world is very different now. For man holds in his mortal hands the power to abolish all forms of human poverty and all forms of human life." (January 20, 1961)

★ "I want every American to stand up for his rights, even if he has to sit down for them." (August 3, 1960)

★ "No one has been barred on account of his race from fighting or dying for America—there are no 'white' or 'colored' signs on the foxholes of graveyards of battle." (June 19, 1963)

★ "It is much easier in many ways for me—and for other presidents, I think, who felt the same way—when Congress is not in town." (June 28, 1962)

★ "Any dangerous spot is tenable if brave men will make it so." (July 26, 1961)

★ "The men who create power make an indispensable contribution to the nation's greatness. But the men who question power make a contribution just as indispensable." (October 1963)

★ "Any system of government will work when everything is going well. It's the system that functions in the pinch that survives." (January 14, 1963)

★ "What we need now in this nation, more than atomic power, or financial, industrial, or even manpower, is brain power. The dinosaur was bigger and stronger than anyone else—but he was also dumber. And look what happened to him." (April 16, 1959)

LYNDON B. JOHNSON

★ "The central lesson of our time is that the appetite of aggression is never satisfied. To withdraw from one battlefield means only to prepare for the next." (April 7, 1965)

★ "We are a nation of lovers and not a nation of haters. We are a land of good homes, decent wages, and decent medical care for the aged. Yes, we want a land of hope and happiness, but never a land of harshness and hate." (September 10, 1964)

★ "This is what America is all about. It is the uncrossed desert and the unclimbed ridge. It is the star that is not reached and the harvest that is sleeping in the unplowed ground." (January 20, 1965)

★ "The promise of America is a simple promise: Every person shall share in the blessings of this land. And they shall share on the basis of their merits as a person. They shall not be judged by their color or by their beliefs, or by their religion, or by where they were born, of the neighborhood in which they live." (March 13, 1965)

★ "No political party can be a friend of the American people which is not a friend of American business." (August 12, 1963)

★ "We must change to master change." (January 12, 1966)

★ "Evil acts of the past are never rectified by evil acts of the present." (July 21, 1964)

★ "We have talked long enough in this country about equal rights. We have talked for 100 years or more. It is time now to write it in the books of law." (November 27, 1963)

★ "The Constitution of the United States applies to every American, of every race, of every religion in this beloved country. If it doesn't apply to every race, to every region, to every religion, it applies to no one." (May 8, 1964)

★ "The test before us as a people is not whether our commitments match our will and courage, but whether we have the will and courage to match our commitments." (August 3, 1967)

★ "Free speech, free press, free religion, the right of free assembly, yes, the right of petition...well, they are still radical ideas." (August 3, 1965)

★ "Once we considered education a public expense. We know now that it is a public investment." (April 27, 1967)

RICHARD M. NIXON

★ "You cannot win a battle in any arena merely by defending yourself." (1962)

★ "(W)inning's a lot more fun." (1972)

★ "The people's right to change what does not work is one of the greatest principles of our system of our government." (March 1972)

★ "The behind-the-scenes power structure in Washington is often called the 'iron triangle': a three-sided set of relationships composed of congressional lobbyists, congressional committee, and subcommittee members and their staffs." (1978)

★ "If being a liberal means federalizing everything, then I'm no liberal. If being a conservative means turning back the clock, denying problems that exist, then I'm no conservative." (1978)

★ "What determines success or failure in handling a crisis is the ability to keep coldly objective when emotions are running high." (1962)

★ "The ability to be cool, confident, and decisive in crisis is not an inherited characteristic, but is the direct result of how well the individual has prepared himself for battle." (1962)

★ "I believe in building bridges, but we should build only our end of the bridge." (July 1967)

★ "Government enterprise is the most inefficient and costly way of producing jobs." (1978)

★ "History makes the man more than the man makes history." (1978)

GERALD R. FORD

★ "One of the enduring truths of the nation's capitals is that bureaucrats *survive*." (1982)

★ "Washington is not the problem, their Congress is the problem." (August 19, 1976)

★ "The Constitution is the bedrock of all our freedoms; guard and cherish it; keep honor and order in your own house; and the republic will endure." (January 12, 1977)

JIMMY CARTER

★ "Three weeks after Pearl Harbor, Winston Churchill came to North America and he said, 'We have not journeyed all this way across the centuries, across the oceans, across the mountains, across the prairies because we are made of sugar candy.' We Americans have courage. Americans have always been on the cutting edge of change. We've always looked forward with anticipation and confidence." (August 14, 1980)

★ "In an all-out nuclear war, more destructive power than in all of World War II would be unleashed every second for the long afternoon it would take for all the missiles and bombs to fall. A World War II every second—more people killed in the first hours than (in) all the wars of history put together. The survivors, if any, would live in despair amid the poisoned ruins of a civilization that had committed suicide." (January 14, 1981)

RONALD REAGAN

★ "You know, by the time you reach my age, you've made plenty of mistakes, and if you've lived properly, you learn. You put things in perspective. You pull your energies together. You change. You go forward." (March 4, 1987)

★ "I've always believed that this land was set aside in an uncommon way, that a divine plan placed this great continent between the oceans to be found by a people from every corner of the earth who had a special love of faith, freedom and peace." (November 11, 1982)

★ "America is too great for small dreams." (January 1, 1984)

★ "A truly successful army is one that, because of its strength and ability and dedication, will not be called upon to fight because no one will dare to provoke it." (May 27, 1981)

★ "It's time we reduced the federal budget and left the family budget alone." (February 2, 1986)

★ "Millions of individuals making their own decisions in the marketplace will always allocate resources better than any centralized government planning process." (September 27, 1983)

★ "Excellence does not begin in Washington." (January 25, 1984)

★ "Somewhere along the way these folks in Washington have forgotten that the economy is business. Business creates new products and services. Business creates jobs. Business creates prosperity for our communities and our nation as a whole." (September 23, 1985)

★ "Entrepreneurs share a faith in a bright future. They have a clear vision of where they are going and what they are doing, and they have a pressing need to succeed. If I didn't know better, I would be tempted to say that 'entrepreneur' is another word for America." (1986)

★ "The very key to our success has been our ability, foremost among nations, to preserve our lasting values by making change work for us rather than against us." (January 25, 1983)

★ "One of the simple, but overwhelming facts of our time is this: Of all the millions of refugees we have seen in the modern world, their flight is always away from, not toward, the communist world." (June 8, 1982)

★ "If the Constitution means anything it means that we, the federal government, are entrusted with preserving life, liberty, and the pursuit of happiness." (June 11, 1986)

★ "Our Constitution is to be celebrated not for being old, but for being young." (January 27, 1987)

★ "Why is the Constitution of the United States so exceptional?...Just three words: We the people. In other constitutions, the government tells the people of those countries what they are allowed to do. In our Constitution, we the people tell the government what it can do." (January 27, 1987)

★ "We do not face large deficits because American families are undertaxed; we face those deficits because the federal government overspends." (February 2, 1986)

★ "Nations do not mistrust each other because they are armed, they are armed because they mistrust each other." (September 22, 1986)

★ "Now what should happen when you make a mistake is this: You take your knocks, you learn your lessons, and then you move on. That's the healthiest way to deal with a problem." (March 4, 1987)

★ "If about 90 percent of the laws that are passed by Congress and the state legislatures each year were lost on the way to the printer, and if all the people in the bureaus went fishing, I don't think they would be missed for quite a while." (December 8, 1972)

GEORGE BUSH

★ "The federal government too often treats government programs as if they are of Washington, by Washington, and for Washington. Once established, federal programs seem to become immortal." (January 29, 1991)

★ "I do believe that some crimes are so heinous, so brutal, so outrageous...and for those real brutal crimes I do believe in the death penalty." (October 13, 1988)

★ "We know what works: Freedom works. We know what's right: Freedom is right. We know how to secure a more just and prosperous life for man on earth: Through free markets, free speech, free elections, and the exercise of free will unhampered by the state." (January 20, 1989)

★ "This is a fact: Strength in the pursuit of peace is no vice. Isolation in the pursuit of security is not virtue." (January 28, 1992)

★ "I see something happening in our towns and in our neighborhoods. Sharp lawyers are running wild. Doctors are afraid to practice medicine. And some moms and pops won't even coach Little League any more. We must sue each other less—and care for each other more." (August 20, 1992)

BILL CLINTON

★ "My doctor ordered me to shut up, which will make every American happy." (April 1992)

★ "We can never again allow the corrupt do-nothing values of the 1980s to mislead us. Today, the average CEO at a major American corporation is paid 100-times more than the average worker. Our government rewards that excess with a tax break for executive pay, no matter how high it is, no matter what performance it reflects. And then the government hands out tax deductions to corporations that shut down their plants here and ship our jobs overseas. That has to change." (1992)

★ "For too long we've been told about 'us' and 'them.' Each and every election we see a new slate of arguments and ads telling us that 'they' are the problem, not 'us.' But there can be no 'them' in America. There's only 'us.'" (1992)

Chapter 66

18 Code Names for NASA's Apollo Command/Service and Lunar Modules

APOLLO 9

Command/Service Module: Gumdrop.
Lunar Module: Spider.

APOLLO 10

Command/Service Module: Charlie Brown.
Lunar Module: Snoopy.

APOLLO 11

Command/Service Module: Columbia.
Lunar Module: Eagle.

APOLLO 12

Command/Service Module: Yankee Clipper.
Lunar Module: Intrepid.

APOLLO 13

Command/Service Module: Odyssey.
Lunar Module: Aquarius.

APOLLO 14

Command/Service Module: Kitty Hawk.
Lunar Module: Antares.

APOLLO 15

Command/Service Module: Endeavor.
Lunar Module: Falcon.

APOLLO 16

Command/Service Module: Casper.
Lunar Module: Orion.

APOLLO 17

Command/Service Module: America.
Lunar Module: Challenger.

Chapter 67

The 10 States that Pollute the Most

A ccording to the U.S. Environmental Protection Agency, these 10 states release the most toxic chemicals into the environment. These pollutants include industrial air releases, surface water releases, underground injections, and on-site land releases.

The industries responsible for the environmental pollution are, in order of most polluting: chemical companies, primary metal companies, paper companies, plastics companies, and transportation equipment.

The leading carcinogenic releases are, in order of volume released, dichloromethane, styrene, formaldehyde, trichlorethylene, acetaldehyde, and chloroform.

The good news is that all of these 10 states have reduced their pollution emissions substantially from 1995 through 1997, the last year for which figures were available. The figures given are for total toxic chemical releases for the year 1997.

1. **Texas**: 262 million pounds.
2. **Louisiana**: 186 million pounds.
3. **Ohio**: 159 million pounds.
4. **Pennsylvania**: 143 million pounds.
5. **Illinois**: 128 million pounds.
6. **Indiana**: 123 million pounds.
7. **Tennessee**: 107 million pounds.
8. **Utah**: 104 million pounds.
9. **Alabama**: 95 million pounds.
10. **Florida**: 95 million pounds.

THE 5 STATES WITH THE MOST HAZARDOUS WASTE SITES

As of 1999, there were 1,285 hazardous waste sites in the United States, including sites already operational, along with proposed sites which are likely to receive federal approval. These five states have the dubious distinction of having the most hazardous waste sites in America:

1. **New Jersey**: 114 sites (110 final, 4 proposed).
2. **Pennsylvania**: 101 sites (98 final, 3 proposed).
3. **California**: 96 sites (93 final, 3 proposed).
4. **New York**: 86 sites (85 final, 1 proposed).
5. **Michigan**: 71 sites (69 final, 2 proposed).

Chapter 68

The 20 Most Popular Breeds of Dogs in the United States

Much like everything else in this country, we like our dogs big. The top four dogs as registered by the American Kennel Club for 1998 are big boys, to say the least. The remainder of the top 20 list does boast a nice showing of little dogs, as well, proving that Americans are (almost) impartial when it comes to their canine preferences! (The number of new dogs registered in 1998 for each particular breed is noted in parentheses following their name. Similar numbers of each dog were registered in 1997, indicating the continuing popularity for these 20 breeds.)

1. **Labrador Retriever** (157,936).
2. **Golden Retriever** (65,681).
3. **German Shepherd** (65,326).
4. **Rottweiler** (55,009).
5. **Dachshund** (53,896).
6. **Beagle** (53,322).
7. **Poodle** (51,935).
8. **Chihuahua** (43,468).
9. **Yorkshire Terrier** (42,900).
10. **Pomeranian** (38,540).
11. **Shih Tzu** (38,468).
12. **Boxer** (36,345).
13. **Cocker Spaniel** (34,632).
14. **Miniature Schnauzer** (31,063).
15. **Shetland Sheepdog** (27,978).
16. **Miniature Pinscher** (22,675).
17. **Pug** (21,487).
18. **Siberian Husky** (21,078).
19. **Boston Terrier** (18,308).
20. **Maltese** (18,013).

Chapter 69

7 Coins That Are No Longer Minted

he half dime seemes to have been the most popular of these discontinued coins: It was in circulation for 79 years. The 20-cent piece, on the other hand, seemed to be as popular as the Susan B. Anthony dollar: It was only in circulation for three years.

1. **The half cent**
   First issued: 1793.
   Last issued: 1857.

2. **The two-cent piece**
   First issued: 1864.
   Last issued: 1873.

3. **The silver three-cent piece**
   First issued: 1851.
   Last issued: 1873.

4. **The nickel three-cent piece**
   First issued: 1865.
   Last issued: 1889.

5. **The half dime**
   First issued: 1794.
   Last issued: 1873.

6. **The 20-cent piece**
   First issued: 1875.
   Last issued: 1878.

7. **The Susan B. Anthony dollar**
   First issued: 1979.
   Last issued: 1999.

Chapter 70

The Leading U.S. Businesses in 47 Categories

These companies were the leaders in their respective categories in 1998, according to *Fortune* magazine. The category is followed by the leader in the field, followed by that company's revenue in 1998.

1. **Aerospace:** Boeing, $56.154 billion.
2. **Airlines:** AMR (American Airlines' parent company), $19.205 billion.
3. **Apparel:** Nike, $9.553 billion.
4. **Beverages:** Pepsico, $22.348 billion.
5. **Building Materials, Glass:** Owens-Illinois, $5.450 billion.
6. **Chemicals:** E.I. du Pont de Nemours, $39.130 billion.
7. **Commercial Banks:** BankAmerica Corporation, $50.777 billion.
8. **Computer and Data Systems:** Electronic Data Systems, $16.891 billion.
9. **Computer Peripherals:** Seagate Technology, $6.819 billion.
10. **Computer Software:** Microsoft, $14.484 billion.
11. **Computers, Office Equipment:** IBM, $81.667 billion.
12. **Diversified Financials:** Citigroup, $76.431 billion.
13. **Electronics, Electrical Equipment:** General Electric, $100.469 billion.
14. **Entertainment:** Walt Disney, $22.976 billion.
15. **Food:** ConAgra, $23.841 billion.
16. **Food and Drug Stores:** Kroger, $28.203 billion.
17. **Food Services:** McDonalds, $12.421 billion.
18. **Forest and Paper Products:** International Paper, $19.500 billion.
19. **Furniture:** Leggett and Platt, $3.370 billion.
20. **General Merchandise:** Wal-Mart Stores, $139.208 billion.
21. **Healthcare:** Cigna, $21.437 billion.

22. **Hotels, Casinos, Resorts**: Marriott International, $7.968 billion.

23. **Industrial and Farm Equipment**: Caterpillar, $20.977 billion.

24. **Insurance, Life and Health**: TIAA-CREF, $35.889 billion.

25. **Insurance, Property and Casualty**: State Farm Insurance, $48.114 billion.

26. **Mail, Package, Freight Delivery**: UPS, $24.788 billion.

27. **Metal Products**: Gillette, $10.056 billion.

28. **Metals**: Alcoa, $15.489 billion.

29. **Motor Vehicles and Parts**: General Motors, $161.315 billion.

30. **Petroleum Refining**: Exxon, $100.697 billion.

31. **Pharmaceuticals**: Merck, $26.898 billion.

32. **Publishing and Printing**: R.R. Donnelley & Sons, $5.9 billion.

33. **Railroads**: Union Pacific, $10.553 billion.

34. **Rubber and Plastic Products**: Goodyear Tire, $12.649 billion.

35. **Scientific, Photographic, and Control Equipment**: Minnesota Mining and Manufacturing, $15.021 billion.

36. **Securities**: Merrill Lynch, $35.853 billion.

37. **Semiconductors**: Intel, $26.273 billion.

38. **Soaps, Cosmetics**: Procter and Gamble, $37.154 billion.

39. **Specialty Retailers**: The Home Depot, $30.219 billion.

40. **Telecommunications**: AT&T, $53.588 billion.

41. **Temporary Help**: Manpower, $8.814 billion.

42. **Textiles**: Shaw Industries, $3.542 billion.

43. **Tobacco**: Phillip Morris, $57.813 billion.

44. **Toys, Sporting Goods**: Mattel, $4.782 billion.

45. **Transportation Equipment**: Brunswick, $3.945 billion.

46. **Utilities, Gas, and Electric**: PG&E Corporation, $19.942 billion.

47. **Wholesalers**: Ingram Micro, $22.034 billion.

Chapter 71

The Presidential Master Reference Table

This table will be a helpful reference, as there are many lists in *The U.S.A. Book of Lists* that deal with America's presidents.

President	Birth	Death	Term
1. George Washington	February 22, 1732	December 14, 1799	1789-1797
2. John Adams	October 30, 1735	July 4, 1826	1797-1801
3. Thomas Jefferson	April 13, 1743	July 4, 1826	1801-1809
4. James Madison	March 16, 1751	June 28, 1836	1809-1817
5. James Monroe	April 28, 1758	July 4, 1831	1817-1825
6. John Quincy Adams	July 11, 1767	February 23, 1848	1825-1829
7. Andrew Jackson	December 29, 1808	June 8, 1845	1829-1837
8. Martin Van Buren	December 5, 1782	July 24, 1862	1837-1841
9. William Henry Harrison	February 9, 1773	April 4, 1841	1841
10. John Tyler	March 29, 1790	January 18, 1862	1841-1845
11. James Polk	November 2, 1795	June 15, 1849	1845-1849
12. Zachary Taylor	November 24, 1784	July 9, 1850	1849-1850
13. Millard Fillmore	January 7, 1800	March 8, 1874	1850-1853
14. Franklin Pierce	November 23, 1804	October 8, 1869	1853-1857
15. James Buchanan	April 23, 1791	June 1, 1868	1857-1861
16. Abraham Lincoln	February 12, 1809	April 15, 1865	1861-1865
17. Andrew Johnson	March 15, 1767	July 31, 1875	1865-1869
18. Ulysses S. Grant	April 27, 1822	July 23, 1885	1869-1877
19. Rutherford B. Hayes	October 4, 1822	January 17, 1893	1877-1881
20. James Garfield	November 19, 1831	September 19, 1881	1881
21. Chester A. Arthur	October 5, 1829	November 18, 1886	1881-1885
22. Grover Cleveland	March 18, 1837	June 24, 1908	1885-1889
23. Benjamin Harrison	August 20, 1833	March 13, 1901	1889-1893
24. Grover Cleveland	March 18, 1837	June 24, 1908	1885-1889
25. William McKinley	January 29, 1843	September 14, 1901	1897-1901

President	Birth	Death	Term
26. Theodore Roosevelt	October 27, 1858	January 6, 1919	1901-1909
27. William Howard Taft	September 15, 1857	March 8, 1930	1909-1913
28. Woodrow Wilson	December 28, 1856	February 3, 1924	1913-1921
29. Warren G. Harding	November 2, 1865	August 2, 1923	1921-1923
30. Calvin Coolidge	July 4, 1872	January 5, 1933	1923-1929
31. Herbert Hoover	August 10, 1874	October 20, 1964	1929-1933
32. Franklin D. Roosevelt	January 30, 1882	April 12, 1945	1933-1945
33. Harry S Truman	May 8, 1884	December 26, 1972	1945-1953
34. Dwight D. Eisenhower	October 14, 1890	March 28, 1969	1953-1961
35. John F. Kennedy	May 29, 1917	November 22, 1963	1961-1963
36. Lyndon B. Johnson	August 27, 1908	January 22, 1973	1963-1969
37. Richard Nixon	January 9, 1913	April 22, 1994	1969-1974
38. Gerald Ford	July 14, 1913	—	1974-1977
39. Jimmy Carter	October 1, 1924	—	1977-1981
40. Ronald Reagan	February 6, 1911	—	1981-1989
41. George Bush	June 12, 1924	—	1989-1993
42. Bill Clinton	August 19, 1946	—	1993-2001

Chapter 72

351 American Firsts and Other Achievments

*"Whatever America hopes to bring to pass in this world
must first come to pass in the heart of America."*
—President Dwight D. Eisenhower, January 20, 1953

*"The American, by nature, is optimistic. He is experimental, an inventor, and a builder
who builds best when called upon to build greatly."*
—President John F. Kennedy, January 1, 1960

America rules! (Sorry. Got caught up in patriotic fervor there for a moment. But who can blame me?) Read through this list of American "firsts" and other major accomplishments and see if you do not swell with pride over what we have achieved as a nation in a little more than a couple of hundred years. Not to mention that we perfected pizza and boast better pies than even Italy can lay claim to. (And that's coming from a sixth-generation Italian-American, too!)

(*Note:* When the historical records do not provide a month and day for a particular event, I listed the achievement under a year heading first. Specifically dated events follow in chronological order.)

1776

★ Benjamin Rush becomes surgeon general of the Continental Army and founds the first free dispensary at the Pennsylvania hospital.

★ The David Bushnell-designed Connecticut *Turtle*, a submarine made of wood, iron, and tar, becomes the first submarine to be used in combat. The *Turtle* had a 30-minute air supply, held one person (who sat on a seat similar to that of a bicycle), and was propelled by pedals and cranks. The fate of the *Turtle* is unclear. Some claim that a sloop on which the *Turtle* was being transported was sunk by a British frigate. Others believe the submarine was dismantled and moved to parts unknown. To this day, no one knows what happened to this historic vehicle. See *www.connix.com/~crm/turtle2.html* for more information.

1780

★   Conveyor belts are used in the first automated flour mill.

1784

★   Benjamin Franklin invents the bifocal lens.

1787

★   The world's first two steamboats are demonstrated, one on the Potomac River and one on the Delaware River.

★   Automation is used to grind grain and sift flour to make bread for the first time.

1790

★   The first working cotton mill opens, marking the start of the Industrial Revolution in the United States.

1792

★   The United States Mint opens.

★   Eli Whitney invents the cotton gin.

1795

★   The Springfield flintlock musket—the first official U.S. military weapon—is created.

1798

★   Eli Whitney invents standardized jigs for mass production.

1799

★   The first suspension bridge is built across Jacob's Creek in Westmoreland, Pa. It was designed and constructed by engineer James Finley and utilized iron chains for support.

1802

★   The first icebox—the forerunner of the modern refrigerator—is built.

1803

★   Hemophilia is identified for the first time.

★   Robert Fulton builds his first steam-powered ship.

1805

★   The first covered bridge in America opens in Pennsylvania.

November 15, 1805
  ★ Lewis and Clark complete the first overland trip across the United States when they reach the Pacific Ocean.

1807
  ★ The S.S. *Clermont* becomes the first commercial cargo steamship.

1809
  ★ A 22-pound ovarian tumor is successfully removed without anesthesia by Ephraim McDowell, creating the new science of ovariotomy.
  ★ Moses Rogers travels from New York City to the Delaware River, completing the first successful ocean steamship voyage.

1811
  ★ The S.S. *New Orleans* becomes the first steamship to cross the Mississippi River Valley.

1817-1818
  ★ The first dental plate is introduced.

1819
  ★ The U.S.S. *Savannah* makes the first successful transatlantic sail/steamship trip.

1820
  ★ Nathan Palmer is the first to explore the Antarctic Peninsula.

1822
  ★ William Church patents the first typesetting machine.

1825
  ★ The Erie Canal opens, linking the Hudson River and the Great Lakes.

1827
  ★ Public transportation begins in New York with a 12-seat horse-drawn bus offering passenger service around town.

1829
  ★ The Tom Thumb is the first American-built locomotive.
  ★ The Tremont House in Boston is the first modern hotel.

1830

★ The first magnetic observatory in the United States is established in Philadelphia.

★ Thaddeus Banks invents the first platform scale.

1831

★ Joseph Henry invents the electric motor.

★ Seth Boyden patents moldable cast iron.

★ Cyrus McCormick invents the horse-drawn reaper.

1832

★ The first clipper ship, the *Ann McKim*, is built in Baltimore. (A clipper ship is a fast-sailing ship, especially one with long slender lines, overhanging bow, a large sail area, and tall, inclining masts.)

1833

★ Augustus Taylor develops the first simple wood frame house.

1836

★ Samuel Colt invents the Colt six-shooter revolver.

1839

★ Charles Goodyear discovers how to vulcanize rubber.

1841

★ Dorothea Dix sets in motion efforts to reform treatment of the mentally ill, resulting in more humane state insane asylums.

1843

★ Oliver Wendell Holmes concludes that fever in children is contagious.

★ Elias Howe Jr. invents the interlocking-stitch sewing machine.

1844

★ Henry Wells creates the first express delivery service, a company that will ultimately become Wells Fargo.

May 24, 1844

★ Samuel Morse sends the first telegraph message. The telegraph is sent from Washington, D.C. to Baltimore, Maryland and consists of the sentence, "What hath God wrought!"

1845

- ★ Claudius Ash invents the single porcelain tooth.
- ★ The first cable suspension aqueduct bridge is opened to traffic. It spans the Allegheny River in Pittsburgh, Penn.

1846

- ★ Elias Loomis develops and publishes the first comprehensive weather map.
- ★ The Smithsonian Institution is founded in Washington, D.C.
- ★ William Morton, in collaboration with John Warren, first uses ether for anesthesia during surgery to remove a tumor from a patient's neck.
- ★ Elias Howe patents the first modern sewing machine.

1847

- ★ Richard Hoe patents a rotary printing press that prints much faster than earlier flatbed-driven printing presses.
- ★ The American Medical Association holds its first meeting in Philadelphia.
- ★ Ebenezer Butterick develops a process for cutting dressmaker patterns using Elias Howe's new sewing machine.
- ★ The United States becomes the first country to use adhesive postage stamps.

October 1, 1847

- ★ Maria Mitchell discovers a comet and becomes the first woman member of the American Academy of Arts and Science a year later.

1849

- ★ Elizabeth Blackwell becomes America's first female physician.
- ★ Walter Hunt invents the safety pin.
- ★ James Bogardus builds the first prefabricated home.

1850

- ★ Isaac Singer patents a foot-operated sewing machine and is sued for patent infringement by Elias Howe. Singer loses. (Howe's 1844 patents were held up in court. Singer, however, went on to form his own company, arrogantly using some of Howe's designs. The cash-strapped Howe could not afford to sue Singer and the subsequent animosities were dubbed "The Sewing Machine Wars" by the media.)

1852

- ★ Kerosene is developed by Boston drug makers.
- ★ A train makes the first successful trip from the East Coast to Chicago.
- ★ Elisah Otis patents the safety elevator.

1855

* Matthew Maury publishes *Physical Geography of the Sea*, the first textbook on oceanography.
* Gail Borden patents a process for making condensed milk.

1856

* Hiram Silbey and Ezra Cornell obtain a charter for a telegraph company they call Western Union.

1858

* Antonio Snider-Pellegrini is one of the first scientists to support the theory of continental drift.
* George Pullman develops the first two-tiered train sleeping car.
* New York City's Central Park opens.
* John Mason invents the zinc-lidded Mason Jar.

AUGUST 28, 1859

* Edwin Drake drills the first petroleum oil well at Titusville, Penn.

1860

* Samuel King and William Black take two photographs of Boston from a balloon, becoming the first aerial photographers.
* The first Winchester repeating rifle is made.
* The Pony Express begins transporting mail between Missouri and California.

1861

* Surgeon Gordon Buck invents the weight-and-pulley device for orthopedic traction.
* James Sims performs the first surgical removal of the cervix.

1862

* Richard J. Gattling patents his invention, the Gattling gun. The gun is a hand-cranked, rapid-fire weapon with 10 rotating barrels. This is considered the first machine gun. Gattling graduated from medical school but never practiced medicine, choosing, instead, to be an inventor. (He also invented a wheat drill and a motorized plow.)

1865

* Francis Pratt and Amos Whitney develop a manufacturing process for interchangeable rifle parts and form the company Pratt & Whitney.
* Linus Yale invents the cylinder lock that will become known as the Yale lock.
* Thaddeus Lowe invents a compression ice-making machine.

1866

★ Cyrus Field lays the first permanent transatlantic telegraph cable.

1867

★ The first elevated railway opens in New York.

1868

★ George Westinghouse invents the air brake for trains. This was just the first invention by a man many believe to be one of the most gifted inventors of all time. (For more information on Westinghouse's many achievements and contributions to industry, visit the Web site: *www.georgewestinghouse.com.*)

★ Christopher Sholes, Carlos Glidden, and Samuel Soule patent the first typewriter.

1869

★ The building of the first U.S. transcontinental railroad is completed.

1870

★ The U.S. Weather Bureau is established.

1871

★ The first U.S. physiology laboratory is established by Henry Pickering with support from Harvard University.

1872

★ Henry Draper becomes the first to photograph a stellar spectrum.
★ The Yellowstone region is declared the first United States National Park.
★ The first U.S. nursing school is established at Bellevue Hospital in New York.
★ George Huntington identifies the neurological disease now known as Huntington's chorea.

1873

★ Barbed wire is invented by Henry Rose.

1875

★ Alexander Graham Bell invents the telephone.
★ Thomas Edison invents a wax-stencil duplicating system that will ultimately become known as mimeographing.

1876

* Melvil Dewey invents the Dewey decimal system for libraries.
* Henry Sherwin develops ready-to-use paint.

1877

* The first telephone switchboard begins operations in Boston, Mass.
* Thomas Edison invents the phonograph. It uses metal cylinders to imprint sound and play it back.

1878

* Thomas Edison figures out how to supply electricity to homes by dividing down the current.
* The Remington Arms Company develops the shift key for typewriters, allowing for the first time the use of upper and lower case when typing.
* Procter & Gamble accidentally invent floating soap when air is injected into the batch of soap during production. They call the new batch "Ivory."

1879

* Ira Remsen and Constantine Fahlberg invent saccharin.
* Thomas Edison develops the long-lasting incandescent light bulb.
* A Brooklyn dairy pioneers the use of milk bottles.

1881

* Edward Barnard is the first to astronomer to identify the image of a comet in a photograph.
* Gustavus Swift invents the refrigerated car for transporting fresh meat over great distances.

1883

* The Brooklyn Bridge opens to pedestrian traffic.

1884

* Dr. Edward Trudeau opens the first tuberculosis sanitarium in the Adirondack Mountains in New York.

1885

* William Stanley invents the electrical transformer.
* The world's first skyscraper is built in Chicago. It is 10-stories high.
* George Westinghouse and William Stanley invent the first electrical transmitter.

1886

* Printer Frederick Ives creates the first halftone photo-engraving process.

1887

- ⋆ The world's first mountaintop refracting telescope begins operation on Mount Hamilton in California.
- ⋆ Thomas Edison invents the first motorized phonograph. It uses imprinted wax cylinders to reproduce recorded sound.

1888

- ⋆ In Virginia, electric trolley cars run for the first time.
- ⋆ George Eastman invents the Kodak, the first inexpensive camera for consumer use.
- ⋆ John Gregg creates the system of shorthand that will ultimately bear his name.
- ⋆ Construction of the 553-foot high Washington Monument, which was first begun in 1848, is complete and opened to the public. At the time, it was the tallest masonry building in the world.

1889

- ⋆ The I.M. Singer company introduces the first electric sewing machine.
- ⋆ The first pay telephone is installed in a Connecticut bank.

1890

- ⋆ The U.S. Congress decides that every state must maintain a state hospital and that they must be called hospitals, not asylums.

1891

- ⋆ Thomas Edison and William K.L. Dickson invent the first motion picture equipment.
- ⋆ The first electric ovens are offered for sale in the U.S.

1892

- ⋆ The cork-lined bottle cap is introduced.

1893

- ⋆ Henry Ford test-drives the first gas-powered motor vehicle. Prior to Ford's invention, some crude steam-powered vehicles were built. These cars were not eagerly embraced by the public because the boilers of these vehicles had a tendency to explode accidentally. Eventually (all explosions aside) a market grew for steam-powered vehicles. Ford's more efficient internal combustion engine effectively wiped out the steam-powered automobile business.

1894

- ⋆ Oil is discovered in Texas for the first time. (The drillers were actually looking for water.)

1896

- ★ Edmund Wilson identifies the cell.
- ★ Graphite, a mixture of coke and clay, is created for the first time by inventor Edward Acheson.
- ★ The Haynes-Duryea is the first motor car to be offered for sale in the United States.

1897

- ★ George Hale plays an important role in placing the world's largest refracting telescope (40 inch diameter) into operation at the Yerkes Observatory in Wisconsin.
- ★ The *Argonaut* is the first submarine to make a successful, independent, open-sea journey from Virginia to New York.

1900

- ★ Benjamin Holt invents the tractor.
- ★ The *Holland* is the first submarine with an internal combustion engine and electric motor to be purchased by the U.S. Navy.
- ★ Eastman Kodak begins selling the one-dollar Brownie camera.
- ★ At Louie's Lunch in New Haven, Conn., Louis Lassen introduces the hamburger on toast. This is believed to be the first time the hamburger was offered in the United States. Lassen and his descendants claim creation of the hamburger. However, "Hamburg steak" is believed to have been brought to America by German immigrants in the early 19th century. Several American establishments claim that they were the first to serve the modern-day hamburger. In fact, some historians feel that Louis's claim is the weakest of the several American restaurants claim on the hamburger.

1901

- ★ Peter Hewitt invents the mercury-vapor electric light.
- ★ The Multigraph, the first real copy machine, is introduced.

1902

- ★ Horn and Hardart open the first Automat in Philadelphia. (The Automat was a "self-serve" restaurant in which foods were in separate compartments behind individual glass doors. They were chosen, cafeteria-style, by patrons.

1903

- ★ Henry Ford introduces his two-cylinder automobile, the Model A.
- ★ William Harley and Arthur and Walter Davidson found the Harley-Davidson motorcycle company.

December 17, 1903

- ★ Orville Wright flies 120 feet in twelve seconds in a 12-horsepower biplane built by him and his brother Wilbur, thus, inaugurating the age of flight.

1907

★ Ross Harrison is the first to successfully culture tissues.

1908

★ Henry Ford introduces his $850.50 automobile known as the Model T. It is available in any color...as long as it's black.

April 6, 1909

★ Commodore Robert Peary is the first person to reach the North Pole.

1910

★ The Ford Motor Company begins to use steel instead of wood for the bodies of its Model T.
★ John Bray creates the cell-process of animation.
★ U.S. physician James Herrick identifies the disease that will come to be called sickle cell anemia.

1911

★ C.F. Kettering invents the electric starter for motor vehicles.
★ The Chevrolet Motor Company is founded.
★ The sturdy brown paper known as Kraft paper is invented.

1913

★ William Coolidge invents a device for manufacturing x-rays known as the Coolidge Tube.
★ Steel-wool pads are introduced for the first time.
★ American biochemist Elmer McCollum isolates Vitamin A.

October 7, 1913

★ The Ford Motor Company uses the assembly line for the first time. An automobile can now be built in 1.5 hours, as compared to 12.5 hours before use of the line.

1914

★ Biochemist Edward Kendall isolates and identifies the thyroid hormone thyroxin, which will eventually lead him to isolate cortisone. Kendall and physician Phillip Hench will win the Nobel Prize for their success with cortisone.

1916

★ Albert Einstein proposes his General Theory of Relativity.

1917

* George Hale installs a 100-inch diameter reflecting telescope on Mount Wilson in California. It is the largest telescope in use at this time.
* AM radio is introduced. (It would be three years before "regularly scheduled programming" on the AM band would start.)

1918

* Charles Strite invents the pop-up toaster.

NOVEMBER 8, 1919

* The American Telegraph & Telephone Company introduces dial telephones in Virginia.

NOVEMBER 2, 1920

* KDKA in Pittsburgh begins operations and becomes the first radio broadcasting station in the world. The first news KDKA broadcasts is the results of the 1920 presidential election (Warren Harding won).

1922

* American biochemist Elmer McCollum discovers Vitamin D. (You'll recall McCollum isolated Vitamin A in 1913.)

1923

* American physiologists Joseph Erlanger and Herbert Gasser determine the rate at which nerve fibers conduct electrical impulses. In 1944, they win the Nobel Prize for their work.
* The B.F. Goodrich Company introduces the zipper.

1924

* Bell Laboratories is established by AT&T and General Electric.
* Americans Lowell Smith and Erik Nelson complete the first around-the-world flight in two U.S. Army Air Corps biplanes.

1925

* Clarence Birdseye and Charles Seabrook invent a deep-freezing process for cooked foods.

1926

* American bacteriologist Thomas Rivera creates the science of virology by successfully distinguishing between bacteria and viruses.
* Waldo Lonsbury Semon, working for the B.F. Goodrich Company, invents what is probably the first synthetic rubber. It is called Koroseal.

★ The first motion picture with synchronized sound is demonstrated.

★ The National Broadcasting Company is founded by David Sarnoff.

March 16, 1926

★ Robert Goddard launches the first liquid-fuel rocket in Auburn, Mass.

May 4, 1926

★ Americans Richard Byrd and Floyd Bennett are the first to fly over the North Pole.

1927

★ Parapsychologist Joseph Rhine begins groundbreaking research into extrasensory perception. This work which will result in concrete evidence for the existence of psychokinesis, clairvoyance, telepathy, and precognition.

★ The Holland Tunnel—the first underwater passage from New York to New Jersey—opens.

★ Transatlantic telephone service between New York and London is offered for the first time.

★ TV is demonstrated for the first time. Images of Herbert Hoover (then Secretary of Commerce) are broadcast from Washington, D.C. to New York.

★ John and Mack Rust perfect the all-mechanical cotton picker.

★ The Borden company begins offering homogenized milk.

May 20-21, 1927

★ Charles Lindbergh makes the first successful solo nonstop transatlantic flight. His plane, The Spirit of St. Louis, takes off from Roosevelt Field, Long Island and lands at Le Bourget Field outside of Paris 33 hours and 29 minutes later.

1928

★ American neurosurgeons Harvey Cushing and W.T. Bowie introduce blood vessel cauterization.

★ Amelia Earhart becomes the first woman to pilot a plane solo across the Atlantic Ocean.

★ Inventor Otto Rohwedder invents the first bread-slicing machine.

1929

★ Astronomer Edwin Hubble confirms that the universe is expanding.

★ Biochemist Edward Doisy (along with German chemist Adolf Butenandt) isolate the female sex hormone estrogen.

★ Eastman Kodak introduces the 16-millimeter camera, projector, and film.

September 24, 1929

★ Pilot James Doolittle makes the first "blind" airplane flight using only instruments to take off and land.

November 28-29, 1929

★ American Richard Byrd and his team are the first to fly over the South Pole.

1930

* Physicist Ernest Lawrence invents the cyclotron, the first subatomic particle accelerator.
* Electrical engineer Vann Bush creates the first computer, a device capable of electronically solving differential equations.

February 18, 1930

* Astronomer Clyde Tombaugh discovers Pluto.

June 11, 1930

* Naturalists Charles Beebe and Otis Barton use the first bathysphere to explore deep ocean depths.

1931

* Karl Jansky of Bell Laboratories establishes the practice of radio astronomy when he discovers radio radiation coming from the sky.
* Pathologist Ernest Goodpasture develops a method of culturing viruses in eggs.
* The George Washington Bridge opens, connecting New York and New Jersey. At 1,644 feet, it is the longest suspension bridge of its time.

1932

* Biochemist Charles King isolates and identifies Vitamin C.
* Heart specialist H.S. Hyman invents the first cardiac pacemaker.
* Edwin Land invents self-developing Polaroid film.

1933

* Thomas Morgan proves that chromosomes carry hereditary traits.
* Edwin Armstrong develops FM radio transmissions.
* Paul Galvin and the U.S. Army Corp of Engineers invent the walkie-talkie.
* Borden sells milk fortified with Vitamin D for the first time.

1935

* Charles Richter develops the Richter scale for measuring the magnitude of earthquakes.
* Alcoholics Anonymous is founded in Akron, Ohio.
* George Gallup develops the scientific method of polling. One of the first things he does is correctly predict the outcome of the 1936 presidential election. (FDR won his second term.)
* Robert Goddard fires the first supersonic liquid-fuel rocket.
* Eastman Kodak introduces Kodachrome color film for movie cameras.
* The U.S. Army introduces the B-17 bomber, one of the most important military aircraft ever built. Known as the "Flying Fortress," the B-17 was extremely fast, could fly high enough to elude enemy fighters, and was very heavily armed. As a strategic bomber, its deadly effectiveness was unparalleled. (One of its strengths was its ability for relentless precision bombing.) Boeing built over 12,000 B-17 bombers for use in World War II.

1936

* The Boulder Dam is completed. It provides inexpensive electrical power to the southwestern American states. In 1947, the dam's name is changed to Hoover Dam.
* Douglas Aircraft introduces the DC-3, a forerunner of the commercial passenger plane. (It carries 21 passengers.)
* Tampax begins selling the tampon.

1937

* The world's first radio telescope is installed in Illinois. (It has a 31-foot dish.)
* D.W. Murray introduces heparin into American medical practice. This anti-blood-clotting factor will soon prove to be an indispensable part of surgery and cardiac medicine.
* Chemist Wallace Carothers (working for DuPont) invents nylon.
* Chester Carlson invents xerography, the first dry-copy photocopying process.
* Grocer Sylvan Goodman invents the shopping cart.

1938

* Chemist Roy Plunkett invents Teflon.

1939

* Robert J. Oppenheimer first theorizes the idea of a "black hole," a star that collapses from its own weight into a single point.
* General Electric invents fluorescent lighting.
* Pan American Airways introduces commercial passenger airline service from New York to France.
* FM radios are sold for the first time.

1940

* Physicist Glenn Seaborg discovers plutonium.
* Nine-year old Milton Sirotta is the first to use the googol, which is 10^{100}, or a 1 followed by 100 zeroes. (Sirotta was the nephew of American mathematician Edward Kasner. It seems that a predilection for numbers ran in the family.)
* Physicist Philip Abelson develops a process for enriching uranium so that it can be used in atomic bombs.
* The Joy Machine, which can cut a continuous, 20-foot tunnel in coal mines, is invented by coal executive Carson Smith and engineer Harold Silver.
* The 160-mile long Pennsylvania Turnpike—the first U.S. superhighway—opens. (Today, the Pennsylvania Turnpike is 359 miles long.)
* Nylon stockings are sold for the first time.

1941

* Cardiac catheterization is performed for the first time.

1942

★   Using an electron microscope, microbiologist Salvador Luria photographs viruses for the first time.

★   Enrico Fermi sets off the first sustained nuclear chain reaction.

★   The first computer that uses vacuum tubes to perform calculations is built.

October 1, 1942

★   The first U.S. jet plane flight takes place at Muroc Army Base in California.

1943

★   Construction begins on the largest office building in the world—The Pentagon. It will ultimately hold 6.5 million square feet and cost $83 million to build.

1944

★   The world's first nuclear reactors begin operation in the state of Washington.

★   The Automatic Sequence Controlled Calculator computer is built at Harvard University in conjunction with IBM. The computer consists of over 750,000 parts and can complete simple mathematical calculations in a few seconds.

★   The United States National System of Interstate Highways—a model for the world's highways—is authorized by a federal Highways Act. The act directs that over 40,000 miles of highway roads be built across America.

★   Eastman Kodak introduces Kodacolor color negative film for color photographs.

1945

★   Grand Rapids, Mich. begins adding fluoride to their water supply to help prevent tooth decay.

★   Frozen orange juice is introduced for the first time in the United States.

July 16, 1945

★   The first atomic bomb is detonated in Alamagordo, New Mexico.

1946

★   Chemist Vincent Schaefer seeds clouds with dry ice and causes a snowstorm. He later succeeds in causing clouds to rain by seeding them with other chemicals.

★   The Atomic Energy Commission authorizes the use of radioisotopes for medical purposes, thereby inaugurating the age of nuclear medicine.

★   The world's first digital computer is built at Harvard.

★   Ford engineer Delmar Harder coins the word "automation" when describing the 14-minute process of building a Ford engine.

1947

★   Chemist Willard Libby invents carbon dating. (The element carbon-14 is used to date objects going back to 4,300 BC.)

★ Alfred Kinsey founds the groundbreaking, Institute of Sex Research at Indiana University.

★ The B.F. Goodrich Company begins selling the first self-sealing, tubeless automobile tires.

★ The first suburban neighborhood of mass-produced, reasonably-priced houses is built in Long Island, New York. It is named "Levittown" after the construction designer Abraham Levitt.

★ Raytheon begins selling the Radarange, the world's first microwave oven designed for commercial use.

October 14, 1947

★ Charles Yeager makes the first successful piloted supersonic (faster than the speed of sound) flight.

1948

★ Albert the monkey is launched into space in the nose cone of a V-2 rocket.

★ The 200-inch diameter Hale telescope begins operating at Mount Palomar in California. It is the largest reflecting telescope in the world (even to this day).

★ Botanist Benjamin Duggar isolates Aureomycin, a form of tetracycline, which will become the second most used antibiotic after penicillin.

★ Scientists for Bell Laboratories develop the transistor.

★ The 12-inch, long-playing, vinyl phonograph record (that plays at 33 1/3 r.p.m.) is developed by a CBS engineer.

1949

★ Astronomer Fred Whipple concludes that comets are composed of ice and dust.

★ The United States uses V-2 rockets to explore the upper atmosphere.

★ A rocket-testing sight opens at Cape Canaveral, Fla.

★ The United States successfully launches the first multi-stage rocket.

1950

★ Du Pont introduces the synthetic fiber Orlon (used for making cloth material).

★ The first Xerox machine is built in New York.

1951

★ The Chrysler Corporation introduces power steering.

★ CBS transmits color television signals for the first time. (But there was no one to watch it—color sets were not available to the consumer until 1954!)

December 1951

★ The first nuclear power reactor generates electricity in Idaho.

1952

★ The antibiotic erythromycin is introduced.

November 1, 1952

★ The U.S. detonates the first hydrogen bomb. The bomb, which is equivalent to 700 of the bombs that destroyed Hiroshima, destroys a Pacific Island.

1953

★ The world's first successful open-heart surgery is performed in the United States.

★ Jonas Salk begins testing his polio vaccine. The vaccine will greatly reduce occurrence of polio in the United States.

★ IBM introduces the first computer for scientific and business use.

★ Robert Abplanalp invents the plastic valve for aerosol cans.

★ Cinemascope, a process of widescreen projection, is used for the first time.

★ The first 3-D movie—*Bwana Devil*—is shown in theaters.

1954

★ Texas Instruments introduces the silicon transistor.

★ Ray Kroc, a milkshake machine salesman, buys franchise rights to the McDonald's brothers hamburger restaurant...and the rest is history!

★ The United States launches the first nuclear-powered submarine, the U.S.S. *Nautilus*.

March 1954

★ The antipsychotic drug Thorazine is sold for the first time in the United States.

June 1954

★ The "not guilty by reason of insanity" defense is allowed for the first time in the United States.

1955

★ Endocrinologist Gregory Pincus develops the first effective birth-control pill.

★ IBM introduces the IBM 752, the first computer designed exclusively for business use.

1956

★ Biologists clone human cells for the first time.

★ The Federal Water Pollution Control Act is enacted in the United States.

★ The Ampex Corporation, an *American* company, demonstrates the first videotape-recording machine.

1957

★ Seismologist Charles Richter develops his soon-to-be-standard Richter scale to measure the intensity of earthquakes.

1958

★ Physicist Eugene Parker discovers the solar wind.

★ After groundbreaking work with hypnosis by Sigmund Freud, the American Medical Association officially validates the therapeutic use of hypnosis.

★ Boeing Aircraft puts their Boeing 707 into operation. The Boeing 707 is the first U.S. passenger service jet.

★ The artificial sweetener saccharin is introduced for consumer use (see 1879).

January 31, 1958

★ The U.S. launches its first satellite, the Explorer I. (This launch was in response to the October 4, 1957 launch of the world's first artificial satellite, Sputnik, by the Soviet Union. The Space Race—which the United States would ultimately win—had begun.)

1959

★ The U.S. launches two monkeys and a chimpanzee into space.

★ The U.S. satellite Vanguard II transmits weather information to Earth for the first time.

★ The U.S. satellite Explorer 6 transmits video images of the Earth's cloud cover for the first time.

★ Jack Kilby of Texas Instruments and Robert Noyce of Fairchild Semiconductors invent the microchip.

★ Glen Raven Mills of North Carolina invents pantyhose.

1960

★ The United States launches Tiros 1, the first weather satellite, into orbit.

★ Physicist Theodore Maiman invents the laser.

★ Bulova introduces the Accutron, the first electronic wristwatch.

★ Aluminum cans are used for the first time for beverages and food products.

MAY 5, 1961

★ U.S. astronaut Alan B. Shepard Jr. is the first American in space.

1962

★ Mariner 2 completes the first fly-by of Venus and sends back pictures to Earth.

★ Telstar, the first commercial telecommunications satellite is launched successfully into orbit by the United States.

★ The first diet soda—Diet-Rite Cola—is introduced in America. It is sweetened with the sugar substitute cyclamate.

★ The Aluminum Corporation of America invents the pull-tab for aluminum cans.

February 20, 1962

★ John Glenn is the first American to orbit the Earth.

1963

★ The tranquilizer Valium becomes widely used and extremely popular. In 1966, the five-milligram Valium tablet (a "little yellow pill") will be immortalized in the Rolling Stones' song "Mother's Little Helper."

* Jersey Central Power's Oyster Creek nuclear reactor begins operations in New Jersey. It is the first commercial nuclear power plant.
* AT&T introduces touch-tone dialing in Pennsylvania.

1964

* Mariner 4 completes the first fly-by of Mars.

1965

* Paleontologist Elso Barghoon discovers the first microfossils, a single-cell organism believed to be at least 3.5 billion years old.

June 3, 1965

* Edward H. White II is the first American to walk in space.

December 15, 1965

* The Gemini 6A and the Gemini 7 are the first spacecraft to rendezvous in space.

1966

* Amantadine, the first antiviral drug for influenza, is licensed in the United States. It will eventually be marketed under the trade name Symmetrel. It will also be found to be an effective drug treatment for Parkinson's Disease.

June 2, 1966

* Surveyor 1 is the first vehicle to land on the moon.

1967

* Cardiovascular surgeon René Favaloro develops the coronary artery bypass operation.
* Maurice Hilleman develops a vaccine that prevents mumps.
* Amana introduces the first microwave oven for home use.

1968

* Cardiovascular surgeons Charles Dotter and Melvin Judkins develop angioplasty, a method of opening up clogged arteries by using a tiny balloon.
* The 911 emergency phone number is used in New York for the first time.
* The Jacuzzi is introduced in California.

December 21-27, 1968

* Astronauts Frank Borman, James Lovell, and William Anders are the first humans to orbit the Moon and see its dark side.

July 20, 1969

* Neil Armstrong is the first man to walk on the surface of the Moon.

1970

★ Intel scientist Ted Hoff invents the microprocessor.

1971

★ Mariner 9 orbits Mars. It is the first space vehicle to orbit another planet.

1972

★ The CAT scan (computerized axial tomography) is used for the first time.

1973

★ The Universal Product Code bar code system is introduced.

1975

★ Bill Gates and Paul Allen found Microsoft.

1976

★ Scientist Baruch Blumberg wins the Nobel Prize for discovering the virus that causes hepatitis B.
★ Stephen Wozniak and Steve Jobs design the first Apple computer.

1977

★ Wozniak and Jobs release the Apple II, the first computer intended for general use by the public.

1980

★ Ted Turner founds CNN, the first, 24-hour all-news cable station.
★ IBM markets the first MS-DOS-based personal computer.

1981

★ A hepatitis vaccine is approved for use in the United States.

April 12, 1981

★ The first reusable spacecraft, the space shuttle Columbia, is launched.

1982

★ The Eli Lilly company markets the first genetically-engineered human insulin for diabetes.

December 2, 1982

★ The first artificial heart is implanted in a 62-year-old man from Utah. He survives a little more than three months with the artificial heart.

1983

★ Carl Sagan develops the theory of nuclear winter, a climactic catastrophe that would occur in the aftermath of an all-out nuclear war.

★ John Buster develops the process of artificial insemination.

★ Cellular phones make their first appearance.

June 18, 1983

★ Sally Ride is the first American woman in space.

1984

★ Geneticists confirm that the chimpanzee is closely related to human beings on a genetic level.

★ Bell Labs invent the first RAM memory chip. It holds one megabit of data.

February 3, 1984

★ Challenger astronauts, using jet-powered backpacks, make the first untethered space walk.

1987

★ The Eli Lilly pharmaceutical company introduces Prozac.

1989

★ The American developers of the drug t-PA, which dissolves blood clots in heart attack patients, are named inventors of the year.

1990

★ Tigers successfully conceived through in-vitro fertilization are born in Omaha, Neb.

★ American doctors perform the first successful fetus-to-fetus tissue graft.

★ The gene that causes osteoarthritis is discovered.

★ Norplant is introduced. It is a hormone-releasing contraceptive that is physically implanted under a woman's skin.

April 15, 1990

★ The Hubble Space Telescope is launched into orbit.

1992

★ The Cosmic Background Explorer provides the strongest evidence yet of the Big Bang Theory of the origin of the universe.

1995

★ The Galileo orbiter reaches Jupiter.

★ The Mars Pathfinder transmits incredible pictures of the surface of Mars to Earth.

1998

★ Viagra is introduced.

1999

★ Princeton neurobiologist Joseph Tsien creates a smarter mouse by altering a single gene...and then patents it.

Index

W

Z

About the Author

Stephen J. Spignesi is a full-time writer who specializes in popular culture subjects, including historical biography, television, film, history, and contemporary fiction.

Mr. Spignesi — christened "the world's leading authority on Stephen King" by *Entertainment Weekly* magazine — has written many authorized entertainment books. He has worked with Stephen King, Turner Entertainment, the Margaret Mitchell Estate, Andy Griffith, Viacom, along with ther entertainment industry personalities and entities on a wide range of projects. Mr. Spignesi has also contributed essays, chapters, articles, and introductions to a wide range of books.

Mr. Spignesi's books have been translated into several languages. He has also written for *Harper's*, *Cinefantastique*, *Saturday Review*, *Mystery Scene*, *Gauntlet*, and *Midnight Graffiti* magazines. He has written for *The New York Times*, the New York *Daily News*, the *New York Post*, the *New Haven Register*, and the French literary journal, *Ténebrés*. Mr. Spignesi has also appeared on CNN, MSNBC, Fox News Channel, among other TV and radio outlets. He appeared in the 1998 E! documentary, *The Kennedys: Power, Seduction, and Hollywood,* as a Kennedy family authority; and in the A&E *Biography* of Stephen King that aired in January 2000. Mr. Spignesi's 1997 book *JFK Jr.* was a *New York Times* bestseller.

In addition to writing, Mr. Spignesi also lectures on a variety of pop culture and historical subjects and teaches writing in the Connecticut area. He is the founder and Editor-in-Chief of the small press publishing company, The Stephen John Press.

Mr. Spignesi is a graduate of the University of New Haven. He lives in New Haven, Conn., with his wife, Pam, and their cat, Carter, named after their favorite character on *ER*.